Shiver

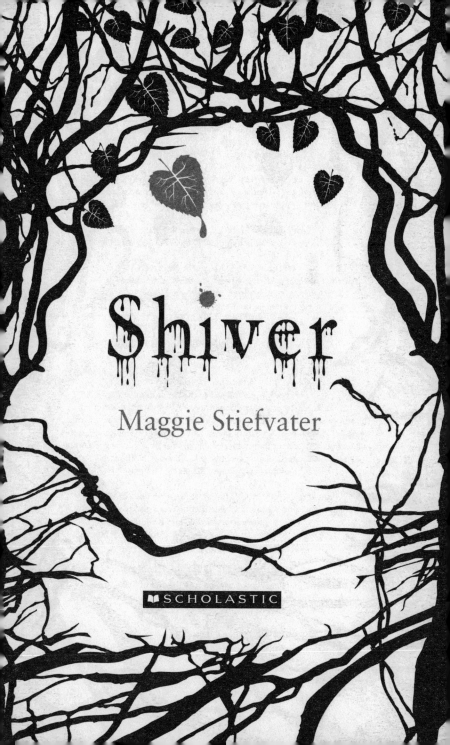

Shiver

Maggie Stiefvater

SCHOLASTIC

Scholastic Children's Books
An imprint of Scholastic Ltd
Euston House, 24 Eversholt Street
London, NW1 1DB, UK
Registered office: Westfield Road, Southam, Warwickshire, CV47 0RA
SCHOLASTIC and associated logos are trademarks and/or
registered trademarks of Scholastic Inc.

First published in the US by Scholastic Inc, 2009
This edition published in the UK by Scholastic Ltd, 2009

Text copyright © Maggie Stiefvater, 2009
The right of Maggie Stiefvater to be identified as the author of this work
has been asserted by her.

ISBN 978 1407 11500 9

A CIP catalogue record for this book is available
from the British Library.

Printed in the UK by CPI Bookmarque, Croydon, CR0 4TD
Papers used by Scholastic Children's Books are made from wood
grown in sustainable forests.

24

www.scholastic.co.uk/zone

For Kate,
because she cried

One
Grace

-9°C

I remember lying in the snow, a small red spot of warm going cold, surrounded by wolves. They were licking me, biting me, worrying at my body, pressing in. Their huddled bodies blocked what little heat the sun offered. Ice glistened on their ruffs and their breath made opaque shapes that hung in the air around us. The musky smell of their coats made me think of wet dog and burning leaves, pleasant and terrifying. Their tongues melted my skin; their careless teeth ripped at my sleeves and snagged through my hair, pushed against my collarbone, the pulse at my neck.

I could have screamed, but I didn't. I could have fought, but I didn't. I just lay there and let it happen, watching the winter-white sky go grey above me.

One wolf prodded his nose into my hand and against my cheek, casting a shadow across my face. His yellow eyes looked into mine while the other wolves jerked me this way and that.

I held on to those eyes for as long as I could. Yellow. And, up close, flecked brilliantly with every shade of gold and hazel. I didn't want him to look away, and he didn't. I wanted to reach out and grab ahold of his ruff, but my hands stayed curled on my chest, my arms frozen to my body.

I couldn't remember what it felt like to be warm.

Then he was gone, and without him, the other wolves closed in, too close, suffocating. Something seemed to flutter in my chest.

There was no sun; there was no light. I was dying. I couldn't remember what the sky looked like.

But I didn't die. I was lost to a sea of cold, and then I was reborn into a world of warmth.

I remember this: his yellow eyes.

I thought I'd never see them again.

Two

Sam

-9°C

They snatched the girl off her tyre swing in the back yard and dragged her into the woods; her body made a shallow track in the snow, from her world to mine. I saw it happen. I didn't stop it.

It had been the longest, coldest winter of my life. Day after day under a pale, worthless sun. And the hunger – hunger that burned and gnawed, an insatiable master. That month nothing moved, the landscape frozen into a colourless diorama devoid of life. One of us had been shot trying to steal trash off someone's back step, so the rest of the pack stayed in the woods and slowly starved, waiting for warmth and our old bodies. Until they found the girl. Until they attacked.

They crouched around her, snarling and snapping, fighting to tear into the kill first.

I saw it. I saw their flanks shuddering with their eagerness. I saw them tug the girl's body this way and that, wearing away the snow beneath her. I saw muzzles smeared with red. Still, I didn't stop it.

I was high up in the pack – Beck and Paul had made sure of that – so I could've moved in immediately, but I hung back, trembling with the cold, up to my ankles in snow. The girl smelled warm, alive, *human* above all else. What was wrong with her? If she was alive, why wasn't she struggling?

I could smell her blood, a warm, bright scent in this dead, cold world. I saw Salem jerk and tremble as he ripped at her clothing. My stomach twisted, painful – it had been so long since I'd eaten. I wanted to push through the wolves to stand next to Salem and pretend that I couldn't smell her humanness or hear her soft moans. She was so little underneath our wildness, the pack pressing against her, wanting to trade her life for ours.

With a snarl and a flash of teeth, I pushed forward. Salem growled back at me, but I was rangier than him, despite my starvation and youth. Paul rumbled threateningly to back me up.

I was next to her, and she was looking up at the endless sky with distant eyes. Maybe dead. I pushed my nose into her hand; the scent on her palm, all sugar and butter and salt, reminded me of another life.

Then I saw her eyes.

Awake. Alive.

The girl looked right at me, eyes holding mine with such terrible honesty.

I backed up, recoiled, starting to shake again – but this time, it wasn't anger that racked my frame.

Her eyes on my eyes. Her blood on my face.

I was tearing apart, inside and outside.

Her life.

My life.

The pack fell back from me, wary. They growled at me, no longer one of them, and they snarled over their prey. I thought she was the most beautiful girl I'd ever seen, a tiny, bloody angel in the snow, and they were going to destroy her.

I saw it. I saw her, in a way I'd never seen anything before.

And I stopped it.

Three

Grace

I saw him again after that, always in the cold. He stood at the edge of the woods in our back yard, his yellow eyes steady on me as I filled the bird feeder or took out the trash, but he never came close. In between day and night, a time that lasted for ever in the long Minnesota winter, I would cling to the frozen tyre swing until I felt his gaze. Or, later, when I'd outgrown the swing, I'd step off the back deck and quietly approach him, hand forward, palm up, eyes lowered. No threat. I was trying to speak his language.

But no matter how long I waited, no matter how hard I tried to reach him, he would always melt into the undergrowth before I could cross the distance between us.

I was never afraid of him. He was large enough to tear me from my swing, strong enough to knock me down and drag me into the woods. But the ferocity of his body wasn't in his eyes. I remembered his gaze, every hue of yellow, and I couldn't be afraid. I knew he wouldn't hurt me.

I wanted him to know I wouldn't hurt him.

I waited. And waited.

And he waited, too, though I didn't know what he was waiting for. It felt like I was the only one reaching out.

But he was always there. Watching me watching him. Never any closer to me, but never any further away, either.

And so it was an unbroken pattern for six years: the wolves' haunting presence in the winter and their even more haunting absence in the summer. I didn't really think about the timing. I thought they were wolves. Only wolves.

Four

Sam

32°C

The day I nearly talked to Grace was the hottest day of my life. Even in the bookstore, which was air-conditioned, the heat crept in around the door and came in through the big picture windows in waves. Behind the counter, I slouched on my stool in the sun and sucked in the summer as if I could hold every drop of it inside me. As the hours crept by, the afternoon sunlight bleached all the books on the shelves to pale, gilded versions of themselves and warmed the paper and ink inside the covers so that the smell of unread words hung in the air.

This was what I loved, when I was human.

I was reading when the door opened with a little *ding*, admitting a stifling rush of hot air and a group of girls. They were laughing too loudly to need my help, so I kept reading and let them jostle along the walls and talk about everything except books.

I don't think I would've given the girls a second thought, except that at the edge of my vision I saw one of them sweep up her dark blonde hair and twist it into a long ponytail. The action itself was insignificant, but the movement sent a gasp of scent into the air. I recognized that smell. I knew immediately.

It was her. It had to be.

I jerked my book up towards my face and risked a glimpse in the girls' direction. The other two were still talking and gesturing at a paper bird I'd hung from the ceiling above the children's book section. She wasn't talking, though; she hung back, her eyes on the books all around her. I saw her face then, and I recognized something of myself in her expression. Her eyes flicked over the shelves, seeking possibilities for escape.

I had planned a thousand different versions of this scene in my head, but now that the moment had come, I didn't know what to do.

She was so real here. It was different when she was in her back yard, just reading a book or scribbling homework in a notebook. There, the distance between us was an impossible void; I felt all the reasons to stay away. Here, in the bookstore, with me, she seemed breathtakingly close in a way she hadn't before. There was nothing to stop me from talking to her.

Her gaze headed in my direction, and I looked away hurriedly, down at my book. She wouldn't recognize my face but she would recognize my eyes. I had to believe she would recognize my eyes.

I prayed for her to leave so I could breathe again.

I prayed for her to buy a book so I would have to talk to her.

One of the girls called, "Grace, come over here and look at this. *Making the Grade: Getting into the College of Your Dreams* – that sounds good, right?"

I sucked in a slow breath and watched her long sunlit back as she crouched and looked at the SAT prep books with the other girls. There was a certain tilt to her shoulders that seemed to indicate only polite interest; she nodded as they pointed to other books, but she seemed distracted. I watched the way the sunlight streamed through the windows, catching the individual flyaway hairs in her ponytail and turning each one into a shimmering gold strand. Her head moved almost imperceptibly back and forth with the rhythm of the music playing overhead.

"Hey."

I jerked back as a face appeared before me. Not Grace. One of the other girls, dark-haired and tanned. She had a huge camera slung over her shoulder and she was looking right into my eyes. She didn't say anything, but I knew what she was thinking. Reactions to my eye colour ranged from furtive glances to out-and-out staring; at least she was being honest about it.

"Do you mind if I take your photo?" she asked.

I cast around for an excuse. "Some native people think if you take their photo, you take their soul. It sounds like a very logical argument to me, so sorry, no pictures." I shrugged apologetically. "You can take photos of the store if you like."

The third girl pushed up against the camera girl: bushy light brown hair, tremendously freckled and radiating so much energy that she exhausted me. "Flirting, Olivia? We don't have time for that. Here, dude, we'll take this one."

I took *Making the Grade* from her, sparing a quick glance around for Grace.

"Nineteen dollars and ninety-nine cents," I said.

My heart was pounding.

"For a paperback?" remarked the freckled girl, but she handed me a twenty. "Keep the penny." We didn't have a penny jar, but I put it on the counter next to the register. I bagged the book and receipt slowly, thinking Grace might come over to see what was taking so long.

But she stayed in the biography section, head tipped to the side as she read the spines. The freckled girl took the bag and grinned at me and Olivia. Then they went to Grace and herded her towards the door.

Turn around, Grace. Look at me, I'm standing right here. If she turned right now, she'd see my eyes, and she'd have to know me.

Freckled girl opened the door – *ding* – and made an impatient sound to the rest of the herd: time to move along. Olivia turned briefly, and her eyes found me again behind the counter. I knew I was staring at them – at Grace – but I couldn't stop.

Olivia frowned and ducked out of the store. Freckled girl said, "Grace, come *on*."

My chest ached, my body speaking a language my head didn't quite understand.

I waited.

But Grace, the only person in the world I wanted to know me, just ran a wanting finger over the cover of one of the new hardcovers and walked out of the store without ever realizing I was there, right within reach.

Five
Grace

6°C

I didn't realize that the wolves in the wood were all werewolves until Jack Culpeper was killed.

September of my junior year, when it happened, Jack was all anybody in our small town could talk about. It wasn't as though Jack had been this amazing kid when he was alive – apart from owning the most expensive car in the car park, principal's car included. Actually, he'd been kind of a jerk. But when he was killed – instant sainthood. With a gruesome and sensational undertow, because of the way it had happened. Within five days of his death, I'd heard a thousand versions of the story in the school halls.

The upshot was this: everyone was terrified of the wolves now.

Because Mom didn't usually watch the news and Dad was terminally not home, the communal anxiety trickled down to our household slowly, taking a few days to really gain momentum. My incident with the wolves had faded from my mother's mind over the past six years, replaced by turpentine fumes and complementary colours, but Jack's attack seemed to refresh it perfectly.

Far be it from Mom to funnel her growing anxiety into something logical like spending more quality time with her only daughter, the one who had been attacked by wolves in the first place. Instead, she just used it to become even more scatterbrained than usual.

"Mom, do you need some help with dinner?"

My mother looked guiltily at me, turning her attention from the television that she could just see from the kitchen back to the mushrooms she was obliterating on the cutting board.

"It was so close to here. Where they found him," Mom said, pointing towards the television with the knife. The news anchor looked insincerely sincere as a map of our county appeared next to a blurry photo of a wolf in the upper right corner of the screen. The hunt for the truth, he said, continued. You'd think that after a week of reporting the same story over and over again, they'd at least get their simple facts straight. Their photo wasn't even the same species as my wolf, with his stormy grey coat and tawny yellow eyes.

"I still can't believe it," Mom went on. "Just on the other side of Boundary Wood. That's where he was killed."

"Or died."

Mom frowned at me, delicately frazzled and beautiful as usual. "What?"

I looked back up from my homework – comforting, orderly lines of numbers and symbols. "He could've just passed out by the side of the road and been dragged into the woods while he was unconscious. It's not the same. You can't just go around trying to cause a panic."

Mom's attention had wandered back to the screen as she chopped the mushrooms into pieces small enough for amoeba consumption. She shook her head. "They *attacked* him, Grace."

I glanced out of the window at the woods, the pale lines of the trees phantoms against the dark. If my wolf was out there, I couldn't see him. "Mom, you're the one who told me over and over and *over* again: wolves are usually peaceful."

Wolves are peaceful creatures. This had been Mom's refrain for years. I think the only way she could keep living in this house was by convincing herself of the wolves' relative harmlessness and insisting that my attack was a one-time event. I don't know if she really believed that they were peaceful, but I did. Gazing into the woods, I'd watched the wolves every year of my life, memorizing their faces and their personalities. Sure, there was the lean, sickly-looking brindle wolf who hung well back in the woods, only visible in the coldest of months. Everything about him – his dull scraggly coat, his notched ear, his one foul running eye – shouted an ill body, and the rolling whites of his wild eyes whispered of a diseased mind. I remembered his teeth grazing my skin. I could imagine him attacking a human in the woods again.

And there was the white she-wolf. I had read that wolves mated for life, and I'd seen her with the pack leader, a heavyset wolf that was as black as she was white. I'd watched him nose her muzzle and lead her through the skeleton trees, fur flashing like fish in water. She had a sort of savage, restless beauty to her; I could imagine her attacking a human, too. But the rest of them? They were silent, beautiful ghosts in the woods. I didn't fear them.

"Right, peaceful." Mom hacked at the cutting board. "Maybe they should just trap them all and dump them in Canada or something."

I frowned at my homework. Summers without my wolf were bad enough. As a child, those months had seemed impossibly long, just time spent waiting for the wolves to reappear. They'd only got worse after I noticed my yellow-eyed wolf. During those long months, I had imagined great adventures where I became a wolf by night and ran away with my wolf to a golden wood where it never snowed. I knew now that the golden wood didn't exist, but the pack – and my yellow-eyed wolf – did.

Sighing, I pushed my maths book across the kitchen table and joined Mom at the cutting board. "Let me do it. You're just messing it up."

She didn't protest, and I hadn't expected her to.

Instead, she rewarded me with a smile and whirled away as if she'd been waiting for me to notice the pitiful job she was doing. "If you finish making dinner," she said, "I'll love you for ever."

I made a face and took the knife from her. Mom was permanently paint-spattered and absentminded. She would never be my friends' moms: apron-wearing, meal-cooking, vacuuming, Betty Crocker. I didn't really want her to be like them. But seriously – I needed to get my homework done.

"Thanks, sweetie. I'll be in the studio." If Mom had been one of those dolls that say five or six different things when you push their tummy, that would've been one of her prerecorded phrases.

"Don't pass out from the fumes," I told her, but she was already running up the stairs. Shoving the mutilated mushrooms into a bowl, I looked at the clock hanging on the bright yellow wall. Still an hour until Dad would be home from work. I had plenty of time to make dinner and maybe, afterwards, to try to catch a glimpse of my wolf.

There was some sort of cut of beef in the fridge that was probably supposed to go with the mangled mushrooms. I pulled it out and slapped it on the cutting board. In the background, an "expert" on the news asked whether the wolf population in Minnesota should be limited or moved. The whole thing just put me in a bad mood.

The phone rang. "Hello?"

"Hiya. What's up?"

Rachel. I was glad to hear from her; she was the exact opposite of my mother – totally organized and great on follow-through. She made me feel less like an alien. I shoved the phone between my ear and my shoulder and chopped the beef as I talked, saving a piece the size of my fist for later. "Just making dinner and watching the stupid news."

She knew immediately what I was talking about. "I know. Talk about surreal, right? It seems like they just can't get enough of it. It's kind of gross, really – I mean, why can't they just shut up and let us get over it? It's bad enough going to school and hearing about it all the time. And you with the wolves and everything, it's got to be really bothering you – and, seriously, Jack's parents have got to be just wanting the reporters to shut up." Rachel was babbling so fast I could barely understand her. I missed a bunch of what she said in the middle, and then she asked, "Has Olivia called tonight?"

Olivia was the third side of our trio, the only one who came anywhere near understanding my fascination with the wolves. It was a rare night when I didn't talk to either her or Rachel by phone. "She's probably out shooting photos. Isn't there a meteor shower tonight?" I said. Olivia saw the world through her camera; half of my school memories seemed to be in four-by-six-inch glossy black-and-white form.

Rachel said, "I think you're right. Olivia will definitely want a piece of that hot asteroid action. Got a moment to talk?"

I glanced at the clock. "Sorta. Just while I finish up dinner, then I have homework."

"OK. Just a second, then. Two words, baby, try them out: *es. cape.*"

I started the beef browning on the stove top. "That's one word, Rach."

She paused. "Yeah. It sounded better in my head. Anyway, so here's the thing: my parents said if I want to go someplace over Christmas break this year, they'll pay for it. I so want to go somewhere. Anywhere but Mercy Falls. God, *any*where but Mercy Falls! Will you and Olivia come over and help me pick something after school tomorrow?"

"Yeah, sure."

"If it's someplace really cool, maybe you and Olivia could come, too," Rachel said.

I didn't answer right away. The word Christmas immediately evoked memories of the scent of our Christmas tree, the dark infinity of the starry December sky above the back yard, and my wolf's eyes watching me from behind the snow-covered trees. No matter how absent he was for the rest of the year, I always had my wolf for Christmas.

Rachel groaned. "Don't do that silent staring-off-into-the-distance-thinking look, Grace! I can tell you're doing it! You can't tell me you don't want to get out of this place!"

I sort of didn't. I sort of belonged here. "I didn't say no," I protested.

"You also didn't say *omigod yes*, either. That's what you were supposed to say." Rachel sighed. "But you will come over, right?"

"You know I will," I said, craning my neck to squint out of the back window. "Now, I really have to go."

"Yeah yeah yeah," Rachel said. "Bring cookies. Don't forget. Love ya. Bye." She laughed and hung up.

I hurried to get the pot of stew simmering on the stove so it could occupy itself without me. Grabbing my coat from the hooks on the wall, I pulled open the sliding door to the deck.

Cool air bit my cheeks and pinched at the tops of my ears, reminding me that summer was officially over. My stocking cap was stuffed in the pocket of my coat, but I knew my wolf didn't always recognize me when I was wearing it, so I left it off. I squinted at the edge of the yard and stepped off the deck, trying to look nonchalant as I did. The piece of beef in my hand felt cold and slick.

I crunched out across the brittle, colourless grass into the middle of the yard and stopped, momentarily dazzled by the violent pink of the sunset through the fluttering black leaves of the trees. This stark landscape was a world away from the small, warm kitchen with its comforting smells of easy survival. Where I was supposed to belong. Where I should've wanted to be. But the trees called to me, urging me to abandon what I knew and vanish into the oncoming night. It was a desire that had been tugging me with disconcerting frequency these days.

The darkness at the edge of the wood shifted, and I saw my wolf standing beside a tree, nostrils sniffing towards the meat in my hand. My relief at seeing him was cut short as he shifted his head, letting the yellow square of light from the sliding door fall across his face. I could see now that his chin was crusted with old, dried blood. Days old.

His nostrils worked; he could smell the bit of beef in my hand. Either the beef or the familiarity of my presence was enough to lure him a few steps out of the wood. Then a few steps more. Closer than he'd ever been before.

I faced him, near enough that I could have reached out and touched his dazzling fur. Or brushed the deep red stain on his muzzle.

I badly wanted that blood to be his. An old cut or scratch earned in a scuffle.

But it didn't look like that. It looked like it belonged to someone else.

"Did you kill him?" I whispered.

He didn't disappear at the sound of my voice, as I had expected. He was as still as a statue, his eyes watching my face instead of the meat in my hand.

"It's all they can talk about on the news," I said, as if he could understand. "They called it 'savage'. They said wild animals did it. Did *you* do it?"

He stared at me for a minute longer, motionless, unblinking. And then, for the first time in six years, he closed his eyes. It went against every natural instinct a wolf should have possessed. A lifetime of an unblinking gaze, and now he was frozen in almost-human grief, brilliant eyes closed, head ducked and tail lowered.

It was the saddest thing I had ever seen.

Slowly, barely moving, I approached him, afraid only of scaring him away, not of his scarlet-stained lips or the teeth they hid. His ears flicked, acknowledging my presence, but he didn't move. I crouched, dropping the meat on to the snow beside me. He flinched as it landed. I was close enough to smell the wild odour of his coat and feel the warmth of his breath.

Then I did what I had always wanted to – I put a hand to his dense ruff, and when he didn't flinch, I buried both my hands in his fur. His outer coat was not soft as it looked, but beneath the coarse guard hairs was a layer of downy fluff. With a low groan, he pressed his head against me, eyes still closed. I held him as if he were no more than a family dog, though his wild, sharp scent wouldn't let me forget what he really was.

For a moment, I forgot where – who – I was. For a moment, it didn't matter.

Movement caught my eye: far off, barely visible in

the fading day, the white wolf was watching at the edge of the wood, her eyes burning.

I felt a rumble against my body and I realized my wolf was growling at her. The she-wolf stepped closer, uncommonly bold, and he twisted in my arms to face her. I flinched at the sound of his teeth snapping at her.

She never growled, and somehow that was worse. A wolf should have growled. But she just stared, eyes flicking from him to me, every aspect of her body language breathing hatred.

Still rumbling, almost inaudible, my wolf pressed harder against me, forcing me back a step, then another, guiding me up to the deck. My feet found the steps and I retreated to the sliding door. He remained at the bottom of the stairs until I pushed the door open and locked myself inside the house.

As soon as I was inside, the white wolf darted forward and snatched the piece of meat I'd dropped. Though my wolf was nearest to her and the most obvious threat for the food, it was me that her eyes found, on the other side of the glass door. She held my gaze for a long moment before she slid into the woods like a spirit.

My wolf hesitated by the edge of the woods, the dim porch light catching his eyes. He was still watching my silhouette through the door.

I pressed my palm flat against the frigid glass.

The distance between us had never felt so vast.

Six

Grace

5°C

When my father got home, I was still lost in the silent world of the wolves, imagining again and again the feeling of my wolf's coarse hairs against my palms. Even though I'd reluctantly washed my hands to finish up dinner, his musky scent lingered on my clothing, keeping the encounter fresh in my mind. It had taken six years for him to let me touch him. Hold him. And now he'd guarded me, just like he'd always guarded me. I desperately wanted to tell *somebody*, but I knew Dad wouldn't share my excitement, especially with the newscasters still droning in the background about the attack. I kept my mouth shut.

In the front hall, Dad stomped in. Even though he hadn't seen me in the kitchen, he called, "Dinner smells good, Grace."

He came into the kitchen and patted me on the head. His eyes looked tired behind his glasses, but he smiled. "Where's your mother? Painting?" He chucked his coat over a chair.

"Does she ever stop?" I narrowed my eyes at his coat. "I know you aren't going to leave that there."

He retrieved it with an affable smile and called up the stairs, "Rags, time for dinner!" His use of Mom's nickname confirmed his good mood.

Mom appeared in the yellow kitchen in two seconds flat. She was out of breath from running down the stairs – she never walked anywhere – and there was a streak of green paint on her cheekbone.

Dad kissed her, avoiding the paint. "Have you been a good girl, my pet?"

She batted her eyelashes. She had a look on her face like she already knew what he was going to say. "The best."

"And you, Gracie?"

"Better than Mom."

Dad cleared his throat. "Ladies and gentlemen, my raise takes effect this Friday. So. . ."

Mom clapped her hands and whirled in a circle, watching herself in the hall mirror as she spun. "I'm renting that place downtown!"

Dad grinned and nodded. "And, Gracie girl, you're trading in your piece of crap car as soon as I find time to get you down to the dealership. I'm tired of taking yours into the garage."

Mom laughed, giddy, and clapped her hands again. She danced into the kitchen, chanting some sort of nonsense song. If she rented the studio in town, I'd probably never see either of my parents again. Well, except for dinner. They usually showed up for food.

But that seemed unimportant in comparison to the promise of reliable transportation. "Really? My own car? I mean, one that runs?"

"A slightly less crappy one," Dad promised. "Nothing nice."

I hugged him. A car like that meant freedom.

That night, I lay in my room, eyes squeezed firmly shut, trying to sleep. The world outside my window seemed silenced, as though it had snowed. It was too early for snow, but every sound seemed muffled. Too quiet.

I held my breath and focused on the night, listening for movement in the still darkness.

I slowly became aware that faint clicks had broken the silence outside, pricking at my ears. It sounded for all the world like toenails on the deck outside my window. Was a wolf on the deck? Maybe it was a raccoon. Then came more soft scrabbling, and a growl – definitely not a raccoon. The hairs rose on the back of my neck.

Pulling my quilt around me like a cape, I climbed out of bed and padded across bare floorboards lit by half a moon. I hesitated, wondering if I'd dreamed the sound, but the *tack tack tack* came through the window again. I lifted the blinds and looked out on to the deck. Perpendicular to my room, I could see that the yard was empty. The stark black trunks of the trees jutted like a fence between me and the deeper forest beyond.

Suddenly, a face appeared directly in front of mine, and I jumped with surprise. The white wolf was on the other side of the glass, paws on the outside sill. She was close enough that I could see moisture caught in the banded hairs of her fur. Her jewel-blue eyes glared into mine, challenging me to look away. A low growl rumbled through the glass, and I felt as if I could read meaning into it, as clearly as if it were written on the pane. *You're not his to protect.*

I stared back at her. Then, without thinking, I lifted my teeth into a snarl. The growl that escaped from me surprised both me and her, and she jumped down from the window. She cast a dark look over her shoulder at me and peed on the corner of the deck before loping into the woods.

Biting my lip to erase the strange shape of the snarl, I picked up my sweater from the floor and crawled back into bed. Shoving my pillow aside, I balled up the sweater to use instead.

I fell asleep to the scent of my wolf. Pine needles, cold rain, earthy perfume, coarse bristles on my face.

It was almost like he was there.

Seven

Sam

5°C

I could still smell her on my fur. It clung to me, a memory of another world.

I was drunk with it, with the scent of her. I'd got too close. My instincts warned against it. Especially when I remembered what had just happened to the boy.

The smell of summer on her skin, the half-recalled cadence of her voice, the sensation of her fingers on my fur. Every bit of me sang with the memory of her closeness.

Too close.

I couldn't stay away.

Eight
Grace

18°C

For the next week, I was distracted in school, floating through my classes and barely taking any notes. All I could think of was the feel of my wolf's fur under my fingers and the image of the white wolf's snarling face outside my window. I snapped to attention, however, when Mrs Ruminski led a policeman into the classroom and to the front of our Life Skills class.

She left him alone at the front of the room, which I thought was pretty cruel, considering it was seventh period and most of us were restlessly anticipating escape. Maybe she thought that a member of law enforcement would be able to handle mere high school students. But criminals you can shoot, unlike a room full of juniors who won't shut up.

"Hi," the officer said. Beneath a gun belt that bristled with holsters and pepper sprays and other assorted weaponry, he looked *young*. He glanced towards Mrs Ruminski, who hovered unhelpfully in the open door of the classroom, and fingered the shiny name tag on his shirt: WILLIAM KOENIG. Mrs Ruminski had told us that he was a graduate of our fine high school, but neither his name nor his face looked particularly familiar to me. "I'm Officer Koenig. Your teacher – Mrs Ruminski – asked me last week if I'd come talk to her Life Skills class."

I glanced over at Olivia in the seat next to me to see what she was making of this. As usual, everything about Olivia looked neat and tidy: straight-A report card made flesh. Her dark hair was plaited in a perfect French braid and her collared shirt was freshly pressed. You could never tell what Olivia was thinking by her mouth. It was her eyes you had to look at.

"He's cute," Olivia whispered to me. "Love the shaved head. Do you think his mom calls him 'Will'?"

I hadn't yet figured out how to respond to Olivia's newfound and very vocal interest in guys, so I just rolled my eyes. He was cute, but not my type. I didn't think I knew what my type was yet.

"I became an officer of the law right after high school," Officer Will said. He looked very serious as he said it, frowning in a sort of *serve-and-protect* way. "It's a profession I always wanted to pursue and one I take very seriously."

"Clearly," I whispered to Olivia. I didn't think his mother called him Will. Officer William Koenig shot a look at us and rested a hand on his gun. I guess it was habit, but it looked like he was considering shooting us for whispering. Olivia disappeared into her seat and a few of the other girls giggled.

"It's an excellent career path and one of the few that doesn't require college yet," he pressed on. "Are – uh – any of you considering going into law enforcement?"

It was the *uh* that did him in. If he hadn't hesitated, I think the class might have behaved.

A hand whipped up. Elizabeth, one of the hordes of Mercy Falls High students still wearing black since Jack's death, asked, "Is it true that Jack Culpeper's body was stolen from the morgue?"

The class erupted in whispers at her audacity, and Officer Koenig looked as if he really did have due cause to shoot her. But all he said was, "I'm not really authorized to talk about the details of any ongoing investigations."

"It's an investigation?" a male voice called out from near the front.

Elizabeth interrupted, "My mom heard it from a dispatcher. Is it true? Why would someone steal a body?"

Theories flew in quick succession.

"It's got to be a cover-up. For a suicide."

"To smuggle drugs!"

"Medical experimentation!"

Some guy said, "I heard Jack's dad has a stuffed polar bear in his house. Maybe the Culpepers stuffed Jack, too." Someone took a swat at the guy who made the last comment; it was still taboo to say anything bad about Jack or his family.

Officer Koenig looked aghast at Mrs Ruminski, who stood in the open door of the classroom. She regarded him solemnly and then turned to the class. "*Quiet down!*"

We quietened down.

She turned back to Officer Koenig. "So was his body stolen?" she asked.

He said again, "I'm not really authorized to discuss the details of any ongoing investigations." But this time, he sounded more helpless, like there might be a question mark at the end of his sentence.

"Officer Koenig," Mrs Ruminski said. "Jack was well loved in this community."

Which was a patent lie. But being dead had done wonders for his reputation. I guess everyone else could forget the way he'd lose his temper in the middle of the hall or even during class. And just what those tempers looked like. But I hadn't. Mercy Falls was all about rumours, and the rumour about Jack was that he got his short fuse from his dad. I didn't know about that. It seemed like you ought to pick the sort of person you would be, no matter what your parents were like.

"We are still in mourning," Mrs Ruminski added, gesturing to the sea of black in the classroom. "This is not about an investigation. This is about giving closure to a close-knit community."

Olivia mouthed at me: "Oh. My. God." I shook my head. Amazing.

Officer Koenig crossed his arms over his chest; it made him look petulant, like a little kid being forced to do something. "It's true. We're looking into it. I understand the loss of someone so young —" this from someone who looked maybe twenty — "has a huge impact on the community, but I ask that everyone respect the privacy of the family and the confidentiality of the investigation process."

He was getting back on firm footing here.

Elizabeth waved her hand again. "Do you think the wolves are dangerous? Do you get lots of calls about them? My mom said you got lots of calls about them."

Officer Koenig looked at Mrs Ruminski, but he should have figured out by now that she wanted to know just as much as Elizabeth did. "I don't think the wolves are a threat to the populace, no. I — and the rest of the department — feel this was an isolated incident."

Elizabeth said, "But she got attacked, too."

Oh, lovely. I couldn't see Elizabeth pointing, but I knew she was, because everyone's faces turned towards me. I bit the inside of my lip. Not because the attention bothered me, but because every time someone remembered I was dragged from my tyre swing, they remembered it could happen to anyone. And I wondered how many someones it would take before they decided to go after the wolves.

To go after my wolf.

I knew this was the real reason why I couldn't forgive

Jack for dying. In between that and his chequered history at the school, it felt hypocritical to go into public mourning along with the rest of the school. It didn't feel right to ignore it, either, though; I wished I knew what I was supposed to be feeling.

"That was a long time ago," I told Officer Koenig, and he looked relieved as I added, "Years. And it might have been dogs."

So I was lying. Who was going to contradict me?

"Exactly," Officer Koenig said emphatically. "Exactly. There's no point vilifying wild animals for a random incident. And there's no point creating panic when it's not warranted. Panic leads to carelessness, and carelessness creates accidents."

My thoughts precisely. I felt a vague kinship with humourless Officer Koenig as he steered the conversation back to careers in law enforcement. After class was over, the other students started talking about Jack again, but Olivia and I escaped to our lockers.

I felt a tug on my hair and turned to see Rachel standing behind me, looking mournfully at both of us. "Babes, I have to rain check on vacation planning this afternoon. Step-freak has demanded a family bonding trip to Duluth. If she wants me to love her, she's going to have to buy me some new shoes. Can we get together tomorrow or something?"

I had barely nodded before Rachel flashed both of us a big smile and surged off through the hall.

"Want to hang out at my place instead?" I asked Olivia. It still felt weird to ask. In middle school, she and Rachel and I had hung out every day, a wordless ongoing agreement. Somehow it had sort of changed after Rachel got her first boyfriend, leaving Olivia and me behind, the geek and the uninterested, and fracturing our easy friendship.

"Sure," Olivia said, grabbing her stuff to follow me down the hall. She pinched my elbow. "Look." She pointed to Isabel, Jack's younger sister, a classmate of ours with more than her fair share of the Culpeper good looks, complete with a cherubic head of blonde curls. She drove a white SUV and had one of those handbag Chihuahuas that she dressed to match her outfits. I always wondered when she would notice that she lived in Mercy Falls, Minnesota, where people just didn't do that kind of thing.

At the moment, Isabel was staring into her locker as if it contained other worlds. Olivia said, "She's not wearing black."

Isabel snapped out of her trance and glared at us as if she realized we were talking about her. I looked away quickly, but I still felt her eyes on me.

"Maybe she's not in mourning any more," I said, after we'd got out of earshot.

Olivia opened the door for me. "Maybe she's the only one who ever was."

★

Back at my house, I made coffee and cranberry scones for us, and we sat at the kitchen table looking at a stack of Olivia's latest photos under the yellow ceiling light. To Olivia, photography was a religion; she worshipped her camera and studied the techniques as if they were rules to live by. Seeing her photos, I was almost willing to become a believer, too. She made you feel as though you were right there in the scene.

"He *was* really cute. You can't tell me he wasn't," she said.

"Are you still talking about Officer No-Smile? What is wrong with you?" I shook my head and shuffled to the next photo. "I've never seen you obsess over a *real* person."

Olivia grinned and leaned at me over a steaming mug. Taking a bite of scone, she spoke around a mouthful, covering her mouth to keep from spraying me with crumbs. "I think I'm turning into one of those girls who likes uniformed types. Oh, c'mon, you didn't think he was cute? I'm feeling ... I'm feeling the boyfriend urge. We should order pizza sometime. Rachel told me there's a really cute pizza boy."

I rolled my eyes again. "All of a sudden you want a boyfriend?"

Olivia didn't look up from the photos, but I got the idea she was paying a lot of attention to my response. "You don't?"

I mumbled, "When the right guy comes along, I guess."

"How will you know if you don't look?"

"As if you have ever had the guts to talk to a guy. Other than your James Dean poster." My voice had got more combative than I'd intended; I added a laugh at the end to soften the effect. Olivia's eyebrows drew closer to each other, but she didn't say anything. For a long time we sat in silence, paging through her photos.

I lingered on a close-up shot of me, Olivia and Rachel together; her mother had come outside to take it right before school started. Rachel, her freckled face contorted into a wild smile, had one arm firmly wrapped around Olivia's shoulders and the other around mine; it looked like she was squeezing us into the frame. Like always, she was the glue that held our threesome together: the outgoing one who made sure us quiet ones stuck together through the years.

In the photo, Olivia seemed to belong in the summer, with her olive skin bronzed and green eyes saturated with colour. Her teeth made a perfect crescent-moon smile for the photo, dimples and all. Next to the two of them, I was the embodiment of winter – dark blonde hair and serious brown eyes, a summer girl faded by cold. I used to think Olivia and I were so similar, both introverts permanently buried in books. But now I realized my seclusion was self-inflicted and Olivia was just painfully shy. This year, it felt like the more time we spent together, the harder it was to stay friends.

"I look stupid in that one," Olivia said. "Rachel looks insane. And you look angry."

I looked like someone who wouldn't take no for an answer – petulant, almost. I liked it. "You don't look stupid. You look like a princess and I look like an ogre."

"You don't look like an ogre."

"I was bragging," I told her.

"And Rachel?"

"No, you called it. She does look insane. Or at least highly caffeinated, as per usual." I looked at the photo again. Really, Rachel looked like a sun, bright and exuding energy, holding us two moons in parallel orbit by the sheer force of her will.

"Did you see that one?" Olivia interrupted my thoughts to point at another one of the photos. It was my wolf, deep in the woods, halfway hidden behind a tree. But she'd managed to get a little sliver of his face perfectly in focus, and his eyes stared right into mine. "You can keep that one. In fact, keep the whole stack. We can put the good ones in a book next time."

"Thanks," I replied, and meant it more than I could say. I pointed at the picture. "This is from last week?"

She nodded. I stared at the photo of him – breath-taking, but flat and inadequate in comparison to the real thing. I lightly ran my thumb over it, as if I'd feel his fur. Something knotted in my chest, bitter and sad. I felt Olivia's eyes on me, and they only made me feel worse, more alone. Once upon a time I would've talked to her about it, but now it felt too personal. Something had changed – and I thought it was me.

Olivia handed me a slender stack of prints that she'd separated from the rest. "This is my brag pile."

Distracted, I paged through them slowly. They were impressive: an autumn leaf floating on a puddle, students reflected in the windows of a school bus, an artfully smudgy black-and-white self-portrait of Olivia. I *oohed* and *aahed* and then slid the photo of my wolf back on top of them to look at it again.

Olivia made a sort of irritated sound in the back of her throat.

I hurriedly shuffled back to the one of the leaf floating on the puddle. I frowned at it for a moment, trying to imagine the sort of thing Mom would say about a piece of art. I managed, "I like this one. It's got great . . . colours."

She snatched them out of my hands and flicked the wolf photo back at me with such force that it bounced off my chest and on to the floor. "Yeah. Sometimes, Grace, I don't know why I even. . ."

Olivia didn't end the sentence, just shook her head. I didn't get it. Did she want me to pretend to like the other photos better than the one of my wolf?

"Hello! Anyone home?" It was John, Olivia's older

brother, sparing me from the consequences of whatever I'd done to irritate Olivia. He grinned at me from the front hall, shutting the door behind him. "Hey, good-looking."

Olivia looked up from her seat at the kitchen table with a frosty expression. "I *hope* you're talking about me."

"Of course," John said, looking at me. He was handsome in a very conventional way: tall, dark-haired like his sister, but with a face quick to smile and befriend. "It would be in very bad taste to hit on your sister's best friend. So. It's four o'clock. How time flies when you're —" he paused, looking at Olivia leaning over the table with a pile of photographs and me across from her with another stack — "doing nothing. Can't you do nothing by yourselves?"

Olivia silently straightened up her pile of photos while I explained, "We're introverts. We like doing nothing together. All talk, no action."

"Sounds fascinating. Olive, we've got to leave now if you want to make it to your lesson." He punched my arm lightly. "Hey, why don't you come with us, Grace? Are your parents home?"

I snorted. "Are you kidding? I'm raising myself. I should get a head of household bonus on my taxes." John laughed, probably more than my comment warranted, and Olivia shot me a look imbued with enough venom to kill small animals. I shut up.

"Come on, Olive," said John, seemingly oblivious to the daggers flying from his sister's eyes. "You pay for the lesson whether you get there or not. You coming, Grace?"

I looked out of the window, and for the first time in months, I imagined disappearing into the trees and running until I found my wolf in a summer wood. I shook my head. "Not this time. Rain check?"

John flashed a lopsided smile at me. "Yep. Come on, Olive. Bye, good-looking. You know who to call if you're looking for some action with your talk."

Olivia swung her backpack at him; it made a solid *thuk* as it hit his body. But it was me who got the dark look again, like I'd done anything to encourage John's flirting. "Go. Just go. Bye, Grace."

I showed them to the door and then returned aimlessly to the kitchen. A pleasantly neutral voice followed me, an announcer describing the classical piece I'd just heard and introducing another one; Dad had left the radio on in his study next to the kitchen. Somehow, the sounds of my parents' presence only highlighted their absence. Knowing that dinner would be canned beans unless I made it, I rummaged in the fridge and put a pot of leftover soup on the stove to simmer until my parents got home.

I stood in the kitchen, illuminated by the slanting cool afternoon light through the deck door, feeling sorry for myself, more because of Olivia's photo than because of the empty house. I hadn't seen my wolf in person since that day I'd touched him, nearly a week ago, and even though I knew it shouldn't, his absence still stabbed. It was stupid, the way I needed his phantom at the edge of the yard to feel complete. Stupid but completely incurable.

I went to the back door and opened it, wanting to smell the woods. I padded out on to the deck in my sock feet and leaned against the railing.

If I hadn't gone outside, I don't know if I would have heard the scream.

Nine
Grace

14°C

From the distance beyond the trees, the scream came again. For a second I thought it was a howl, and then the cry resolved itself into words: "Help! Help!"

I *swore* the voice sounded like Jack Culpeper's.

But that was impossible. I was just imagining it, remembering it from the cafeteria, where it had always seemed to carry over the others around him as he catcalled girls in the hallway.

Still, I followed the sound of the voice, moving impulsively across the yard and through the trees. The ground was damp and prickly through my sock feet; I was clumsier without my shoes. The crashing of my own steps through fallen leaves and tangled brush drowned out any other sounds. I hesitated, listening. The voice was gone, replaced by just a whimper, distinctly animal-sounding, and then by silence.

The relative safety of the back yard was far behind me now. I stood for a long moment, listening for any indication of where the first scream had come from. I knew I hadn't imagined it.

But there was nothing but silence. And in that silence, the smell of the woods seeped under my skin and reminded me of him. Crushed pine needles and wet earth and wood smoke.

I didn't care how idiotic it was. I'd come into the woods this far. Going a little further to try to see my wolf again wouldn't hurt anybody. I retreated to the house, just long enough to get my shoes, and headed back out into the cool autumn day. There was a bite behind the breeze that promised winter, but the sun shone bright, and under the shelter of the trees, the air was warm with the memory of hot days not so long ago.

All around me, leaves were dying gorgeously in red and orange; crows cawed to each other overhead in a vibrant, ugly soundtrack. I hadn't been this far into these woods since I was eleven, when I'd awoken surrounded by wolves, but strangely, I didn't feel afraid.

I stepped carefully, avoiding the little streams that snaked through the underbrush. This should have been unfamiliar territory, but I felt confident, assured. Silently guided, as though by a weird sixth sense, I followed the same worn paths that the wolves used over and over again.

Of course I knew it wasn't really a sixth sense. It was just me, acknowledging that there was more to my senses than I normally let on. I gave in to them and they became efficient, sharpened. As it reached me, the breeze seemed to carry the information of a stack of maps, telling me which animals had travelled where and how long ago. My ears picked up faint sounds that before had gone unnoticed: the rustling of a twig as a bird built a nest overhead, the soft step of a deer dozens of feet away.

I felt like I was home.

The woods rang with an unfamiliar cry, out of place in this world. I hesitated, listening. The whimper came again, louder than before.

Rounding a pine tree, I came upon the source: three wolves. It was the white wolf and the black pack leader; the sight of the she-wolf made my stomach twist with nerves. The two of them had pounced on a third wolf, a scraggly young male with an almost-blue tint to his grey coat and an ugly, healing wound on his shoulder. The other two wolves were pinning him to the leafy ground in a show of dominance; they all froze when they saw me. The pinned male twisted his head to stare at me, eyes entreating. My heart thudded in my chest. I knew those eyes. I remembered them from school; I remembered them from the local news.

"Jack?" I whispered.

The pinned wolf whistled pitifully through his nostrils. I just kept staring at those eyes. Hazel. Did wolves have hazel eyes? Maybe they did. Why did they look so wrong? As I stared at them, that one word just kept singing through my head: *human, human, human.*

With a snarl in my direction, the she-wolf let him

up. She snapped at his side, pushing him away from me. Her eyes were on me the entire time, daring me to stop her, and something in me told me that maybe I should have tried. But by the time my thoughts stopped spinning and I remembered the pocketknife in my jeans, the three wolves were already dark smudges in the distant trees.

Without the wolf's eyes before me, I had to wonder if I'd imagined the likeness to Jack's. After all, it had been two weeks since I'd seen Jack in person, and I'd never really paid close attention to him. I could have been misremembering his eyes. What was I thinking, anyway? That he'd turned into a wolf?

I let out a deep breath. Actually, that *was* what I was thinking. I didn't think I had forgotten Jack's eyes. Or his voice. And I hadn't imagined the human scream or the desperate howl. I just knew it was Jack, in the way I'd known how to find my way through the trees.

There was a knot in my stomach. Nerves. Anticipation. I didn't think Jack was the only secret these woods held.

That night I lay in bed and stared at the window, my blinds pulled up so I could see the night sky. One thousand brilliant stars punched holes in my consciousness, pricking me with longing. I could stare at the stars for hours, their infinite number and depth pulling me into a part of myself that I ignored during the day.

Outside, deep in the woods, I heard a long, keening wail, and then another, as the wolves began to howl. More voices pitched in, some low and mournful, others high and short, an eerie and beautiful chorus. I knew my wolf's howl; his rich tone sang out above the others as if begging me to hear it.

My heart ached inside me, torn between wanting them to stop and wishing they would go on for ever. I imagined myself there among them in the golden wood, watching them tilt their heads back and howl underneath a sky of endless stars. I blinked a tear away, feeling foolish and miserable, but I didn't go to sleep until every wolf had fallen silent.

Ten
Grace

15°C

"Do you think we need to take the book home – you know, *Exploring Guts*, or whatever it's called?" I asked Olivia. "For the reading? Or can I leave it here?"

She shoved her locker shut, her arms full of books. She was wearing reading glasses, complete with a chain on the ear pieces so that she could hang them around her neck. On Olivia, the look kind of worked, in a sort of charming librarian way. "It's a lot of reading. I'm bringing it."

I reached back into my locker for the textbook. Behind us, the hall hummed with noise as students packed up and headed home. All day long, I'd tried to work up the nerve to tell Olivia about the wolves. Normally I wouldn't have had to think about it, but after our almost-fight the day before, the moment hadn't seemed to come up. And now the day was over. I took a deep breath. "I saw the wolves yesterday."

Olivia paged idly through the book on top of her stack, not realizing how momentous my confession was. "Which ones?"

"The nasty she-wolf, the black one, and a new one." I debated again whether or not to tell her. She was way more interested in the wolves than Rachel was, and I didn't know who else to talk to. Even inside my head, the words sounded crazy. But since the evening before, the secret had surrounded me, tight around my chest and throat. I let the words spill out, my voice low. "Olivia, this is going to sound stupid. The new wolf – I think something happened when the wolves attacked Jack."

She just stared at me.

"Jack Culpeper," I said.

"I know who you meant." Olivia frowned at the front of her locker.

Her knotted eyebrows were making me regret starting the conversation. I sighed. "I thought I saw him in the woods. Jack. As a. . ." I hesitated.

"Wolf?" Olivia clicked her heels together – I'd never known anyone to actually do that, outside of *The Wizard of Oz* – and spun on them to face me with a raised eyebrow. "You're crazy." I could barely hear her over the students pressed all around us in the hall. "I mean, it's a nice fantasy, and I can see why you'd want to believe it – but you're crazy. Sorry."

I leaned in close, although the hall was so loud that even I had to struggle to hear our conversation. "Olive, I know what I saw. They were Jack's eyes. It was *his* voice." Of course, her doubt made me doubt, but I wasn't about to admit that. "I think the wolves turned him into one of them. Wait – what do you mean? About me wanting to believe it?"

Olivia gave me a long look before setting off towards our homeroom. "Grace, seriously. Don't think I don't know what this is about."

"What is this about?"

She answered with another question. "Are they *all* werewolves then?"

"What? The whole pack? I don't know. I didn't think about that." It hadn't occurred to me. It should have, but it hadn't. It was impossible. That those long absences were because my wolf vanished into human form? The idea was immediately unbearable, only because I wanted it to be true so badly that it hurt.

"Yeah, sure you didn't. Don't you think this obsession is getting kind of creepy, Grace?"

My reply sounded more defensive than I meant it to. "I'm not obsessed."

Students shot annoyed looks at us as Olivia stopped in the hall and put a finger on her chin. "Hmm, it's all you think about, all you talk about, and all you want us to talk about. What in the world would we call something like that? Oh, yeah! An obsession!"

"I'm just interested," I snapped. "And I thought you were, too."

"I *am* interested in them. Just not like all-consuming, involving, whatever, interested. I don't fantasize about being one." Her eyes were narrowed behind her reading glasses. "We're not thirteen any more, but you haven't seemed to figure that out yet."

I didn't say anything. All I could think was that she was being tremendously unfair, but I didn't feel like telling her that. I didn't want to say anything to her. I wanted to walk away and leave her standing there in the hallway. But I didn't. Instead, I kept my voice super flat and even. "Sorry to have bored you for so long. Must've killed you to look entertained."

Olivia grimaced. "Seriously, Grace. I'm not trying to be a jerk. But you're being impossible."

"No, you're just telling me that I'm creepy obsessed with something that's important to me. That's very –" the word I wanted took too long to surface in my head and ruined the effect – "*philanthropic* of you. Thanks for the help."

"Oh, grow *up*," snapped Olivia, and pushed around me.

The hallway seemed too quiet after she'd gone, and my cheeks felt hot. Instead of heading home, I trailed back into my empty homeroom, flopped into a chair, and put my head in my hands. I couldn't remember the last time I'd fought with Olivia. I'd looked at every photograph she'd ever taken. I'd listened to countless rants about her family and the pressure to perform. She owed it to me to at least hear me out.

My thoughts were cut short by the sound of cork heels *squelching* into the room. The scent of expensive perfume hit me a second before I lifted my eyes to Isabel Culpeper standing over my desk.

"I heard that you guys were talking about the wolves yesterday with that cop." Isabel's voice was pleasant, but the expression in her eyes belied her tone. The sympathy conjured up by her presence vanished at her words. "I'm giving you the benefit of the doubt and assuming you're innocently misinformed and not out-and-out retarded. I heard you're telling people the wolves aren't a problem. You must not have heard the newsflash: those animals killed my brother."

"I'm sorry about Jack," I said, automatically wanting to jump to my wolf's defence. For a second, I thought about Jack's eyes and what a revelation like that might mean to Isabel, but I discounted the idea almost immediately. If Olivia thought I was crazy for believing in werewolves, Isabel would probably be on the phone to the local mental institution before I could even finish a sentence.

"Shut. Up," Isabel interrupted my thoughts. "I know you're about to tell me the wolves aren't dangerous. Well, obviously they are. And obviously, someone's going to have to do something about that."

My mind flicked to the conversation in the classroom: Tom Culpeper and his stuffed animals. I imagined my wolf, stuffed and glassy-eyed. "You don't know that the wolves did it. He could've been—" I stopped. I knew the wolves had done it. "Look, something went really wrong. But it could've been just one wolf. The odds are that the rest of the pack had nothing to do with—"

"How beautiful objectivity is," Isabel snapped. She just looked at me for a long moment. Long enough for me to wonder what it was she was thinking. And then she said, "Seriously. Just get the last of your Greenpeace wolf-love done soon, because they won't be around much longer, whether you like it or not."

My voice was tight. "Why are you telling me this?"

"I'm sick of you telling people they're harmless. They killed him. But you know what? It's over now. Today." Isabel tapped my desk. "Ta."

I grabbed her wrist before she could go; I had a handful of fat bracelets. "What's that supposed to mean?"

Isabel stared at my hand on her wrist but didn't pull it away. She'd wanted me to ask. "What happened to Jack is never happening again. They're killing the wolves. Today. Now."

She slipped out of my now-slack grip and glided through the door.

For a single moment, I sat at the desk, my cheeks burning, pulling her words apart and putting them back together again.

And then I jumped from my chair, my notes fluttering to the floor like listless birds. I left them where they fell and ran for my car.

★

I was breathless by the time I slid behind the wheel of my car, Isabel's words playing over and over again in my head. I'd never thought of the wolves as vulnerable, but once I started imagining what a small-town attorney and big-time egomaniac like Tom Culpeper was capable of – fuelled by pent-up anger and grief, helped along by wealth and influence – they suddenly seemed terribly fragile.

I shoved my key in the ignition, feeling the car rattle reluctantly to life as I did. My eyes were on the yellow line of school buses waiting at the kerb and the knots of loud students still milling on the pavement, but my brain was picturing the chalk-white lines of the birches behind my house. Was a hunting party going after the wolves? Hunting them now?

I had to get home.

My car stalled, my foot uncertain on the dodgy clutch.

"God," I said, glancing around to see how many people had seen my car gasp to a halt. It wasn't as if it were difficult to stall my car these days, now that the heat sensor was crapping out, but usually I could finesse the clutch and get on the road without too much humiliation. I bit my lip, pulled myself together, and managed to restart.

There were two ways to get home from the school. One was shorter but involved stoplights and stop signs – impossible today, when I was too distracted to baby my car. I didn't have time to sit by the side of the road. The other route was slightly longer, but with only two stop signs. Plus, it ran along the edge of Boundary Wood, where the wolves lived.

As I drove, pushing my car as hard as I dared, my stomach twisted, sick with nerves. The engine gave an unhealthy shudder. I checked the dials; the engine was starting to overheat. Stupid car. If only my father had taken me to the dealership like he kept promising he would.

As the sky began to burn brilliantly red on the horizon, turning the thin clouds to streaks of blood above the trees, my heart thumped in my ears, and my skin felt tingly, electric. Everything inside me screamed that something was wrong. I didn't know what bothered me most – the nerves that shook my hands or the urge to curl my lips and fight.

Up ahead, I spotted a line of pickup trucks parked by the side of the road. Their four-ways blinked in the failing light, sporadically illuminating the woods next to the road. A figure leaned over the truck at the back of the line, holding something I couldn't quite make out at this distance. My stomach turned over again, and as I eased off the gas, my car gasped and stalled, leaving me coasting in an eerie quiet.

I turned the key, but between my jittery hands and the redlining heat sensor, the engine just shuddered under the hood without turning over. I wished

I'd just gone to the dealership myself. I had Dad's chequebook.

Growling under my breath, I braked and let the car drift to a stop behind the pickup trucks. I called Mom's studio on my mobile, but there was no answer – she must have been at her gallery opening already. I wasn't really worried about getting home; it was close enough to walk. What I was worried about was those trucks. Because they meant that Isabel had been telling the truth.

As I climbed out on to the shoulder of the road, I recognized the guy standing next to the pickup ahead. It was Officer Koenig, out of uniform, drumming his fingers on the hood. When I got closer, my stomach still churning, he looked up and his fingers stilled. He was wearing a bright orange cap and held a shotgun in the crook of his arm.

"Car problems?" he asked.

I turned abruptly at the sound of a car door slamming behind me. Another truck had pulled up, and two orange-capped hunters were making their way down the side of the road. I looked past them, to where they were heading, and my breath caught in my throat. Dozens of hunters were knotted on the shoulder, all carrying rifles, visibly restless, voices muffled. Squinting into the dim trees beyond a shallow ditch, I could see more orange caps dotting the woods, infesting them.

The hunt had already begun.

I turned back to Koenig and pointed at the gun he held. "Is that for the wolves?"

Koenig looked at it as if he'd somehow forgotten it was there. "It's—"

There was a loud *crack* from the woods behind him; both of us jerked at the sound. Cheers rose from the group down the road.

"What was that?" I demanded. But I knew what it was. It was a gunshot. In Boundary Wood. My voice was steady, which surprised me. "They're hunting the wolves, aren't they?"

"With all due respect, miss," Koenig said, "I think you should wait in your car. I can give you a ride home, but you'll have to wait a little bit."

There were shouts in the woods, distant, and another popping sound, further away. God. The wolves. My wolf. I grabbed Koenig's arm. "You have to tell them to stop! They can't shoot back there!"

Koenig stepped back, pulling his arm from my grip. "Miss—"

There was another distant *pop*, small and insignificant-sounding. In my head, I saw a perfect image of a wolf rolling, rolling, a gaping hole in its side, eyes dead. I didn't think. The words just came out. "Your phone. You have to call them and tell them to stop. I have a friend in there! She was going to take photos this afternoon. In the woods. Please, you have to call them!"

"What?" Koenig froze. "There's someone in there? Are you sure?"

"Yes," I said, because I was sure. "Please. Call them!"

God bless humourless Officer Koenig, because he didn't ask me for any more details. Pulling his mobile phone from his pocket, he punched a quick number and held the phone to his ear. His eyebrows made a straight, hard line, and after a second, he pulled the phone away and stared at the screen. "Reception," he muttered, and tried again. I stood by the pickup truck, my arms crossed over my chest as cold seeped into me, watching the grey dusk take over the road as the sun disappeared behind the trees. Surely they had to stop when it got dark. But something told me that just because they had a cop standing watch by the road didn't make what they were doing legal.

Staring at his phone again, Koenig shook his head. "It's not working. Hold on. You know, it'll be fine – they're being careful – I'm sure they wouldn't shoot a person. But I'll go and warn them. Let me lock my gun up. It will only take a second."

As he started to put his shotgun in the pickup truck, there was another gunshot from the woods and something buckled inside me. I just couldn't wait any more. I jumped the ditch and scrambled up into the trees, leaving Koenig behind. I heard him calling after me, but I was already well into the woods. I had to stop them – warn my wolf – do something.

But as I ran, slipping between trees and jumping over fallen limbs, all I could think was, *I'm too late*.

Eleven

Sam

10°C

We ran. We were silent, dark drops of water, rushing over brambles and around the trees as the men drove us before them.

The woods I knew, the woods that protected me, were punched through by their sharp odours and their shouts. I scrambled here and there amongst the other wolves, guiding and following, keeping us together. The fallen trees and underbrush felt unfamiliar beneath my feet; I kept from stumbling by flying – long, endless leaps, barely touching the ground.

It was terrifying to not know where I was.

We traded simple images amongst ourselves in our wordless, futile language: dark figures behind us, figures topped with bright warnings; motionless, cold wolves; the smell of death in our nostrils.

A crack deafened me, shook me out of balance. Beside me, I heard a whimper. I knew which wolf it was without turning my head. There was no time to stop; nothing to do even if I had.

A new smell hit my nostrils: earthy rot and stagnant

water. The lake. They were driving us to the lake. I formed a clear image in my head at the same time that Paul, the pack leader, did. The slow, rippling edge of the water, thin pines growing sparsely in the poor soil, the lake stretching for ever in both directions.

A pack of wolves, huddled on the shore. No escape.

We were the hunted. We slid before them, ghosts in the woods, and we fell, whether or not we fought.

The others kept running, towards the lake.

But I stopped.

Twelve
Grace

9°C

These were not the woods that I'd walked through just a few days earlier, painted all the vivid hues of autumn. These were close woods made of a thousand dark tree trunks turned black by dusk. The sixth sense I'd imagined guiding me before was gone; all the familiar paths destroyed by crashing hunters in orange caps. I was completely disoriented; I had to keep stopping to listen for shouts and faraway footsteps through the dry leaves.

My breath was burning my throat by the time I saw the first orange cap, glowing distantly out of the twilight. I shouted, but the cap didn't even turn; the figure was too far away to hear me. And then I saw the others – orange dots scattered through the woods, all moving slowly, relentlessly, in the same direction. Making a lot of noise. Driving the wolves ahead of them.

"Stop!" I shouted. I was close enough to see the outline of the nearest hunter, shotgun in his hands. I closed the distance between us, my legs protesting, stumbling a little because I was tired.

He stopped walking and turned, surprised, waiting until I approached. I had to get very close to see his face; it was so close to night in these trees. His face, older and lined, seemed vaguely familiar to me, though I couldn't remember where in town I'd seen him before. The hunter frowned a strange frown at me; I thought he looked guilty, but I could've been reading into it. "Well, what are you doing here?"

I started to speak before realizing that I was so out of breath that I could hardly get the words out. Seconds ticked by as I struggled to find my voice. "You – have – to – stop. I have a friend in the woods here. She was going to take photographs."

He squinted at me, and then looked at the darkening woods. "*Now?*"

"Yes, now!" I said, trying not to snap. I saw a black box at his waist – a walkie-talkie. "You've got to call them and tell them to stop. It's almost dark. How would they see her?"

The hunter stared at me for an agonizingly long moment before nodding. He reached for his walkie-talkie and unstrapped it and lifted it up and brought it towards his mouth. It felt like he was doing everything in slow motion.

"Hurry!" Anxiety shot through me, a physical pain.

The hunter clicked the button down on the walkie-talkie to speak.

And suddenly a volley of shots snapped and snarled,

not far away. Not little pops, like they were from the roadside, but crackling fireworks, unmistakably gunshots. My ears rang.

In a weird way, I felt totally objective, like I was standing outside my own body. So I could feel that my knees were weak and trembling without knowing why, and I heard my heartbeat racing inside me, and I saw red trickling down behind my eyes, like a dream of crimson. Like a viciously clear nightmare of death.

There was such a convincing metallic taste in my mouth that I touched my lips, expecting blood. But there was nothing. No pain. Just the absence of feeling.

"There's someone in the woods," the hunter said into his walkie-talkie, as if he couldn't see that part of me was dying.

My wolf. My wolf. I couldn't think of anything but his eyes.

"Hey! Miss." This voice was younger than the hunter's, and the hand that took my shoulder was firm. Koenig said, "What were you thinking, taking off like that? There are people with guns here."

Before I could reply to that, Koenig turned to the hunter. "And I heard those shots. I'm fairly sure everyone in Mercy Falls heard those shots. It's one thing, doing this —" he jerked a hand towards the gun in the hunter's hands — "and something else flaunting it." I started to twist out from under Koenig's hand; he tightened his fingers reflexively and then released me when he realized what he was doing. "You're from the school. What's your name?"

"Grace Brisbane."

Recognition dawned on the hunter's face. "Lewis Brisbane's daughter?"

Koenig looked at him.

"The Brisbanes have a house right over there. On the edge of the woods." The hunter pointed in the direction of home. The house was invisible behind a black tangle of trees.

Koenig seized upon this bit of information. "I'll escort you back there and then come back to find out what's going on with your friend. Ralph, use that thing to tell them to *stop shooting things*."

"I don't need an escort," I said, but Koenig walked with me anyway, leaving Ralph the hunter talking into his walkie-talkie. The cold air was beginning to bite and prickle on my cheeks, the evening getting cold quickly as the sun disappeared. I felt as frozen on the inside as I was on the outside. I could still see the curtain of red falling over my eyes and hear the crackling gunfire.

I was so sure that my wolf had been there.

At the edge of the woods, I stopped, looking at the dark glass of the back door on the deck. The entire house looked shadowed, unoccupied, and Koenig sounded dubious as he said, "Do you need me to—"

"I can make it back from here. Thanks."

He hesitated until I stepped into our yard, and then I heard him go crashing back the way we'd come. For a long moment, I stood in the silent twilight, listening to the faraway voices in the woods and the wind rattling the dry leaves in the trees above me.

And as I stood there in what I had thought was silence, I started to hear sounds that I hadn't before. The rustling of animals in the woods, turning over crisp leaves with their paws. The distant roar of trucks on the highway.

The sound of fast, ragged breathing.

I froze. I held my breath.

But the uneven gasps weren't mine.

I followed the sound, climbing cautiously on to the deck, painfully aware of the sound of each stair sighing beneath my weight.

I smelled him before I saw him, my heart instantly revving up into high gear. My wolf. Then the motion detector light above the back door clicked on and flooded the porch with yellow light. And there he was, half sitting, half lying against the glass back door.

My breath caught painfully in my throat as I moved still closer, hesitant. His beautiful ruff was gone and he was naked, but I knew it was my wolf even before he opened his eyes. His pale yellow eyes, so familiar, flicked open at the sound of my approach, but he didn't move. Red was smeared from his ear to his desperately human shoulders – deadly war paint.

I can't tell you how I knew it was him, but I never doubted it.

Werewolves didn't exist.

Despite telling Olivia I'd seen Jack, I hadn't really believed it. Not like this.

The breeze carried the smell to my nostrils again, grounding me. Blood. I was wasting time.

I pulled out my keys and reached over the top of him to open the back door. Too late, I saw one of his hands reach out, snatching air, and he crashed inside the open door, leaving a smear of red on the glass.

"I'm sorry!" I said. I couldn't tell if he'd heard me. Stepping over him, I hurried into the kitchen, hitting light switches as I did. I grabbed a wad of dishcloths from a drawer; as I did, I noticed my dad's car keys on the counter, hastily thrown next to a pile of papers from work. So I could use Dad's car, if I had to.

I ran back to the door. I was afraid the boy might've disappeared while my back was turned, a figment of my imagination, but he hadn't moved. He lay half in and half out, shaking violently.

Without thinking, I grabbed him under his armpits and dragged him far enough inside that I could shut the door. In the light of the breakfast area, blood smearing a path across the floor, he seemed tremendously real.

I crouched swiftly. My voice was barely a whisper. "What happened?" I knew the answer, but I wanted to hear him speak.

His knuckles were white where his hand was pressed against his neck, brilliant red leaking around his fingers. "Shot."

My stomach squeezed with nerves, not from what he said, but the voice that said it. It was him. Human words, not a howl, but the timbre was the same. It was *him*. "Let me see."

I had to pry his hands away from his neck. There was too much blood to see the wound, so I just pressed one of the dishcloths over the mess of red that stretched from his chin to his collarbone. It was well beyond my first-aid abilities. "Hold this." His eyes flicked to me, familiar but subtly different. The wildness was tempered with a comprehension that had been absent before.

"I don't want to go back." The agony in his words immediately transported me to a memory: a wolf standing in silent grief before me. The boy's body jerked, a weird, unnatural movement that hurt to think about. "Don't – don't let me change."

I laid a second, bigger dishcloth over his body, covering the goosebumps as best I could. In any other context, I would've been embarrassed by his nakedness, but here, his skin smeared with blood and dirt, it just made his condition seem more pitiful. My words were gentle, as though he might still leap up and run. "What's your name?"

He groaned softly, one hand shaking just a bit as he held the cloth against his neck. It was already soaked through with his blood, and a thin red trail ran along his jaw and dripped to the floor. Lowering himself slowly to the floor, he laid his cheek against the wood, his breath clouding the shiny finish. "Sam."

He closed his eyes.

"Sam," I repeated. "I'm Grace. I'm going to go start my dad's car. I have to take you to the hospital."

He shuddered. I had to lean very close to hear his voice. "Grace – Grace, I—"

I only waited a second for him to finish. When he didn't, I jumped up and grabbed the keys from the counter. I still couldn't quite believe that he wasn't my own invention – years of wishing made real. But whatever he was, he was here now, and I wasn't about to lose him.

Thirteen

Sam

7°C

I was not a wolf, but I wasn't Sam yet, either.

I was a leaking womb bulging with the promise of conscious thoughts: the frozen woods far behind me, the girl on the tyre swing, the sound of fingers on metal strings. The future and the past, both the same, snow and then summer and then snow again.

A shattered spider's web of many colours, cracked in ice, immeasurably sad.

"Sam," the girl said. "Sam."

She was past present future. I wanted to answer, but I was broken.

Fourteen

Grace

7°C

It's rude to stare, but the great thing about staring at
a sedated person is that they don't know you're doing
it. And the truth was, I couldn't stop staring at Sam.
If he'd gone to my school, he probably would've been
dismissed as an emo kid or maybe a long-lost member
of the Beatles. He had that sort of mop-top black hair
and interestingly shaped nose that a girl could never
get away with. He looked nothing like a wolf, but
everything like my wolf. Even now, without his
familiar eyes open, a little part of me kept jumping
with irrational glee, reminding myself – *it's him*.

"Oh, honey, are you still here? I thought you'd left."

I turned as the green curtains parted to admit a
broad-shouldered nurse. Her name tag read SUNNY.

"I'm staying until he wakes up." I held on to the side
of the hospital bed as if to prove how difficult it would
be to remove me.

Sunny smiled pityingly at me. "He's been heavily
sedated, hon. He won't wake up until the morning."

I smiled back at her, my voice firm. "Then that's how

long I'm staying." I'd already waited hours while they removed the bullet and stitched the wound; it had to be after midnight by now. I kept waiting to feel sleepy, but I was wired. Every time I saw him it was like another jolt. It occurred to me, belatedly, that my parents hadn't bothered to call my mobile phone when they got back from Mom's gallery opening. They probably hadn't even noticed the bloody towel I'd used to hurriedly wipe up the floor, or the fact that Dad's car was missing. Or maybe they just hadn't got home yet. Midnight was early for them.

Sunny's smile stayed in place. "OK, then," she said. "You know, he's awfully lucky. For the bullet to just graze him?" Her eyes glittered. "Do you know why he did it?"

I frowned at her, nerves prickling. "I don't follow. Why he was in the woods?"

"Hon, you and I both know he wasn't in the woods."

I raised an eyebrow, waiting for her to say something else, but she didn't. I said, "Uh, yeah. He was. A hunter accidentally shot him." It wasn't a lie. Well, all but the "accidentally" part. I was pretty confident it was no accident.

Sunny clucked. "Look — Grace, isn't it? Grace, are you his girlfriend?"

I grunted in a way that could be interpreted as either yes or no, depending on how the listener was leaning.

Sunny took it as a yes. "I know you're really close to the situation, but he does need help."

Realization dawned on me. I almost laughed. "You think he shot himself. Look — Sunny, isn't it? Sunny, you're wrong."

The nurse glared at me. "Do you think we're stupid? That we wouldn't notice this?" On the other side of the bed, she took Sam's limp arms and turned them so his palms faced towards the ceiling in a silent entreaty. She gestured at the scars on his wrists, memories of deep, purposeful wounds that should've been lethal.

I stared at them, but they were like words in a foreign language. They meant nothing to me. I shrugged. "Those are from before I knew him. I'm just telling you he didn't try and shoot himself tonight. It was some insane hunter."

"Sure, hon. Fine. Let me know if you need anything." Sunny glared at me before backing out of the curtain and leaving me alone with Sam.

Face flushed, I shook my head and stared at my white-knuckled grip on the bed. Of all my pet peeves, condescending adults were probably at the top of the list.

A second after Sunny was gone, Sam's eyes flicked open, and I jumped out of my skin, heart pounding in my ears. It took a long moment of staring at him for my pulse to return to normal. Logic told me to read his eyes as hazel, but really, they were still yellow, and they were definitely fixed on me.

My voice came out a lot quieter than I meant it to. "You're supposed to be asleep."

"Who are you?" His voice had the same complicated, mournful tone I remembered from his howl. He narrowed his eyes. "Your voice seems so familiar."

Pain flickered through me. It hadn't occurred to me that he might not remember his time as a wolf. I didn't know what the rules were for this. Sam reached his hand towards mine, and I automatically put my fingers in his. With a guilty little smile, he pulled my hand towards his nose and took a sniff, and then another one. His smile widened, though it was still shy. It was absolutely adorable, and my breath got caught somewhere in my throat. "I know that smell. I didn't recognize you; you look different. I'm sorry. I feel stupid for not remembering. It takes a couple hours for me – for my brain – to come back."

He didn't release my fingers, and I didn't take them away, even though it was hard to concentrate with his skin against mine. "Come back from what?"

"Come back from *when*," he corrected. "Come back from when I was. . ."

Sam waited. He wanted me to say it. It was harder than I thought it would be, to admit it out loud, even though it shouldn't have been.

"When you were a wolf," I whispered. "Why are you here?"

"Because I was shot," he said pleasantly.

"I meant like *this*." I gestured towards his body, so clearly human underneath the silly hospital gown.

He blinked. "Oh. Because it's spring. Because it's warm. Warm makes me *me*. Makes me Sam."

I finally pulled my hand away and closed my eyes, trying to gather what was left of my sanity for a moment. When I opened my eyes and spoke, I said the most mundane thing possible. "It's not spring. It's September."

I'm not the best at reading people, but I thought I saw a glimmer of anxiety behind his eyes before they cleared. "That's not good," he remarked. "Can I ask you a favour?"

I had to close my eyes again at the sound of his voice, because it shouldn't have been familiar, but it was, speaking to me on some deep level just like his eyes always had as a wolf. It was turning out to be more difficult to accept this than I'd thought. I opened my eyes. He was still there. I tried again, closing and then opening them once more. But he was still there.

He laughed. "Are you having an epileptic fit? Maybe *you* should be in this bed."

I glared at him, and he turned bright red as he realized another meaning for his words. I spared him from his mortification by answering his question. "What's the favour?"

"I, uh, need some clothing. I need to get out of here before they figure out I'm a freak."

"How do you mean? I didn't see a tail."

Sam reached up and began to prise at the edge of the dressings on his neck.

"Are you crazy?" I reached forward and grabbed at his hand, too late. He peeled away the gauze to reveal four new stitches dotting a short line through old scar tissue. There was no fresh wound still oozing blood, no evidence of the gunshot except for the pink, shiny scar. My jaw dropped.

Sam smiled, clearly pleased by my reaction. "See, don't you think they'd suspect something?"

"But there was so much blood—"

"Yeah. My skin just couldn't heal when it was bleeding so much. Once they stitched me up—" He shrugged and made a little gesture with his hands, like he was opening a small book. "Abracadabra. There are some perks to being me." His words were light, but his expression was anxious, watching me, seeing how I was taking all this. How I was taking the fact of his existence.

"OK, I just have to see something here," I told him. "I just—" I stepped forward and touched the end of my fingers to the scar tissue on his neck. Somehow feeling the smooth, firm skin convinced me in a way that his words couldn't. Sam's eyes slid to my face and away again, unsure of where to look while I felt the lump of old scar beneath the prickling black sutures. I let my hand linger on his neck for slightly longer than necessary, not on the scar, but on the smooth, wolf-scented skin beside it. "OK. So obviously you need to leave before they look at it. But if you sign out against medical advice or just take off, they'll try to track you down."

He made a face. "No, they won't. They'll just figure I'm some derelict without insurance. Which is true. Well, the insurance part."

So much for being subtle. "No, they'll think you left to avoid counselling. They think you shot yourself because of—"

Sam's face was puzzled.

I pointed to his wrists.

"Oh, that. I didn't do that."

I frowned at him again. I didn't want to say something like, "It's OK, you have an excuse" or "You can tell me, I won't judge", because, really, that'd be just as bad as Sunny, assuming that he'd tried to kill himself. But it wasn't as though he could've got those scars tripping on the stairs.

He rubbed a thumb over one of his wrists, thoughtful. "My mom did this one. Dad did the other one. I remember they counted backwards so they'd do it at the same time. I still can't stand to look at a bathtub."

It took me a moment to process what he meant. I don't know what did it – the flat, emotionless way he said it, the image of the scene that swam in my head, or just the shock of the evening in general, but I suddenly felt dizzy. My head whirled, my heartbeat crashed in my ears, and I hit the sticky linoleum floor hard.

I don't know how many seconds I was out, but I saw the curtain slide open at the same time that Sam thumped back down on the bed, slapping the bandage back over his neck. Then a male nurse was kneeling beside me, helping me sit up.

"Are you OK?"

I'd fainted. I'd never fainted in my life. I closed my eyes and opened them again, until the nurse had one head instead of three heads floating side by side. Then I began to lie. "I just thought about all the blood when I found him ... *ohhhh*. . ." I still felt woozy, so the *ohhhh* sounded very convincing.

"Don't think about it," suggested the nurse, smiling in a very friendly way. I thought his hand was slightly too close to my boob for casual contact, and that fact steeled my resolve to follow through with the humiliating plan that had just popped into my head.

"I think – I need to ask an embarrassing question," I muttered, feeling my cheeks heat. This was almost as bad as if I had been telling the truth. "Do you think I could borrow a pair of scrubs? I – uh – my trousers—"

"Oh!" cried the poor nurse. His embarrassment at my condition was probably sharpened by his earlier flirtatious smile. "Yes. Absolutely. I'll be right back."

Good as his word, he returned in a few minutes,

holding a folded pair of sick-green scrubs in his hands. "They might be a little big, but they have strings that you can – you know."

"Thanks," I mumbled. "Uh, do you mind? I'll just change here. He's not looking at anything at the moment." I gestured towards Sam, who was looking convincingly sedated.

The nurse vanished behind the curtains. Sam's eyes flashed open again, distinctly amused.

He whispered, "Did you tell that man you went potty on yourself?"

"You. Shut. Up," I hissed back furiously and chucked the scrubs at his head. "Hurry up before they find out I didn't wet myself. You seriously owe me."

He grinned and slid the scrubs beneath the thin hospital sheet, wrestling them on, then tugged the dressing from his neck and the blood pressure cuff from his arm. As the cuff dropped to the bed, he ripped off his gown and replaced it with the scrubs top. The monitor squealed in protest, flatlining and announcing his death to the staff.

"Time to go," he said, and led the way out behind the curtains. As he paused, quickly taking in the room around us, I heard nurses rustling into his curtained area behind us.

"He was *sedated*." Sunny's voice rose above the others.

Sam reached out and grabbed my hand, the most

natural thing in the world, and pulled me into the bright light of the hall. Now that he was clothed – in scrubs, no less – and not drowning in blood, nobody blinked an eye as he wended his way past the nurses' station and on towards the exit. All the while, I could see his wolf's mind analysing the situation. The tilt of his head told me what he was listening to, and the lift of his chin hinted of the scents he was gathering. Agile despite his lanky, loose-jointed build, he cut a deft path through the clutter until we were crossing the general lobby.

A syrupy country song was playing over the speaker system as my sneakers scrubbed across the ugly dark-blue tartan carpet; Sam's bare feet made no sound. At this time of night, the lobby was empty, without even a receptionist at the desk. I felt so high on adrenaline I thought I could probably fly to Dad's car. The eternally pragmatic corner of my mind reminded me that I needed to call the tow company to get my own car off the side of the road. But I couldn't really work up proper annoyance about it, because all I could think about was Sam. My wolf was a cute guy and he was holding my hand. I could die happy.

Then I felt Sam's hesitation. He held back, eyes fixed on the darkness that pressed against the glass door. "How cold is it out there?"

"Probably not too much colder than it was when I brought you. Why – will it make that much of a difference?"

Sam's face darkened. "It's right on the edge. I hate this time of year. I could be either."

I heard the pain in his voice. "Does it hurt to change?"

He looked away from me. "I want to be human right now."

I wanted him to be human, too. "I'll go start the car and get the heater going. That way you'll only be in the cold for a second."

He looked a little helpless. "But I don't know where to go."

"Where do you normally live?" I was afraid he'd say something pitiful, like the homeless shelter downtown. I assumed he didn't live with the parents who had cut his wrists.

"Beck – one of the wolves – once he changes, a lot of us stay at his house, but if he's not changed, the heat might not be turned up. I could—"

I shook my head and let go of his hand. "No. I'm getting the car and you're coming home with me."

His eyes widened. "Your parents—?"

"What they don't know won't kill them," I said, pushing open the door. Wincing at the blast of cold night air, Sam backed away from the door, wrapping his arms around himself. But even as he shuddered with the cold, he bit his lip and gave me a hesitant smile.

I turned towards the dark car park, feeling more alive and more happy and more afraid than I ever had before.

Fifteen
Grace

6°C

"Are you sleeping?" Sam's voice was barely a whisper, but in the dark room where he didn't belong, it was like a shout.

I rolled in my bed towards where he lay on the floor, a dark bundle curled in a nest of blankets and pillows. His presence, so strange and wonderful, seemed to fill the room and press against me. I didn't think I'd ever sleep again. "No."

"Can I ask you a question?"

"You already have."

He paused, considering. "Can I ask you *two* questions, then?"

"You already have."

Sam groaned and threw one of the small sofa pillows in my direction. It arced through the moonlit room, a blackened projectile, and thumped harmlessly by my head. "So you're a smart-ass, then."

I grinned in the darkness. "OK, I'll play. What do you want to know?"

"You were bitten." But it wasn't a question. I could

hear the interest in his voice, sense the tension in his body, even across the room. I slid down into my blankets, hiding from what he'd said.

"I don't know."

Sam's voice rose above a whisper. "How can you not know?"

I shrugged, though he couldn't see it. "I was young."

"I was young, too. I knew what was happening." When I didn't answer, he asked, "Is that why you just lay there? You didn't know they were going to kill you?"

I stared at the dark square of night through the window, lost in the memory of Sam as a wolf. The pack circled around me, tongues and teeth, growls and jerks. One wolf stood back, ice-decked ruff bristling all along his neck, quivering as he watched me in the snow. Lying in the cold, under a white sky going dark, I kept my eyes on him. He was beautiful: wild and dark, yellow eyes filled with a complexity I couldn't begin to fathom. And he gave off a scent the same as the other wolves around me – rich, feral, musky. Even now, as he lay in my room, I could smell the wolf on him, though he was wearing scrubs and a new skin.

Outside, I heard a low, keening howl, and then another. The night chorus rose, missing Sam's plaintive voice but gorgeous nonetheless. My heart quickened, sick with abstract longing, and on the floor, I heard

Sam give a low whimper. The miserable sound, caught halfway between human and wolf, distracted me.

"Do you miss them?" I whispered.

Sam climbed from his makeshift bed and stood by the window, an unfamiliar silhouette against the night, his arms clutched around his lanky body. "No. Yeah. I don't know. It makes me feel – sick. Like I don't belong here."

Sounds familiar. I tried to think of something to say to comfort him, but couldn't settle on anything that would sound genuine.

"But this is me," he insisted, his chin jerking to refer to his body. I didn't know if he meant to convince me or himself. He remained by the window as the wolves' howls reached a crescendo, pricking my eyes to tears.

"Come up here and talk to me," I said, to distract both of us. Sam half turned, but I couldn't see his expression. "It's cold down there on the floor and you'll get a crick in your neck. Just come up here."

"What about your parents?" he said, the same question he'd asked in the hospital. I was about to ask him why he worried about them so much, when I remembered Sam's story about his own parents and the shiny, puckered scars on his wrists.

"You don't know my parents."

"Where are they?" Sam asked.

"Gallery opening, I think. My mom's an artist."

His voice was dubious. "It's three o'clock in the morning."

My voice was louder than I'd meant for it to be. "Just get in. I trust you to behave. And to not hog the sheets." When he still hesitated, I said, "Hurry up, before there's no more night left."

Obediently, he retrieved one of the pillows from the floor, but hesitated again on the opposite side of the bed. In the dim light, I could just make out his mournful expression as he regarded the forbidden territory of the bed. I wasn't sure if I was charmed by his reluctance to share a bed with a girl or insulted that, apparently, I wasn't hot enough for him to charge the mattress like a bull.

Finally, he climbed in. The bed creaked under his weight, and he winced before settling on the very far edge of it, not even under the blanket. I could smell the faint wolf scent better now, and I sighed with a strange contentedness. He sighed, too.

"Thank you," he said. Formal, considering he was lying in my bed.

"You're welcome."

The truth of it struck me then. Here I was with a shape-shifting boy in my bed. Not just any shape-shifting boy, but my wolf. I kept reliving the memory of the deck light clicking to life, revealing him for the first time. A weird combination of excitement and nervousness tingled through me.

Sam turned his head to look at me, as though my thrill of nerves had sent up a flare. I could see his eyes glinting in the dim light, a few feet away. "They bit you. You should've changed, too, you know."

In my head, the wolves circled a body in the snow, their lips bloody, teeth bared, growling over the kill. A wolf, Sam, dragged the body from the circle of wolves. He carried it through the trees on two legs that left human footprints in the snow. I knew I was falling asleep, so I shook myself awake; I couldn't remember whether I'd answered Sam.

"Sometimes I wish I had," I told him.

He closed his eyes, miles away on the other side of the bed. "Sometimes I do, too."

Sixteen

Sam

5°C

I woke up all in a rush. For a moment, I lay still, blinking, trying to determine what had woken me. The events of the previous night rushed back to me as I realized it wasn't a sound that had woken me, but a sensation: a hand resting on my arm. Grace had rolled over in her sleep, and I couldn't stop staring at her fingers resting on my skin.

Here, lying next to the girl who had rescued me, my simple humanity felt like a triumph.

I rolled on to my side and for a while, I just watched her sleep, long, even breaths that moved the flyaway hairs by her face. In slumber, she seemed utterly certain of her safety, utterly unconcerned by my presence beside her. That felt like a subtle victory, too.

When I heard her father get up, I lay perfectly still, heart beating fast and silent, ready to leap from the edge of the mattress in case he came to wake her for school. But he left for work in a cloud of juniper-scented aftershave that billowed towards me from under the door. Her mother left soon after, noisily dropping something in the kitchen and swearing in a pleasant voice as she shut the door behind her. I couldn't believe they wouldn't glance into Grace's room to make sure she was still alive, especially considering they hadn't seen her when they came home in the dead of the night. But the door stayed shut.

Anyway, I felt foolish in the scrubs, and they were useless to me in this awful in-between weather, so I slipped out while Grace slept; she didn't even stir as I left. I hesitated on the back deck, looking at the frost-tipped blades of grass. Even though I'd borrowed a pair of her father's boots, the early-morning air still bit at the skin of my bare ankles beneath the rubber. I could almost feel the nausea of the change rolling over in my stomach.

Sam, I told myself, willing my body to believe. *You're Sam*. I needed to be warmer; I retreated inside to find a coat. Damn this weather. What had happened to summer? In an overstuffed wardrobe that smelled of stale memories and mothballs, I found a puffy, bright blue jacket that made me look like a blimp and ventured out into the back yard with more confidence. Grace's father had feet the size of a yeti, so I tramped into the woods with all the grace of a polar bear in a dollhouse.

Despite the chilly air that made ghosts of my breath, the woods were beautiful this time of year, all bold primary colours: crisp leaves in startling yellow and red, bright cerulean sky. Details I never noticed as a wolf.

But as I made my way towards my stash of clothing, I missed all the things I didn't notice as a human. Though I still had heightened senses, I couldn't smell the many subtle tracks of animals in the underbrush or the damp promise of warmer weather later in the day. Normally, I could hear the industrial symphony of cars and trucks on the distant highway and detect the size and speed of each vehicle. But now all I could smell was the smokiness of autumn, its burning leaves and half-dead trees, and all I could hear was the low, barely audible hum of traffic far in the distance.

As a wolf, I would have smelled Shelby's approach long before she'd come into sight. But not now. She was nearly on top of me when I got the feeling that something was close. The tiny hairs on my neck stood to attention, and I had the uneasy sense that I was sharing my breath with someone else. I turned and saw her, big for a female, white coat ordinary and yellowish in this full daylight. She seemed to have survived the hunt without so much as a scratch. Ears slightly back, she observed my ridiculous apparel with a cocked head.

"Shhh," I said, and held my hand out, palm up, letting what was left of my scent waft towards her. "It's me."

Her muzzle curled in distaste as she backed slowly away, and I guessed she recognized Grace's scent layered on top of mine. I knew I did; even now, her spare, soapy aroma clung to my hair where I'd lain on her bed and to my hand where she'd held it.

Wariness flashed in Shelby's eyes, mirroring her human expression. This was how it was with Shelby and me – I couldn't remember a time we hadn't been subtly at odds. I clung to my humanity – and to my obsession with Grace – like a drowning man, but Shelby welcomed the forgetting that came with her lupine skin. Of course, she had plenty of reasons to forget.

Now, in these September woods, we regarded each other. Her ears tipped towards me and away, collecting dozens of sounds that escaped my human ears, and her nostrils worked, discovering where I'd been. I found myself remembering the sensation of dried leaves beneath my paws and the sharp, rich, slumber-heavy scent of these autumn woods when I was a wolf.

Shelby stared into my eyes – a very human gesture, considering my rank in the pack was too high for wolves other than Paul or Beck to challenge me like that – and I imagined her human voice saying to me, as it had so many times before, *Don't you miss it?*

I closed my eyes, shutting out the vividness of her gaze and the memory of my wolf body, and instead thought of Grace, back at the house. There was nothing in my wolf experience that could ever compare to the feeling of Grace's hand in mine. I immediately turned this thought over in my head, creating lyrics. *You're my change of skin / my summer-winter-fall / I spring to follow you / this loss is beautiful.* In the second it took me to compose the lyric and imagine the guitar riff that would go with it, Shelby had vanished into the woods, soft as a whisper.

That she could disappear with the same silent stealth as she had arrived reminded me of my vulnerable state, and I clumped hurriedly to the shed where my clothing was stashed. Years ago, Beck and I had dragged the old shed, piece by piece, from his back yard to a small clearing deep in the woods.

Inside were a space heater, a boat battery and several plastic bins with names written on the sides. I opened the bin marked with my name and pulled out the stuffed backpack inside. The other bins were loaded with food and blankets and spare batteries – equipment for holing up in this shack, waiting for other pack members to change – but mine contained supplies for escape. Everything I kept here was designed to get me back to humanity as quickly as possible, and for that, Shelby couldn't forgive me.

I hurriedly changed into my several layers of long-sleeved shirts and a pair of jeans and traded Grace's father's oversized boots for wool socks and my scuffed leather shoes, getting my wallet with my summer-job money in it and stuffing everything left over into the backpack. As I shut the shed door behind me, I caught dark movement out of the corner of my eye.

"Paul," I said, but the black wolf, our wolf pack leader, was gone. I doubted he even knew me now: to him, I was just another human in these woods, despite my vaguely familiar scent. The knowledge prickled a kind of regret somewhere in the back of my throat. Last year, Paul hadn't become human until the end of August. Maybe he wouldn't change at all this year.

I knew my own remaining shifts were numbered, too. Last year I had changed in June, a frighteningly huge jump from the previous year's shift in early spring, when there had still been snow on the ground. And this year? How late would I have got my body back if Tom Culpeper hadn't shot me? I didn't even really understand how being shot had given me back my human form in this cool weather. I thought of how frigid it had been when Grace knelt over me, pressing a cloth to my neck. It hadn't been summer for a long time.

The brilliant colours of the brittle leaves all around the shed mocked me then, evidence that a year had lived and died without my being aware of it. I knew with sudden, chilling certainty that this was my last year.

To meet Grace only now seemed like an intensely cruel twist of fate.

I didn't want to think about it. Instead, I jogged back to the house, checking to make sure that Grace's parents' cars were still gone. Letting myself back in, I hovered outside the bedroom door for a second, then loitered for a long time in the kitchen, looking through the cabinets even though I wasn't really hungry.

Admit it. You're too nervous to go back in there. I wanted so badly to see her again, this iron-willed ghost that had haunted my years in the woods. But I was afraid, too, of how seeing her face-to-face in damning daylight might change things. Or worse, wouldn't change things. Last night, I'd been bleeding to death on her back deck. Anyone might have saved me. Today, I wanted more than saving. But what if I was just a freak to her?

You're an abomination to God's creation. You're cursed. You're the Devil. Where is my son? What have you done with him? I closed my eyes, wondering why, considering all the things I had lost, memories of my parents couldn't have been among them.

"Sam?"

I jerked, hearing my name. Grace called again in her room, barely above a whisper, wondering where I was. She didn't sound afraid.

I pushed open her door and looked around her room. In the strong late-morning light, I could see now that it was a grown-up's room. No leftover pink whimsy or stuffed animals for Grace, if she'd ever had them. Framed photographs of trees on the walls, all matching black frames with no frills. Matching black furniture, all very square and useful looking. Her towel and washcloth tidily folded on top of the dresser next to another clock – black and white, all smooth lines – and a stack of library books, mostly narrative non-fiction and mysteries, judging by the titles. Probably alphabetized or organized according to length.

I was suddenly struck by how dissimilar we were. It occurred to me that if Grace and I were objects, she would be an elaborate digital clock, synced up with the World Clock in London with technical perfection, and I'd be a snow globe – shaken memories in a glass ball.

I struggled to find something to say that wouldn't sound like the greeting of an interspecies stalker. "Good morning," I managed.

Grace sat up, her hair frizzy on one side and flat against her head on the other, her dark eyes filled with open delight. "You're still here! Oh. You have clothes. I mean, instead of scrubs."

"I went to get them while you were sleeping."

"What time is it? Ohhh – I'm really late for school, aren't I?"

"It's eleven."

Grace groaned and then shrugged. "You know what? I haven't missed class since I started high school. I got an award for it last year. And a free pizza or something." She climbed out of bed; in the daylight, I could see just how clingy and unbearably sexy her camisole top was. I turned away.

"You don't have to be so chaste, you know. It's not like I'm naked." Pausing in front of her wardrobe, she looked back at me, her expression canny. "You haven't seen me naked, have you?"

"No!" My answer came out distinctly rushed.

She grinned at my lie and pulled some jeans from

the wardrobe floor. "Well, unless you want to see me now, you'd better turn around."

I lay down on the bed, face buried in the cool pillows that smelled of her. I listened to the rustling sounds she made as she pulled on her clothing, my heart pounding a million miles an hour. I sighed, guilty, unable to contain the lie. "I didn't mean to."

The mattress groaned as she crashed onto it, her face close to mine. "Are you always this apologetic?"

My voice was muffled by her pillow. "I'm trying to make you think I'm a decent person. Telling you I saw you naked while I was another species does not help my case."

She laughed. "I'll grant you leniency, since I should've pulled the blinds." There was a long silence, filled with a thousand unspoken messages. I could smell her nervousness, faintly wafting from her skin, and could hear the fast beat of her heart carried through the mattress to my ear. It would have been so easy for my lips to span the centimetres between our mouths. I thought I could hear the hope in her heartbeat: *kiss me kiss me kiss me*. Normally I was good at sensing others' feelings, but with Grace, everything I thought I knew was clouded by what I wanted.

She giggled quietly; it was a terribly cute noise, and also completely at odds with how I normally thought of her. "I'm starving," she said finally. "Let's go find breakfast. Or brunch, I guess."

I rolled out of bed and she rolled after me. I was acutely aware of her hands on my back, pushing me through the bedroom door. Together we padded softly out into the kitchen. Sunlight, too bright, blared in the glass door to the deck, reflecting off the white counter and tiles in the kitchen, covering us both with white light. Because of my previous exploration, I knew where things were, so I started to take out supplies.

As I moved about the kitchen, Grace shadowed me, her fingers finding my elbow and her palm brushing along my back, finding excuses to touch me. Out of the corner of my eye, I could see her staring unabashedly at me when she thought I wouldn't notice. It was as though I had never changed, as though I still gazed at her from the woods and she still sat on her tyre swing and watched me with admiring eyes. *Peeling off my skin / leaving just my eyes behind / You see inside my head / Still know that you are mine.*

"What are you thinking?" I asked, cracking an egg into a skillet and pouring her a glass of orange juice with human fingers that seemed suddenly precious.

Grace laughed. "That you're making me breakfast."

It was too simple an answer; I wasn't sure if I could believe it. Not when I had a thousand thoughts competing for space in my head at the same moment. "What else are you thinking?"

"That it's very sweet of you. That I hope you know how to cook eggs." But her eyes lifted from the skillet to my mouth, just for a second, and I knew she wasn't only thinking about eggs. She whirled away and pulled the blinds, instantly changing the mood in the kitchen. "And it's too bright in here." The light filtered through the blinds, casting horizontal stripes across her wide brown eyes and the straight line of her lips.

I turned back to the scrambled eggs and tipped them on to a plate just as the toast popped out of the toaster. I reached for it at the same time as Grace, and it was just one of those perfect movie moments where the hands touch and you know the characters are going to kiss. Only this time it was my arms somehow accidentally circling her, pinning her against the counter as I reached for the toast, and bracing against the edge of the fridge as I leaned forward. Lost in embarrassment over my bumbling, I didn't even realize it was the perfect moment until I saw Grace's eyes close, face lifted towards mine.

I kissed her. Just the barest brush of my lips against hers, nothing animal. Even in that moment, I deconstructed the kiss: her possible reactions to, her possible interpretations of, the way it made a shudder tighten my skin, the seconds between when I touched her lips and when she opened her eyes.

Grace smiled at me. Her words were taunting, but her voice was gentle. "Is that all you've got?" I touched my lips to hers again, and this time, it was a very different sort of kiss. It was six years' worth of kissing, her lips coming to life under mine, tasting of orange and of desire. Her fingers ran through my sideburns and into my hair before linking around my neck, alive and cool on my warm skin. I was wild and tame and pulled into shreds and crushed into being all at once. For once in my human life, my mind didn't wander to compose a song lyric or store the moment for later reflection.

For once in my life,

I was here

and nowhere else.

And then I opened my eyes and it was just Grace and me – nothing anywhere but Grace and me – she pressing her lips together as though she were keeping my kiss inside her, and me, holding this moment that was as fragile as a bird in my hands.

Seventeen

Sam

15°C

Some days seem to fit together like a stained-glass window. A hundred little pieces of different colour and mood that, when combined, create a complete picture. The last twenty-four hours had been like that. The night at the hospital was one pane, sickly green and flickering. The dark hours of the early morning in Grace's bed were another, cloudy and purple. Then the cold blue reminder of my other life this morning, and finally the brilliant, clear pane that was our kiss.

In the current pane, we sat on the worn bench seat of an old Bronco at the edge of a run-down, overgrown car lot on the outskirts of town. It seemed like the complete picture was starting to come into focus, a shimmering portrait of something I thought I couldn't have.

Grace ran her fingers over the Bronco's steering wheel with a thoughtful, fond touch, and then turned to me. "Let's play twenty questions."

I was lying back in the passenger seat, eyes closed, and letting the afternoon sun cook me through the windshield. It felt good. "Shouldn't you be looking at other cars? You know, car shopping usually involves . . . shopping."

"I don't shop very well," Grace said. "I just see what I need and I get it."

I laughed at that. I was beginning to see how very *Grace* such a statement was.

She narrowed her eyes at me in mock irritation and crossed her arms over her chest. "So, questions. These aren't optional."

I glanced out across the car lot to make sure that the owner hadn't returned from towing her car yet – here in Mercy Falls, the towing company and the used car company were one and the same. "OK. Better not be anything embarrassing."

Grace slid over a little closer to me on the bench seat and slouched down in a mirror image of my posture. I felt like this was the first question: her leg pressed against my leg, her shoulder pressed against my shoulder, her tightly laced shoe resting on top of my scuffed leather one. My pulse raced, a wordless answer.

Grace's voice was pragmatic, as if she didn't know the effect she was having on me. "I want to know what makes you a wolf."

That one was easy. "When the temperature drops, I become a wolf. When it's cold at night and warm during the day, I can feel it coming on, and then, finally, it's cold enough that I shift into a wolf until spring."

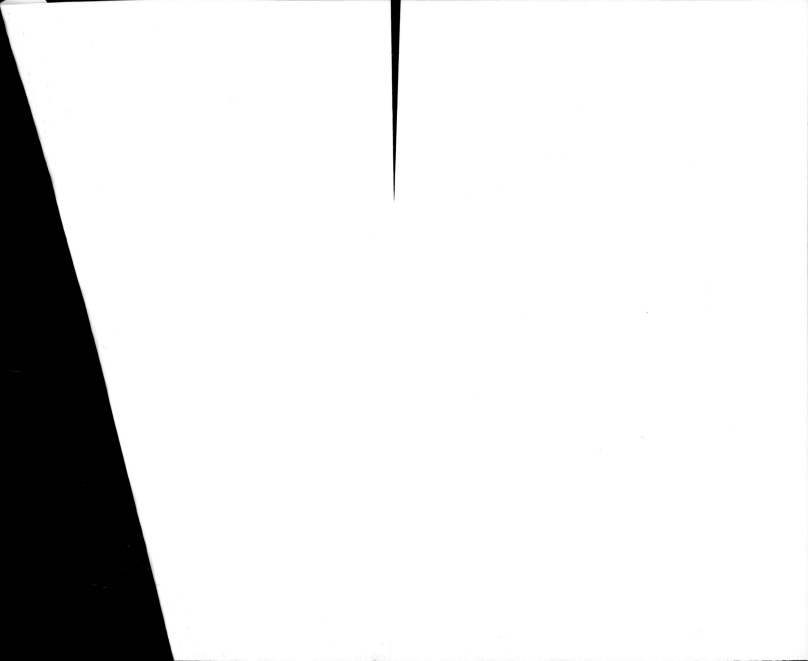

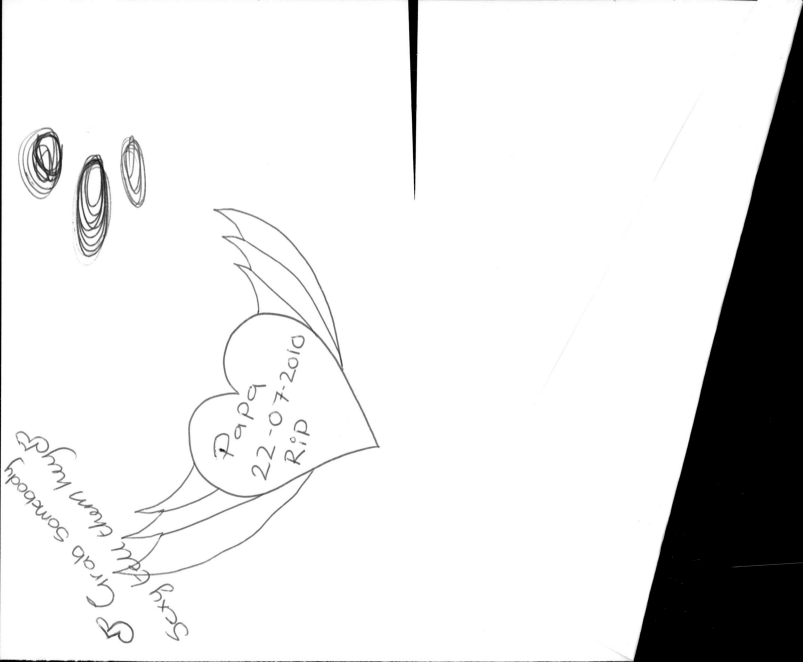

Papa
22-07-2010
RiP

By Cirob Someboody
Say you will clean him off

"The others, too?"

I nodded. "The longer you're a wolf, the warmer it has to be for you to become human." I paused for a moment, wondering if now was the time to tell her. "Nobody knows how many years you get of switching back and forth. It's different for every wolf."

Grace just looked at me — the same long look she'd given me when she was younger, lying in the snow, looking up at me. I couldn't read it any better now than I could then. I felt my throat tighten in anticipation of her reply, but, mercifully, she changed her line of questioning. "How many of you are there?"

I wasn't sure, just because so many of us didn't become humans any more. "About twenty."

"What do you eat?"

"Baby bunnies." She narrowed her eyes, so I grinned and said, "Adult bunnies, too. I'm an equal-opportunity bunny-eater."

She didn't skip a beat. "What was on your face the night you let me touch you?" Her voice stayed the same for this question, but something around her eyes tightened, as though she wasn't sure she wanted to hear the answer.

I had to struggle to remember that night — her fingers in my ruff, her breath moving the fine hairs on the side of my face, the guilty pleasure of being so close to her. The boy. The one who was bitten. That was what she was really asking. "Do you mean there was blood on my face?"

Grace nodded.

Part of me felt a little sad that she had to ask, but of course she did. She had every reason not to trust me. "It wasn't his – that boy's."

"Jack," she said.

"Jack," I repeated. "I knew the attack happened, but I wasn't there for it." I had to dig deeper into my memory to trace the source of the blood on my muzzle. My human brain supplied logical answers – rabbit, deer, roadkill – all of them instantly stronger than my actual wolf memories. Finally, I snatched the real answer from my thoughts, though I wasn't proud of it. "It was a cat. The blood. I'd caught a cat."

Grace let out a breath.

"You aren't upset that it was a cat?" I asked.

"You have to eat. If it wasn't Jack, I don't care if it was a wallaby," she said. But it was obvious her mind was still on Jack. I tried to remember what little I knew of the attack, hating for her to think badly of my pack.

"He provoked them, you know," I said.

"He what? You weren't there, were you?"

I shook my head and struggled to explain. "We can't – the wolves – when we communicate, it's with images. Nothing complicated. And not across great distances. But if we're right by each other, we can share an image with another wolf. And so the wolves that attacked Jack, they showed me images."

"You can read each other's minds?" Grace asked, incredulous.

I shook my head vigorously. "No. I – it's hard to explain as a hu – as me. It's just a way of talking, but our brains are different as wolves. There's no abstract concepts, really. Things like time and names and complicated emotions are all out of the question. Really, it's for things like hunting or warning each other of danger."

"And what did you see about Jack?"

I lowered my eyes. It felt strange, recalling a wolf memory from a human mind. I flipped through the blurry images in my head, recognizing now that the red blotches on the wolves' coats were bullet wounds, and that the stains on their lips were Jack's blood. "Some of the wolves showed me something about being hit by him. A – gun? He must have had a BB gun. He was wearing a red shirt." Wolves saw colour poorly, but red we could see.

"Why would he do that?"

I shook my head. "I don't know. That's not the sort of thing we told each other."

Grace was quiet, still thinking about Jack, I suppose. We sat in the close silence until I started to wonder whether she was upset. Then she spoke. "So you never get to open Christmas presents."

I looked at her, not knowing how to respond. Christmas was something that happened in another life, one before the wolves.

Grace looked down at the steering wheel. "I was just thinking that you were never around in the summer, and I always loved Christmas, because I knew you'd always be there. In the woods. As a wolf. I guess it's because it's cold, right? But that must mean that you never get to open Christmas presents."

I shook my head. I changed too early now to even see Christmas decorations in stores.

Grace frowned at the steering wheel. "Do you think of me when you're a wolf?"

When I was a wolf, I was a memory of a boy, struggling to hold on to meaningless words. I didn't want to tell her the truth: that I couldn't remember her name.

"I think of the way you smell," I said, truthfully. I reached over and lifted a few strands of her hair to my nose. The scent of her shampoo reminded me of the scent of her skin. I swallowed and let her hair fall back down to her shoulder.

Grace's eyes followed my hand from her shoulder to my lap, and I saw her swallow, too. The obvious question – when I would change back again – hung between us, but neither of us put words to it. I wasn't ready to tell her yet. My chest ached at the thought of leaving all this behind.

"So," she said again, and put her hand on the steering wheel. "Do you know how to drive?"

I pulled my wallet from my jeans pocket and proffered it. "The State of Minnesota seems to think so."

She extracted my driver's licence, held it up against the steering wheel, and read out loud: "Samuel K. Roth." She added, with some surprise, "This is an actual licence. You must really be real."

I laughed. "You still doubt it?"

Instead of answering, Grace handed my wallet back and asked, "Is that your real name? Aren't you supposedly dead, like Jack?"

I wasn't sure I wanted to talk about this, but I answered anyway. "It wasn't the same. I wasn't bitten as badly, and some strangers saved me from being dragged off. Nobody pronounced me dead, like they did with Jack. So, yes, that's my real name."

Grace looked thoughtful, and I wondered what she was thinking. Then, abruptly, she looked at me, her expression dark. "So your parents know what you are, right? That's why they—" She stopped and sort of half closed her eyes. I could see her swallowing again.

"It makes you sick for weeks afterwards," I said, rescuing her from finishing the sentence. "The wolf toxin, I guess. While it's changing you. I couldn't stop shifting back and forth, no matter how warm or cold I was." I paused, the memories flickering through my head like photos from someone else's camera. "They thought

I was possessed. Then it got warm and I improved – became stable, I mean, and they thought I was cured. Saved, I suppose. Until winter. For a while they tried to get the church to do something about me. Finally they decided to do something themselves. They're both serving life sentences now. They didn't realize that we're harder to kill than most people."

Grace's face was nearing a pale shade of green and the knuckles on her hand clutching the steering wheel had turned white. "Let's talk about something else."

"I'm sorry," I said, and I really was. "Let's talk about cars. Is this one your betrothed? I mean, assuming it runs OK? I don't know anything about cars, but I can at least pretend. 'Runs OK' sounds like something someone would say if they knew what they were talking about, right?"

She seized the subject, petting the steering wheel. "I do like it."

"It's very ugly," I said generously. "But it looks as though it would laugh at snow. And, if you hit a deer, it would just hiccup and keep going."

Grace added, "Plus, it's got a pretty appealing front seat. I mean, I can just—" Grace leaned across the bench seat towards me, lightly resting one of her hands on my leg. Now she was a couple of centimetres away from me, close enough that I felt the heat of her breath on my lips. Close enough that I could feel her waiting for me to lean into her, too.

In my head, an image flashed of Grace in her back yard, her hand outstretched, imploring me to come to her. But I couldn't, then. I was in another world, one that demanded I keep my distance. Now, I couldn't help but wonder whether I still lived in that world, bound by its rules. My human skin was only mocking me, taunting me with riches that would vanish at the first freeze.

I sat back from her, and looked away before I could see her disappointment. The silence was thick around us. "Tell me about after you were bitten," I said, just to say something. "Did you get sick?"

Grace leaned back in her seat and sighed. I wondered how many times I'd disappointed her before. "I don't know. It seems like such a long time ago. I guess – maybe. I remember having the flu right afterwards."

After I was bitten, it had felt like the flu, too. Exhaustion, hot and cold shakes, nausea burning the back of my throat, bones aching to change form.

Grace shrugged. "That was the year I got locked in the car, too. It was a month or two after the attack. It was spring, but it was really hot. My dad took me along with him to run some errands, because I guess I was too young to leave behind." She glanced at me to see if I was listening. I was.

"Anyway, I had the flu, I guess, and I was just stupid with sleep. So on the way home I fell asleep in the back seat . . . and the next thing I remember was waking up in the hospital. I guess Dad had got home and got the groceries out and forgotten about me. Just left me locked in the car, I guess. They said I tried to get out, but I don't remember that, really. I don't remember anything until the hospital, where the nurse was saying that it was the hottest May day on record for Mercy Falls. The doctor told my dad the heat in the car should've killed me, so I'm a miracle girl. How's that for responsible parenting?"

I shook my head in disbelief. There was a brief silence that gave me enough time to notice the consternation in her expression and remind me that I sincerely regretted not kissing her a moment ago. I thought about saying, *Show me what you meant earlier, when you said that you liked this front seat.* But I couldn't imagine my mouth forming those words, so instead I just took her hand and ran my finger along her palm and between her fingers, tracing the lines in her hand and letting my skin memorize her fingerprints.

Grace made a small sound of appreciation and closed her eyes as my fingers whispered circles on her skin. Somehow this was almost better than kissing.

Both of us jerked when someone tapped on the glass on my side of the car. The tow-truck driver and car-lot owner stood there, peering in at us. His voice came through, muffled by the glass. "You find what you were looking for?"

Grace reached across and rolled down the window. She was talking to him but looking at me, gaze intense, when she said, "Absolutely."

Eighteen
Grace

3°C

That night, Sam stayed in my bed again, chastely perched on the furthest edge of the mattress, but somehow, during the night, our bodies migrated together. I half woke early in the morning, long before dawn, the room washed clean by pale moonlight, and found that I was pressed up against Sam's back, my hands balled up to my chest like a mummy. I could just barely see the dark curve of his shoulder, and something about the shape it made, the gesture it suggested, filled me with a sort of fierce, awful affection. His body was warm and he smelled so good – like wolf, and trees, and home – that I buried my face in his shoulder and closed my eyes again. He made a soft noise and rolled his shoulders back against me, pressing closer.

Right before I drifted back to sleep again, my breathing slowing to match his, I had a brief, burning thought: *I can't live without this*.

There had to be a cure.

Nineteen
Grace

22°C

The next day was unseasonably fair, too beautiful to be going to school, but I couldn't skip a second day without coming up with a really good excuse. It wasn't that I'd get too far behind; it just seemed that when you never miss school for a certain length of time, people tend to notice when you do. Rachel had already called twice and left an ominous voicemail saying I'd picked the *wrong day to cut class, Grace Brisbane*! Olivia hadn't called since our argument in the hall, so I guessed that meant we weren't on speaking terms.

Sam drove me to school in the Bronco while I hastily caught up on some of the English homework I hadn't done the day before. Once he'd parked, I opened the door, letting in a gust of unseasonably warm air. Sam turned his face towards the open door, his eyes half-closed.

"I love this weather. I feel so me."

Watching him bask in the sun, winter seemed a million miles away, and I couldn't imagine him leaving me. I wanted to memorize the crooked line of his nose for later daydreaming. For a moment, I felt an irrational stab of guilt that my feelings for Sam were replacing those that I'd had for my wolf – until I remembered that he *was* my wolf. All over again, I had the weird sensation of the ground shifting beneath me at the fact of his existence, immediately followed by relief. My obsession was so – easy now. The only thing I had to explain to my friends was where my new boyfriend had come from.

"I guess I have to go," I said. "I don't want to."

Sam's eyes opened the rest of the way and focused on me. "I'll be here when you come back, promise." He added, very formal, "May I use your car? I'd like to see if Beck's still human, and if not, whether his house has the power turned on."

I nodded, but part of me hoped the power would be off at Beck's house. I kind of wanted Sam back in my bed, where I could keep him from disappearing like the dream that he was. I climbed out of the Bronco with my backpack. "Don't get any tickets, speed racer."

As I came around the front of the vehicle, Sam rolled down his window. "Hey!"

"What?"

Shyly, he said, "Come here, Grace." I smiled at the way he said my name and returned to the window, smiling wider when I realized what he wanted. His careful kiss didn't fool me; as soon as I parted my lips slightly, he sighed and pulled back. "I'll make you late for school."

I grinned. I was on top of the world. "You'll be back at three?"

"Wouldn't miss it."

I watched him pull out of the car park, already feeling the length of the school day stretching before me.

A notebook smacked my arm. "Who was that?!"

I turned to Rachel and tried to think of something that was easier than the truth. "My ride?"

Rachel didn't push the issue, mostly because her brain was already on to something else. She grabbed my elbow and began steering me towards the school. Surely, surely, there had to be some kind of eternal reward waiting for me for going to school on a gorgeous day like this with Sam in my car. Rachel wiggled my arm to get my attention. "Grace. Focus. There was a wolf outside of the school yesterday. In the car park. Like, everyone saw it when school got out."

"What?" I turned and looked over my shoulder at the car park, trying to imagine a wolf amongst the cars. The sparse pine trees that bordered the car park didn't connect with Boundary Wood; the wolf would've had to cross several streets and gardens to get to it. "What did it look like?"

Rachel gave me a weird look. "The wolf?"

I nodded.

"Like a wolf. Grey." Rachel saw my withering

look and shrugged. "I don't know, Grace. Bluish-grey? With mucky gross scratches on its shoulder. It looked scruffy."

So it was Jack. It had to be. "It must have been total chaos," I said.

"Yeah, you should've been here, wolf-girl. Seriously. Nobody got hurt, thank God, but Olivia completely freaked out. The whole school was freaked out. Isabel was totally hysterical and made a huge scene." Rachel squeezed my arm. "So why didn't you pick up your phone, anyway?"

We walked into the school; the doors were propped open to let in the balmy air. "Battery died."

Rachel made a face and spoke louder to be heard over the crush of students in the halls. "So, are you sick? I never thought I'd live to see the day that you didn't make it to class. Between you not being in class and wild animals roaming the car park, I thought the world was coming to an end. I was waiting for the rains of blood."

"I think I got some sort of twenty-four-hour bug," I replied.

"Ew, should I not touch you?" But instead of moving away, Rachel slammed her shoulder into mine with a grin. I laughed and shoved her off, and as I did, I saw Isabel Culpeper. My smile faded. She was leaning against the wall by one of the drinking fountains, her shoulders hunched forward. At first I thought she was looking at her mobile phone, but then I realized her hands were empty and she was just staring at the ground. If she hadn't been such an ice princess, I would've thought she was crying. I wondered if I should talk to her.

As if reading my thoughts, Isabel looked up then, and her eyes, so similar to Jack's, met mine. I could read the challenge in them: *So what are you looking at, huh?*

I looked away quickly and kept walking with Rachel, but I had the uncomfortable sense of things left unsaid.

Twenty

Sam

4°C

As I lay in Grace's bed that night, jarred by the news of Jack's appearance at the school, I stared, sleepless, out into a blackness interrupted only by the dim halo of her hair on her pillow. And I thought about wolves who didn't act like wolves. And I thought about Christa Bohlmann.

It had been years since the memory of Christa had crossed my mind, but Grace's frowning account of Jack lurking where he didn't belong had brought it all back.

I remembered the last day I saw her, when Christa and Beck were fighting in the kitchen, the living room, the hall, the kitchen again, growling and shouting at each other like circling wolves. I'd been young, about eight, so Beck had seemed like a giant then – a narrow, furious god barely containing his anger. Round and round the house he went with Christa, a heavyset young woman with a face made blotchy by rage.

"You killed two people, Christa. When are you going to face up to that?"

"Killed? Killed?" Her voice was shrill to my ears,

claws on glass. "What about me? Look at me. My life is over."

"It's not over," Beck snapped. "You're still breathing, aren't you? Your heart's still beating? I can't say the same for your two victims."

I remember shrinking back at Christa's voice – a throaty, barely understandable scream. "This is not a life!"

Beck raged at her about selfishness and responsibility, and she shot back with a string of profanity that I was shocked by; I'd never heard the words before.

"How about that guy in the basement?" Beck snapped. I could just see Beck's back from my vantage point in the hall. "You bit him, Christa. You've ruined *his* life now. And you killed two people. Just because they called you some nasty words. I keep waiting to see some remorse. Hell, I'll just take a guarantee that this won't happen again."

"Why would I guarantee you anything? What have you ever given me?" Christa snarled. Her shoulders hunched and twitched. "You call yourselves a pack? You're a coven. You're an abomination. You're a cult. I'll do what I want. I'll get through this life how I want."

Beck's voice was terribly, terribly even. I remember being suddenly sorry for Christa then, because Beck stopped sounding angry when he was at his worst. "Promise me this won't happen again."

She looked straight at me then – no, not at me.

Through me. Her mind was someplace far away, escaping the reality of her changing body. I could see a vein standing out right down the middle of her forehead, and I noticed that her fingernails were claws. "I don't owe you anything. Go to hell."

Beck said, very quietly, "Get out of my house."

She did. She slammed the glass door so hard that the dishes in the kitchen cabinets rattled. A few moments later, I heard the door open and shut again, much quieter, as Beck went after her.

I remembered that it had been cold enough out that I was worried Beck would change for the winter and leave me alone in the house. That fear was enough to make me slide out of the hallway into the living room, just as I heard a massive *crack*.

Beck quietly let himself back into the house, shivering with the cold and the threat of the change, and he carefully laid a gun on the counter as though it was made of glass. Then he noticed me, standing in the living room, arms across my chest, my fingers clutching my biceps.

I still remembered the way his voice sounded when he said, "Don't touch that, Sam." Hollow. Ragged. He'd gone into his office and laid his head down on his arms for the rest of the day. At dusk, he and Ulrik had gone outside, voices low and hushed; through the window, I'd seen Ulrik get a shovel from the garage.

And now, here I was, lying in Grace's bed, and

somewhere out there was Jack. Angry people didn't make good werewolves.

While Grace was in school, I had driven by Beck's house. The driveway was empty and the windows were dark; I hadn't the heart to go inside and see how long it had been unoccupied. Without Beck to enforce the pack's safety, who was supposed to keep Jack in line?

An unwelcome sense of responsibility was starting to pinch at the back of my throat. Beck had a mobile phone, but I couldn't remember the number, no matter how long I riffled through my memories. I pressed my face against the pillow and prayed that Jack wouldn't bite anyone, because if he became a problem, I didn't think I was strong enough to do what would have to be done.

Twenty-One
Sam

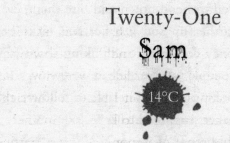

14°C

When Grace's alarm went off the next morning at 6:45 for school, screaming electronic obscenities into my ear, I instantly shot straight up into the air, heart pounding, just as I had the day before. My head was stuffed full of dreams: wolves and humans and blood smeared on lips.

"Ummmm," Grace mumbled, unconcerned, and pulled up the sheets around her neck. "Turn that off, would you? I'm getting up. I'll ... be up in a second." She rolled over, her blonde head barely visible above the edge of the blanket, and sank into the bed as if she had grown into the mattress.

And that was it. She was asleep and I was not.

I leaned back against her headboard and let her lie by my side, warm and dreaming, for a few minutes more. I stroked her hair with careful fingers, tracing a line from her forehead around her ear and down to just the top of her long neck, where her hair stopped being hair proper and was instead little baby fluffs that went every which way. They were fascinating, these

119

soft feathers that would grow up to be her hair. I was incredibly tempted to bend down and bite them, ever so softly, to wake her up and kiss her and make her late for school, but I couldn't stop thinking about Jack and Christa and people who made bad werewolves. If I went to the school, would I still be able to follow Jack's trail with my weaker sense of smell?

"Grace," I whispered. "Wake up."

She made a soft noise that, roughly translated, meant *piss off* in sleep language.

"Time to wake up," I said, and stuck my finger in her ear.

Grace squealed and smacked at me. She was up.

Our mornings together were beginning to have the comfort of routine. While Grace, still dogged by sleep, stumbled towards the shower, I put a bagel in the toaster for each of us and convinced the coffeemaker to do something that sounded like making coffee. Back in her bedroom, I listened to Grace sing tunelessly in the shower while I pulled on my jeans and checked her drawers for socks that didn't look too girly for me to borrow.

I heard my breathing stop without feeling it. Photographs, nestled amongst her neatly folded socks. Pictures of the wolves. Of us. Carefully, I lifted the stack out of the drawer and retreated to the bed. Turning my back to the door as if I were doing something illicit, I paged through the pictures with slow fingers. There was something fascinating about seeing these images with my human eyes. Some of the wolves I could attach human names to; the older ones who had always changed before me. Beck, big, bulky, blue-grey. Paul, black and clean-looking. Ulrik, brownish-grey. Salem, with his notched ear and running eye. I sighed, though I didn't know why.

The door behind me opened, letting in a gust of steam that smelled like Grace's soap. Grace stepped behind me and rested her head on my shoulder; I breathed in the scent of her.

"Looking at yourself?" she asked.

My fingers, flicking between the photos, froze. "I'm in here?"

Grace came round the side of the bed and sat down facing me. "Of course. Most of them are of you – you don't recognize yourself? Oh. Of course you wouldn't. Tell me who's who."

Slower, I paged through the images again as she shifted to sit next to me, the bed groaning with her movements. "That's Beck. He's always taken care of the new wolves." Though there'd only been two newly made wolves since me: Christa and the wolf that she'd created, Derek. The fact was, I wasn't used to younger newcomers – our pack usually grew by other, older wolves finding us, not by the addition of savagely born newbies like Jack. "Beck's like a father to me." It sounded weird to say it like that, even if it was true. I'd never had to explain it to anyone before. He had been the one to take me under his wing after I'd escaped from my house, and the one who carefully glued the fragments of my sanity back together.

"I could tell how you felt about him," Grace said, and she sounded surprised at her own intuition. "Your voice is different whenever you talk about him."

"It is?" Now it was my turn to be surprised. "Different how?"

She shrugged, looking a little shy. "I dunno. Proud, I guess. I think it's sweet. Who's that?"

"Shelby," I said, and there was no pride in my voice for her. "I told you about her before."

Grace watched my face.

The memory of the last time Shelby and I had seen each other made my gut twist uncomfortably. "She and I don't see things the same way. She thinks being a wolf is a gift."

Beside me, Grace nodded, and I was grateful to leave it at that.

I flipped through the next few photographs, more of Shelby and Beck, until I paused at Paul's black form. "That's Paul. He's our pack leader when we're wolves. That's Ulrik next to him." I pointed to the brown-grey wolf beside Paul. "Ulrik's like a crazy uncle, sort of. A German one. He swears a lot."

"Sounds great."

"He's a lot of fun." Actually, I should've said *was* a lot

of fun. I didn't know if this had been his last year, or if he might still have another summer in him. I remembered his laugh, like a flock of crows taking off, and the way he held on to his German accent, like he couldn't be Ulrik without it.

"Are you OK?" Grace asked, frowning at me.

I shook my head, staring at the wolves in the photographs, so clearly animals when seen through my human eyes. My family. Me. My future. Somehow, the photographs blurred a line I wasn't ready to cross yet.

I realized Grace had her arm around my shoulder, her cheek leaning against me, comforting me even though she couldn't possibly understand what was bothering me.

"I wish you could've met them," I said, "when everybody was human." I didn't know how to explain to her what an enormous part of me they were, their voices and faces as humans, and their scents and forms as wolves. How lost I felt now, the only one wearing human skin.

"Tell me something about them," Grace said, her voice muffled against my T-shirt.

I let my mind flit over memories. "Beck taught me how to hunt when I was eight. I hated it." I remembered standing in Beck's living room, staring out at the first ice-covered tree branches of the winter, brilliant and winking in the morning sun. The back yard seemed like a dangerous and alien planet.

"Why did you hate it?" Grace asked.

"I didn't like the sight of blood. I didn't like hurting things. I was eight." In my memories, I seemed small, ribby, innocent. I had spent all of the previous summer letting myself believe that this winter, with Beck, would be different, that I wouldn't change and that I'd go on eating the eggs Beck cooked for me for ever. But as the nights grew colder and even short trips outside made my muscles shake, I knew the time was coming soon when I wouldn't be able to avoid the change, and that Beck wouldn't be around to cook much longer. But that didn't mean I would go willingly.

"Why hunt, then?" Grace asked, ever logical. "Why not just leave food out for yourselves?"

"Ha. I asked Beck that same question, and Ulrik said, '*Ja*, and the raccoons and possums, too?'"

Grace laughed, unduly delighted by my lousy impression of Ulrik's accent.

I felt a rush of warmth in my cheeks; it felt good to talk to her about the pack. I loved the glow in her eyes, the curious quirk in her mouth – she knew what I was and she wanted to know more. But that didn't mean it was right to tell her, someone outside the pack. Beck had always said, *The only people we have to protect us is us*. But Beck didn't know Grace. And Grace wasn't only human. She may not have changed, but she had been bitten. She was wolf on the inside. She had to be.

"So what happened?" Grace asked. "What did you hunt?"

"Bunnies, of course," I replied. "Beck took me out while Paul waited in a van to collect me afterwards in case I was unstable enough to change back." I couldn't forget how Beck had stopped me by the door before we went out, bending double so he could look into my face. I was motionless, trying not to think about changing bodies and snapping a rabbit's neck between my teeth. About saying goodbye to Beck for the winter. He had taken my thin shoulder in his hand and said, "Sam, I'm sorry. Don't be scared."

I hadn't said anything, because I was thinking it was cold, and Beck wouldn't change back after the hunt, and then I'd have no one who knew how to cook my eggs right. Beck made perfect eggs. More than that. Beck kept me Sam. Back then, with the scars on my wrists still so fresh, I'd been so dangerously close to fracturing into something that was neither human nor wolf.

"What are you thinking about?" Grace asked. "You stopped talking."

I looked up; I hadn't realized I'd looked away from her. "Changing."

Grace's chin pressed into my shoulder as she looked into my face; her voice was hesitant. She asked me a question she'd asked me before. "Does it hurt?"

I thought of the slow, agonizing process of the change, the bending of muscles, the bulging of skin, the grinding of bones. The adults had always tried to hide their shifts from me, wanting to protect me. But it wasn't seeing them change that scared me – the sight only made me pity them, since even Beck groaned with the pain of it. It was changing myself that terrified me, even now. Forgetting Sam.

I was a bad liar, so I didn't bother to try. "Yes."

"It kind of makes me sad to think of you having to do that as a little kid," Grace said. She was frowning at me, blinking too-shiny eyes. "Actually, it bothers me a lot. Poor little Sam." She touched my chin with a finger; I leaned into her hand.

I remembered being so proud that I hadn't cried while I changed that time, unlike when I was younger and my parents had watched me, eyes round with horror. I remembered Beck the wolf, bounding away and leading me into the woods, and I remembered the warm, bitter sensation of my first kill on my muzzle. I had changed back again after Paul, bundled up in a coat and hat, had retrieved me. It was in the van on the way home that loneliness hit me. I was alone; Beck wouldn't be human again that year.

Now, it was like I was eight years old all over again, alone and newly scarred. My chest ached, my breath squeezed out of me.

"Show me what I look like," I asked Grace, tilting the photos towards her. "Please."

I let her take the stack from my hand and watched

her face light up as she flipped through the pictures, looking for one in particular. "There. That one's my favorite of you."

I looked at the photo she had handed me. A wolf looked back at me, wearing my eyes, a still wolf watching from the woods, sunlight touching the edges of its fur. I looked and looked, waiting for it to mean something. Waiting for a prickling of recognition. It seemed unfair that the other wolves' identities were so clear to me in their photographs, but that mine was hidden. What was it in this photo, in that wolf, that made Grace's eyes light up?

What if it wasn't me? What if she was in love with some other wolf and she only thought it was me? How would I ever know?

Grace was oblivious to my doubts and misread my silence for fascination. She unfolded her legs and stood up, facing me, then ran a hand through my hair. She lifted her palm to her nose, inhaling deeply. "You know, you still smell like you do when you're a wolf."

And just like that, she'd said maybe the one thing that could've made me feel better. I handed her the photo on her way out.

Grace stopped in the door, dimly silhouetted by the dull grey morning light, and looked back at me, at my eyes, my mouth, my hands, in a way that made something inside me knot and unknot unbearably.

I didn't think I belonged here in her world, a boy

stuck between two lives, dragging the dangers of the wolves with me, but when she said my name, waiting for me to follow, I knew I'd do anything to stay with her.

Twenty-Two
Sam

16°C

I spent too long after dropping Grace off circling the car park, frustrated with Jack, frustrated with the rain, frustrated with the limitations of my human body. I could smell that a wolf had been there – just a faint, musky trace of wolf odour – but I couldn't pinpoint a direction or even say for sure that it had been Jack. It was like being blind.

I gave up finally and, after sitting in the car for several minutes, decided to give in to the pull of Beck's house. I couldn't think of anywhere else in particular to start a search for Jack, but the woods behind the house were a logical place to find wolves in general. So I headed back towards my old summer home.

I didn't know if Beck had been a human at all this year; I couldn't even clearly recall my own summer months. Memories blurred into each other until they became a composite of seasons and scents, their origins obscured.

Beck had been shifting for more years than I had, so it seemed unlikely that he'd been human this year when

I hadn't. But it also felt like I should have had more years of changing back and forth than this. I hadn't been shifting for that long. Where had my summers gone?

I wanted Beck. I wanted his guidance. I wanted to know why the gunshot had made me human. I wanted to know how long I had with Grace. I wanted to know if this was the end.

"You're the best of them," he had told me once, and I still remembered the way his face looked when he said it. Square, trustworthy, solid. An anchor in a churning sea. I had known what he meant: the most human of the pack. That was after they'd pulled Grace from her tyre swing.

But when I drove up to the house, it was still empty and dark, and my hopes dissipated. It occurred to me that all of the other wolves must've already shifted for the winter; there weren't many young wolves left. Except for Jack, now. The mailbox was stuffed with envelopes and slips from the post office advising Beck to pick up more at the main office. I took all of it out and put it in Grace's car. I had a key for his post office box, but I'd get it later.

I refused to think I wouldn't see Beck again.

But the fact remained that if Beck wasn't around, Jack hadn't been shown the ropes. And someone had to get him away from the school and civilization until he stopped the unpredictable shifting that came with being a new wolf. His death had done enough damage to the pack. I wasn't going to let him expose us, either through shifting in public or through biting someone.

Since Jack had already paid a visit to the school, I decided to operate under the assumption that he had tried going home as well, and so I headed over towards the Culpepers' place. It wasn't any secret where they lived; everybody in town knew the gigantic Tudor mansion that could be just glimpsed from the highway. The only mansion in Mercy Falls. I didn't think anybody would be home at this time of the day, but I parked Grace's Bronco about a kilometre away just in case and cut through the pine woods on foot.

Sure enough, the house was empty, towering over me like a massive structure out of an old folk tale. A quick poking around the doors turned up the unmistakable odour of wolf.

I couldn't tell whether he'd got inside already, or if, like me, he'd come while everyone was away and returned to the woods. Remembering how vulnerable I was in my human form, I whirled around and sniffed the air, scanning the surrounding pines for signs of life. Nothing. Or at least nothing close enough that my human senses could pick it up.

In the cause of thoroughness, I broke into the house to see whether Jack was there, already sequestered in a locked room reserved for monsters. I wasn't tidy about my breaking-and-entering job, either; I shattered a window in the back door with a brick and reached through the jagged hole to turn the knob.

Inside, I scented the air again. I thought I smelled wolf, but it was faint and somewhat stale. I wasn't sure why Jack would smell that way, but I followed the scent through the house. My path led to a massive set of oak doors; I felt sure the trail was leading to the other side.

Carefully I pushed them open, then inhaled sharply.

The massive foyer in front of me was filled with animals. Stuffed ones. And not the cuddly kind. The dim, high-ceilinged room had the feel of a museum exhibit: Animals of North America, or some sort of shrine to death. My mind snatched for song lyrics, but could only settle on a single line: *We bear the grins of the smiling dead*.

I shuddered.

In the half-light that filtered through the round windows high above my head, it seemed as though there were enough animals to populate Noah's ark. Here was a fox, stiffly holding a stuffed quail in its mouth. There, a black bear, rising above me with claws outstretched. A lynx, creeping eternally along a log. And a polar bear, complete with stuffed fish in his paws. Could you stuff a fish? I hadn't ever considered it.

And then, amidst a herd of deer of all sizes and shapes, I saw the source of the smell I had detected earlier: a wolf stared over its shoulder at me, teeth bared, glass eyes menacing. I walked towards it, reaching out to touch its brittle fur. Under my fingers, the stale smell blossomed, releasing secrets in my nostrils, and I recognized the unique scent of my woods. I curled my fingers into a fist, stepping back from the wolf with crawling skin. One of us. Maybe not. Maybe just a wolf. Except I'd never met a normal wolf in our woods before.

"Who were you?" I whispered. But the only common feature between a werewolf's two forms – the eyes – had long since been gouged out in favour of a pair of glass ones. I wondered whether Derek, riddled with bullets the night I was shot, would join this wolf in this macabre menagerie. The thought twisted my stomach.

I glanced around the hall once more and retreated towards the front door. Every bit of animal still left in me was screaming to get away from the dull odour of death that filled the hall. Jack wasn't here. I didn't have any reason to stay.

Twenty-Three
Grace

11°C

"Good morning." Dad glanced at me as he poured coffee into a travel mug. He was very sharply dressed for a Saturday; he must have been trying to sell a resort to some rich investor. "I have to meet Ralph at the office at eight-thirty. About the Wyndhaven resort."

I blinked a few times, eyes bleary. My whole body felt sticky and slow from sleep. "Don't talk to me yet. I'm not awake." Through my fog, I felt a twinge of guilt for not being more friendly; I hadn't really seen him for days, much less properly spoken with him. Sam and I had spent last night talking about the strange room of stuffed animals at the Culpepers' and wondering, with the constant irritation of a scratchy sweater, where Jack was going to make his next appearance. This ordinary morning with Dad felt like an abrupt return to my pre-Sam life.

Dad gestured at me with the coffee pot. "Want some of this?"

I cupped my hands and held them towards him. "Just pour it in there. I'll splash some on my face. Where's

Mom?" I didn't hear her crashing around upstairs. Mom's getting ready to leave the house normally required a lot of indiscriminate banging and shoe-scraping noises from the bedroom.

"Some gallery down in Minneapolis."

"Why'd she leave so early? It's practically yesterday." Dad didn't answer; he was looking over the top of my head at the TV, which was blaring some morning talk show. The show's guest, dressed in khaki, was surrounded by all sorts of baby animals in boxes and cages. It reminded me vividly of the room of animals that Sam had described. Dad frowned as one of the two hosts gingerly petted a baby possum, who hissed. I cleared my throat. "Dad. Focus. Get me a coffee mug and fill it or I'll die. And I'm not cleaning up my body if I do."

Dad, still watching the TV, felt around in the cabinet for a mug. His fingers found my favourite – a robin's-egg-blue mug that one of Mom's friends had made – and pushed it and the coffee pot across the counter to me. The steam rushed into my face as I poured.

"So, Grace, how's school?" I asked myself.

Dad nodded, eyes on the baby koala now struggling in the guest's arms.

"Oh, it's fine," I continued, and Dad made a mumbling noise of agreement. I added, "Nothing special, aside from the load of pandas they brought in, and the teachers abandoning us to cannibalistic savages—" I paused to see if I'd caught his attention yet, then pressed on. "The whole building caught fire, then I failed drama, and then sex sex sex *sex*."

Dad's eyes abruptly focused, and he turned to me and frowned. "What did you say they were teaching you in school?"

Well, at least he'd caught more of the beginning than I'd given him credit for. "Nothing interesting. We're writing short stories for English. They're hateful. I have absolutely no talent for writing fiction."

"Fiction about sex?" he asked doubtfully.

I shook my head. "Go to work, Dad. You're going to be late."

Dad scratched his chin; he'd missed a hair shaving. "That reminds me. I need to take that cleaner back to Tom. Have you seen it?"

"You need to take *cleaner* back to who?"

"The gun cleaner. I think I put it on the counter. Or maybe under it—" He crouched and began to rummage in the cabinet under the sink.

I frowned at him. "Why did you have gun cleaner?"

He gestured towards his study. "For the gun."

Little warning bells were going off in my head. I knew my dad had a rifle; it hung on the wall in his study. But I couldn't remember him ever cleaning it before. You cleaned guns after you'd used them, right? "Why were you borrowing cleaner?"

"Tom loaned it to me to clean my rifle after we

were out. I know I should clean it more, but I just don't think about it when I'm not using it."

"Tom Culpeper?" I said.

He withdrew his head from the cabinet, bottle in hand. "Yes."

"You went shooting with Tom Culpeper? That was you the other day?" My cheeks were beginning to feel hot. I prayed for him to say no.

Dad gave me a look. The sort that was usually followed by him saying something like, *Grace, you're usually so reasonable.* "Something had to be done, Grace."

"You were part of that hunting party? The one that went after the wolves?" I demanded. "I can't believe that you—" The image of Dad creeping through the trees, rifle in hand, the wolves fleeing before him, was suddenly too strong, and I had to stop.

"Grace, I did it for you, too," he said.

My voice came out very low. "Did you shoot any of them?"

Dad seemed to realize that the question was important. "Warning shots," he said.

I didn't know if it was true or not, but I didn't want to talk to him any more. I shook my head and turned away.

"Don't sulk," Dad said. He kissed my cheek – I remained motionless as he did – and gathered up his coffee and briefcase. "Be good. See you later."

Standing in the kitchen, hands cupped around the

blue mug, I listened as Dad's Taurus rumbled to life in the driveway and then faded slowly away. After he'd gone, the house settled into its familiar silence, both comforting and depressing. It could've been any other morning, just the quiet and the coffee in my hands – but it wasn't. Dad's voice – *warning shots* – still hung in the air.

He knew how I felt about the wolves, and he'd gone behind my back and made plans with Tom Culpeper, anyway.

The betrayal stung.

A soft noise from the doorway caught my attention. Sam stood in the hallway, his hair wet and spiky from a shower, his eyes on me. There was a question written on his face, but I didn't say anything. I was wondering what Dad would do if he knew about Sam.

Twenty-Four

Grace

11°C

I spent the better part of the morning and afternoon slogging through my English homework while Sam stretched on the couch, a novel in hand. It was a vague sort of torture to be in the same room with him but separated quite effectively by an English textbook. After several hours only punctuated by a brief lunch break, I couldn't take it any more.

"I feel like I'm wasting our time together," I confessed.

Sam didn't answer, and I realized he hadn't heard me. I repeated my statement, and he blinked, eyes slowly focusing on me as he returned from whatever world he'd been in. He said, "I'm happy just to be here with you. That's enough."

I studied his face for a long moment, trying to decide if he really meant it.

Noting his page number, Sam folded the novel shut with careful fingers and said, "Do you want to go somewhere? If you've got enough done, we can go poke around Beck's house, to see if Jack's made his way back over there."

I liked the idea. Ever since Jack's appearance at school, I'd felt uneasy about where and how he might turn up next. "Do you think he'll be there?"

"I don't know. The new wolves always seemed to find their way there, and that's where the pack tends to live, in that stretch of Boundary Wood behind the house," Sam said. "It'd be nice to think he'd finally found his way to the pack." His face looked worried then, but he stopped short of saying why. I knew why I wanted Jack to fit in with the pack – I didn't want anyone exposing the wolves for what they were. But Sam seemed to be concerned about something more, something bigger and more nameless.

In the golden afternoon light, I drove the Bronco to Beck's house while Sam navigated. We had to follow the winding road around Boundary Wood for a good thirty-five minutes to get to the house. I hadn't realized how far the wood stretched until we drove all the way around it. I guess it made sense; how could you hide an entire pack of wolves without hundreds of unpopulated acres to help? I pulled the Bronco into the driveway, squinting up at the brick facade. The dark windows looked like closed eyes; the house was overwhelmingly empty. When Sam cracked his door open, the sweet smell of the pines that stood guard around the yard filled my nostrils.

"Nice house." I stared at the tall windows glinting in

the afternoon sun. A brick house of this size could easily look imposing, but there was an atmosphere about the property that seemed disarming – maybe the sprawling, unevenly cut hedges at the front or the weathered bird feeder that looked as if it had grown out of the lawn. It was a *comfortable* sort of place. It looked like the sort of place that would create a boy like Sam. I asked, "How did Beck get it?"

He frowned. "The house? He used to be a lawyer for rich old guys, so he's got money. He bought it for the pack."

"That's awfully generous of him," I said. I shut the car door. "*Crap.*"

Sam leaned over the hood of the Bronco towards me. "What?"

"I just locked the keys in the car. My brain was on autopilot."

Sam shrugged dismissively. "Beck's got a slim-jim in the house. We can get it when we get back from the woods."

"A slim-jim? How intriguing," I said, grinning at him. "I like a man with hidden depths."

"Well, you've got one," Sam replied. He jerked his head toward the trees in the back yard. "Are you ready to head in?"

The idea was both compelling and terrifying. I hadn't been in the woods since the night of the hunt, and before that, the evening I'd seen Jack pinned by the other wolves. It seemed like my only memories of these woods were of violence.

I realized Sam was holding his hand out towards me. "Are you afraid?"

I wondered if there was a way to take his hand without admitting my fear. Not fear, really. Just some emotion that crawled along my skin and lifted the hairs on my arms. It was cool weather, not the barren dead of winter. Plenty of food for the wolves without them having to attack us. *Wolves are shy creatures.*

Sam took my hand; his grip was firm and his skin warm against mine in the cool autumn air. His eyes studied me, large and luminescent in the afternoon glow, and for a moment I was caught in his gaze, remembering those eyes studying me from a wolf's face. "We don't have to look for him now," he said.

"I want to go." It was true. Part of me wanted to see where Sam lived in these cold months, when he wasn't lingering at the edge of our yard. And part of me, the part that ached with loss when the pack howled at night, was begging to follow that faint scent of the pack into the woods. All of that outweighed any bit of me that was anxious. To prove my willingness, I headed towards the back yard, nearing the edge of the woods, still holding Sam's hand.

"They'll stay away from us," Sam said, as if he still had to convince me. "Jack's the only one who would approach us."

I looked over to him with a crooked eyebrow. "Yeah, about that. He's not going to come at us all slathering and horror movie, is he?"

"It doesn't make you a monster. It just takes away your inhibitions," Sam said. "Did he slather a lot when he was in school?"

Like the rest of the school, I had heard the story about how Jack had put some kid in the hospital after a party; I had dismissed it as gossip until I'd seen the guy for myself, walking the halls with half his face still swollen. Jack didn't need a transformation to become a monster.

I made a face. "He slathered a bit, yeah."

"If it makes you feel any better," Sam said, "I don't think he's here. But I still hope he is."

So we went into the woods. This was a different sort of forest from the one that bordered my parents' yard. These trees were pressed tightly together, the underbrush crammed between the trunks as if holding them upright. Brambles caught on my jeans, and Sam kept stopping to pick burrs off our ankles. We saw no sign of Jack, or any of the wolves, during our slow progress. In truth, I didn't think Sam was doing a very good job of scanning the woods around us. I made a big show of looking around so I could pretend I didn't notice him glancing at me every few seconds.

It didn't take me long to get a headful of burrs, tugging my hairs painfully as they worked their way into knots.

Sam stopped me to pick at the burrs. "It gets better," he promised. It was sweet that he thought I would get put out enough to go back to the car. As if I had anything better to do than feel him carefully worry the barbs of the burrs out of my hair.

"I'm not worried about that," I assured him. "I'm just thinking we'd never know if there was anyone else here. The woods go on for ever."

Sam ran his fingers through my hair as if he were checking for more burrs, though I knew they were all gone, and he probably did, too. He paused, smiling at me, and then inhaled deeply. "Doesn't smell like we're alone."

He looked at me, and I knew he was waiting for me to verify – to admit that if I tried, I could smell the scent of the pack's hidden life all around us. Instead, I reached for his hand again. "Lead the way, bloodhound."

Sam's expression turned a bit wistful, but he led me through the underbrush, up a gradual hill. As he'd promised, it got better. The thorns thinned out and the trees grew taller and straighter, their branches not beginning until a few feet over our heads. The white, peeled bark of the birches looked buttery in the long, slanting afternoon light, and their leaves were a delicate gold. I turned to Sam, and his eyes reflected the same brilliant yellow back at me.

I stopped in my tracks. It was my woods. The golden woods I'd always imagined running away to. Sam, watching my face, dropped his hand out of mine and stepped back to look at me.

"Home," he said. I think he was waiting for me to say something. Or maybe he wasn't waiting for me to say something. Maybe he saw it on my face. I didn't have anything to say – I just looked around at the shimmering light and the leaves hanging on the branches like feathers.

"Hey." Sam caught my arm, looking at my face sideways, as if searching for tears. "You look sad."

I turned in a slow circle; the air seemed dappled and vibrant around me. I said, "I used to always imagine coming here, when I was younger. I just can't figure out how I would've seen it." I probably wasn't making any sense, but I kept talking, trying to reason it out. "The woods behind my house don't look like this. No birches. No yellow leaves. I don't know how I would recognize it."

"Maybe someone told you about it."

"I think I would remember someone telling me every little detail about this part of the woods, down to the colour of the glittering air. I don't even know how someone could've told me all that."

Sam said, "I told you. Wolves have funny ways of communicating. Showing each other pictures when they're close to one another."

I turned back to where he was standing, a dark blot against the light, and gave him a look. "You aren't going to stop, are you?"

Sam just gazed at me steadily, the silent lupine stare that I knew so well, sad and intent.

"Why do you keep bringing it back up?"

"You were bitten." He walked in a slow circle around me, scuffing up leaves with his foot, glancing at me underneath his dark eyebrows.

"So?"

"So it's about who you are. It's about you being one of us. You couldn't have recognized this place if you weren't a wolf, too, Grace. Only one of us would've been able to see what I showed you." His voice was so serious, his eyes so intense. "I couldn't – I couldn't even talk to you right now if you weren't like us. We aren't supposed to talk about who we are with regular people. It's not as if we have a ton of rules to live by, but Beck told me that's one rule we just don't break."

That didn't make sense to me. "Why not?"

Sam didn't say anything, but his fingers touched his neck where he'd been shot; as he did, I saw the pale, shiny scars on his wrist. It seemed wrong for someone as gentle as Sam to have to always wear evidence of human violence. I shivered in the growing chill of the afternoon. Sam's voice was soft. "Beck's told me stories. People kill us in all kinds of awful ways. We die in labs and we get shot and we get poisoned. It might be science that changes us, Grace, but all people see is magic. I believe Beck. We can't tell people who aren't like us."

I said, "I don't change, Sam. I'm not really like

you." Disappointment stuck a lump in my throat that I couldn't swallow.

He didn't answer. We stood together in the wood for a long moment before he sighed and spoke again.

"After you were bitten, I knew what would happen. I waited for you to change, every night, so I could bring you back and keep you from getting hurt." A chilly gust of wind lifted his hair and sent a shower of golden leaves glimmering down around him. He spread out his arms, letting them fall into his hands. He looked like a dark angel in an eternal autumn wood. "Did you know you get one happy day for every one you catch?"

I didn't know what he meant, even after he opened his fist to show me the quivering leaves crumpled in his palm.

"One happy day for every falling leaf you catch." Sam's voice was low.

I watched the edges of the leaves slowly unfold, fluttering in the breeze. "How long did you wait?"

It would've been unbearably romantic if he'd had the courage to look into my face and say it, but instead, he dropped his eyes to the ground and scuffed his boot in the leaves – countless possibilities for happy days – on the ground. "I haven't stopped."

And I should've said something romantic, too, but I didn't have the courage, either. So instead, I watched the shy way he was chewing his lip and studying the leaves, and said, "That must've been very boring."

Sam laughed, a funny, self-deprecating laugh. "You did read a lot. And spent too much time just inside the kitchen window, where I couldn't see you very well."

"And not enough time mostly naked in front of my bedroom window?" I teased.

Sam turned bright red. "That," he said, "is so not the point of this conversation."

I smiled sweetly at his embarrassment, beginning to walk again, kicking up golden leaves. I heard him scuffing leaves behind me. "And what was the point of it again?"

"Forget it!" Sam said. "Do you like this place or not?"

I stopped in my tracks, spinning to face him. "Hey." I pointed at him; he raised his eyebrows and stopped in his tracks. "You didn't think Jack would be here at all, did you?"

His thick dark eyebrows went up even further.

"Did you really intend to look for him at all?"

He held his hands up as if in surrender. "What do you want me to say?"

"You were trying to see if I would recognize it, weren't you?" I took another step, closing the distance between us. I could feel the heat of his body, even without touching him, in the increasing cold of the day. "*You* told me about this wood somehow. How did you show it to me?"

"I keep trying to tell you. You won't listen. Because

you're stubborn. It's how we speak — it's the only words we have. Just pictures. Just simple little pictures. You *have* changed, Grace. Just not your skin. I want you to believe me." His hands were still raised, but he was starting to grin at me in the failing light.

"So you only brought me here to see this." I stepped forward again, and he stepped back.

"Do you like it?"

"Under false pretences." Another step forward; another back. The grin widened.

"So do you like it?"

"When you knew we wouldn't come across anybody else."

His teeth flashed in his grin. "Do you like it?"

I punched my hands into his chest. "You know I love it. You knew I would." I went to punch him again, and he grabbed my wrists. For a moment we stood there like that, him looking down at me with the grin half-caught on his face, and me looking up at him: Still Life with Boy and Girl. It would've been the perfect moment to kiss me, but he didn't. He just looked at me and looked at me, and by the time I realized I could just as easily kiss him, I noticed that his grin was slipping away.

Sam slowly lowered my wrists and released them. "I'm glad," he said, very quietly.

My arms still hung by my sides, right where Sam had put them. I frowned at him. "You were supposed to kiss me."

"I thought about it."

I just kept looking at the soft, sad shape of his lips, looking just like his voice sounded. I was probably staring, but I couldn't stop thinking about how much I wanted him to kiss me and how stupid it was to want it so badly. "Why don't you?"

He leaned over and gave me the lightest of kisses. His lips, cool and dry, ever so polite and incredibly maddening. "I have to get inside soon," he whispered. "It's getting cold."

For the first time I paid attention to the icy wind that cut through my long sleeves. One of the frigid gusts hurled thousands of fallen leaves back into the air, and for a single second, I thought I smelled wolf.

Sam shuddered.

Squinting at his face in the dim light, I realized suddenly that his eyes were afraid.

Twenty-Five

Sam

3°C

We didn't run back to the house. Running would've meant acknowledging something that I wasn't ready to face in front of her – something that I *was*. Instead, we walked with a giant's strides, dried leaves and branches snapping under our feet, our breaths drowning out the other sounds of the evening. Cold snaked under my collar, tightening my skin into goosebumps.

If I didn't let go of her hand, I'd be all right.

A wrong turn would lead us away from the house, but I couldn't concentrate on the trees around me. My vision flashed with jerky memories of humans shifting into wolves, hundreds of shifts over my years with the pack. The memory of the first time I'd seen Beck shift was vivid in my mind – more real than the screaming red sunset through the trees in front of Grace and me. I remembered the frigid white light streaming in the living-room windows of Beck's house, and I remembered the shaking line of his shoulders as he braced his arms against the back of the sofa.

I stood beside him, looking up, no words in my mouth.

"Take him out!" Beck shouted, his face towards the hallway but his eyes half-closed. "Ulrik, take Sam out of here!"

Ulrik's fingers around my arm then were as tight as Grace's fingers around my hand were now, pulling me through the woods, leading us back over the trail we'd left earlier. Night crouched in the trees, waiting to overtake us, cold and black. But Grace didn't look away from the sun glowing through the trees as she headed towards it.

The brilliant nimbus of the sun half blinded me, making stark silhouettes of the trees, and suddenly I was seven again. I saw the star pattern of my old bedspread so clearly that I stumbled. My fingers clutched the fabric, balling and tearing it under my grip.

"Mama!" My voice broke on the second syllable. "Mama, I'm going to be sick!"

I was tangled on the floor in blankets and noise and puke, shaking and clawing at the floor, trying to hold on to something, when my mother came to the bedroom door, a familiar silhouette. I looked at her, my cheek resting against the floor, and I started to say her name, but no sound came out.

She dropped to her knees and she watched me change for the first time.

"Finally," Grace said, tearing my brain back to the

woods around us. She sounded out of breath, as if we'd been running. "There it is."

I couldn't let Grace see me change. I couldn't change now.

I followed Grace's gaze to the back of Beck's house, a flash of warm red-brown in this chilly blue evening.

And now I ran.

Two steps from the car, all my hopes of getting warm in the Bronco were crushed in the moment it took for Grace to uselessly tug the locked door handle. Inside, the keys swung from the ignition with her effort. Grace's face twisted with frustration.

"We'll have to try the house," she said.

We didn't have to break into Beck's house. He always left a spare key stuck in the weather lining of the back door. I tried not to think of the car keys hanging in the Bronco's ignition; if we had them, I would've been warm again already. My hands shook as I pulled the spare key from the lining and tried to slide it into the dead bolt. I was hurting already. *Hurry up, you idiot. Hurry up.*

I just couldn't stop shaking.

Grace carefully took the key from me, with not even a hint of fear, though she had to know what was happening. She closed one of her warm hands over my cold, shuddering ones, and with the other she shoved the key into the knob and unlocked it.

God, please let the power be on. Please let the heat be on.

Her hand on my elbow pushed me inside the dark kitchen. I couldn't shed the cold; it clung to every bit of me. My muscles began to cramp and I put my fingers over my face, shoulders hunched.

"No," Grace said, her voice even and firm, just like she was answering a simple question. "No, come on."

She pulled me away from the door and shut it behind me. Her hand slid along the wall by the door, finding the light switches, and miraculously, the lights flickered on, coming to ugly, fluorescent life above us. Grace pulled on me again, dragging me further away from the door, but I didn't want to move. I just wanted to curl in on myself and give in. "I can't, Grace. I can't."

I didn't know if I'd said it out loud or not, but she wasn't listening to me if I had. Instead, she sat me on the floor directly on top of an air vent, and she pulled off her jacket to wrap around my shoulders and over the top of my head. Then she crouched in front of me and gathered my cold hands against her body.

I shook and clenched my teeth to keep them from chattering, trying to focus on her, on being human, on getting warm. She was saying something; I couldn't understand her. She was too loud. Everything was too loud. It smelled in here. This close, her scent was exploding in my nostrils. I hurt. Everything hurt. I whined, very softly.

She leaped up and ran down the hall, her hands smacking light switches as she did, and then she disappeared. I groaned and put my head down on my knees. *No, no, no, no.* I didn't even know what I was supposed to be fighting any more. The pain? The shuddering?

She was back. Her hands were wet. She grabbed my wrists and her mouth moved, her voice ringing out, indecipherable. Sounds meant for someone else's ears. I stared at her.

She pulled again; she was stronger than I thought she was. I got to my feet; my height somehow surprised me. I shivered so violently that her jacket fell from my shoulders. The cold air hitting my neck racked me with another shudder and I nearly went to my knees.

The girl got a better grip on my arms and pulled me along, talking all the time, low, soothing sounds with an edge of iron beneath them. She pushed me into a doorway; heat emanated from inside it.

God, no. No. *No.* I pulled and fought against her hold, eyes locked on the far wall of the little tiled room. A bathtub lay in front of me like a tomb. Steam rolled off the water, the heat tempting and wonderful, but every part of my body resisted.

"Sam, don't fight me! I'm sorry. I'm sorry, I don't know what else to do."

Eyes fixed on the tub, I hooked my fingers on the edge of the door. "Please," I whispered.

In my head, the hands held me down in the tub, hands that smelled of childhood and familiarity, of hugs and clean sheets and everything I'd ever known. They pushed me into the water. It was warm, the temperature of my body. The voices counted together. They didn't say my name. *Cut. Cut. Cut. Cut.* They were poking holes in my skin, letting what was inside get out. The water turned red in little wispy strands. I gasped, struggled, cried. They didn't speak. The woman cried into the water as she held me down. *I'm Sam,* I told them, holding my face above the red water. *I'm Sam. I'm Sam. I'm*

"Sam!" The girl ripped me from the door and pushed off the wall against me; I stumbled and fell towards the tub. She shoved me as I fought to regain my balance, sending my head smacking against the wall and into the steaming water.

I lay perfectly still, sinking, water closing over my face, scalding my skin, boiling my body, drowning my shudders. Grace gently lifted my head above water, cradling it in her arms, one foot in the tub behind me. She was sopping wet and shivering.

"Sam," she said. "God, I'm sorry. I'm so sorry. I'm sorry. I didn't know what else to do. Please forgive me. I'm sorry."

I couldn't stop shaking, my fingers gripped on the side of the tub. I wanted out. I wanted her to hold me, so I could feel safe. I wanted to forget the blood running from the scars on my wrists. "Get me out," I whispered. "Please get me out."

"Are you warm enough?"

I couldn't answer. I was bleeding to death. I balled my hands into fists and drew them to my chest. Every caress of water over my wrists sent a new wave of shivers through me. Her face was full of pain.

"I'm going to find the thermostat and turn the heat up. Sam, you have to stay in there until I come back with towels. I'm so sorry."

I closed my eyes.

I passed a lifetime with my head held barely above water, unable to move, and then Grace came back, holding a stack of mismatched towels. She knelt by the tub and reached past me; I heard a gurgle behind my head. I felt myself slipping down the drain with the water in red circling swirls.

"I can't get you out if you don't help. Please, Sam." She stared at me as if she was waiting for me to move. The water drained away from my wrists, my shoulders, my back, until I lay in an empty tub. Grace laid a towel on top of me; it was very warm, as if she'd heated it somehow. Then she took one of my scarred wrists in her hands and looked at me. "You can come out now."

I looked back at her, unblinking, my legs folded up the side of the tiled wall like a giant insect.

She reached down and traced my eyebrows. "You do have really beautiful eyes."

"We get to keep them," I said.

Grace started at my voice. "What?"

"It's the one thing we keep. Our eyes stay the same."
I unclenched my fists. "I was born with these eyes. I was
born for this life."

As if there was no bitterness in my voice, Grace
replied, "Well, they're beautiful. Beautiful and sad." She
reached down and took my fingers, her eyes locked on
mine, holding my gaze. "Do you think you can stand
up now?"

And I did. Looking at her brown eyes and nothing
else, I stepped out of the tub, and she led me out of the
bathroom and back into my life.

Twenty-Six
Grace

I couldn't keep my thoughts together. I stood in the kitchen, staring at the cabinets, which were covered with pinned-up photographs of smiling people – the pack members as humans. Normally, I would've looked through them to find Sam's face, but I kept seeing the broken shape of his body in the bathtub and hearing the terror in his voice. The vision of him shaking in the woods right before I realized what was happening to him replayed over and over in my head.

Saucepan. Can of soup. Bread from freezer. Spoons. Beck's kitchen was obviously stocked by someone who was familiar with a werewolf's peculiar schedule; it was full of canned goods and boxed foods with long shelf lives. I lined up all of the ingredients for a makeshift dinner on the counter, forcing myself to concentrate on the task at hand.

In the next room, Sam sat on the couch under a blanket, his clothing running through the wash. My jeans were still soaking, but they'd have to wait. Turning on a burner for the soup, I tried to focus on the slick black controls, the shiny aluminium surface.

But instead I remembered Sam convulsing on the floor, eyes vacant, and the animal whimper he made as he realized that he was losing himself.

My hands shook as I tipped the soup from the can to the saucepan.

I couldn't keep it together.

I would keep it together.

I saw the look on his face as I shoved him into the bathtub, just like his parents must have—

God, I couldn't think about that. Opening the fridge, I was surprised to see a gallon of milk, the first perishable food I'd found in the house. It looked so out of place that I felt my thoughts sharpen. Checking the expiration date – only three weeks ago – I poured the odiferous milk down the drain and frowned into the fridge for other signs of recent life.

Sam was still curled on the couch when I emerged from the kitchen to hand him a bowl of soup and some toast. He accepted it with a more mournful look than usual. "You must think I'm a total freak."

I sat on a tartan chair across from him, tucking my legs beneath me, and held my bowl of soup against my chest for warmth. The living-room ceiling went all the way up to the roof and the room was still draughty. "I am so sorry."

Sam shook his head. "It was the only thing you could do. I just – I shouldn't have lost it that way."

I winced, remembering the crack of his head hitting the wall and his splayed fingers, reaching through the air as he careened into the tub.

"You did really well," Sam said, glancing at me as he picked at the toast. He seemed to consider his words, and then just repeated, "You did really well. Are you—" He hesitated and then looked to where I sat, several feet away from him. Something in his glance made the empty stretch of couch next to him painfully obvious.

"I'm not afraid of you!" I said. "Is that what you think? I just thought you'd like some elbow room while you ate."

Actually, any other time I'd have happily crawled under the blanket with him – especially with him looking warm and sexy in a set of old sweats he'd got from his room. But I just wanted – I just needed to put my thoughts in order, and didn't think I could do that while sitting next to him just yet.

Sam smiled, relief all over his face. "The soup's good."

"Thanks." It wasn't actually that good – in fact, it tasted completely canned and bland, but I was hungry enough that I didn't care. And the mechanical action of eating helped dull the images of Sam in the bathtub.

"Tell me more about the mind-meld thing," I said, wanting to keep him talking, to hear his human voice.

Sam swallowed. "The what?"

"You said you showed me the woods, when you were a wolf. And that the wolves talked to each other that way. Tell me more about it. I want to know how it works."

Sam leaned forward to set his bowl on the floor, and when he sat back and looked at me, his face looked tired. "It's not like that."

"I didn't say it was like anything!" I said. "Not like what?"

"It's not a superpower," he replied. "It's a consolation prize." When I just looked at him, he added, "It's the only way we get to communicate. We can't remember words. We couldn't say them even if we could wrap our wolf brains around them. So all we get are little images that we can send to each other. Simple images. Postcards from the other side."

"Can you send me one now?"

Sam slouched down on the couch, tightening the blanket around himself. "I can't even remember how to do it now. While I'm *me*. I only do it when I'm a wolf. Why would I need it now? I have words. I can say anything I want to you."

I thought about saying *But words aren't enough*, but just thinking it made me ache in an unfamiliar way. So instead I said, "But I wasn't a wolf when you showed me the woods. So can the wolves talk to other pack members when those members are human?"

Sam's heavy-lidded eyes flicked over my face. "I

don't know. I don't think I ever tried with anyone else. Just wolves." He said, again, "Why would I need to?"

There was something bitter and tired in his voice. I set my bowl down on the end table and joined him on the couch. He lifted the blanket so that I could press myself against his side, and then he leaned his forehead against mine, closing his eyes. For a long moment, he just rested there, and then he opened his eyes again.

"All I cared about was showing you how to get home," he said, voice low. His breath warmed my lips. "When you changed, I wanted to make sure you knew how to find me."

I ran my fingers across the triangle of bare chest that was visible above the loose collar of his sweatshirt. My voice came out a little uneven. "Well, I found you."

The dryer buzzed from down the hall, a strange sound of occupation in this empty house. Sam blinked and leaned back. "I should get my clothing." He opened his mouth as if he was going to say something else and blushed instead.

"The clothing's not going anywhere," I said.

"Neither are we, if we don't break into the Bronco to get the keys," Sam pointed out. "I'm thinking sooner rather than later for that. Especially since it's going to have to be you doing it. I can't stand out there that long."

I reluctantly moved back so that he could stand, holding the blanket around him like some sort of primitive chieftain. I could see the outline of his square shoulders underneath it and thought about the feel of his skin underneath my fingers. He saw me looking and held my gaze for half a second before vanishing into the dark hallway.

Something gnawed inside me, hungry and wanting.

I sat on the couch after he left, debating whether or not to follow him to the laundry room, until reason won over. I took the plates to the kitchen, then returned to the living room to poke around the bits and pieces on the mantel. I wanted to get a handle on the werewolf he called Beck, the one who owned the house. The one who had raised Sam.

The living room, like the exterior of the house, looked comfortable and lived in. It was all tartans and rich reds and dark wood accents. One wall of the living room was almost entirely made up of tall windows, and the now-dark winter night seemed to enter the room without permission. I turned my back on the windows and looked at a photo on the mantel: a loosely posed group of faces smiling at the camera. It made me think of the picture of Rachel, Olivia and me, and I felt a twinge of loss before focusing on the people in this photo. Out of the six figures in the photo, my eyes immediately found Sam. This was a slightly younger version of him, with summer-tanned skin. The one girl in the photograph stood next to him, about his age, her white-blonde hair reaching beyond her shoulders. She was the only one not smiling at the camera. Instead, she was looking at Sam in an intense way that made my stomach churn.

A soft touch on my neck made me whirl around, defensive, and Sam jumped back, laughing, hands up in the air. "Easy!"

I swallowed the growl in my throat, feeling stupid, and rubbed the still-tingling skin on my neck where he'd kissed it. "You should make some noise." I gestured to the photo, still feeling uncharitable towards the unnamed girl beside him. "Who's that?"

Sam lowered his hands and stood behind me, wrapping his arms around my stomach. His clothing smelled clean and soapy; his skin gave off hints of wolf from his near-transformation earlier. "Shelby." He leaned his head on my shoulder, his cheek against mine.

I kept my voice light. "She's pretty."

Sam growled in a soft, wild way that made my gut tense with longing. He pressed his lips against my neck, not quite a kiss. "You've met her, you know."

It didn't take rocket science to figure it out. "The white she-wolf." And then I just asked it, because I wanted to know. "Why is she looking at you like that?"

"Oh, Grace," he said, taking his lips from my neck. "I don't know. She's – I don't know. She thinks she's in love with me. She wants to be in love with me."

"Why?" I asked.

He gave a little laugh, not at all amused. "Why do

you ask such hard questions? I don't know. She had a bad life, I think, before she came to the pack. She likes being a wolf. She likes belonging. I guess maybe she sees how Beck and I are around each other and thinks that being with me would make her belong even more."

"It is possible to be in love with you just because of who you are," I pointed out.

Sam's body tensed behind me. "But it's not because of who I am. It's ... obsession."

"I'm obsessed," I said.

Sam let out a long breath and pulled away from me.

I sighed. "Shhhhh. You didn't have to *move*."

"I'm trying to be a gentleman."

I leaned back against him, smiling at his worried eyes. "You don't have to try so hard."

He sucked in his breath, waited a long moment, and then carefully kissed my neck, just underneath my jawbone. I turned around in his arms so I could kiss his lips, still charmingly hesitant.

"I was thinking about the refrigerator," I whispered.

Sam pulled back, ever so slightly, without removing himself from my arms. "You were thinking about the refrigerator?"

"Yes. I was thinking about how you didn't know if the power would be turned on here for the winter. But it is."

He frowned at me, and I rubbed the crease between his eyebrows.

"So who pays the power bill? Beck?" When he nodded, I went on, "There was milk in the fridge, Sam. It was only a few weeks old. Someone has been in here. Recently."

Sam's arms around me had loosened and his sad eyes had gone even sadder. His entire expression was complicated, his face a book in a language I didn't understand.

"Sam," I said, wanting to bring him back to me.

But his body had gone stiff. "I should get you home. Your parents will be worried."

I laughed, short and humourless. "Yeah. I'm sure. What's wrong?"

"Nothing." Sam shook his head, but he was clearly distracted. "I mean, not nothing. It's been a hell of a day, that's all. I'm just – I'm just tired, I guess."

He did look tired, something dark and sombre in his expression. I wondered if almost changing had affected him, or if I should've just stayed quiet about Shelby and Beck. "You're coming home with me, then."

He jerked his chin towards the house around him.

"C'mon," I said. "I'm still worried that you'll disappear."

"I won't disappear."

Inadvertently, I thought of him on the floor in the hallway, curled up, making a soft noise as he struggled to stay human. I immediately wished I hadn't. "You can't promise that. I don't want to go home. Not unless you're coming with me."

Sam groaned softly. His palms brushed the bare skin at the bottom edge of my T-shirt, his thumbs tracing desire on my sides. "Don't tempt me."

I didn't say anything; just stood in his arms looking up at him.

He pushed his face against my shoulder and groaned again. "It's so hard to behave myself around you." He pushed away from me. "I don't know if I should keep staying with you. God, you're only, what – you're only seventeen."

"And you're so old, right?" I said, suddenly defensive.

"Eighteen," he said, as if it were something to be sad about. "At least I'm legal."

I actually laughed, though nothing was funny. My cheeks felt hot and my heart pounded in my chest. "Are you kidding me?"

"Grace," he said, and the sound of my name slowed my heart immediately. He took my arm. "I just want to do things right, OK? I only get this one chance to do things right with you."

I looked at him. The room was silent except for the rattle of leaves blowing up against the windows. I wondered what my face looked like just then, turned up at Sam. Was it the same intense gaze that Shelby wore in the photograph? Obsession?

The frigid night pressed up against the window beside us, a threat that had become abruptly real tonight. This wasn't about lust. It was about fear.

"Please come back with me," I said. I didn't know what I'd do if he said no. I couldn't stand to return here tomorrow and find him a wolf.

Sam must have seen it in my eyes, because he just nodded and picked up the slim-jim.

Twenty-Seven

Sam

3°C

Grace's parents were home.

"They're never home," Grace said, her voice clearly spelling out her annoyance. But there they were, or at least their cars: her father's Taurus, looking either silver or blue in the moonlight, and her mother's little VW Rabbit tucked in front of it.

"Don't even think of saying 'I told you so'," Grace said. "I'm going to go inside and see where they are, and then I'll come back out to debrief."

"You mean, for me to debrief you," I corrected, tensing my muscles to keep from shivering. Whether from nerves or the memory of cold, I didn't know.

"Yes," Grace replied, turning off the headlights. "That. Right back."

I watched her run in the house and slunk down into my seat. I couldn't quite believe that I was hiding in a car in the middle of a freezing cold night, waiting for a girl to come running back out and tell me the coast was clear to come sleep in her room. Not just any girl. *The* girl. Grace.

She appeared at the front door and made an elaborate gesture. It took me a moment to realize she meant for me to turn off the Bronco and come in. I did so, sliding out of the car as quickly as possible and hurrying quietly up into the front hallway; cold tugged and bit at my exposed skin. Without even letting me pause, Grace gave me a shove, launching me down the hall while she shut the front door and headed in towards the kitchen.

"I forgot my backpack," she announced loudly in the other room.

I used the cover of their conversation to creep into Grace's bedroom and softly shut the door. Inside the house, it was easily fifteen degrees warmer, a fact for which I was very grateful. I could still feel the trembling in my muscles from being outside; the sensation of *in between* that I hated.

The cold exhausted me and I didn't know how long Grace would be up with her parents, so I climbed into bed without turning on the light. Sitting there in the dim moonlight, leaning against the pillows, I rubbed life back into my frozen toes and listened to Grace's distant voice down the hall. She and her mother were having some amiable conversation about the romantic comedy that had just been on TV. I'd already noticed that Grace and her parents had no problem talking about unimportant things. They seemed to have an endless capacity for laughing pleasantly together about inane topics, but I'd never once heard them talk about anything meaningful.

It was so strange to me, coming from the environment of the pack. Ever since Beck had taken me under his wing, I'd been surrounded by family, sometimes suffocatingly so, and Beck had never failed to give me his undivided attention when I wanted it. I'd taken it for granted, but now I felt spoiled.

I was still sitting up in bed when the doorknob turned quietly. I froze, absolutely still, and then exhaled when I recognized the sound of Grace's breathing. She shut the door behind her and turned towards the window.

I saw her teeth in the low light. "You in here?" she whispered.

"Where are your parents? Are they going to come in here and shoot me?"

Grace went silent. In the shadows, without her voice, she was invisible to me.

I was about to say something to dispel the strangely awkward moment when she said, "No, they're upstairs. Mom's making Dad sit for her to paint him. So you're clear to go brush your teeth and stuff. If you do it fast. Just sing in a high-pitched voice, so they think it's me." Her voice hardened when she said *Dad*, though I couldn't imagine why.

"A tone-deaf voice," I corrected.

Grace passed by me on the way to the dresser, swatting at my butt. "Just go."

Leaving my shoes in her room, I padded quietly down the hall to the downstairs bathroom. It only had a stand-up shower, for which I was intensely grateful, and Grace had made sure to pull the curtain shut so that I wouldn't have to look into it, anyway.

I brushed my teeth with her toothbrush. Then I stood there, a lanky teenager in a big green T-shirt she had borrowed from her father, looking at my floppy hair and yellow eyes in the mirror. *What are you doing, Sam?*

I closed my eyes as if hiding my pupils, so wolflike even when I was a human, would change what I was. The fan for the central heating hummed, sending subtle vibrations through my bare feet, reminding me that it was the only thing keeping me in this human form. The new October nights were already cold enough to rip my skin from me, and by next month, the days would be, too. What was I going to do, hide in Grace's house all winter, fearing every creeping draught?

I opened my eyes again, staring at them in the mirror until their shape and colour didn't mean anything. I wondered what Grace saw in me, why I fascinated her. What was I without my wolf skin? A boy stuffed so full of words that they spilled out of me.

Right now, every phrase, every lyric that I had in my head ended with the same word: *love*.

I had to tell Grace that this was my last year.

I peered into the hallway for signs of her parents and

crept back into the bedroom, where Grace was already in bed, a long, soft lump under the covers. For a moment, I let my imagination run wild as to what she was wearing. I had a dim wolf memory of her climbing out of bed one spring morning, wearing just an oversized T-shirt, her long legs exposed as she slid them out from under the covers. So sexy it hurt.

Immediately, I felt embarrassed for fantasizing. I sort of paced around at the end of the bed for a few minutes, thinking about cold showers and barré chords and other things that weren't Grace.

"Hey," she whispered, voice muzzy as if she had been asleep already. "What're you doing?"

"Shhh," I said, my cheeks flushing. "Sorry I woke you up. I was just thinking."

Her reply was broken by a yawn. "Stop thinking then."

I climbed into bed, keeping to the edge of the mattress. Something about this evening had changed me – something about Grace seeing me at my worst, immobile in the bathtub, ready to give up. Tonight, the bed seemed too small to escape her scent, the sleepy sound of her voice, the warmth of her body. I discreetly stuffed a bunch of blankets between us and rested my head on the pillow, willing my doubts to fly away and let me sleep.

Grace reached over and began stroking her fingers through my hair. I closed my eyes and let her drive me crazy. *She draws patterns on my face / These lines make shapes that can't replace / the version of me that I hold inside / when lying with you, lying with you, lying with you.* "I like your hair," she said.

I didn't say anything. I was thinking about a melody to go with the lyrics in my head.

"Sorry about tonight," she whispered. "I don't mean to push your boundaries."

I sighed as her fingers curled around my ears and neck. "It's just so fast. I want you to —" I stopped short of saying *love me*, because it seemed presumptive — "want to be with me. I've wanted it for ever. I just never thought it would actually happen." It felt too serious, so I added, "I am just a mythological creature, after all. I technically shouldn't exist."

Grace laughed, low, just for me. "Silly boy. You feel very real to me."

"You do, too," I whispered.

There was a long pause in the darkness.

"I wish I changed," she said finally, barely audible. I opened my eyes, needing to see the way her face looked when she said that. It was more descriptive than any expression I'd ever seen her wear: immeasurably sad, lips set crookedly with longing.

I reached out for her, cupped the side of her face with my hand. "Oh, no, you don't, Grace. No, you don't."

She shook her head against the pillow. "I feel so

miserable when I hear the howling. I felt so awful when you disappeared for the summer."

"Oh, angel, I would take you with me if I could," I said, and I was simultaneously surprised that the word *angel* came out of my mouth and that it felt right to call her that. I ran a hand over her hair, fingers catching in the strands. "But you don't want this. I lose more of myself every year."

Grace's voice was strange. "Tell me what happens, at the end."

It took me a moment to figure out what she meant. "Oh, the end." There were one thousand ways to tell her, a thousand ways to colour it. Grace wouldn't fall for the rose-coloured version that Beck had told me at first, so I just told it straight. "I become me – become human – later in the spring every year. And one year – I guess I just won't change. I've seen it happen to the older wolves. One year, they don't become human again, and they're just ... a wolf. And they live a little longer than natural wolves. But still – fifteen years, maybe."

"How can you talk about your own death like that?"

I looked at her, eyes glistening in the dim light. "How else could I talk about it?"

"Like you regret it."

"I regret it every day."

Grace was silent, but I *felt* her processing what I'd

said, pragmatically putting everything into its proper place in her head. "You were a wolf when you got shot."

I wanted to press my fingers to her lips, push the words she was forming back into her mouth. It was too soon. I didn't want her to say it yet.

But Grace went on, her voice low. "You missed the hottest months this year. It wasn't that cold when you got shot. It was cold, but not winter cold. But you were a wolf. When were you a human this year?"

I whispered, "I don't remember."

"What if you hadn't been shot? When would you have become you again?"

I closed my eyes. "I don't know, Grace." It was the perfect moment to tell her. *This is my last year.* But I couldn't say it. Not yet. I wanted another minute, another hour, another night of pretending this wasn't the end.

Grace inhaled a slow, shaky breath, and something in the way she did it made me realize that somehow, on some level, she knew. She'd known all along.

She wasn't crying, but I thought I might.

Grace put her fingers back into my hair, and mine were in hers. Our bare arms pressed against each other in a cool tangle of skin. Every little movement against her arm rubbed off a tiny spark of her scent, a tantalizing mix of flowery soap, faint sweat, and desire for me.

I wondered if she knew how transparent her scent

made her, how it told me what she was feeling when she didn't say it out loud.

Of course, I'd seen her smelling the air just as often as I did. She had to know that she was driving me crazy right now, that every touch of her skin on mine tingled, electric.

Every touch pushed the reality of the oncoming winter further away.

As if to prove me right, Grace moved closer, kicking away the blankets between us, pressing her mouth to mine. I let her part my lips and sighed, tasting her breath. I listened to her almost inaudible gasp as I wrapped my arms around her. Every one of my senses was whispering to me over and over to get closer to her, closer to her, as close as I could. She twined her bare legs in mine and we kissed until we had no more breath and got closer until distant howls outside the window brought me back to my senses.

Grace made a soft noise of disappointment as I disentangled my legs from hers, aching with wanting more. I shifted to lie next to her, my fingers still caught in her hair. We listened to the wolves howling outside the window, the ones who hadn't changed. Or who would never change again. And we buried our heads against each other so we couldn't hear anything but the racing of our hearts.

Twenty-Eight
Grace

9°C

School felt like an alien planet on Monday. It took me a long moment of sitting behind the wheel of the Bronco, watching the students milling on the pavements and the cars circling the car park and the buses filing neatly into place, to realize that school hadn't changed. I had.

"You have to go to school," Sam said, and if I hadn't known him, I wouldn't have heard the hopeful questioning note. I wondered where he would go while I was sitting in class.

"I know," I replied, frowning at the multicoloured sweaters and scarves trailing into the school, evidence of winter's approach. "It just seems so..." What it seemed was irrelevant, disconnected from my life. It was hard to remember what was important about sitting in a classroom with a stack of notes that would be meaningless by next year.

Beside me, Sam jumped in surprise as the driver's-side door came open. Rachel climbed into the Bronco with her backpack, shoving me across the bench seat to make room for herself.

She slammed the door shut and let out a big sigh. The car seemed very full with her in it. "Nice truck." She leaned forward and looked over at Sam. "Ooh, a boy. Hi, Boy! Grace, I'm so *hyper*. Coffee! Are you mad at me?"

I leaned back in surprise, blinking. "No?"

"Good! Because when you didn't call me in for *ever*, I figured you'd either died or were mad at me. And you're obviously not dead, so I thought it was the mad thing." She drummed her fingers on the steering wheel. "But you *are* pissed at Olivia, right?"

"Yes," I said, although I wasn't sure if it was still true. I remembered why we fought, but I couldn't really remember why it had been meaningful. "No. I don't think so. It was stupid."

"Yeah, I thought so," Rachel said. She leaned forward and rested her chin on the steering wheel so that she could look at Sam. "So, Boy, why are you in Grace's car?"

Despite myself, I smiled. I knew what Sam *was* needed to be a secret, but Sam himself didn't have to be, did he? I was suddenly filled with the need for Rachel to approve of him. "Yeah, Boy," I said, craning my neck to see Sam right beside me. He wore an expression caught somewhere between amusement and doubt. "Why are you in my car?"

"I'm here for visual interest," Sam said.

"Wow," Rachel replied. "Like, long-term, or short-term?"

"For as long as I'm interesting." He turned his face into my shoulder for a moment in a wordless gesture of affection. I tried not to smile like an idiot.

"Oh, it's that way, is it? Well, then, I'm Rachel, and I'm hyper, and I'm Grace's best friend," she said, and stuck her hand out to him. She was wearing rainbow-coloured fingerless gloves that stretched up to her elbows. Sam shook her hand.

"Sam."

"Nice to meet you, Sam. Do you go here?" When he shook his head, Rachel took my hand and said, "Yeah, I didn't think so. Well, then, I'm going to steal this nice person from you and take her to class because we're going to be late and I have lots of stuff to talk to her about and she's missed out on so much freaky wolf stuff because she's not talking to her other best friend. So you can see we have to go. I would say I'm not normally this hyper, but I kinda am. Let's go, Grace!"

Sam and I exchanged looks, his eyes fleetingly worried, and then Rachel opened the door and pulled me out. Sam slid behind the wheel. For a second I thought he might kiss me goodbye, but instead he glanced at Rachel before resting his fingers on my hand for a moment. His cheeks were pink.

Rachel didn't say anything, but she smiled crookedly before pulling me towards the school. She wiggled my arm. "So that's why you haven't been calling, huh? The Boy is supercute. What's he, homeschooled?"

As we pushed through the school doors, I looked over my shoulder at the Bronco. I saw Sam lift a hand in a wave before he started to back out of the parking space.

"Yeah, he is, on both counts," I said. "More on that later. What is going on with the wolves?"

Rachel dramatically clutched her arms around my shoulders.

"Olivia saw one. It was up on their front porch and there were *claw marks*, Grace. On the door. Creep. Factor."

I halted in the middle of the hallway; students behind us made irritated noises and pushed around us. I said, "Wait. At Olivia's house?"

"No, at your mom's." Rachel shook her head and peeled off her rainbow gloves. "Yes, at Olivia's house. If you guys would stop fighting, she could tell you herself. What are you fighting about, anyway? It pains me to see my peeps not playing nice with each other."

"I told you, it's just stupid stuff," I said. I kind of wanted her to stop talking so I could try and think about the wolf at Olivia's house. Was it Jack again? Why at Olivia's?

"Well, you guys need to start getting along because I want you both to go with me over Christmas break. And that's not that far off, you know. I mean, not really, once you start planning stuff. Come *on*, Grace, just say yes!" Rachel wailed.

"Maybe." It wasn't really the wolf at Olivia's that bothered me. It was the claw marks bit. I needed to talk to Olivia and find out how much of this was real and how much of it was Rachel's love of a good story.

"Is this about The Boy? He can come! I don't care!" Rachel said.

The hall was slowly emptying; the bell rang overhead. "We'll talk about it later!" I said, and hurried with Rachel into first period. I found my usual seat and began sorting through my homework.

"We need to talk."

I jerked to attention at the sound of an entirely different voice: Isabel Culpeper's. She slid her giant cork heels the rest of the way under the other desk and leaned towards me, highlighted hair framing her face in perfect, shiny ringlets.

"We're sort of in class right now, Isabel," I said, gesturing towards the taped morning announcements playing on the TV at the front of the classroom. The teacher was already at the front of the class, bent over her desk. She wasn't paying attention, but I still wasn't thrilled with the idea of a conversation with Isabel. Best-case scenario was that she needed help with her homework or something; I had a reputation for being good at maths, so it was sort of possible.

Worst case was that she wanted to talk about Jack.

Sam had said that the only rule the pack had was

that they didn't talk about werewolves to outsiders. I wasn't about to break that rule.

Isabel's face was still wearing a pretty pout, but I saw storms destroying small villages in her eyes. She glanced towards the front of the room and leaned closer to me. I smelled perfume – roses and summer in this Minnesota cold. "It will only take a second."

I looked over at Rachel, who was frowning at Isabel. I really didn't want to talk to Isabel. I didn't really know much about her, but I knew she was a dangerous gossip who could quickly reduce my standing in the school to cafeteria target practice. I wasn't really one who tried to be popular, but I remembered what had happened to the last girl who had got on Isabel's bad side. She was still trying to get out from under a convoluted rumour that involved lap dancing and the football team. "Why?"

"*Privately*," hissed Isabel. "Across the hall."

I rolled my eyes as I pushed out of my desk and tiptoed out of the back of the room. Rachel gave me a brief, pained look. I was sure I wore a matching one. "Two seconds. That's it," I told Isabel as she shuffled me across the hall into an empty classroom. The corkboard on the opposite wall was covered with anatomical drawings; someone had pinned a thong over one of the figures.

"Yeah. Whatever." She shut the door behind us and eyed me as if I would spontaneously break into song or something. I didn't know what she was waiting for.

I crossed my arms. "OK. What do you want?"

I'd thought I was prepared for it, but when she said, "My brother. Jack," my heart still raced.

I didn't say anything.

"I saw him while I was running this morning."

I swallowed. "Your brother."

Isabel pointed at me with a perfect nail, glossier than the hood of the Bronco. Her ringlets bounced. "Oh, don't give me that. I *talked* to him. He's not dead."

I briefly wrestled with the image of Isabel jogging. I couldn't see it. Maybe she meant running from her Chihuahua. "Um."

Isabel pressed on. "There was something screwed up with him. And don't say 'That's because he's dead'. He's not."

Something about Isabel's charming personality – and maybe the fact that I knew Jack was actually alive – made it very difficult to empathize with her. I said, "Isabel, it seems to me like you don't need me to have this conversation. You're doing a great job all by yourself."

"Shut up," Isabel said, which only supported my theory. I was about to tell her so, but her next words stopped me cold. "When I saw Jack, he said he hadn't really died. Then he started – twitching –

and said he had to go *right then*. When I tried to ask him what was wrong with him, he said that you knew."

My voice came out a little strangled sounding. "Me?" But I remembered his eyes imploring me as he lay pinned beneath the she-wolf. *Help me.* He had recognized me.

"Well, it's not exactly a shock, is it? Everyone knows that you and Olivia Marx are freaks for those wolves, and clearly this has something to do with them. So what's going on, Grace?"

I didn't like the way she asked the question – like maybe she already knew the answer. Blood was rushing in my ears; I was in way over my head. "Look. You're upset, I get that. But seriously, get help. Leave me and Olivia out of this. I don't know what you saw, but it wasn't Jack."

The lie left a bad taste in my mouth. I could see the reasoning behind the pack's secrecy, but Jack was Isabel's brother. Didn't she have a right to know?

"I wasn't seeing things," Isabel snapped as I opened the door. "I'm going to find him again. And I'm going to find out what your part is in all this."

"I don't have a part," I said. "I just like the wolves. Now I need to get to class."

Isabel stood in the doorway, watching me go, and I wondered what, at the beginning of all this, she had thought I was going to say.

She looked almost forlorn, or maybe it was just an act.

In any case, I said, "Isabel, just get help."

She crossed her arms. "I thought that's what I was doing."

Twenty-Nine

Sam

12°C

While Grace was at school, I spent a long time in the car park, thinking about meeting wild Rachel and wondering what she'd meant by the wolf comment. I debated hunting for Jack, but I wanted to hear what Grace found out at school before I went on any wild-goose chase.

I didn't quite know how to occupy my time without Grace and without my pack. I felt like someone who has an hour until his bus arrives – not really enough time to do anything important, but too much time to just sit and wait.

The subtle cold bite behind the breeze told me that I couldn't put off getting on my bus for ever.

I finally drove the Bronco to the post office. I had the key to Beck's post office box, but mostly, what I wanted to do was conjure up memories and pretend that I'd run into him there.

I remembered the day Beck had brought me there to pick up my books for school – even now, I remembered it had been a Tuesday, because back then, Tuesdays were my favourite day. I don't remember why – it was just something about the way that *u* looked when it was next to *e* that seemed very friendly. I always loved going to the post office with Beck; it was a treasure cave with rows and rows of little locked boxes holding secrets and surprises only for those with the proper key.

I remembered that conversation with peculiar clarity, down to the expression on Beck's face: "Sam. Come on, bucko."

"What's that?"

Beck shoved his back ineffectually against the glass door, suffering under the weight of a huge box. "Your brain."

"I already have a brain."

"If you did, you'd have opened the door for me."

I shot him a dark look and let him shove against the door a moment longer before I ducked under his arms to push it open. "What is it really?"

"Schoolbooks. We're going to educate you properly, so you don't grow up to be an idiot."

I remembered being intrigued by the idea of school-in-a-box, just-add-water-and-Sam.

The rest of the pack was equally intrigued. I was the first in the pack to be bitten before finishing school, so the novelty of educating me was fascinating to the others. For several summers, they all took turns with the massive lesson manual and the lovely, ink-smelling new textbooks. They would stuff my brain full all day long:

Ulrik for maths; Beck for history; Paul for vocabulary, and later, science. They shouted test questions at me across the dinner table, invented songs for the timelines of dead presidents, and converted one of the dining-room walls into a giant whiteboard that was always written with words of the day and dirty jokes that no one would admit to.

When I was done with the first box of books, Beck packed them up and another box came to take its place. When I wasn't studying my school-in-a-box, I was surfing the internet for a different sort of education. I surfed for photos of circus freaks and synonyms for the word *intercourse* and for answers to why staring at the stars in the evening tore my heart with longing.

With the third box of books came a new pack member: Shelby, a tanned, slender girl covered in bruises and stumbling under the weight of a heavy Southern accent. I remembered Beck telling Paul, "I couldn't just leave her there. God! Paul, you didn't see where she came from. You didn't see what they were doing to her."

I'd felt sorry for Shelby, who'd made herself inaccessible to the others. I'd been the only one who had managed to float a life raft to the island that was Shelby, coaxing words out of her and, sometimes, a smile. She was strange, a breakable animal that would do anything to reassert control over her life. She'd steal things from Beck so that he would have to ask where they'd gone, play with the thermostat to watch Paul get up from the couch to fix it, hide my books so that I would talk with her instead of reading. But we were all broken in that house, weren't we? After all, I was the kid who couldn't bear to look into a bathroom.

Beck had picked up another box of books from the post office for Shelby, but they didn't mean the same thing to her as they did to me. She left them to collect dust and looked up wolf behaviour online instead.

Now, here in the post office, I stopped in front of Beck's PO box, 730. I touched the chipped paint of the numbers; the three was nearly gone and had been for as long as I'd been coming here. I put the key into the box, but I didn't turn it. Was it so wrong to want *this* so bad? An ordinary life of ordinary years with Grace, a couple of decades of turning keys in PO boxes and lying in bed and putting up Christmas trees in winter?

And now I was thinking of Shelby, again, and the memories bit, sharp as cold next to memories of Grace. Shelby had always thought my attachment to my human life was ludicrous. I still remembered the worst fight we had about it. Not the first, or the last, but the most cruel. I was lying on my bed, reading a copy of Yeats that Ulrik had bought for me, and Shelby jumped on to the mattress and stepped on the pages of the book, wrinkling them beneath her bare foot.

"Come listen to the howls I found online," she said.

"I'm reading."

"Mine's more important," Shelby said, towering above me, her toes curling and crinkling the pages further. "Why do you bother reading that stuff?" She gestured to the stack of schoolbooks on the desk beside my bed. "That's not what you're going to be when you grow up. You're not going to be a man. You're going to be a wolf, so you should be learning wolf things."

"Shut up," I said.

"Well, it's true. You're not going to be Sam. All those books are a waste. You're going to be alpha male. I read about that. And I'll be your mate. The alpha female." Her face was excited, flushed. Shelby wanted nothing more than to leave her past behind.

I ripped Yeats out from beneath her foot and smoothed the page. "I *will be Sam*. I'm never going to stop being Sam."

"You won't be!" Shelby's voice was getting louder. She jumped off my bed and shoved my stack of books over; thousands of words crashed on to the floor. "This is just pretending! We won't have names, we'll just be wolves!"

I shouted, "Shut up! I can still be Sam when I'm a wolf!"

Beck burst into the room then, looking at the scene in his silent way: my books, my life, my dreams, spread under Shelby's feet, and me on my bed, clutching my wrinkled Yeats in white-knuckled hands.

"What's going on here?" Beck said.

Shelby jerked a finger at me. "Tell him! Tell him he's not going to be Sam any more, when we're wolves. He can't be. He won't even know his name. And I won't be Shelby." She was shaking, furious.

Beck's voice was so quiet I could barely hear him. "Sam will always be Sam." He took Shelby's upper arm and marched her out of the room, her feet skidding on my books. Her face was shocked; Beck had been careful to never lay a hand on her since she'd come. I'd never seen him so angry. "Don't you ever tell him differently, Shelby. Or I will take you back where you came from. I will *take you back*."

In the hallway, Shelby began to scream, and she didn't stop until Beck slammed her bedroom door.

He walked back past my room and paused in the doorway. I was gently stacking my books back on the desk. The words shook in my hands as I did.

I thought Beck would say something, but he just picked up a book by his feet and added it to my pile before he left.

Later, I heard Ulrik and Beck; they didn't realize there weren't many places in the house a werewolf couldn't hear. "You were too hard on Shelby," Ulrik said. "She has a point. What is it you think he's going to do with all this wonderful book learning, Beck? It's not as if he'll ever be able to do what you do."

There was a long pause and Ulrik said, "What, you

can't be surprised. It doesn't take a genius to figure out what you were thinking. But tell me, how did you think Sam would go to college?"

Another pause. Beck said, "Summer school. And some online credits."

"Right. Let's say Sam gets his degree. What's he going to do with it? Go to law school online, too? And then what kind of lawyer would he be? People put up with your eccentric gone-for-the-winter routine because you were established when you were bitten. Sam will have to try to get jobs that ignore his unscheduled disappearance every year. For all the learning you're stuffing in his head, he's going to have to get jobs at gas stations like the rest of us. If he even makes it past twenty."

"You want to tell him to give up? You tell him. I'll never tell him that."

"I'm not telling him to give up. I'm telling *you* to give up."

"Sam doesn't do anything he doesn't want to. He wants to learn. He's smart."

"Beck. You're going to make him miserable. You can't give him all the tools to succeed and then let him discover — *poof* — that he can't use any of them. Shelby's right. In the end, we're wolves. I can read him German poetry and Paul can teach him about past participles and you can play Mozart for him, but in the end, it's a long, cold night and those woods for all of us."

Another pause before Beck answered, sounding tired and unlike himself.

"Just leave me alone, Ulrik, OK? Just leave me alone."

The next day Beck told me I didn't have to do my schoolwork if I didn't want to, and he went driving by himself. I waited until he was gone, and then I did the work, anyway.

Now, I wished more than anything that Beck was here with me. I turned the key in the lock, knowing what I'd find – a box stuffed with months' worth of envelopes and probably a slip to collect more from behind the desk.

But when I opened the box, there were two lonely letters and some junk fliers.

Someone had been here. Recently.

Thirty

Sam

5°C

"Do you mind if I go by Olivia's?" Grace asked, climbing into the car, bringing in a rush of cold air with her. In the passenger seat, I recoiled, and she hurriedly shut the door behind her. She said, "Sorry about that. It got really cold, didn't it? Anyway, I don't want to, you know, actually go inside. Just drive by. Rachel said that a wolf had been scratching around Olivia's house. So maybe we could pick up a trail near there?"

"Go for it," I said. Taking her hand from where it rested, I kissed her fingertips before replacing it on the wheel. I slouched down in my seat and got my translation of Rilke I'd brought to read while I waited for her.

Grace's lips lifted slightly at my touch, but she didn't say anything as she pulled out of the car park. I watched her face, etched into concentration, mouth set in a firm line, and waited to see if she was ready to say what was on her mind. When she didn't, I picked up the volume of Rilke and slouched down in my seat.

"What are you reading?" Grace asked, after a long space of silence.

I was fairly certain that pragmatic Grace would not have heard of Rilke. "Poetry."

Grace sighed and gazed out at the dead white sky that seemed to press down on the road before us. "I don't get poetry." She seemed to realize her statement might offend, because she hurriedly added, "Maybe I'm reading the wrong stuff."

"You're probably just reading it wrong," I said. I'd seen Grace's to-be-read pile: non-fiction, books about things, not about how things were described. "You have to listen to the pattern of the words, not just what they're saying. Like a song." When she frowned, I paged through my book and scooted closer to her on the bench seat, so that our hip bones were pressed together.

Grace glanced down at the page. "That's not even in English!"

"Some of them are," I said. I sighed, remembering. "Ulrik was using Rilke to teach me German. And now I'm going to use it to teach you poetry."

"Clearly a foreign language," Grace said.

"Clearly," I agreed. "Listen to this. '*Was soll ich mit meinem Munde? Mit meiner Nacht? Mit meinem Tag? Ich habe keine Geliebte, kein Haus, keine Stelle auf der ich lebe.*'"

Grace's face was puzzled. She chewed her lip in a cute, frustrated sort of way. "So what's it mean?"

"That's not the point. The point is what it sounds like. Not just what it means." I struggled to find words for what I meant. What I wanted to do was remind her of how she'd fallen in love with me as a wolf. Without words. Seeing beyond the obvious meaning of my wolf skin to what was inside. To whatever it was that made me Sam, always.

"Read it again," Grace said.

I read it again.

She tapped her fingers against the steering wheel. "It sounds sad," she said. "You're smiling – I must be right."

I flipped to the English translation. "'What then would I do with my lips? With my night? With my day? I have no—' bah. I don't like this translation. I'm going to get my other one from the house tomorrow. But yeah, it's sad."

"Do I get a prize?"

"Maybe," I said, and slid my hand underneath one of hers, twining our fingers. Without looking away from the road, she lifted our tangled fingers to her mouth. She kissed my index finger and then put it between her teeth, biting down softly.

She glanced over at me, her eyes holding an unspoken challenge.

I was completely caught. I wanted to tell her to pull over right then because I *needed* to kiss her.

But then I saw a wolf.

"Grace. Stop – stop the car!"

She jerked her head around, trying to see what I saw,

but the wolf had already jumped the ditch on the side of the road and headed into the sparse woods.

"Grace, *stop*," I said. "Jack."

She hit the brakes; the Bronco shimmied back and forth as she guided it to the shoulder. I didn't wait for the car to stop. Just shoved open the door and stumbled out, my ankles crying out as I slammed on to the frozen ground. I scanned the woods in front of me. Clouds of sharp-smelling smoke drifted through the trees, mingling with the heavy white clouds that pushed down from above; someone was burning leaves on the other side of the woods. Through the smoke, I saw the blue-grey wolf hesitating in the woods ahead of me, not sure he was being pursued. Cold air clawed at my skin, and the wolf looked over his shoulder at me. Hazel eyes. Jack. It had to be.

And then he was gone, just like that, plunging into the smoke. I jumped after him, taking the ditch by the side of the road in one leap and running over the cold, hard stubble of the dying winter woods.

As I leaped into the forest, I heard Jack crashing ahead, more interested in escape than stealth. I could smell the stink of fear as he bolted ahead of me. The wood smoke was heavier here, and it was hard to tell where the smoke ended and the sky began, snared in the bare branches overhead. Jack was half-invisible in front of me, faster and nimbler than me on his four legs, and impervious to the cold.

My fingers, half-numb, stabbed with pain, and cold pinched the skin of my neck and twisted my gut. I was losing sight of the wolf ahead of me; the one inside me seemed closer all of a sudden.

"Sam!" Grace shouted. She grabbed the back of my shirt, pulling me to a stop, and threw her coat around me. I was coughing, gasping for air and trying to swallow the wolf rising up in me. Wrapping her arms around me as I shuddered, she said, "What were you thinking? What were you—"

She didn't finish. She pulled me back through the woods, both of us stumbling, my knees buckling. I slowed, especially when we got to the ditch, but Grace didn't falter, hooking my elbow to haul me up to the Bronco.

Inside, I buried my cold face into the hot skin of her neck and let her wrap her arms around me as I shook uncontrollably. I was acutely aware of the tips of my fingers, of each little pinprick of pain throbbing individually.

"What were you doing?" Grace demanded, squeezing me hard enough to force the breath out of me. "Sam, you can't do that! It's freezing out there! What did you think you were going to do?"

"I don't know," I said into her neck, balling my hands into fists between us to get them warm. I didn't know. I just knew that Jack was an unknown, and that I didn't know what kind of person he was, what sort of a wolf he was. "I don't know," I said again.

"Sam, it's not worth it," Grace said, and she pressed her face, hard, against my head. "What if you'd changed?" Her fingers were tight on the sleeves of my shirt, and now her voice was breathy. "What were you thinking?"

"I wasn't," I said, truthfully. I sat back, finally warm enough to stop shivering. I pressed my hands against the heating vents. "I'm sorry."

For a long moment, there wasn't any sound but the uneven rumbling of the idling engine. Then Grace said, "Isabel talked to me today. She's Jack's sister." She paused. "She said she'd talked to him."

I didn't say anything, just curled my fingers tighter over the vents as if I could physically grab the heat.

"But you can't just go running after him. It's getting too cold, and it's not worth the risk. Promise me you won't do anything like that again?"

I dropped my eyes. I couldn't look at her when she sounded like she did now. I said, "What about Isabel? Tell me what she said."

Grace sighed. "I don't know. She knows Jack's alive. She thinks the wolves have something to do with it. She thinks I know something. What should we do?"

I pressed my forehead against my hands. "I don't know. I wish Beck were here."

I thought about the two lonely envelopes in the

post office box and the wolf in the woods and my still-tingling fingertips. Maybe Beck *was* here.

Hope hurt more than the cold.

Maybe it wasn't Jack I should've been looking for.

Thirty-One
Sam

11°C

Once I'd let myself think that Beck might still be human, the idea possessed me. I slept badly, my mind skipping over all the ways I could try to track him down. Doubts crowded in there, too – it could've been any of the pack members that had got the mail or bought milk – but I couldn't help it. Hope won over all of it. At breakfast the next morning, I chatted with Grace about her calculus homework – it looked entirely incomprehensible to me – and about her rich, hyper friend Rachel and about whether or not turtles had teeth, but really, what I was thinking about was Beck.

After I dropped Grace off at school, I tried for a brief moment to pretend that I wasn't heading straight back to Beck's house.

He wasn't there. I already knew that.

But it couldn't hurt to just check again.

On the way over, I kept thinking about what Grace had said the other night about the electricity and the milk in the fridge. Maybe, just maybe, Beck would be there, relieving me of the responsibility of Jack and eliminating the unbearable weight of being the last one of my kind. Even if the house was still empty, I could still get some more clothing and my other copy of Rilke and walk through the rooms, smelling the memories of kinship.

I remembered three short years ago, back when more of us were in our prime, able to return to our real, human forms at the first kiss of spring's warmth. The house was full then – Paul, Shelby, Ulrik, Beck, Derek and even crazy Salem were human at the same time. Spiralling through insanity together made it seem more sane.

I slowed as I headed down Beck's road, my heart jumping as I saw a vehicle pulling into his driveway, and then sinking when I saw that it was an unfamiliar Tahoe. Brake lights glowed dully in the grey day, and I rolled down my window to try and catch a bit of scent. Before I'd caught anything, I heard the driver's-side door open and shut on the far side of the SUV. Then the breeze played the driver's scent right to me, clean and vaguely smoky.

Beck. I parked the Bronco on the side of the road and jumped out, grinning as I saw him come around the side of the SUV. His eyes widened for a moment, and then he grinned, too, an expression that his smile-lined face fell into easily.

"Sam!" Beck's voice held something weird –

surprise, I think. His grin widened. "Sam, thank God. Come here!"

He hugged me and patted my back in that touchy-feely way that he always managed to pull off without seeming gropey. Must've come from being a lawyer; he knew how to schmooze people. I couldn't help but notice that he was wider around the middle; not from fat. I don't know how many shirts he must've been wearing underneath his coat to keep himself warm enough to be human, but I saw the mismatched collars of at least two. "Where have you been?"

"I—" I was about to tell him the whole story in a nutshell of getting shot, meeting Grace, seeing Jack, but I didn't. I don't know why I didn't. Certainly it wasn't because of Beck, who was watching me earnestly with his intense blue eyes. It was something, some strange scent, faint but familiar, that was making my muscles clench and pasting my tongue to the top of my mouth. This wasn't how it was supposed to be. It wasn't supposed to feel like this. My answer came out more guarded than I'd intended. "I've been around. Not here. *You* weren't here, either, I noticed."

"Nope," Beck admitted. He headed around to the back of the Tahoe. I noticed then that the van was filthy – thick with dirt. Dirt that smelled of somewhere else, stuffed up into the wheel wells and splattered along the fenders. "Salem and I were up in Canada."

So that's why I hadn't seen Salem anywhere recently.

Salem had always been problematic: he wasn't quite right as a human, so he wasn't quite right when he was a wolf, either. I was pretty sure Salem was the one who had dragged Grace from her swing. How Beck had managed a car trip with him was beyond me. *Why* he managed a car trip with him was even further beyond me.

"You smell like hospital." Beck squinted at me. "And you look like hell."

"Thanks," I said. Guess I was telling after all. I really didn't think the hospital smell could still linger after a week, but Beck's wrinkled nose said otherwise. "I was shot."

Beck pushed his fingers against his lips and spoke through them. "God. Where? Nowhere that'd make me blush, I hope."

I gestured to my neck. "Nowhere near that interesting."

"Is everything OK?"

He meant were we still OK? Did anybody know? *There's a girl. She's amazing. She knows, but it's OK.* I tried out the words in my head, but there wasn't any way to make them sound all right. I just kept hearing Beck tell me how we couldn't trust our secret with anyone but us. So I just shrugged. "As OK as we ever are."

And then my stomach dropped out from under me. He was going to smell Grace in the house.

"God, Sam," Beck said. "Why didn't you call my mobile? When you were shot?"

"I don't have your number. For this year's phone." Every year, we got new phones, since we didn't use them over the winter.

Another look that I didn't like. Sympathy. No, pity. I pretended not to see it.

Beck fumbled in his pocket and pulled out a mobile phone. "Here, take this. It's Salem's. Like he's going to use it any more."

"Bark once for yes, twice for no?"

Beck grinned. "Exactly. Anyway, it's got my number in its brain already. So use it. You might have to buy a charger for it."

I thought he was about to ask me where I'd been staying, and I didn't want to answer. So instead I jerked my chin towards the Tahoe. "So why all the dirt? Why the trip?" I knocked a fist on the side of the car, and to my surprise, something knocked back inside. More like a thud. Like a kick. I raised an eyebrow. "Is Salem in here?"

"He's back in the woods. He changed in Canada, the bastard, I had to bring him back like that and he sheds like it's going out of style. And you know, I think he's crazy."

Beck and I both laughed at that – as if that needed to be said.

I looked back to the place where I'd *felt* the thump against my fist. "So what's thumping?"

Beck raised his eyebrows. "The future. Want to see?"

I shrugged and stepped back so he could open the doors to the back. If I thought I was prepared for what was inside, I was wrong in about forty different ways.

The backseats of the Tahoe were folded down to make more room, and inside the extended trunk were three bodies. Humans. One was sitting awkwardly against the back of the seats, one was curled into a fetal position, and the other lay crookedly alongside the door. Their hands were all zip tied.

I stared, and the boy sitting against the seats stared back, his eyes bloodshot. My age, maybe a little younger. Red was smeared along his arms, and I saw now that it continued all over the inside of the vehicle. And then I smelled them: the metallic stink of blood, the sweaty odour of fear, the earthy scent that matched the dirt on the outside of the Tahoe. And wolf, wolf, everywhere – Beck, Salem and unfamiliar wolves.

The girl curled into a ball was shuddering, and when I squinted at the boy, staring back at me in the darkness, I saw that he was shivering, too, his fingers clenching and unclenching one another in a tangled knot of fear.

"Help," he said.

I fell back, several feet into the driveway, my knees weak beneath me. I covered my mouth, then came closer to stare at them. The boy's eyes pleaded.

I was vaguely aware that Beck was standing nearby, just watching me, but I couldn't stop looking back at those kids. My voice didn't sound like mine. "No. *No*. These kids have been bitten. Beck, they've been bitten."

I spun, laced my hands behind my head, spun back to look at the three of them again. The boy shuddered violently, but his eyes never left mine. *Help.* "Oh, hell, Beck. What have you done? What the hell have you done?"

"Are you finished yet?" Beck asked calmly.

I turned again, squeezing my eyes shut and then open again. "Finished? How can I be finished? Beck, these kids are changing."

"I'm not going to talk to you until you're done."

"Beck, are you *seeing* this?" I leaned against the Tahoe, looking in at the girl, fingers clawed into the bloodstained carpet of the back. She was maybe eighteen, wearing a tight tie-dyed shirt. I pushed off, backing away, as if that would make them disappear. "What is going on?"

In the back of the car, the boy began to groan, pushing his face into his bound wrists. His skin was dusky as he began to change in earnest.

I turned away. I couldn't watch. Not remembering what it was like, those first days. I just kept my fingers laced behind my head and pressed my arms against my ears like a vice grip, saying, *Oh hell oh hell oh hell*, over and over until I convinced myself I couldn't hear his wails. They weren't even calls for help; maybe he already sensed that Beck's house was too isolated for anyone to hear him. Or maybe he'd given up.

"Will you help me take them inside?" Beck asked.

I spun to face him, seeing a wolf stepping from the too-large zip ties and a shirt, growling and starting back as tie-dye-girl moaned at his feet. In an instant, Beck had leaped into the back of the SUV, lithe and animal, and had thrown the wolf on to its back. He grabbed its jaws with one hand and stared into the wolf's eyes. "Don't even think of fighting," he snarled at the wolf. "You aren't in charge here."

Beck dropped the wolf's muzzle, and its head hit the carpet with a dull thud, unprotesting. The wolf was beginning to shake again; already getting ready to change back again.

God. I couldn't watch this. It was as bad as going through it myself all over again, never sure which skin I'd be wearing. I looked away, to Beck. "You did this on purpose, didn't you?"

Beck sat on the tailgate as if there wasn't a spasming wolf behind him and a wailing girl beside him. And that other one – still not moving. Dead? "Sam, it's probably my last year. I don't think I'll change next year. It took a lot of quick thinking this year to keep myself human once I finally had changed." He saw my eyes looking at the different-coloured collars at his neck and he nodded. "We need this house. The pack needs this house. And the pack needs protectors still able to change. You already know. We can't rely on humans. We are the only ones who can protect us."

I didn't say anything.

He sighed heavily. "This is your last year, too, isn't it, Sam? I didn't think you would change at all this year. You were still a wolf when I changed, and it should've been the other way around. I don't know why you got so few years. Maybe because of what your parents did to you. It's a damn shame. You're the best of them."

I didn't say anything, because I had no breath to say it with. All I could focus on was how his hair had a little bit of blood in it. I hadn't noticed it before, because his hair was dark auburn, but the blood had dried just one lock into a stiff cowlick.

"Sam, who was supposed to watch over the pack, huh? Shelby? We had to have more wolves. More wolves at the beginning of their years, so this isn't a problem again for another eight or ten years."

I stared at the blood in his hair. My voice was dull. "What about Jack?"

"The kid with the gun?" Beck grimaced. "We can thank Salem and Shelby for that. I can't go looking for him. It's too cold. He's going to have to find us. I just hope to hell he doesn't do anything stupid before then. Hopefully, he'll have the brains God gave him and stay away from people until he's stable."

Beside him, the girl screamed, a high, thin wail lacking any force, and between one shudder and the next, her skin was the creamy blue of a black wolf's. Her shoulders rippled, arms forcing her upwards, on to new toes where fingers had been. I remembered the pain as clearly as if I were shifting – the pain of loss. I felt the agony of the single moment that I lost myself. Lost what made me Sam. The part of me that could remember Grace's name.

I rubbed a tear out of one of my eyes, watching her struggle. Part of me wanted to shake Beck for doing this to them. And part of me was just thinking, *Thank God Grace never had to go through this*. "Beck," I said, blinking before looking at him. "You're going to hell for this."

I didn't wait to see what his reaction was. I just left. I wished I'd never come.

That night, like every other night since I'd met her, I curled Grace into my arms, listening to her parents' muffled movements in the living room. They were like busy little brainless birds, fluttering in and out of their nest at all hours of the day or night, so involved in the pleasure of nest building that they hadn't noticed that it had been empty for years.

They were noisy, too, laughing, chatting, clattering dishes in the kitchen although I'd never seen evidence of either of them cooking. They were college kids who had found a baby in a rush basket and didn't know what to do with it. How would Grace have been different if she'd had my family – the pack? If she'd had Beck.

In my head, I heard Beck acknowledging what I'd feared. It really was true, that this was my last year.

I breathed, "The end." Not really out loud. Just trying out the shape of the words in my mouth.

In the cautious fortress of my arms, Grace sighed and pressed her face into my chest. She was already asleep. Unlike me, who had to stalk sleep with poisoned arrows, Grace could fall asleep in a second. I envied her.

All I could see was Beck and those kids, a thousand different permutations of the scene dancing before my eyes.

I wanted to tell Grace about it. I didn't want to tell her about it.

I was ashamed of Beck, torn between loyalty to him and loyalty to me – and I hadn't even realized until now they could be two different things. I didn't want Grace to think badly of him – but I wanted a confessional, someplace to put this unbearable weight in my chest.

"Go to sleep," she murmured, barely audible, hooking her fingers in my T-shirt in a way that didn't make me think of sleep. I kissed her closed eyes and sighed. She made an appreciative noise and whispered, eyes still closed, "Shh, Sam. Whatever it is will keep till morning. And if it doesn't, it isn't worth it anyway. *Sleep.*"

Because she told me to, I could.

Thirty-Two
Grace

7°C

The first thing Sam said to me the next day was, "It's time to take you on a proper date." Actually, the very first thing he said was, "Your hair is all funky in the morning." But the very first lucid thing he said (I refused to believe my hair looked funky in the morning) was the date statement. It was a "work day" for the teachers at school, so we had the entire day to ourselves – which felt indulgent. He said this while stirring some oatmeal and looking over his shoulder towards the front door. Even though my parents had disappeared early for some sort of business outing of my dad's, Sam still seemed worried that they would reappear and hunt him down with pitchforks.

I joined him at the counter and leaned against it, peering down into the pan. I wasn't thrilled by the prospect of oatmeal. I had tried to make it before, and it had tasted very ... *healthy*. "So about this date. Where are you taking me? Someplace exciting, like the middle of the woods?"

He pressed his finger against my lips, right where

they parted. He didn't smile. "On a normal date. Food and fun fun fun."

I turned my face so his hand was against my hair instead. "Yeah, sounds like it," I said, sarcastically, because he still wasn't smiling. "I didn't think you did normal."

"Get me two bowls, would you?" Sam said. I set them on the counter and Sam divided the oatmeal between them, releasing a sweet scent. "I just really want to do a proper date, so you'll have something real to rem—"

He stopped and looked down into the bowls, arms braced against the counter, shoulders shrugged up by his ears. Finally, he turned and said, "I want to do things right. Can we try to do normal?"

With a nod, I accepted one of the bowls and tried a spoonful — it was all brown sugar and maple and something sort of spicy. I pointed an oatmeal-covered spoon at Sam. "I have no problem doing normal. This stuff is sticky."

"Ingrate," Sam said. He looked dolefully at his bowl. "You don't like it."

"It's actually OK."

Sam said, "Beck used to make it for me, after I got over my egg fixation."

"You had an egg fixation?"

"I was a peculiar child," Sam said. He gestured to my bowl. "You don't have to eat it if you don't like it. When you're done, we'll go."

"Go where?"

"Surprise."

That was all I needed to hear. That oatmeal was gone instantly and I had my hat, coat and backpack in hand.

For the first time that morning, Sam laughed, and I was ridiculously glad to hear it. "You look like a puppy. Like I'm jingling my keys and you're jumping by the door waiting for your walk."

"Woof."

Sam patted my head on the way out and together we ventured into the cold pastel morning. Once we were in the Bronco and on the road, I pressed again, "So you won't tell me where we're going?"

"Nope. The only thing I'll tell you is to pretend that this is what I did with you the first day I met you, instead of being shot."

"I don't have that much imagination."

"I do. I'll imagine it for you, so strongly that you'll have to believe it." He smiled to demonstrate his imagining, a smile so sad that my breath caught in my throat. "I'll court you properly and then it won't make my obsession with you so creepy."

"Seems to me that mine's the creepy one." I looked out of the window as we pulled out of the driveway. The sky was relinquishing one slow snowflake after another. "I have that, you know, what's it called? That syndrome where you identify with the people who save you?"

Sam shook his head and turned the opposite way

from school. "You're thinking of that Munchausen syndrome, where the person identifies with their kidnapper."

I shook my head. "That's not the same. Isn't Munchausen when you invent sicknesses to get attention?"

"Is it? I just like saying 'Munchausen'. I feel like I can actually speak German when I say it."

I laughed.

"Ulrik was born in Germany," Sam said. "He has all kinds of interesting children's stories about werewolves." He turned on to the main road through downtown and started looking for a parking space. "He said people would get bitten willingly, back in the old days."

I looked out of the window at Mercy Falls. The shops, all shades of brown and grey, seemed even more brown and grey under the leaden sky, and for October, it felt ominously close to winter. There were no green leaves left on the trees that grew by the side of the street, and some were missing their leaves entirely, adding to the bleak appearance of the town. It was concrete as far as the eye could see. "Why would they want to do that?"

"In the folk tales, they'd turn into wolves and steal sheep and other animals when food was scarce. And some of them changed just for the fun of it."

I studied his face, trying to read his voice. "Is there fun in it?"

He looked away – ashamed of his answer, I thought,

until I realized he was just looking over his shoulder to parallel park in front of a row of shops. "Some of us seem to like it, maybe better than being human. Shelby loves it – but like I said, I think her human life was pretty awful. I don't know. The wolf half of my life is such a part of me now, it's hard to imagine living without it."

"In a good way or a bad way?"

Sam looked at me, yellow eyes catching and holding me. "I miss being me. I miss you. All the time."

I dropped my eyes to my hands. "Not now you don't."

Sam reached across the bench seat and touched my hair, running a hand down it until he caught just the ends of it between his fingers. He studied the hairs like they might contain the secrets of Grace in their dull blonde strands. His cheeks flushed slightly; he still blushed when he complimented me. "No," he admitted, "right in this moment, I can't even remember what unhappy feels like."

Somehow that made tears prick at the corners of my eyes. I blinked, glad he was still looking at my hair. There was a long pause.

He said, "You don't remember being attacked."

"What?"

"You don't remember being attacked at all, do you?"

I frowned and pulled my backpack on to my lap,

startled by the seemingly random change of topic. "I don't know. Maybe. It seems like there were a lot of wolves, way more than I think there actually could've been. And I remember you – I remember you standing back, and then just touching my hand –" Sam touched my hand – "and my cheek –" he touched my cheek – "when the others were rough with me. I guess they wanted to eat me, right?"

His voice was soft. "You don't remember what happened after that? How you survived?"

I tried to remember. It was all a flash of snow, and red, and breath on my face. Then Mom screaming. But there must've been something between all that. I must've got from the woods to the house somehow. I tried to imagine walking, stumbling through the snow. "Did I walk?"

He looked at me, waiting for me to answer my own question.

"I know I didn't. I can't remember. Why can't I remember?" I was frustrated now, with my own brain's inability to comply. It seemed like such a simple request. But I only remembered the scent of Sam, Sam everywhere, and then the unfamiliar sound of Mom's panic as she scrambled for the phone.

"Don't worry about it," Sam said. "It doesn't matter." But I thought it probably did.

I closed my eyes, recalling the scent of the woods that day and the jolting feeling of moving back towards the house, arms tight around me. I opened my eyes again. "You carried me."

Sam looked at me abruptly.

It was coming back, in the way you remember fever dreams. "But you were human," I said. "I *remember* seeing you as a wolf. But you must've been human to carry me. How did you do that?"

He shrugged, helplessly. "I don't know how I shifted. It's the same as when I was shot, and I was human when you found me."

I felt something fluttering in my chest, like hope. "You can make yourself change?"

"It's not like that. It was only two times. And I haven't been able to do it again, ever, no matter how badly I've wanted to. And believe me, I've wanted it pretty badly." Sam turned off the Bronco with an air of ending the conversation, and I reached into my backpack to pull out a hat. As he locked the car, I stood on the pavement and waited.

Sam came around the back of the car and stopped dead when he saw me. "Oh my God, what is *that*?"

I used my thumb and middle finger to flick the multicoloured pom-pom on top of my head. "In my language, we call it a *hat*. It keeps my ears warm."

"Oh my God," Sam said again, and closed the distance between us. He cupped my face in his hands and studied me. "It's horribly cute." He kissed me, looked at the hat, and then he kissed me again.

I vowed never to lose the pom-pom hat. Sam was still holding my face; I was sure everyone in town was looking now. But I didn't want to pull away, and I let him kiss me one more time, this time soft as the snow, barely a touch, and then he released me and took my hand instead.

It took me a moment to find my voice, and when I did, I couldn't stop grinning. "OK. Where are we going?" It was cold enough that I knew it had to be close; we couldn't stay out here much longer.

Sam's fingers were laced tightly with mine. "To a Grace-shop first. That's what a proper gentleman would do."

I giggled, completely unlike me, and Sam laughed because he knew it. I was drunk with Sam. I let him walk me down the stark concrete block to The Crooked Shelf, a little independent bookstore; I hadn't been there for a year. It seemed stupid that I hadn't, given how many books I read, but I was just a poor high schooler with a very limited allowance. I got my books from the library.

"This is a Grace-shop, right?" Sam pushed open the door without waiting for my answer. A wonderful wave of new-book smell came rushing out, reminding me immediately of Christmas. My parents always got me books for Christmas. With a melodic *ding*, the shop door swung shut behind us, and Sam released my hand. "Where to? I'll buy you a book. I know you want one."

I smiled at the stacks, inhaling again. Hundreds of thousands of pages that had never been turned, waiting for me. The shelves were a warm, blond wood, piled with spines of every colour. Staff picks were arranged on tables, glossy covers reflecting the light back at me. Behind the little cubby where the cashier sat, ignoring us, stairs covered with rich burgundy carpet led up to worlds unknown. "I could just live here," I said.

Sam watched my face with obvious pleasure. "I remember watching you reading books on the tyre swing. Even in the most stupid weather. Why didn't you read inside when it was so cold?"

My eyes followed the rows and rows of books. "Books are more real when you read them outside." I bit my lip, eyes flitting from shelf to shelf. "I don't know where to go first."

"I'll show you something," Sam said. The way he said it made me believe that it was not only *something* but a very amazing something that he had waited all day to show me. He took my hand again and led me through the store, past the uninterested cashier, and up the silent stairs that swallowed the sounds of our footsteps and kept them.

Upstairs was a little loft, less than half the size of the store below, with a railing to keep us from tumbling back down to the ground floor.

"One summer, I worked here. Sit. Wait." Sam guided me to a battered burgundy love seat that took up a large part of the floor space. I took off my hat and sat, charmed by his orders, and checked out his butt while he searched on the shelves for whatever he was looking for. Unaware of my stare, he crouched, running his fingers along spines like they were old friends. I watched the slope of his shoulders, the tilt of his head, the way one hand braced, fingers spread crablike on the floor, as he knelt by the shelves. Finally he found what he was looking for and he came over to the love seat.

"Close your eyes," he said. Without waiting, he pressed his hand over my eyelids, shutting them for me. I felt the love seat shift as he slid in beside me, heard the inexplicably loud sound of the cover opening, the pages inside scraping against each other as he turned them.

Then I felt his breath on my ear as he said, voice barely audible, "'*I am alone in the world, and yet not alone enough to make each hour holy. I am lowly in this world, and yet not lowly enough for me to be just a thing to you, dark and shrewd. I want my will and I want to go with my will as it moves towards action.*'" He paused, long, the only sound his breath, a little ragged, before he went on, "'*And I want, in those silent, somehow faltering times, to be with someone who knows, or else alone. I want to reflect everything about you, and I never want to be too blind or too ancient to keep your profound wavering image with me. I want to unfold. I don't want to be folded anywhere, because there, where I'm folded, I am a lie.*'"

I turned my face towards his voice, eyes still fast shut, and he put his mouth on mine. I felt his lips pull from mine slightly, just for a moment, and heard the rustle of the book laid gently on the floor, and then he wrapped his arms around me.

His lips tasted cool and sharp, peppermint, winter, but his hands, soft on the back of my neck, promised long days and summer and for ever. I felt light-headed, like I wasn't getting enough air, as if my breath was stolen as soon as I took it. Sam lay back on the couch, just a little, and pulled me into the circle his body made, and kissed me and kissed me, so careful, like my lips were a flower and if he touched them too roughly, they might bruise.

I don't know how long we were curled against each other on the couch, silently kissing, before Sam noticed that I was crying. I felt him hesitate, salt water on his tongue, before he realized what the taste meant.

"Grace. Are you – crying?"

I didn't say anything, because that would only make the reason for my tears more real. Sam rubbed them away with his thumb, then pulled his sleeve over his fist to wipe the tracks away with the fabric.

"Grace, what's wrong? Did I do something wrong?" Sam's yellow eyes were flickering over my face, looking for clues as I shook my head. Downstairs, I heard the cashier ringing up another customer. It seemed very far away.

"No," I said finally. I rubbed another tear out of my eye before it could fall. "No, you did everything right. It's just that—" I couldn't say it. I couldn't.

Sam didn't flinch. "—that this is my last year."

I bit my lip, hard, and rubbed away another tear. "I'm not ready. I'll never be ready."

He didn't say anything. Maybe there wasn't anything to say. Instead, he wrapped his arms around me again, only this time he guided my cheek on to his chest and ran his hand over the back of my head, clumsy but comforting. I closed my eyes and listened to the thud of his heart until mine matched pace with his. Finally, he rested his cheek on the top of my head and whispered, "We don't have time to be sad."

The sun had become brilliant by the time we walked out of the bookstore, and with a shock I realized how much time had passed. On cue, my stomach pinched with hunger.

"Lunch," I said. "Immediately. I'm going to wither away to absolutely nothing. Then you'll be racked with guilt."

"I don't doubt it." Sam took my little bag of new books and turned to put them in the Bronco, but he froze partway towards the car, his eyes fixed somewhere behind me. "Crap. Incoming."

He turned his back to me and unlocked the car, shoving the books on to the passenger seat, trying to look inconspicuous. I turned around and found Olivia, looking dishevelled and tired. Then John appeared behind her and gave me a big grin. I hadn't seen him since before I met Sam, and in comparison, I couldn't fathom how I'd ever imagined he was good-looking. He looked dusty and ordinary in comparison beside Sam's black flop of hair and golden eyes.

"Hey, gorgeous," John said.

That turned Sam around in a hurry. He didn't move towards me, but he didn't have to – his yellow eyes stopped John in his tracks. Or maybe it was just Sam's stance beside me, shoulders stiff. In the space of a second, I had a flashing thought that Sam might be dangerous – that maybe he normally quietened the wolf inside him far more than he let on.

John had a weird, unreadable expression that made me wonder if all those months of pretend flirting had been more real than I'd thought.

"Hi," Olivia said. She glanced at Sam, whose gaze had been fixed on the camera slung over her shoulder. He looked down and rubbed his eyes as though he'd got something in one of them.

Sam's discomfort was catching, and my smile felt insincere. "Hi. Funny bumping into you guys here."

"We're just running some errands for Mom." John's eyes flicked towards Sam and he smiled a little too pleasantly. My cheeks warmed at the silent testosterone battle waging; it was kind of flattering, if a little weird.

"And Olivia wanted to hit up the bookstore while we were out. It's friggin' cold out here. I'm going to go on in."

"They let illiterate people in there?" I teased, like old times.

John grinned then, all tension gone, and grinned at Sam, too, like, *Yeah, good luck with that,* before heading into the store. Sam sort of smiled back, eyes squinted shut, still acting like he had something in them. Olivia remained on the pavement just outside the door, arms hugged around herself.

"I never thought I'd see you out of the house this early on a non-schoolday," she told me. Talking to me, but looking at Sam. "I thought you hibernated on days off."

"Nope, not today," I said. After this much time not talking to her, it felt like I didn't know how to do it any more. "Up early to see what it feels like."

"Amazing," Olivia said. She was still looking at Sam, an unasked question hanging in the air. I didn't want to introduce them, since Sam seemed so uncomfortable around Olivia and her camera, but I was hyperaware of the way she was looking at us: the space between the two of us, how it shifted as either of us moved, connected by invisible strings. And the casual contact. Her eyes followed his hand to my arm as he touched my sleeve lightly, and then moved to his other hand, still rested on the handle of the car door – comfortable, like he'd opened it many times before. Like he belonged with the Bronco and with me. Finally, Olivia said, "Who's this?"

I glanced at Sam, for approval. His eyelids were still lowered, shadowing his eyes.

"Sam," he said softly.

There was something wrong with the tenor of his voice. He wasn't looking at the camera, but it seemed like I could *feel* his attention on it. My voice inadvertently echoed his anxiety when I said, "This is Olivia. Olive, Sam and I are going out. I mean, dating."

I expected her to comment, but instead she said, "I recognize you." Beside me, Sam stiffened until she added, "From the bookstore, right?"

Sam flicked his eyes up to her, and she nodded, almost imperceptibly. "Yes. From the bookstore."

Olivia, arms still crossed, fingered the edge of her sweater but didn't take her eyes from Sam's. She seemed to be struggling to find words. "I – do you wear contacts? Sorry to be so blunt. You must get asked a lot."

"I do," Sam said. "Get asked a lot. And I do wear them."

Something like disappointment flashed across Olivia's face. "Well, they're really cool. Um. It was nice to meet you." Turning to me, she said, "I'm sorry. It was a really stupid thing to fight over."

Whatever I had been planning to say disappeared when she said *I'm sorry.*

"I'm sorry, too," I replied, a little feebly, because I wasn't really sure what I was apologizing for.

Olivia looked at Sam and then back at me. "Yeah. I just... Could you call me? Later on?"

I blinked with surprise. "Yeah, of course! When?"

"I – actually, can I call you? I don't know when will be a good time. Is that OK? Can I just call your mobile?"

"Anytime. You sure you don't want to go somewhere and talk now?"

"Um, no, not now. I can't, because of John." She shook her head and looked at Sam again. "He wants to hang out. Later will be good, though, definitely. Thanks, Grace. I mean it. I'm so sorry about our stupid argument."

I pressed my lips together. Why was she thanking me?

John stuck his head out of the bookstore's door. "Olive? Are you coming, or what?"

Olivia waved at us and disappeared into the bookstore with a little *ding* from the bookstore's doorbell.

Sam cupped his hands around the back of his head and heaved a huge, shaky sigh. He paced a small circle on the pavement without lowering his hands.

I stepped past him and pulled open the passenger-side door. "Are you going to tell me what's going on? Are you just camera shy, or is it something more?"

Sam came around the other side of the Bronco and

got in, slamming the door shut, as if shutting Olivia and all the weirdness of the conversation out. "I'm sorry. I just — I saw one of the wolves the other day and this Jack thing just has me on edge. And Olivia — she took pictures of all of us. As wolves. And my eyes... I was afraid that Olivia knew more about me than she was saying and I just — freaked out. I know. I acted totally whacked, didn't I?"

"Yeah, you did. You're lucky that she was acting more whacked than you. I hope she calls later." Unease crept through me.

Sam touched my arm. "Do you want to go someplace to eat or just head home?"

I groaned and put my forehead into my hand. "Let's just go home. Man. I feel so weird, not finding out what she was talking about."

Sam didn't say anything, but it was all right. I was going over and over what Olivia had said, trying to figure out why the conversation seemed so awkward. Trying to figure out what wasn't being said. I should've said more to her after she told me that she was sorry. But what else was there to say?

We travelled along in silence back towards the house, until I realized how intensely selfish I was being.

"I'm sorry, I'm ruining our date." I reached over and took Sam's free hand; he squeezed his fingers around mine. "First I bawled — which I never do, for the record — and now I'm totally distracted by Olivia."

"Shut up," Sam said pleasantly. "We've got plenty of day left. And it's nice to see you ... *emote* ... for once. Instead of being so damn stoic."

I smiled at the thought. "Stoic? I like it."

"Figured you would. But it was nice to not be the wishy-washy one for once."

I burst out laughing. "Those aren't the words I'd use to describe you."

"You don't think of me as a delicate flower in comparison to you?" When I laughed again, he pressed, "OK, what words *would* you use, then?"

I leaned back in the seat, thinking, as Sam looked at me doubtfully. He was right to look doubtful. My head didn't work with words very well – at least not in this abstract, descriptive sort of way. "Sensitive," I tried.

Sam translated: "Squishy."

"Creative."

"Dangerously emo."

"Thoughtful."

"Feng shui."

I laughed so hard I snorted. "How do you get *feng shui* out of 'thoughtful'?"

"You know, because in feng shui, you arrange furniture and plants and stuff in thoughtful ways." Sam shrugged. "To make you calm. Zenlike. Or something. I'm not one hundred per cent sure how it all works, besides the thoughtful part."

I playfully punched his arm and looked out

of the window as we got closer to home. We were driving through a stand of oak trees on the way to my parents' house. Dull orange-brown leaves, dry and dead, clung to the branches and fluttered in the wind, waiting for the gust of wind that would knock them to the ground. That was what Sam was: transient. A summer leaf clinging to a frozen branch for as long as possible.

"You're beautiful and sad," I said finally, not looking at him when I did. "Just like your eyes. You're like a song that I heard when I was a little kid but forgot I knew until I heard it again."

For a long moment there was only the *whirring* sound of the tyres on the road, and then Sam said softly, "Thank you."

We went home and slept on my bed all afternoon, our jean-covered legs tangled together and my face buried in his neck, the radio murmuring in the background. Around dinner time, we wandered out to the kitchen to find food. As Sam carefully assembled sandwiches, I tried calling Olivia.

John answered. "Sorry, Grace. She's out. Do you want me to tell her anything, or just to call you?"

"Just have her call me," I said, somehow feeling like I'd let Olivia down. I hung up the phone and ran a finger along the counter absently. I kept thinking about what she had said: *Stupid thing to argue about.* "Did you notice," I asked Sam, "when we came in, that it smelled out the front? By the front step?"

Sam handed me a sandwich. "Yeah."

"Like pee," I said. "Like wolf pee."

Sam's voice sounded unhappy. "Yeah."

"Who do you think it was?"

"I don't think," Sam said. "I *know*. It's Shelby. I can smell her. She peed on the deck again, too. I smelled it when I was out there yesterday."

I remembered her eyes, looking at mine through my bedroom window, and made a face. "Why is she doing this?"

Sam shook his head, and he sounded uncertain when he said, "I just hope it's about me and not about you. I hope she's just following me." His eyes slid towards the front hallway; distantly, I heard a car coming down the road. "I think that's your mom. I'm going to vanish." I frowned after him as he retreated into my room with his sandwich, the door closing softly behind him, leaving all the questions and doubts about Shelby out here with me.

Out the front, the car's tyres rolled into the driveway. I got my backpack and settled down so that by the time Mom came in, I was sitting at the kitchen table staring at a problem set.

Mom whirled in and tossed a pile of papers on the kitchen counter, dragging a rush of cold air in with her. I winced, hoping Sam was impervious behind my bedroom door. Her keys jangled as they slid on to the floor. She picked them up, swearing lightly, and threw them back on to the papers. "Have you eaten yet? I'm feeling snacky. We did paintball on the outing! I mean, his work paid for it."

I frowned at her. Half of my brain was still thinking about Shelby, lurking around the house, watching Sam, or watching me. Or watching us together. "What, for group bonding, I guess?"

Mom didn't answer. She opened the fridge and asked, "Do we have anything I can eat while I watch TV? God! What is this?"

"It's a pork loin, Mom. It's for the slow cooker tomorrow."

She shuddered and closed the fridge. "It looks like a giant, chilled slug. Do you want to watch a movie with me?"

I looked past her towards the hall, looking for Dad, but the hall was empty. "Where's Dad?"

"He went out for wings with the new guys from work. You act like I'd only ask you because he's not here." Mom banged around the kitchen, pouring herself granola and leaving the box open on the counter before retreating towards the sofa.

Once upon a time, I would've leaped at the rare opportunity of curling up with Mom on the couch. But now, it sort of felt like too little, too late. I had someone else waiting for me.

"I'm feeling a little off," I told Mom. "I think I'd rather just go to sleep early."

I hadn't realized that I'd wanted her face to fall until it didn't. She just jumped on to the couch and grabbed the remote control. As I turned to go, she said, "By the way, don't leave rubbish bags on the back deck, OK? Animals are getting into it."

"Yeah," I said. I had a feeling I knew which animal in particular. I left her watching the movie on the couch, swept up my homework, and carried it all to my room. Opening my bedroom door, I found Sam curled on my bed, reading a novel by the light of my bedside lamp, looking like he belonged there. I knew he must've heard me enter, but he didn't glance up from his book for a moment, finishing his chapter. I loved looking at the shape his body made while he read, from the curved slope of his neck bent over the pages to the long forms of his sock feet.

Finally, he stuck his finger in the book and closed it, smiling up at me, his eyebrows tipped together in their permanently mournful way. He reached out an arm as an invitation, and I dumped my textbooks at the end of the bed and joined him. He held his novel with one hand and stroked my hair with the other, and together we read the last three chapters. It was a strange book where everyone had been taken from earth except for the main character and his lover, and they had to choose whether to make their ultimate mission finding the ones who had been taken or having earth all to themselves and repopulating at their leisure. When we were done, Sam rolled on to his back and stared at the ceiling. I drew slow circles on his flat stomach with my fingers.

"Which would you choose?" he asked.

In the book, the characters had searched for the others, only to get separated and end up alone. For some reason, Sam's question made my heart beat a little faster, and I gripped a handful of his T-shirt in my fist.

"Duh," I said.

Sam's lips curled up.

It wasn't until later that I realized that Olivia hadn't returned my call. When I called her house, her mother told me she was still out.

A little voice inside me said, *Out where? Where is there to be* out *in Mercy Falls?*

That night when I fell asleep, I dreamed of Shelby's face in my window and Jack's eyes in the woods.

Thirty-Three

Sam

5°C

That night, for the first time in a long time, I dreamed of Mr Dario's dogs.

I woke, sweaty and shuddering, the taste of blood in my mouth. I rolled away from Grace, feeling like my pounding heart would wake her, and licked my bloody lips. I'd bitten my tongue.

It was so easy to forget the primitive violence of my world when I was human, safe in Grace's bed. It was easy to see us as she must see us: ghosts in the woods, silent, magical. And if we were only wolves, maybe she would be right. Real wolves wouldn't be a threat. But these weren't real wolves.

The dream whispered that I was ignoring the signs. The ones that said I was bringing the violence of my world to Grace's. Wolves at her school, her friend's house, and now hers. Wolves that hid human hearts within their pelts.

Lying there in Grace's bed in the dark room, I strained my ears, listening. I thought I could hear toenails on the deck, and imagined I could smell Shelby's scent even through the window. I knew she wanted me – wanted what I stood for. I was the favourite of Beck, the human pack leader, and also of Paul, the wolf pack leader, and the logical successor to both. In our little world, I had a lot of power.

And, oh, Shelby wanted power.

Dario's dogs proved that. When I was thirteen and living in Beck's house, our nearest neighbour (some seventy-five acres away) moved out and sold his gigantic house to a wealthy eccentric by the name of Mr Dario. Personally, I didn't find Mr Dario himself very impressive. He had a peculiar smell that suggested he'd died and then been preserved. He spent most of the time we were in his house explaining the complicated alarm device he'd installed to protect his antiques business ("He means drugs," Beck told me later) and waxing poetic about the guard dogs he turned out of his house while he was gone.

Then he showed them to us. They were gargoyles come to life, snarling masks of froth and wrinkled, pale skin. A South American breed meant to guard cattle, Mr Dario said. He looked pleased when he explained that they would rip a man's face off and eat it. Beck's expression was dubious as he said he hoped Mr Dario didn't let them off the property. Pointing to collars with metallic prongs on the inside ("Shocks the hell out of the dogs," Beck said later, and made a jiggling motion to indicate voltage), Mr Dario assured us that the only people getting their faces ripped off would be the ones sneaking on to the property at night to steal his antiques. He showed us the power box that controlled the dogs' shock collars and kept them near the house; it was covered with a powdery black paint that left dark smudges on his hands.

Nobody else seemed to think about those dogs, but I was obsessed with them. All I could think about was them getting loose and tearing Beck or Paul to pieces, ripping one of their faces off and eating it. For weeks, I was preoccupied with the idea of the dogs, and in the heat of summer, I found Beck in the kitchen, in shorts and a T-shirt, basting ribs for the barbecue.

"Beck?"

He didn't look up from his careful painting. "What do you need, Sam?"

"Would you show me how to kill Mr Dario's dogs?" Beck spun to face me, and I added, "If I had to?"

"You won't have to."

I hated to beg, but I did it, anyway. "Please?"

Beck winced. "You don't have the stomach for that sort of work." It was true — as a human, I had an agonizing sensitivity to the sight of blood.

"Please?"

Beck made a face and told me no, but the next day, he brought home half a dozen raw chickens and taught me how to find the weak part of the joints and break them. When I didn't pass out at the sight of snapping chickens, he brought red meat that oozed blood and made my jaw slack with nausea. The bones were hard, cold, unforgiving under my hands, impossible to break without finding the joint.

"Tired of this yet?" Beck asked after a few days. I shook my head; the dogs haunted my dreams and ran through the songs that I wrote. So we kept on. Beck found home videos of dog fights; together we watched the dogs tear each other apart. I kept a hand pressed over my mouth, my stomach churning at the sight of gore, and watched how some dogs went for the jugular and some went for the front legs, snapping them and rendering their opponents powerless. Beck pointed out one particularly unequal fight, a huge pit bull and a little mixed terrier. "Look at the little dog. That would be you. When you're human, you're stronger than most people, but you're still not going to be as strong as one of Dario's dogs. Look how the little one fights. He weakens the big dog. Then suffocates him."

I watched the little terrier kill the bigger dog. And then Beck and I went outside and fought – big dog, little dog.

Summer vanished. We began to change, one by one, the oldest and most careless of us first. Soon there was just a handful of humans left: Beck, out of stubbornness, Ulrik, from sheer cunning, Shelby, to be closer to Beck and me. Me, because I was young and not yet fragile.

I will never forget the sounds of a dog fight. Someone

who hasn't heard it can't imagine the sort of primal savagery of two dogs bent on destroying each other. Even as a wolf, I never came across that sort of struggle – pack members fought for dominance, not to kill.

I was in the woods; Beck had told me not to leave the house, so of course I was out walking in the evening. I had half an idea that I was going to write a song in the exact moment between day and night, and I had just seized a scrap of a lyric when I heard the dog fight. The sound was close, here in the woods, not near Mr Dario's, but I knew it couldn't be wolves. I recognized that rippling snarl immediately.

And then they came into sight. Two giant white ghosts of dogs in the dim evening: Dario's monsters. With them, a black wolf, struggling, bleeding, rolling in the underbrush. The wolf, Paul, was doing everything pack behaviour dictated – ears back, tail down, half-turned head – everything he did screamed submission. But the dogs knew no pack behaviour; all they knew was attack. And so they began to pull Paul to shreds.

"Hey!" I shouted, my voice not as strong as I'd expected. I tried again, and this time it was halfway to a growl. "*Hey!*"

One of the dogs broke off and rushed me; I spun and rolled, my eyes on the other white demon, its teeth clasped on the black wolf's throat. Paul was gasping for breath, and the side of his face was soaked with crimson. I threw myself against the dog that held him, and the three of us crashed to the ground. The monster was heavy, blood-streaked, and all muscle. I grabbed for its throat with a pitifully weak human hand and missed.

Dead weight hit my back and I felt hot drool on my neck. I twisted just in time to avoid a killing bite from one dog and got the other's teeth in my shoulder instead. I felt bone grate against bone – the sick, fiery sensation of the dog's tooth sliding up against my collarbone.

"*Beck!*" I yelled. It was maddeningly hard to think through the pain and with Paul dying in front of me. Still, I remembered that little terrier – fast, deadly, brutal. I snaked a hand forward to the dog that had the murder grip on Paul's neck. I grabbed the front leg, found the joint, and I didn't think about the blood. I didn't think about the sound it was going to make. I didn't think about anything but the mechanical action of

snap.

The dog's eyes rolled. It whistled through its nose but didn't release its grip.

My survival instinct was screaming at me to get the other animal off me; it was shaking and grinding my shoulder in jaws that felt iron-heavy and fire-hot. I imagined I could feel my bones wrenching free from their proper positions. I imagined my arm was being torn from its socket. But Paul couldn't wait.

I couldn't feel my right arm very well, but with my left I grabbed a handful of dog throat in my hand and twisted, tightened, suffocated, until I heard the monster gasping. I was that little terrier. The dog was tireless in its grip on Paul's neck, but I was equally tireless in mine. Reaching up from under the other dog that was grinding my shoulder down, I flopped my dead right hand over the first dog's nose and pressed its nostrils closed. I didn't think of anything – my mind was far away, in the house, someplace warm, listening to music, reading a poem, anywhere but here, killing.

For a terrible minute nothing happened. Sparks flashed before my eyes. Then the dog flopped to the ground, and Paul fell out of its grip. There was blood everywhere – mine, Paul's, the dog's.

"Don't let go!" It was Beck's voice, and now I heard the dull crash of footsteps in the woods. "Don't let go – he's not dead yet!"

I couldn't feel my hands any more – couldn't feel anything any more – but I thought I was still clutching the dog's neck, the one that had been biting Paul. And then I felt the teeth in my shoulder jerk as the dog gripping my neck lurched. A wolf, Ulrik, was snarling, going for its neck, dragging it off me. There was a *pop*, and I realized it was a gun. Another *pop* again, much closer, and a jerk beneath my fingers. Ulrik backed away from us, breathing hard, and then there was so much silence that my ears rang.

Beck gently peeled my hands off the dead dog's throat and pressed them against my shoulder instead. The blood flow slowed; immediately I started to feel better as my incredible, messed-up body started to heal itself.

Beck knelt in front of me. He was shaking with the cold, his skin grey, the bend of his shoulders wrong. "You had it right, didn't you? You saved him. Those poor damn chickens didn't go to waste."

Behind him, Shelby stood silently, arms crossed, watching Paul gasping in the dry, dead leaves. Watching me and Beck with our heads together. Her hands were fists, and one of them had a black, powdery smear on it.

Now, in the soft darkness of Grace's room, I rolled over and pressed my face into her shoulder. Strange that my most violent moments had been as a human, not as a wolf.

Outside, I heard the distinct scratching of toenails on the deck. I closed my eyes and tried to concentrate on the sound of Grace's beating heart.

The taste of blood in my mouth reminded me of winter.

I knew Shelby had let those dogs out.

She wanted me at the top, with her beside me, and Paul was in my way. And now Grace was in hers.

Thirty-Four
Grace

9°C

Days blurred into a collage of common images: cool walks across the school car park, Olivia's empty seat in class, Sam's breath in my ear, pawprints in our yard's frosted blades of grass.

By the time the weekend arrived, I felt breathless with waiting, although I wasn't sure what I was waiting for. Sam had tossed and turned the night before, plagued by a nightmare, and he looked so terrible on Saturday morning that instead of making any plans to go out, I just parked him on the couch after my parents had gone to brunch at a friend's house.

I lay in the curve of Sam's arm as he flipped between various bad made-for-TV movies. We settled on a sci-fi thriller that had probably cost less to produce than the Bronco. Rubbery tentacles were *everywhere* when Sam finally said something.

"Does it bother you? That your parents are the way they are?"

I nuzzled my face into his armpit. It smelled very Sam in there. "Let's not talk about them."

"Let's do talk about them."

"Oh, *why*? What's there to tell? It's fine. They're fine. They're the way they are."

Sam's fingers gently found my chin and lifted my face up. "Grace, it's not fine. I've been here for – how many weeks now? I don't even know. But I know how it is, and it's *not* fine."

"They are who they are. I never knew anybody's parents were any different until I started school. Until I started reading. But seriously, Sam, it's *OK*."

My skin felt hot. I pulled my chin away from his hand and looked at the screen, where a compact car was drowning in slime.

"Grace," Sam said softly. He was sitting so still, as if, for once, I was the wild animal that might vanish if he moved a muscle. "You don't have to pretend around me."

I watched the car crumble into pieces, along with the driver and the passenger. It was hard to tell what was going on with the sound turned down, but it looked like the pieces were reforming into tentacles. There was a guy walking a dog in the background, and he didn't even seem to notice. How could he not notice?

I didn't look at Sam, but I knew he was watching me, not the television.

I didn't know what he thought I was going to say. I had nothing to say. This was not a problem. It was a way of life.

The tentacles on the screen began to drag along the ground, looking for the original tentacled monster so that they could reattach themselves. There was no way they would be able to; the original alien was on fire in Washington, DC, melting around a model of the Washington Monument. The new tentacles were just going to have to torment the world on their own.

"Why can't I make them love me any more than they do?"

Did I say that? It didn't sound like my voice. Sam's fingers brushed my cheek, but there weren't any tears. I was nowhere close to tears.

"Grace, they love you. It's not *about* you. It's their problem."

"I've tried *so* hard. I never get into trouble. I always do my homework. I cook their damn meals, when they're home, which is never—" Definitely not my voice. I didn't swear. "And I nearly got killed, twice, but that didn't change anything. It's not like I want them to jump all over me. I just want, one day, just want—" I couldn't finish the sentence, because I didn't know how it ended.

Sam dragged me into his arms. "Oh, Grace, I'm sorry. I didn't mean to make you cry."

"I'm not crying."

He wiped my cheeks with his thumb, carefully, and showed me the tear trapped on his fingertip. Feeling foolish, I let him ball me up in his lap and tuck me under his chin. I had my own voice back again, here in the muffled shelter of his arms. "Maybe I'm too good. If I got into trouble at school or burned down people's garages, they'd have to notice me."

"You're not like that. You know you're not," he said. "They're just silly, selfish people, that's all. I'm sorry I asked, OK? Let's just watch this dumb movie."

I laid my cheek against his chest and listened to the *thump-thump* of his heart. It sounded so normal, just a regular human heart. He'd been human long enough now that I almost couldn't detect the faint odour of the woods on him or remember what it felt like to bury my fingers in his ruff. Sam turned up the volume on the aliens and we sat like that, one creature in two bodies, for a long time, until I forgot what I'd been upset about and I was myself again.

"I wish I had what you have," I said.

"What do I have?"

"Your pack. Beck. Ulrik. When you talk about them, I can see how important they are to you," I said. "They made you this person." I pushed a finger into his chest. "They're wonderful, so you're wonderful."

Sam closed his eyes. "I don't know about that." He opened them again. "Anyway, your parents made you who you are, too. Do you think you'd be so independent if they were around more? At least you're *someone* when they're not around. I feel like I'm not who I was before. Because so much of being me is being with Beck and Ulrik and the others."

I heard a car pull into the driveway and straightened up. I knew Sam had heard it, too. "Time to vanish," he said.

But I held on to his arm. "I'm tired of sneaking around. I think it's time for you to meet them."

He didn't argue, but he threw a worried glance in the direction of the front door.

"And now we come to the end," he said.

"Don't be melodramatic. They won't kill you."

He looked at me.

Heat flushed my cheeks. "Sam, I didn't mean it like – God. I'm sorry." I wanted to look away from his face, but I couldn't seem to, like watching a car crash. I kept waiting for the collision, but his expression never changed. It was as if there was a little disconnect between the memories of Sam's parents and his emotions, a slight misfire that mercifully kept him whole.

Sam rescued me by changing the subject, which was incredibly generous. "Should I play the friendly boyfriend or are we just friends?"

"Boyfriend. I'm not pretending."

Sam edged a few centimetres away from me and pulled his arm from behind my head, resting it on the back of the couch behind me instead. To the wall, he said, "Hello, Grace's parents. I'm Grace's boyfriend. Please notice the chaste distance between us. I am very responsible and have never had my tongue in your daughter's mouth."

The door cracked open and both of us jumped with matching nervous laughs.

"Is that you, Grace?" Mom's voice called lightly from the hallway. "Or are you a burglar?"

"Burglar," I called back.

"I'm going to wet myself," Sam whispered in my ear.

"Are you sure that's you, Grace?" Mom sounded suspicious; she wasn't used to me laughing. "Is Rachel here?"

Dad came first into the living-room doorway and stopped, immediately spotting Sam.

In a barely perceptible movement, Sam turned his head just enough that the light didn't catch his yellow eyes, an automatic gesture that made me realize for the first time that Sam had been an oddity even before he'd been a wolf.

Dad's eyes were on Sam, just looking. Sam was looking back, tense but not terrified. Would he be sitting so calmly if he knew that Dad had been one of the hunting party in the woods? I was suddenly ashamed of my father, just another human that the wolves had to fear; I was glad I hadn't said anything to Sam.

My voice was tight. "Dad, this is Sam. Sam, this is Dad."

Dad looked at him for a split second more, and then smiled widely. "Please tell me you're a boyfriend."

Sam's eyes became perfectly round and I let out a big breath.

"Yes, he's a boyfriend, Dad."

"Well, that's nice. I was beginning to think you didn't do that kind of thing."

"*Dad.*"

"What's going on in there?" Mom's voice was distant. She was already in the kitchen, rummaging in the fridge. The food at the brunch must've been bad. "Who's Sam?"

"My boyfriend."

With Mom's presence came an ever-present cloud of turpentine vapours; she had paint smeared on her lower arms. Knowing Mom, I guessed she'd intentionally left herself that way when she went out. She looked from me to Sam and back to me again, her expression quizzical.

"Mom, this is Sam. Sam, Mom."

I smelled emotions rolling off both of them, though I couldn't tell which ones, exactly. Mom was staring at Sam's eyes, just staring and staring, and Sam seemed fixed in place. I punched his arm.

"Nice to meet you," he said, voice automatic.

"Mom," I hissed. "*Mom*. Earth to Mom."

To her credit, she looked slightly abashed when she snapped out of it. She said to Sam, apologetic, "Your face looks very familiar." Yeah. Right. As if even an infant couldn't tell it was a transparent excuse for staring at his eyes.

"I used to work at the bookstore downtown?" Sam's voice was hopeful.

Mom wagged a finger at him. "I'll bet that's it." She beamed at Sam then, used her hundred-watt smile, erasing any social atrocity she may have just committed. "Well, it's nice to meet you. I'm going to go upstairs and work for a while." She displayed her painted arms, indicating what she meant by "work", and I felt a brief flash of irritation towards her. I knew her serial flirtation was just habitual, a knee-jerk reaction to any unfamiliar guy who had reached puberty, but still. Grow up.

Sam surprised me by saying, "I'd like to see the studio, while I'm here, if you don't mind. Grace told me a little bit about your art and I'd love to see it." This was partially true. I'd told him about a particularly nauseating show of hers I'd gone to where all of the paintings were named after types of clouds but were portraits of women in bathing suits. "Meaningful" art sailed over my head. I didn't get it. I didn't *want* to get it.

Mom smiled in a plastic sort of way. She probably thought Sam's understanding of meaningful art was similar to mine.

I looked at Sam dubiously. This sort of sucking up seemed unlike him. After Mom had vanished upstairs and Dad had vanished into his study, I demanded, "Are you a sucker for punishment?"

Sam unmuted the television in time for a woman to be eaten by something with tentacles. All that was left after the attack was a fake-looking severed arm lying on the pavement. "I just think I need to make her like me."

"The only person in this house who has to like you is me. Don't worry about them."

Sam picked up a sofa cushion and hugged it to himself, pressing his face into it. His voice was muffled. "She might have to put up with me for a long time, you know?"

"How long?"

His smile was amazingly sweet. "The longest."

"For ever?"

Sam's lips smiled, but above his grin, his yellow eyes turned sad, as if he knew it was a lie. "Longer."

I closed the distance between us and settled into the crook of his arm, and we went back to watching the tentacled alien slowly creep through the sewer system of an unsuspecting town. Sam's eyes flickered around the screen, as if he was actually watching the futile intergalactic battle, but I sat there and tried to figure out why Sam had to change and I didn't.

Thirty-Five
Sam

9°C

After the sci-fi flick ended (the world was saved, but civilian casualties were high), I sat with Grace at the little breakfast table near the door to the deck and watched her do her homework for a while. I was unimaginably tired – the colder weather gnawed at me like an ache, even when it couldn't get a tight enough grip to change me – and I would've liked to crawl into Grace's bed or on to the couch for a nap. But the wolf side of me felt restless and unable to sleep with unfamiliar people around. So to keep myself awake, I left Grace downstairs doing her homework in the dying light from the windows and went upstairs to see the studio.

It was easy to find; there were only two doors in the hallway upstairs and an orange, chemical smell wafted out from one of them. The door was slightly ajar. I pushed it open and blinked. The entire room was brilliantly lit by lamps fitted with bulbs meant to mimic natural light, and the effect was a cross between a desert at noon and a Wal-Mart.

The walls were hidden behind towering canvases that leaned against every available surface. Gorgeous riots of colour, realistic figures in unrealistic poses, normal shapes in abnormal colours, the unexpected in ordinary places. The paintings were like falling into a dream, where everything you know is presented in an unfamiliar way. *Anything's possible in this lush rabbit hole / Is it mirror or portrait you've given to me? / All of these permutations of dreams will patrol / this lovely wasteland of colour I see.*

I stood before two larger-than-life paintings leaning against one of the walls. Both were of a man kissing a woman's neck, poses identical but colours radically different. One was shot through with reds and purples. It was bright, ugly, commercial. The other was dark, blue, lavender, hard to read. Understated and lovely. It reminded me of kissing Grace in the bookstore, how she felt in my arms, warm and real.

"Which one do you like?"

Her mom's voice sounded bright and approachable. I imagined it as her gallery voice. The one she used to lure viewers' wallets into sight so that she could shoot them.

I tilted my head towards the blue one. "No contest."

"Really?" She sounded genuinely surprised. "No one has ever said that before. That one's much more popular." She stepped into my view so that I could see that she was pointing at the red one. "I've sold hundreds of prints of it."

"It's very pretty," I said kindly, and she laughed.

"It's hideous. Do you know what they're called?" She pointed to the blue one, then the red one. "*Love* and *Lust*."

I smiled at her. "Guess I failed my testosterone test, didn't I?"

"Because you chose *Love*? I don't think so, but that's just me. Grace told me it was stupid of me to paint the same thing twice. She said his eyes are too close together in both of them, anyway."

I grinned. "Sounds like something she would say. But she's not an artist."

Her mouth twisted into a rueful shape. "No. She's very practical. I don't know where she got that from."

I walked slowly to the next set of paintings – wildlife walking through clothing racks, deer perched on high-rise windows, fish peering up through storm drains. "That disappoints you."

"Oh, no. No. Grace is just Grace, and you just have to take her the way she is." She hung back, letting me look, years of good sales training in subconscious practice. "And I suppose she'll have an easier time in life because she'll get a nice normal job and be good and stable."

I didn't look at her when I answered. "Methinks the mom doth protest too much."

I heard her sigh. "I guess everyone wants their kid to turn out like them. All Grace cares about is numbers and books and the way things work. It's hard for me to understand her."

"And vice versa."

"Yes. But you're an artist, aren't you? You must be."

I shrugged. I had noticed a guitar case sitting close to the door of her studio, and I was itching to find chords for some of the tunes in my head. "Not with paint. I play a little guitar."

There was a long pause as she watched me looking at a painting of a fox peering out from beneath a parked car, and then she said, "Do you wear contacts?"

I'd been asked the question so many times that I didn't even wonder any more at how much nerve it had taken to ask it. "Nope."

"I'm having a terrible painter's block right now. I would love to do a quick study of you." She laughed. It was a very self-conscious sound. "That's why I was ogling you downstairs. I just thought it would make an amazing colour study, your black hair and your eyes. You remind me of the wolves in our woods. Did Grace tell you about them?"

My body stiffened. It felt too close, like she was prying, especially after the run-in with Olivia. My immediate wolfish instinct was to bolt. Tear down the stairs, rip open the door, and melt into the safety of the trees. It took me several long moments to battle the desire to run and convince myself that she couldn't possibly know, and that I was reading too much into her words. Another long moment to realize that I had been standing for too long not saying anything.

"Oh – I don't mean to make it awkward for you." Her words tumbled over each other. "You don't have to sit for me. I know some people feel really self-conscious. And you probably want to be getting back downstairs to Grace."

I felt obliged to make up for my rudeness. "No – no, that's OK. I mean, I do feel sort of self-conscious about it. Can I do something while you paint me? I mean, so I don't have to just sit and stare off into space?"

She literally ran over to her easel. "No! Of course not. Why don't you play the guitar? Oh, this is going to be great. Thank you. You can just sit over there, under those lights." While I retrieved the guitar case, she ran across her studio several more times, getting a chair for me, adjusting the spotlights, and draping a yellow sheet to reflect golden light on one side of my face.

"Do I have to try to stay still?"

She waved a paintbrush at me, as if that would answer my question, then propped a new canvas against her easel and squeezed gobs of black paint onto a palette. "No, no, just play away."

So I tuned the guitar, and I sat there in the golden light and played and hummed the songs under my breath, thinking of all the times I'd sat on Beck's couch and played songs for the pack, of Paul playing his guitar with me and us singing harmonies. In the background, I heard the *scrape, scrape* of the palette knife and the *whuff* of the brush on the canvas and wondered what she was doing with my face while I wasn't paying attention.

"I can hear you humming," she said. "Do you sing?"

I grunted, still fingerpicking idly.

Her brush never ceased moving. "Are those your songs?"

"Yup."

"Have you written one for Grace?"

I had written a thousand songs for Grace. "Yes."

"I'd like to hear it."

I didn't stop playing, just modulated carefully into a major key. For the first time this year, I sang out loud. It was the happiest tune I'd ever written, and the simplest.

I fell for her in summer, my lovely summer girl
From summer she is made, my lovely summer girl
I'd love to spend a winter with my lovely summer girl
But I'm never warm enough for my lovely summer girl

It's summer when she smiles, I'm laughing like a child
It's the summer of our lives; we'll contain it for a while
She holds the heat, the breeze of summer in the circle
*   of her hand*
I'd be happy with this summer if it's all we ever had.

She looked at me. "I don't know what to say." She showed me her arm. "I have goosebumps."

I set the guitar down, very carefully, so the strings wouldn't make any sound. Suddenly it seemed very pressing to spend my moments, so precious and numbered, with Grace.

And in the moment I made that decision, there was a terrific crash from downstairs. It was so loud and so *wrong* that for a moment her mother and I just frowned at each other as if we couldn't believe that the sound had happened.

Then there was the scream.

Right after, I heard a snarl, and was out of the room before I could hear any more.

Thirty-Six

Sam

9°C

I remembered Shelby's face when she asked, "Would you like to see my scars?"

"From what?" I replied.

"From when I was attacked. From the wolves."

"No."

She showed me anyway. Her belly was lumpy with scar tissue that disappeared under her bra. "It looked like hamburger after they bit me."

I didn't want to know.

Shelby didn't pull her shirt back down. "It must be hell when we kill something. We must be the worst way to die."

Thirty-Seven

Sam

5°C

A riot of sensations assaulted me as soon as I got into the living room. Viciously cold air stung my eyes and twisted my stomach. My eyes quickly found the ragged hole in the door to the back deck; partially cracked glass hung precariously in the frame and thin, pink-stained shards lay all over the floor, winking light back up at me.

The chair at the breakfast nook was knocked over. It looked like someone had splattered red paint on the floor, endless erratic shapes dropped and smeared from the door to the kitchen. Then I smelled Shelby. For a moment I stood there, frozen by the absence of Grace and the frigid air and the stench of blood and wet fur.

"Sam!"

It had to be Grace, though her voice sounded strange and unrecognizable – someone pretending to be Grace. I scrambled, slipping in the spots of blood, gripping the doorjamb to pull myself into the kitchen.

The scene was surreal in the pleasant light of the kitchen. Bloody pawprints pointed the direction to where Shelby shook and twisted, Grace pinned to the cupboards. Grace was struggling, kicking, but Shelby was massive and reeked of adrenaline. I saw a flash of pain in Grace's eyes, honest and wide, before Shelby jerked her body away. I'd seen this image before.

I didn't feel the cold any more. I saw an iron skillet sitting on the stove and grabbed it; my arm ached with the weight of it. I didn't want to hit Grace – I smashed it on Shelby's hip.

Shelby snarled back at me, teeth snapping together. We didn't have to speak the same language to know what she was telling me. *Stay back.* An image filled my field of vision, clear, perfect, riveting: Grace lying on the kitchen floor, flopping, dying, while Shelby watched. I was paralysed by this clarion picture dropped into my thoughts – this is how it must've felt when I showed Grace the image of the golden wood. It felt like a razor-sharp memory, a memory of Grace gasping for breath.

I dropped the skillet and threw myself at Shelby.

I found her muzzle where she was clamped on to Grace's arm, and I felt back to her jaw. Pressing my fingers into the tender skin, I jammed upwards, into her windpipe, until Shelby yelped. Her grip loosened enough for me to push off the cabinets with my feet and roll her off Grace. We scrabbled across the floor, her nails clicking and scraping on the tiles and my shoes squeaking and slipping in the blood she dripped.

She snarled beneath me, furious, snapping at my face but stopping short of biting me. The image of Grace lifeless on the floor just kept going through my head.

I remembered snapping chicken bones.

In my mind, I could see perfectly what it would look like to kill Shelby.

She jerked away from me, out of my hands, as if she'd read my thoughts.

"Dad, no, watch *out!*" Grace shouted.

A gun exploded, close by.

For a brief moment, time stood still. Not really still. It sort of danced and shimmered in place, the lights flickering and dimming before reappearing. If that moment had been a real thing, it would've been a butterfly, flapping and fluttering toward the sun.

Shelby fell out of my grip, dead weight, and I fell back into the cabinets behind me.

She was dead. Or at least close, because she was jerking. But all I could seem to think about was how I'd made a mess of the kitchen floor. I just stared at the white squares of linoleum, my eyes following the streaky lines my shoes had made through the blood and finding the one red pawprint in the centre of the kitchen that had somehow been perfectly preserved.

I couldn't figure how I could smell the blood so strongly, and then I looked down at my shaking arms and saw the red smeared on my hands and over my wrists. I had to struggle to remember that it was Shelby's blood. She was dead. This was her blood. Not mine. Hers.

My parents counted backwards, slowly, and blood welled up from my veins.

I was going to throw up.

I was ice.

I

"We have to move him!" The girl's voice was piercingly loud in the silence. "Get him someplace warm. I'm all right. I'm *all right*. I just – help me move him!"

Their voices tore into my head, too loud and too many. I sensed movement all around me, their bodies and my skin whirling and spinning, but deep inside me, there was a part that held completely still.

Grace. I held on to that one name. If I kept that in my head, I would be OK.

Grace.

I was shaking, shaking; my skin was peeling away.

Grace.

My bones squeezed, pinched, pressed against my muscles.

Grace.

Her eyes held me even after I stopped feeling her fingers gripping my arms.

"Sam," she said. "Don't go."

Thirty-Eight
Grace

3°C

"Who could do that to a child?" Mom made a face. I wasn't sure if the face was because of what I'd just told her or because of the pee-and-antiseptic smell of the hospital.

I shrugged and wriggled uncomfortably on the hospital bed. I didn't really need to be here. The gash on my arm hadn't even needed stitches. I just wanted to see Sam.

"So he's really messed up then." Mom frowned at the television above the hospital bed, though it was turned off. She didn't wait for me to respond. "Well, of course. Of course he is. He would have to be. You don't live through that without being messed up. Poor kid. He looked like he was really in pain."

I hoped Mom would quit babbling about this by the time Sam was done talking to the nurse. I didn't want to think about the curve of his shoulders, the unnatural shape that his body had formed in response to the cold. And I hoped Sam would understand why I'd told Mom about his parents – her knowing about them had to be better than her knowing about the wolves. "I told you, Mom. It *really* bothers him to remember. Of course he freaked out when he saw the blood on his arms. It's classical conditioning, or whatever they call it. Google it."

Mom squeezed her arms around herself. "If he hadn't been there, though..."

"Yes, I would've died, blah blah blah. But he *was* there. Why is everyone more worked up about this than I am?" Many of Shelby's teeth marks had already become ugly bruises instead – though I didn't heal nearly as quickly as Sam had when he was shot.

"Because you have no survival instinct, Grace. You're like a tank, you just chug along, thinking nothing can stop you, until you meet up with a bigger tank. Are you sure you want to go out with someone with that kind of history?" Mom seemed to warm to her theory. "He could have a psychotic break. I read that people get those when they're twenty-eight. He could be almost normal and then suddenly go slasher. I mean, you know I've never told you what to do with your life before now. But what if – what if I asked you to not see him?"

I hadn't expected that. My voice was brittle. "I would say that by virtue of your not acting parental up to this point, you've relinquished your ability to wield any power now. Sam and I are together. It's not an option."

Mom threw her hands up as if trying to stop the

Grace-tank from running over her. "OK. Fine. Just be careful, OK? Whatever. I'm going to go get a drink."

And just like that, her parental energies were expended. She had played Mom by driving us to the hospital, watching the nurse tend to my wounds, and warning me off my psychotic boyfriend, and now she was done. It was obvious I was going to live, so she was off duty.

A few minutes after she'd left, the door clicked open, and Sam came to the side of my bed, looking pale and tired under the greenish lights. Tired, but human.

"What did they do to you?" I asked.

His mouth quirked into a smile completely without humour. "Gave me a bandage for a cut that has healed since they put it on. What did you tell her?" He glanced around for Mom.

"I told her about your parents and said that's what was wrong with you. She believed me. It's cool. Are you all right? Are you—" I wasn't sure what I was asking. Finally, I said, "Dad said she was dead. Shelby. I guess she couldn't heal like you did. It was too fast."

Sam laid his palms on either side of my neck and kissed me. He pressed his forehead against mine so that we were staring at each other and it looked like he had only one eye. "I'm going to hell."

"What?"

His one eye blinked. "Because I should be feeling bad about her being dead."

I pulled back so I could see his expression; it was strangely empty. I wasn't sure what to say in light of that information, but Sam saved me by taking my hands and squeezing them tightly. "I know I should be upset right now. But I just feel like I've dodged this huge missile. I didn't change, you're all right, and for the moment, she's just one less thing for me to worry about. I just feel – I feel *drunk*."

"Mom thinks you're damaged goods," I told him.

Sam kissed me again, closed his eyes for a moment, and then kissed me a third time, lightly. "I am. Do you want to run away?"

I didn't know if he meant from the hospital, or from him.

"Mr Roth?" a nurse appeared in the door. "You can stay in here, but you should sit down for this."

Like me, Sam had to get a series of rabies shots – standard hospital procedure for unprovoked animal attacks. It wasn't like we could tell the staff that Sam knew the animal personally and that said animal had been homicidal, not rabid. I shuffled over to make room for Sam, who sat beside me with an uneasy glance towards the syringe in the nurse's hands.

"Don't look at the needle," the nurse advised as she pushed up his bloody sleeve with rubber-gloved hands. Sam looked away, to my face, but his eyes were distant and unfocused, his mind somewhere else as the nurse stuck the needle into his skin. As I watched her depress the syringe, I fantasized that it was a cure for Sam – liquid summer injected right into his veins.

There was a knock on the door and another nurse stuck her face in. "Brenda, are you done?" the second nurse asked. "I think they need you in 302. There's a girl going crazy in there."

"Oh, wonderful," Brenda said, with deep sarcasm. "You two are done." To me, she said, "I'll get your paperwork to your mom when I'm done."

"Thanks," Sam said, and took my hand. Together we walked down the hall, and for a strange moment, it felt like the first night that we'd met, like no time at all had passed.

"Wait," I said as we passed through the emergency room waiting area, and Sam let me pull him to a halt. I squinted across the busy room, but the woman I thought I'd seen was gone.

"Who are you looking for?"

"I thought I saw Olivia's mom." I squinted across the waiting room again, but there were only unfamiliar faces.

I saw Sam's nostrils flare and his eyebrows draw a little closer to his eyes, but he didn't say anything as we made our way to the glass hospital doors. Outside, Mom had already pulled the car up to the kerb, not knowing what a favour she had done for Sam.

Beyond the car, tiny snowflakes swirled, the cold delicately embodied. Sam's eyes were on the trees on the other side of the car park, barely visible in the streetlights. I wondered if he was thinking about the deadly chill that seeped through the cracks in the door, or about Shelby's broken body that would never be human again, or if, like me, he was still thinking about that imaginary syringe full of liquid summer.

Thirty-Nine
Sam

5°C

My patchwork life: quiet Sunday, coffee on Grace's breath, the unfamiliar landscape of the lumpy new scar on my arm, the dangerous smell of snow in the air. Two different worlds circling each other, getting closer and closer, knotting together in ways I'd never imagined.

My near-change of the day before still hung over me, the dusky memory of wolf odour caught in my hair and on the tips of my fingers. It would've been so easy to give in. Even now, twenty-four hours later, I felt like my body was still fighting it.

I was so tired.

I tried to lose myself in a novel, curled in a squashy leather chair, half dozing. Ever since the evening temperatures had begun to pitch sharply downwards in the last few days, we'd been spending our free time in her father's largely unused study. Other than her bedroom, it was the warmest and least draughty place in the house. I liked the room. The walls were lined with dark-spined encyclopaedias, too old to be useful, and stacked with dark wooden award plaques for marathon running, too old to be meaningful. The entire study was very small and brown, a rabbit hole made of dark leather, smoky-smelling wood, and manila folders: it was a place to be safe and productive.

Grace sat at the desk doing homework, her hair illuminated like an old painting by a couple of dull gold desk lamps. The way she sat, head bent in stubborn concentration, held my attention in the way that my book didn't.

I realized that Grace's pen hadn't moved in a long while. I asked, "What are you thinking about?"

She spun the desk chair around to face me and tapped her pen on her lip; it was a charming gesture that made me want to kiss her. "Washer and dryer. I was thinking about how when I move out, I'll either have to use the laundromat or buy a washer and dryer."

I just looked at her, equal parts entranced and horrified by this strange look into the workings of her mind. "*That* was distracting you from your homework?"

"I was not distracted," Grace said stiffly. "I was giving myself a break from reading this stupid short story for English." She whirled around and leaned back over the desk.

There was quiet for several long moments; she still didn't put pen to paper. Finally, without lifting her head, she said, "Do you think there's a cure?"

I closed my eyes and sighed. "Oh, Grace."

Grace persisted, "Tell me, then. Is it science? Or is it magic? What you are?"

"Does it matter which?"

"Of course," she said, and her voice was frustrated. "Magic would be intangible. Science has cures. Haven't you ever wondered how it all started?"

I didn't open my eyes. "One day a wolf bit a man and the man caught it. Magic or science, it's all the same. The only thing magical about it is that we can't explain it."

Grace didn't say anything more, but I could *feel* her disquiet. I sat there silently, hiding behind my book, knowing that she needed words from me – words I wasn't willing to give. I wasn't sure which of us was being more selfish – her, for wanting something that no one could promise, or me, for not promising her something that was too painfully impossible to want.

Before either of us could break the uneasy silence, the door to the study pushed open and her father came in, his wire frames fogged from the temperature change. He scanned the room, taking in the changes we'd made to it. The underused guitar from her mother's studio leaning against my chair. My pile of tattered paperbacks on the side table. The neat stack of sharpened pencils on his desk. His eyes lingered on the coffee maker Grace had brought in to satisfy her caffeine cravings; he seemed as fascinated by it as

I had been. A child-sized coffee maker. For toddlers who needed a quick pick-me-up. "We're home. Have you guys taken over my room?"

"It was being neglected," Grace said, without looking up from her homework. "It was too useful to let it go to waste. And now you can't have it back."

"Obviously," he observed. He looked at me, sunk into his chair. "What are you reading?"

I said, "*Bel Canto.*"

"I've never heard of it. What's it about?"

He squinted at the cover; I held it out so that he could see it. "Opera singers and chopping onions. And guns."

To my surprise, her father's expression cleared and filled with understanding. "Sounds like something Grace's mother would read."

Grace turned around in the desk chair. "Dad, what did you do with the body?"

He blinked. "What?"

"After you shot it. What did you do with the body?"

"*Oh.* I put it on the deck."

"And?"

"And what?"

Grace pushed away from the desk, exasperated. "And what did you do with it after that? I know you didn't leave it to rot on the deck."

A slow, sick feeling was beginning to knot in the bottom of my stomach.

"Grace, why is this such an issue? I'm sure Mom took care of it."

Grace pressed her fingers into her forehead. "Dad, how can you think that *Mom* moved it? She was with us at the hospital!"

"I didn't really think about it. I was going to call animal control to pick it up, but it was gone the next morning, so I thought one of you guys must've called them."

Grace made a little strangled noise. "Dad! Mom can't even call to order pizza! How would she call animal control?"

Her father shrugged and stirred his soup. "Stranger things have happened. It's not worth getting worked up about, anyway. So it was dragged off the deck by a wild animal. I don't think other animals can catch rabies from a dead animal."

Grace just crossed her arms and glared at him, as if this comment was just too stupid to dignify with a response.

"Don't sulk," he said, and pushed the door further open with his shoulder to leave. "It's not becoming."

Her voice was ice-cold. "I have to take care of everything myself."

He smiled at her fondly, somehow reducing the value of her anger. "We'd be lost without you, obviously. Don't stay up too late."

The door softly clicked shut behind him, and Grace

stared at the bookshelves, the desk, the closed door. Anything but my face.

I closed my novel without noting the page. "She's not dead."

"Mom might've called animal control," Grace said to the desk.

"Your mom didn't call animal control. Shelby's alive."

"Sam. Shut up. Please. We don't know. One of the other wolves could've dragged her body off the deck. Don't jump to conclusions." She looked at me, finally, and I saw that Grace, despite her complete inability to read people, had puzzled out what Shelby was to me. My past clawing out at me, trying to steal me even before winter did.

I felt like things were getting away from me. I'd found heaven and grabbed it as tightly as I could, but it was unravelling, an insubstantial thread sliding between my fingers, too fine to hold.

Forty

Sam

14°C

And so I looked for them.

Every day that Grace was at school, I searched for them, the two wolves I didn't trust, the ones who were supposed to be dead. Mercy Falls was small. Boundary Wood was – not as small, but more familiar, and maybe more willing to give up its secrets to me.

I would find Shelby and Jack and I'd confront them on my own terms.

But Shelby had left no trail off the deck, so maybe she really was gone. And Jack, too, was nowhere – a dead, cold trail. A ghost that left no corpse behind. I felt like I had combed the entire county for signs of him.

I thought – vaguely hoped – that he'd died, too, and ceased to be a problem. Been hit by some Department of Transportation vehicle and scooped into a dump somewhere. But there were no tracks leading to roads, no trees marked, no scent of a new-made wolf lingering at the school car park. He had disappeared as completely as snow in summer.

I should've been glad. Disappearing meant discreet. Disappearing meant he wasn't my problem any more.

But I just couldn't accept it. We wolves did many things: change, hide, sing underneath a pale, lonely moon – but we never disappeared entirely. Humans disappeared. Humans made monsters out of us.

Forty-One
Grace

12°C

Sam and I were like horses on a merry-go-round. We followed the same track again and again – home, school, home, school, bookstore, home, school, home, etc. – but really, we were circling the big issue without ever getting any closer to it. The real heart of it: winter. Cold. Loss.

We didn't talk about the looming possibility, but I felt I could always sense the chill of the shadow it cast over us. I'd read a story once, in a really dire collection of Greek myths, about a man called Damocles who had a sword dangling over his throne, hung by a single hair. That was us – Sam's humanity dangling by a tight thread.

On Monday, as per the merry-go-round, it was back to school as usual. Although it had only been two days since Shelby attacked me, even the bruising had disappeared. It seemed I had a little bit of the werewolf healing in me after all.

I was surprised to find Olivia still absent. Last year, she'd never missed a single day.

I kept waiting and waiting for her to walk into one of the two classes we shared before lunch, but she didn't. I kept looking at her empty desk in class. She could've just been sick, but a part of me that I was trying to ignore said it was more. In fourth period, I slid into my usual seat behind Rachel. "Rachel, hey, have you seen Olivia?"

Rachel turned to face me. "Huh?"

"Olivia. Doesn't she have science with you?"

She shrugged. "I haven't heard from her since Friday. I tried calling her and her mom said she was sick. But what about you, buttercup? Where were you this weekend? You never call, you never write."

"I got bitten by a raccoon," I said. "I had to get rabies shots and I took Sunday to sleep it off. To make sure I didn't start foaming at the mouth and savaging people."

"Gross. Where did it bite you?"

I gestured towards my jeans. "Ankle. It doesn't look like much. I'm worried about Olive, though. I haven't been able to get her on the phone."

Rachel frowned and crossed her legs; she was, as ever, wearing stripes, this time, striped tights. She said, "Me, neither. Do you think she's avoiding us? Is she still mad at you?"

I shook my head. "I don't think so."

Rachel made a face. "*We're* OK, though, right? I mean, we haven't really been talking. About stuff, I mean. Stuff's been happening. But we haven't been, you know, talking. Or over at each other's houses. Or whatever."

"We're OK," I said firmly.

She scratched her rainbow tights and bit her lip before saying, "Do you think we should, you know, go over to her house and see if we can catch her?"

I didn't answer right away, and she didn't push it. This was unfamiliar territory for both of us: we'd never had to really work to make our trio stick together. I didn't know if tracking Olivia down was the right thing or not. It seemed kind of drastic, but how long had it been since we'd seen her or talked to her, really? I said, slowly, "How about we wait until the end of the week? If we haven't heard from her by then, then we. . . ?"

Rachel nodded, looking relieved. "Coolio."

She turned back around in her seat as Mr Rink, at the front of the classroom, cleared his throat to get our attention. He said, "OK, you guys will probably hear this several times today from the teachers, but don't go around licking the water fountains or kissing perfect strangers, OK? Because the Health Department has reported a couple of cases of meningitis in this part of the state. And you get that from – anyone? Snot! Mucus! Kissing and licking! Don't do it!"

There was appreciative hooting in the back of the classroom.

"Since you can't do any of that, we'll do something

almost as good. Social studies! Open up your books to page one hundred and twelve."

I glanced at the doorway again for the thousandth time, hoping to see Olivia come through it, and opened my book.

When classes broke for lunch, I snuck into the hall and phoned Olivia's house. It rang twelve times and went to voicemail. I didn't leave a message; if she was cutting class for a reason other than sickness, I didn't want her mother to get a message asking where she was during the school day. I was about to shut my locker when I noticed that the smallest pouch of my backpack was partially unzipped. A piece of paper jutted out with my name written on it. I unfolded it, my cheeks warming unexpectedly when I recognized Sam's messy, ropy handwriting.

"AGAIN AND AGAIN, HOWEVER, WE KNOW THE LANGUAGE OF LOVE,
AND THE LITTLE CHURCHYARD WITH ITS LAMENTING NAMES AND
THE STAGGERINGLY SECRET ABYSS IN WHICH OTHERS FIND THEIR
END: AGAIN AND AGAIN THE TWO OF US GO OUT UNDER THE
ANCIENT TREES, MAKE OUR BED AGAIN AND AGAIN BETWEEN
THE FLOWERS, FACE TO FACE WITH THE SKIES."

THIS IS RILKE. I WISH I HAD WRITTEN IT FOR YOU.

I didn't understand it entirely, but, thinking of Sam, I read it out loud, whispering the words to myself. In my mouth, the shapes of the words became beautiful. I felt a smile on my face, even with no one around to see it. My worries were still there, but for the moment, I floated above them, warm with the memory of Sam.

I didn't want to dispel my quiet, buoyant feelings in the noisy cafeteria, so I retreated back to my next period's empty classroom and took a seat. Dropping my English text on the desk, I flattened the note on my desk to read it again.

Sitting in the empty classroom and listening to the faraway sounds of noisy students in the cafeteria, I was reminded of feeling sick in class and being sent to the school nurse. The nurse's office had that same muffled sense of distance, like a satellite to the loud planet that was the school. I had spent a lot of time there after the wolves attacked me, suffering from that flu that probably hadn't really been a flu.

For a measureless amount of time, I stared at the open mobile phone, thinking about getting bitten. About getting sick from it. About getting better. Why was I the only one who had?

"Have you changed your mind?"

My chin jerked up at the sound of the voice, and I found myself facing Isabel at the desk next to mine. To my surprise, she didn't look quite as perfect as usual; she had bags under her eyes that were only partially hidden by make-up, and there was nothing to disguise her bloodshot eyes. "Excuse me?"

"About Jack. About knowing anything about him."

I looked at her, wary. I had heard once that lawyers never ask a question they didn't already know the answer to, and Isabel's voice was surprisingly sure.

She reached a long, unnaturally tanned arm into her bag and pulled out a sheaf of paper. She tossed it on top of my poetry book. "Your friend dropped these."

It took me a moment to realize that it was a stack of glossy photo paper and that these images in front of me must've been digital prints of Olivia's. My stomach flip-flopped. The first few photos were of woods, nothing particularly remarkable. Then there were the wolves. The crazy brindle wolf, half-hidden by trees. And that black wolf – had Sam told me his name? I hesitated, my fingers on the edge of the page, ready to flip to the next one. Isabel had tensed visibly next to me, preparing for me to see what was on the next sheet. I knew whatever Olivia had caught on film was going to be difficult to explain.

Finally, impatient, Isabel leaned across the aisle and snatched the top few prints from the stack. "Just turn the page."

It was a photo of Jack. Jack as a wolf. A close-up of his eyes in a wolf's face.

And the next one was of Jack himself. As a person. Naked.

The shot had a kind of raw, artistic power, almost posed-looking, the way Jack's arms curled around his body, his head turned back over his shoulder towards the camera, showing scratches on the long, pale curve of his back.

I chewed my lip and looked at his face in both of them. No shot of him changing, but the similarity of the eyes was devastating. That close-up of the wolf's face – that was the money shot. And then it hit me, what these photos really meant, the true importance. Not that Isabel knew. But that Olivia did. Olivia had taken these photos, so of course she must know. But for how long, and why hadn't she told me?

"*Say* something."

Finally, I looked up from the photos to Isabel. "What do you want me to say?"

Isabel made an irritated little noise. "You see the photos. He's alive. He's *right there*."

I looked back at Jack, staring out of the woods. He looked cold in his new skin. "I don't know what you want me to say. What do you want from me?"

She seemed to be struggling with herself. For a second, she looked like she might snap at me, and then she closed her eyes. She opened them and looked away, at the whiteboard. "You don't have a brother, do you? Any siblings, right?"

"No. I'm an only child."

Isabel shrugged. "Then I don't know how I can explain. He's my brother. I thought he was dead. But he's not. He's alive. He's *right there*, but I don't know where there is. I don't know *what* that is. But I think – I think you do. Only you won't help me." She looked at me and her eyes flashed, fierce. "What have I ever done to you?"

I stumbled over the words. The truth was, Jack was her brother. It seemed like she ought to know. If only it wasn't *Isabel* asking. I said, "Isabel . . . you have to know why I'm afraid to talk to you. I know you haven't done anything to me personally. But I know people you've *destroyed*. Just . . . tell me why I should trust you."

Isabel snatched back the photos and stuffed them back in her bag. "What you said. Because I've never done anything to you. Or maybe because I think whatever's wrong with Jack – I think that's what's wrong with your boyfriend, too."

I was abnormally paralysed by the thought of the photos that I *hadn't* seen in that stack. Was Sam in there? Maybe Olivia had known about the wolves for longer than I had – I tried to replay exactly what Olivia had said during our argument, trying to remember any double meaning. Isabel was staring at me, waiting for me to say something, and I didn't know what to say. Finally, I snapped, "OK, stop staring at me. Let me *think*." The classroom door thumped as students began strolling in for class. I ripped a page out of my notebook and jotted my phone number on it. "That's my mobile. Call me after school sometime and we'll figure out someplace to meet. I guess."

Isabel took the number. I expected to see satisfaction

on her face, but to my surprise, she looked as sick as I felt. The wolves were a secret no one wanted to share.

"We have a problem."

Sam turned in the driver's seat to look at me. "Aren't you supposed to still be in class?"

"I got out early." Last class was art. Nobody was going to miss me and my hideous clay-and-wire sculpture, anyway. "Isabel knows."

Sam blinked, slowly. "Who's Isabel?"

"Jack's sister, remember?" I turned down the heat – Sam had it set to *hell* – and shoved my backpack down by my feet. I explained the confrontation to him, leaving out how creepy the Jack-human photo was. "I have no idea what the other photos were."

Sam immediately bypassed the Isabel question. "They were Olivia's photos?"

"Yeah."

Worry was written all over his face. "I wonder if this has something to do with the way Olivia was at the bookstore. With me." When I didn't answer, he looked at the steering wheel, or at something just past it. "If she knew what we were, it makes her entire eye comment very logical. She was trying to get us to confess."

I said, "Yeah, actually. That would make a lot of sense."

He sighed heavily. "Suddenly I'm thinking about

what Rachel said. About the wolf that was at Olivia's house."

I closed my eyes and opened them again, still seeing the image of Jack with his arms wrapped around himself. "Ugh. I don't want to think about that. What about Isabel? I can't really avoid her. And I can't keep lying; I just look like an idiot."

Sam half smiled at me. "Well, I *would* ask you what sort of person she is and what you thought we ought to do—"

"—but I suck at reading people," I finished for him.

"You said it, not me. Just remember that."

"OK, so what do we do? Why do I feel like I'm the only one in panic mode here? You're completely . . . calm."

Sam shrugged. "Total lack of preparedness for such a thing, probably. I don't think I know what to plan for without meeting her. If I had talked to her when she had the photos, maybe I'd be worried, but right now, I can't think of it concretely. I don't know, Isabel sounds like a pleasant sort of name."

I laughed. "Barking up the wrong tree there."

He made a melodramatic face, and the twisted rueful agony in it was so overdone that it made me feel better. "Is she awful?"

"I used to think so. Now?" I shrugged. "Jury's still out. So what do we do?"

"I think we have to meet her."

"Both of us? Where?"

"Yes, both. This isn't just your problem. I dunno. Someplace quiet. Someplace I can get a feel for her before we decide what to tell her." He frowned. "She wouldn't be the first family member to find out."

I knew from his frown that he couldn't be talking about his parents – his expression wouldn't have changed if he had. "She wouldn't?"

"Beck's wife knew."

"Past tense?"

"Breast cancer. It was long before me. I never knew her. I only found out about her from Paul, and by accident then. Beck didn't want me to know about her. I guess because most people don't do well with us, and he didn't want me thinking I could just go out and get me a nice little wife of my own, or something."

It seemed unfair, that two such tragedies should strike a couple. I realized, too late to comment on it, that I'd almost missed the unfamiliar bitterness in his voice. I thought about saying something, asking him about Beck, but the moment was gone, lost in noise as Sam turned up the radio and hit the accelerator.

He backed the Bronco out of the parking space, his forehead furrowed with thought. "To heck with the rules," Sam said. "I want to meet her."

Forty-Two
Sam

12°C

The first words I ever heard Isabel say were: "Can I ask why the hell we're making quiche instead of talking about my brother?" She had just climbed out of a massive white SUV that basically took over the Brisbanes' entire driveway. My first impression of her was *tall* – probably because of the five-inch heels on the ass-kicking boots she wore – followed by *ringlets* – because her head had more of them than a porcelain doll.

"No," Grace said, and I loved her because of the way she said it, no negotiation allowed.

Isabel made a noise that, if converted into a missile, had enough vitriol to obliterate a small country. "So can I ask who he is?"

I glanced at her in time to see her checking out my butt. She looked away quickly as I echoed, "No."

Grace led us into the house. Turning to Isabel in the front hallway, she said, "Don't ask any questions about Jack. My mom's home."

"Is that you, Grace?" Grace's mom called from upstairs.

"Yes! We're making quiche!" Grace hung up her coat and motioned for us to do the same.

"I brought some stuff back from the studio, just shove it out of your way!" her mom shouted back.

Isabel wrinkled her nose and kept her fur-lined jacket on, stuffing her hands in the pockets and standing back while Grace shoved boxes towards the walls of the room to clear a path through the clutter. Isabel looked profoundly out of place in the comfortably crowded kitchen. I couldn't decide whether her perfect artificial ringlets made the not-quite-white linoleum floor look more pathetic or whether the old cracked floor made her hair look more perfect and fake. Until now, I hadn't ever seen the kitchen as shabby.

Isabel shuffled back even further as Grace shoved up her sleeves and washed her hands at the sink.

"Sam, turn on that radio and find something good, will you?"

I found a little boom box on the counter amongst some tins of salt and sugar and turned it on.

"God, we really are going to make quiche," Isabel moaned. "I thought it was code for something else." I grinned at her and she caught my eye and made an anguished face. But her expression was too much – I didn't believe her angst entirely. Something in her eyes made me think she was at least curious about the situation. And the situation was this: I wasn't going to confide in Isabel until I was damn certain what kind of person she was.

Grace's mom came in then, smelling of orange-scented turps. "Hi, Sam. You're making quiche, too?"

"Trying," I said earnestly.

She laughed. "How fun. Who's this?"

"Isabel," Grace said. "Mom, do you know where that green cookbook is? I had it right here for ever. It's got the quiche recipe in it."

Her mom shrugged helplessly and knelt by one of the boxes on the floor. "It must've walked off. What in the world is on the radio? Sam, you can make it do something better than that."

While Grace fumbled through some cookbooks tucked away on a corner of the counter, I clicked through the radio stations until Grace's mom said, "Stop right there!" when I got to some rather funky-sounding pop station. She stood, holding a box. "I think my work here is done. Have fun, kids. I'll be back ... sometime."

Grace barely seemed to notice her leaving. She gestured at me. "Isabel, eggs and cheese and milk are in the fridge. Sam, we need to make plain old piecrusts. Would you preheat the oven to two-thirty and get us some pans?"

Isabel was staring inside the fridge. "There's, like, eight thousand kinds of cheese in here. It all looks the same to me."

"You do the oven, let Sam get the cheese and stuff. He knows food," Grace said. She was standing on her tiptoes to get flour out of an overhead cupboard; it stretched her body gorgeously and made me want in the worst way to touch the bare skin exposed on her lower back. But then she heaved the flour down and I'd missed my chance, so I traded places with Isabel, grabbed some sharp cheddar and eggs and milk, and threw it all on the counter.

Grace was already involved with cutting shortening and flour in a bowl by the time I'd finished cracking eggs and whisking in some mayonnaise. The kitchen was suddenly full of activity, as if we were legion.

"What the hell is this?" Isabel demanded, staring at a package Grace had handed her.

Grace snorted with laughter. "It's a mushroom."

"It looks like it came out of a cow's rear end."

"I'd like that cow," Grace said, leaning past Isabel to slap some butter into a saucepan. "Its butt would be worth a million. Sauté those in there for a few minutes till they're nice and yummy."

"How long?"

"Till they're yummy," I repeated.

"You heard the boy," Grace said. She reached out a hand. "Pan!"

"Help her," I told Isabel. "I'll take care of yummy, since you can't."

"I'm *already* yummy," muttered Isabel. She handed two pans to Grace, and Grace deftly unfolded the pie pastry – magic – into the bottom of each. She began to show Isabel how to crimp the edges. The entire process seemed very well-worn; I got the idea that Grace could've done this whole thing a lot faster without me and Isabel in her way.

Isabel caught me smiling at the sight of the two of them crimping piecrusts. "What are you smiling at? Look at your mushrooms!"

I rescued the mushrooms in time and added the spinach that Grace pushed into my hands.

"My *mascara*." Isabel's voice rose above the increasing clamour, and I looked to see her and Grace laughing and crying while cutting onions. Then the little onions' powerful odour hit my nose and burned my eyes, too.

I offered my sauté pan to them. "Throw them in here. It'll kill it a bit."

Isabel scraped them off a cutting board into the pan and Grace slapped my butt with a flour-covered hand. I craned my neck, trying to see if she'd left a print, while Grace rubbed her hand in leftover flour to get better coverage and tried again.

"*This is my song!*" Grace suddenly announced. "Turn it up! Turn it up!"

It was Mariah Carey in the worst possible way, but it was so right at the moment. I turned it up until the little speakers buzzed against the tins next to them. I grabbed Grace's hand and tugged her over to me and we started to dance like we were cool, terribly clumsy and unbearably sexy, her grinding up against me, hands in the air, my arms around her waist, too low to be chaste.

I thought to myself, *A life is measured by moments like these.* Grace leaned her head back, neck long and pale against my shoulder, to reach my mouth for a kiss, and just before I gave her one, I saw Isabel's wistful eyes watch my mouth touch Grace's.

"Tell me how long to set the timer for," Isabel said, catching my eye and looking away. "And then maybe we can talk...?"

Grace was still leaning back against me, secure in my arms, covered in flour and so entirely edible that I ached with wanting to be alone with her, here, now. She gestured lazily towards the open cookbook on the counter, drunk with my presence. Isabel consulted the recipe and set the timer.

There was a moment's silence when we realized we were done, and then I took a breath and faced Isabel. "OK, I'll tell you what's wrong with Jack."

Isabel and Grace both looked startled.

"Let's go sit down," Grace suggested, removing herself from my arms. "Living room's that way. I'll get coffee."

So Isabel and I made our way into the living room. Like the kitchen, it was cluttered in a way I hadn't noticed until Isabel was in it. She had to move a pile of unfolded laundry to sit on the sofa. I didn't want to sit next to her, so I sat on the rocker across from her.

Looking at me out of the corner of her eye, Isabel

asked, "Why aren't you like Jack? Why aren't you changing back and forth?"

I didn't flinch; if Grace hadn't warned me of how much Isabel had guessed, I probably would have. "I've been this way longer. You get more stable the longer it's been. At first you just switch back and forth all the time. Temperature has a little bit to do with it, but not as much as later."

She immediately fired another one off: "Did you do this to Jack?"

I let the revulsion show on my face. "I don't know who did it. There are quite a few of us and not all of us are nice people." I didn't say anything about his BB gun.

"Why is he so angry?"

I shrugged. "I dunno. Because he's an angry person?"

Isabel's expression became ... *pointy*.

"Look, getting bitten doesn't make you into a monster. It just makes you into a wolf. You are what you are. When you're a wolf, or when you're shifting, you don't have human inhibitions, so if you're naturally angry or violent, you get worse."

Grace walked in, precariously carrying three mugs of coffee. Isabel took one with a beaver on the side and I took one with a bank name on it. Grace joined Isabel on the sofa.

Isabel closed her eyes for a second. "OK. So let me

get this straight. My brother wasn't *really* killed by wolves. He was just mauled by them and then turned into a *werewolf*? Sorry, I'm missing the whole undead thing. And isn't there supposed to be something about moons and silver bullets and a bunch of crap like that?"

"He healed himself, but it took a while," I told her. "He wasn't ever really dead. I don't know how he escaped from the morgue. The moon and silver stuff is all just myth. I don't know how to explain it. It's – it's a disease that's worse when it's cold. I think the moon myth is because it gets cold overnight, so when we're new, we change into wolves overnight a lot. So people thought it was the moon that caused it."

Isabel seemed to be taking this pretty well. She wasn't fainting, and she didn't smell afraid. She sipped her coffee. "Grace, this is disgusting."

"It's instant," Grace apologized.

Isabel asked, "So does my brother recognize me when he's a wolf?"

Grace looked at my face; I couldn't look back at her when I answered. "Probably a little. Some of us don't remember anything about our lives when we're wolves. Some of us remember a little."

Grace looked away, sipped her coffee, pretended she didn't care.

"So there's a pack?"

Isabel asked good questions. I nodded. "But Jack hasn't found them yet. Or they haven't found him."

Isabel ran a finger around the rim of her coffee mug for a long moment. Finally she looked from me to Grace and back again. "OK, so what's the catch here?"

I blinked. "What do you mean?"

"I mean, you're sitting here just talking, and Grace is here trying to pretend like everything's just fine, but everything *isn't* just fine, is it?"

I guess I couldn't be surprised by her intuition. You didn't claw your way to the top of the high-school food chain without being able to read people. I looked into my still-full coffee cup. I didn't like coffee – too strong and bitter a flavour. I'd been a wolf too long; I'd lost my taste for it. "We've got expiration dates. The longer it's been since we've been bitten, the less cold we need to turn us into wolves. And the more heat we need to turn us into humans. Eventually, we just don't turn, become human again."

"How long?"

I didn't look at Grace. "It varies from wolf to wolf. Years and years for most wolves."

"But not for you."

Shut up, Isabel. I didn't want to test Grace's even expression any further. I just shook my head, very slightly, hoping that Grace really was looking out of the window and not at me.

"So what if you lived in Florida, or someplace really warm?"

I was relieved to get the topic off me. "A couple of us

tried it. It doesn't work. It just makes you supersensitive to the slightest temperature change." Ulrik and Melissa and a wolf named Bauer had gone down to Texas one year in the hope of outrunning the winter. I still remembered the excited phone call from Ulrik after weeks of not changing – and then his dejected return, minus Bauer, after they'd walked past the slightly ajar door of an air-conditioned shop and Bauer had instantly changed forms. Apparently, Texas Animal Control didn't believe in tranquilizer guns.

"What about the equator? Where the temperature never changes?"

"I don't know." I tried not to sound exasperated. "None of us ever decided to go to the rain forest, but I'll keep that in mind for when I win the lottery."

"No need to be a jerk," Isabel said, setting her coffee mug down on a stack of magazines. "I was just asking. So anybody who gets bitten changes, then?"

Everyone except the one I wish I could take with me. "Pretty much." I heard my voice, how tired it sounded, and didn't care.

Isabel pursed her lips and I thought she'd press it further, but she didn't. "So that's really it. My brother's a werewolf, a real werewolf, and there's no cure."

Grace's eyes narrowed, and I wished I knew what she was thinking. "Yeah. You got it. But you already knew all this. So why did you ask us?"

Isabel shrugged. "I guess I was waiting for someone

to jump out of the curtain and say, 'Whoopdie-friggin-doo, fooled you! No such thing as werewolves. What were you thinking?'"

I wanted to tell her that there really *wasn't* such a thing as werewolves. That there were humans, and there were wolves, and there were those of us that were on the way from one to another. But I was just tired, so I didn't say anything.

"Tell me you won't tell anyone." Grace spoke abruptly. "I don't think you have yet, but you can't tell anyone now."

"Do you think I'm an idiot? My dad fricking shot one of the wolves because he was angry about it. Do you think I'm going to try and tell him Jack's one of them? And my mother's already medicated out the wazoo. Yeah, big help she would be. I'm just going to have to deal with this on my own."

Grace exchanged a look with me that said, *Good guess, Sam.*

"And with us," Grace added. "We'll help you when we can. Jack doesn't have to be alone, but we have to find him first."

Isabel flicked an invisible piece of dust off one of her boots, as if she didn't know what to do with the kindness. Finally, she said, still looking at her boot, "I don't know. He wasn't a very nice person last time I saw him. I don't know if I want to find him."

"Sorry," I said.

"For what?"

For not being able to tell you that his nasty temper was from the bite and would go away. I shrugged. It felt like I was doing a lot of that. "For not having happier news."

There was a low, irritating buzz from the kitchen.

"The quiche is done," Isabel said. "At least I get a consolation prize." She looked at me and then at Grace. "So soon he'll stop switching back and forth, right? Because winter's almost here?"

I nodded.

"Good," Isabel said, looking out of the window at the naked branches of the trees. Looking out to the woods that were Jack's home now, and soon, mine. "Can't get here soon enough."

Forty-Three
Grace

7°C

I was a zombie of sleeplessness. I was

English essay

Mr Rink's voice

Flickering fluorescent light above my desk

AP Biology

Isabel's stone face

Heavy eyes

"Earth to Grace," Rachel said, pinching my elbow as she passed me on the pavement. "There's Olivia. I didn't even see her in class, did you?"

I followed Rachel's gaze to the kids waiting for the school bus. Olivia was among them, jumping up and down to stay warm. No camera. I thought about the photos. "I have to talk to her."

"Yes. You do," Rachel said. "Because you need to be on speaking terms before our vacation to hot, sunny places this Christmas. I would go with you, but Dad's waiting, and he's got an appointment in Duluth. He'll go all fanged if I don't get out there this second. Tell me what she says!"

She ran towards the parking lot and I jogged towards Olivia. "Olivia."

She jerked, and I caught her elbow, as if she would fly away if I didn't. "I've been trying to call you."

Olivia pulled her stocking cap down and balled herself up against the chill. "Yeah?"

For a single moment, I thought about waiting to see what she would say. To see if she would confess to knowledge about the wolves without prompting. But the buses were pulling in, and I didn't want to wait. I lowered my voice and said in her ear, "I saw your photographs. Of Jack."

She abruptly turned to face me. "*You* were the one who took them?"

I tried, with some success, to keep the accusation out of my voice. "*Isabel* showed them to me."

Olivia's face went pale.

I demanded, "Why wouldn't you tell me? Why wouldn't you call me?"

She bit her lip and looked across the car park. "I was going to, at first. To tell you that you were right. But then I ran across Jack, and he told me I couldn't tell anyone about him, and I just felt guilty, like I was doing something wrong."

I stared at her. "Have you *talked* to him?"

Olivia shrugged, unhappy, and shivered in the growing chill of the afternoon. "I was taking photos of the wolves, like always, and I saw him. I saw him —"

she lowered her voice and leaned towards me – "change. Become human again. I couldn't believe it. And he had no clothing, and my house wasn't far, so I had him come over and get some of John's clothes. I guess I was just trying to convince myself that I wasn't crazy."

"Thanks," I said sarcastically.

It took her a moment. Then she said, quickly, "Oh, Grace, I know. I know you told me at the very beginning, but what was I supposed to do – believe you? It sounds impossible. It *looks* impossible. But I felt sorry for him. He doesn't belong anywhere now."

"How long has this been going on?!" Something was stinging at me. Betrayal, or something. I'd told Olivia at the very beginning about my suspicions, and she'd waited until I came to her to admit anything.

"I don't know. A while. I've been giving him food and washing his clothes and stuff. I don't know where he's been staying. We talked a lot, until we had a fight about the cure. I was cutting class to talk to him and to try to get more photos of the wolves. I wanted to see if any of the others would change." She paused. "Grace, he said you'd been bitten and cured."

"That's true. Well, that I was bitten. You knew that. But I didn't ever change into a wolf, obviously."

Her eyes were intent on me. "Ever?"

I shook my head. "No. Have you told anybody else?"

Olivia gave me another withering look. "I'm not an idiot."

"Well, Isabel got those photos somehow. If she can, anyone can."

"I don't have any photos that really show what's going on," Olivia said. "I told you, I'm not a total idiot. I just have the photos of the before and after. And who would believe anything from that?"

"Isabel," I said.

Olivia frowned at me. "I'm being careful. Anyway, I haven't seen him since we fought. I have to go." She gestured at the bus. "You really never changed?"

Now it was my turn to give her a withering look. "I never lie to you, Olive."

She looked at me for a long beat. Then she said, "Do you want to come back to my house?"

I kind of wanted her to say that she was sorry. For not confiding in me. For not answering my calls. For fighting with me. For not saying *you were right*. So I just said, "I'm waiting for Sam."

"OK. Maybe another day this week?"

I blinked. "Maybe."

And then she was gone, on to the bus, just a silhouette in the windows making her way towards the back. I had thought that hearing her admit to knowing about the wolves would give me some ... closure, but all I felt was an uneasy disquiet. After all this time looking for Jack, and Olivia had known where to find him all along. I wasn't sure what to think.

In the car park, I saw the Bronco pulling in slowly, heading in my direction. Seeing Sam behind the wheel gave me peace in a way that the conversation with Olivia hadn't. Strange how just seeing my own car could make me so happy.

Sam leaned over to unlatch the passenger-side door for me. He still looked a little tired. He handed me a steaming Styrofoam cup of coffee. "Your phone rang just a few minutes ago."

"Thanks." I climbed into the Bronco and gratefully accepted the coffee. "I'm a zombie today. I was dying for caffeine and I just had the weirdest conversation with Olivia. I'll tell you about it once I'm properly caffeinated. Where's my phone?" Sam pointed to the glove compartment.

Climbing into the Bronco, I opened the glove compartment and retrieved the phone. *One new message.* I dialled my voicemail, put it on speakerphone, and set the phone on the dash while I turned to Sam.

"I'm ready now," I told him.

Sam looked at me, eyebrows doubtful. "For?"

"My kiss."

Sam chewed his lip. "I prefer the surprise attack."

"*You have one new message,*" said the recorded mobile-phone babe.

I grimaced, throwing myself back in the seat. "You drive me crazy."

He grinned.

"*Hi, honey! You'll never guess who I ran into today!*" Mom's voice buzzed out of the mobile-phone speaker.

"You could just throw yourself at me," I suggested. "That would be fine with me."

Mom sounded excited. "*Naomi Ett! You know, from my school.*"

"I didn't think you were that sort of girl," Sam said. I thought he might be joking.

Mom continued, "*She's all married and everything now, and in town for just a little bit, so Dad and I are going to spend some time with her.*"

I frowned at him. "I'm not. But with you, all bets are off."

"*So we won't be back until late tonight,*" Mom's message concluded. "*Remember there's leftovers in the fridge, and of course, we have our phone if you need us.*"

My leftovers. From the casserole I'd made.

Sam was staring at the phone as mobile-phone babe took up where Mom had left off. "*To hear this message again, press one. To delete this message. . .*"

I deleted it. Sam was still looking at the phone, his eyes sort of distant. I didn't know what he was thinking. Maybe, like me, his head was full of a dozen different problems, all too amorphous and intangible to be solved.

I snapped the phone shut, and the sound seemed to break his spell. Sam's eyes were suddenly intense on me. "Come away with me."

I raised an eyebrow.

"No, seriously. Let's go somewhere. Can I take you somewhere, tonight? Someplace better than leftovers?"

I didn't know what to say. I think maybe what I wanted to say was, *Do you really think you have to even ask?*

I watched Sam intently while he babbled on, words tumbling over each other in their hurry to get out. If I hadn't scented the air at that moment, I probably wouldn't have realized that anything was wrong. But coming off him in waves was the too-sweet scent of anxiety. Anxious about me? Anxious about something that had happened today? Anxious because he had heard the weather report?

"What's up?" I asked.

"I just want to get out of town tonight. I want to just get away for a little bit. Mini holiday. A few hours in someone else's life, you know? I mean, we don't have to if you don't want to. And if you think that it's not—"

"Sam," I said. "Shut up."

He shut up.

"Start driving."

We started driving.

★

Sam got on to the interstate and we drove and drove until the sky grew pink above the trees and birds flying over the road were black silhouettes. It was cold enough that cars just getting on to the highway puffed visible white exhaust into the frosty air. Sam used one hand to drive and used the other to twine his fingers with mine. This was so much better than staying at home with a casserole.

By the time we got off the interstate, I had either got used to the smell of Sam's anxiety, or he had calmed down, because the only odour in the car was his musky, wolf wood scent.

"So," I said, and ran a finger over the back of his cool hand. "Where are we going, anyway?"

Sam glanced over at me, the dash lights illuminating his doleful smile. "There's a wonderful sweet shop in Duluth."

It was incredibly cute that he'd driven us an hour just to go to a sweet shop. Incredibly stupid, given the weather report, but incredibly cute nonetheless. "I've never been."

"They have the most amazing caramel apples," Sam promised. "And these gooey things, I don't even know what they are. Probably a million calories. And hot chocolate – oh, man, Grace. It's amazing."

I couldn't think of anything to say. I was idiotically entranced by the way he said "Grace". The tone of it. The way his lips formed the vowels. The timbre of his voice stuck in my head like music.

"I even wrote a song about their truffles," he confessed.

That caught my attention. "I heard you playing the guitar for my mom. She told me it was a song about me. Why don't you ever sing it for me?"

Sam shrugged.

I looked past him at the brilliantly illuminated city, every building and bridge lit bravely against the early-winter darkness; we were heading downtown. I couldn't remember the last time I'd been there. "It would be very romantic. And add to your walking stereotype street cred."

Sam didn't look away from the road, but his lips curled up. I grinned, then looked away to watch our progress downtown. He didn't even look at the road signs as he navigated his way down the evening streets. Streetlights striped light across the windshield and the white lines striped below us, marking time above and below.

Finally, he parallel parked and gestured to a warmly lit shop a few doors ahead of us. He turned to me. "Heaven."

Together we got out of the car and jogged the distance. I didn't know how cold it was, but my breath formed a shapeless cloud in front of me as I pushed open the glass door to the sweet shop. Sam pushed into the warm yellow glow after me, arms clasped around himself. The bell was still dinging from our entrance when Sam came from behind me and pulled me to him, crushing his arms over my chest. He whispered in my ear, "Don't look. Close your eyes and smell it. *Really* smell it. I know you can."

I leaned my head back against his shoulder, feeling the heat of his body against me, and closed my eyes. My nose was centimetres away from the skin on his neck, and *that* was what I smelled. Earthy, wild, complex.

"Not me," he said.

"It's all I smell," I murmured, opening my eyes to look up at him.

"Don't be stubborn." Sam turned me slightly, so that I was facing the centre of the shop; I saw shelves of tinned cookies and sweets and the glint of a glass sweets counter beyond them. "Give in for once. It's worth it."

His sad eyes implored me to explore something I'd left untouched for years. Something more than untouched – something I'd buried alive. Buried when I had thought I was alone. Now I had Sam behind me, holding me tightly to his chest as if he held me upright, his breath blowing warm over my ear.

I closed my eyes, flared my nostrils, and let the scents flood in. The strongest of them, caramel and brown sugar, smell as yellow-orange as the sun, came first. That one was easy. The one that anyone would notice coming into the shop. And then chocolate, of course, the bitter dark and the sugary milk chocolate. I don't think a normal girl would've smelled anything else, and part of me wanted to stop there. But I could feel Sam's heart pounding behind me, and for once, I gave in.

Peppermint swirled into my nostrils, sharp as glass, then raspberry, almost too sweet, like too-ripe fruit. Apple, crisp and pure. Nuts, buttery, warm, earthy, like Sam. The subtle, mild scent of white chocolate. Oh, God, some sort of mocha, rich and dark and sinful. I sighed with pleasure, but there was more. The butter cookies on the shelves added a floury, comforting scent, and the lollipops, a riot of fruit scents too concentrated to be real. The salty bite of pretzels, the bright smell of lemon, the brittle edge of anise. Smells I didn't even know names for. I groaned.

Sam rewarded me with the lightest of kisses on my ear before he spoke into it. "Isn't it amazing?"

I opened my eyes; colours seemed dull in comparison with what I had just experienced. I couldn't think of anything that didn't sound trivial, so I just nodded. He kissed me again, on my cheek, and gazed at my face, his expression bright and delighted with whatever he saw in mine. It occurred to me that he hadn't shared this place, this experience, with anyone else. Just me.

"I love it," I said finally, in a voice so low I'm not even sure he could hear it. But of course he could. He could hear everything I could.

I wasn't sure if I was ready to admit how not normal I was.

Sam released all of me but my hand, and tugged me

deeper into the shop. "Come on. Now the hard part. Pick something. What do you want? Pick something. Anything. I'll get it for you."

I want you. Feeling the grip of his hand in mine, the brush of his skin on mine, seeing the way he moved in front of me, equal parts human and wolf, and remembering his smell – I ached with wanting to kiss him.

Sam's hand squeezed on mine as if he was reading my thoughts, and he led me to the sweets counter. I stared at the rows of perfect chocolates, petit fours, coated pretzels and truffles.

"Cold out tonight, isn't it?" the girl behind the counter asked. "It's supposed to snow. I can't wait." She looked up at us and gave us a silly, indulgent smile, and I wondered just how stupidly happy we looked, holding hands and drooling over chocolates.

"What's the best?" I asked.

The girl immediately pointed out a few racks of chocolates. Sam shook his head. "Could we get two hot chocolates?"

"Whipped cream?"

"Do you have to ask?"

She grinned at us and turned around to prepare it. A *whuff* of rich chocolate gusted over the counter when she opened the tin of cocoa. While she dribbled peppermint extract into the bottom of paper cups, I turned to Sam and took his other hand. I stood on my toes and stole a soft kiss from his lips. "Surprise attack," I said.

Sam leaned down and kissed me back, his mouth lingering on mine, teeth grazing my lower lip, making me shiver. "Surprise attack back."

"Sneaky," I said, my voice breathier than I intended.

"You two are too cute," the counter girl said, setting two cups piled with whipped cream on the counter. She had a sort of lopsided, open smile that made me think she laughed a lot. "Seriously. How long have you been going out?"

Sam let go of my hands to get his wallet and took out some bills. "Six years."

I wrinkled my nose to cover a laugh. Of course he would count the time that we'd been two entirely different species.

"Whoa." Counter girl nodded appreciatively. "That's pretty amazing for a couple your age."

Sam handed me my hot chocolate and didn't answer. But his yellow eyes gazed at me possessively – I wondered if he realized that the way he looked at me was far more intimate than copping a feel could ever be.

I crouched to look at the almond bark on the bottom shelf in the counter. I wasn't quite bold enough to look at either of them when I admitted, "Well, it was love at first sight."

The girl sighed. "That is just so romantic. Do me a

favour, and don't you two ever change. The world needs more love at first sight."

Sam's voice was husky. "Do you want some of those, Grace?"

Something in his voice, a catch, made me realize that my words had more of an effect than I'd intended. I wondered when the last time someone had told him they loved him was.

That was a really sad thing to think about.

I stood up and took Sam's hand again; his fingers gripped mine so hard it almost hurt. I said, "Those buttercreams look fantastic, actually. Can we get some of those?"

Sam nodded at the girl behind the counter. A few minutes later, I was clutching a small paper bag of sweets and Sam had whipped cream on the end of his nose. I pointed it out and he grimaced, embarrassed, wiping it off with his sleeve.

"I'm going to go start the car," I said, handing him the bag. He looked at me without saying anything, so I added, "To warm it up."

"Oh. Right. Good thinking."

I think he'd forgotten how cold it was outside. I hadn't, though, and I had a horrible picture in my head of him spasming in the car while I tried to get the heat higher. I left him in the store and headed out into the dark winter night.

It was weird how as soon as the door closed behind

me, I felt utterly alone, suddenly assaulted with the vastness of the night, lost without Sam's touch and scent to anchor me. Nothing here was familiar to me. If Sam became a wolf right now, I didn't know how long it would take me to find my way home or what I'd do with him – I wouldn't be able to just leave him here, miles of interstate away from his woods. I'd lose him in both his forms. The street was already dusted with white, and more snowflakes drifted down around me, delicate and ominous. As I unlocked the car door, my breath made ghostly shapes in front of me.

This increasing unease was unusual for me. I shivered and waited in the Bronco until it was warmed up, sipping my hot chocolate. Sam was right – the hot chocolate was amazing, and immediately I felt better. The little bit of mint shot my mouth through with cold at the same time that the chocolate filled it with warmth. It was soothing, too, and by the time the car was warm, I felt silly for imagining anything would go wrong tonight.

I jumped out of the Bronco and stuck my head in the candy shop, finding Sam where he lingered by the door. "It's ready."

Sam shuddered visibly when he felt the blast of cold air come in the door, and without a word, he bolted for the Bronco. I called a thanks to the counter girl before following Sam, but on the way to the car, I saw something on the pavement that made me pause. Beneath the scuffed footsteps Sam had made were another, older set that I hadn't noticed before, pacing back and forth through the new snow in front of the sweet shop.

My eyes followed their path as they crossed back and forth by the shop, steps long and light, and then I let my gaze follow them down the sidewalk. There was a dark pile about fifteen feet away, out of the bright circle of light of the street lamp. I hesitated, thinking, *Just get in the Bronco*, but then instinct pricked me, and I went to it.

It was a dark jacket, a pair of jeans and a turtleneck, and leading away from the clothing was a trail of pawprints through the light dusting of snow.

Forty-Four

Sam

0°C

It sounds stupid, but one of the things that I loved about Grace was how she didn't have to talk. Sometimes, I just wanted my silences to stay silent, full of thoughts, empty of words. Where another girl might have tried to lure me into conversation, Grace just reached for my hand, resting our knotted hands on my leg, and leaned her head against my shoulder until we were well out of Duluth. She didn't ask how I knew my way around the city, or why my eyes lingered on the road that my parents used to turn down to get to our neighbourhood, or how it was that a kid from Duluth ended up living in a wolf pack near the Canadian border.

And when she did finally speak, taking her hand off mine to retrieve a buttercream from the sweet shop bag, she told me about how, as a kid, she'd once made cookies with leftover boiled Easter eggs instead of raw ones. It was exactly what I wanted – beautiful distraction.

Until I heard the musical tone of a mobile phone, a descending collection of digital notes, coming from my pocket. For a second I couldn't think why a phone would be in my coat, and then I remembered Beck stuffing it into my hand while I stared past him. *Call me when you need me* was what he had said.

Funny how he had said *when*, not *if*.

"Is that a phone?" Grace's eyebrows drew down over her eyes. "You have a phone?"

Beautiful distraction crashed around me as I dug it out of my pocket. "I didn't," I said weakly. She kept looking at me, and the little bit of hurt in her eyes killed me. Shame coloured my cheeks. "I just got one," I said. The phone rang again, and I hit the ANSWER button. I didn't have to look at the screen to know who was calling.

"Where are you, Sam? It's cold." Beck's voice was full of the genuine concern that I'd always appreciated.

I was aware of Grace's eyes on me.

I didn't want his concern. "I'm fine."

Beck paused, and I imagined him dissecting the tone of my voice. "Sam, it's not so black-and-white. Try to understand. You won't even give me a chance to talk to you. When have I ever been wrong?"

"Now," I said, and hung up. I shoved the phone back in my pocket, half expecting it to ring again. I sort of hoped it would so that I could not answer.

Grace didn't ask me who it was. She didn't ask me to tell her what was said. I knew she was waiting for me to volunteer the information, and I knew I should, but I didn't want to. I just – I just couldn't bear the idea of her seeing Beck in that light. Or maybe I just couldn't bear the idea of *me* seeing him in that light.

I didn't say anything.

Grace swallowed before pulling out her own phone. "That reminds me, I should check for messages. Ha. As if my family would call."

She studied her mobile phone; its blue screen lit up the palm of her hand and cast a ghostly light on her chin.

"Did they?" I asked.

"Of course not. They're rubbing elbows with old friends." She punched in their number and waited. I heard a murmur on the other end of the phone, too quiet for me to make out. "Hi, it's me. Yeah. I'm fine. Oh. OK. I won't wait up then. Have fun. Bye." She slapped the phone shut, rolled her brown eyes towards me, and smiled wanly. "Let's elope."

"We'd have to drive to Vegas," I said. "No one around here to marry us at this hour except deer and a few drunk guys."

"It would have to be the deer," Grace said firmly. "The drunk guys would slur our names and that would ruin the moment."

"Somehow, having a deer preside over the ceremony of a werewolf and a girl seems oddly appropriate, anyway."

Grace laughed. "And it would get my parents'

attention. 'Mom, Dad, I've got married. Don't look at me like that. He only sheds part of the year.'"

I shook my head. I felt like telling her *thanks*, but instead, I said, "It was Beck on the phone."

"*The* Beck?"

"Yeah. He was in Canada with Salem – one of the wolves who's gone completely crazy." It was only part of the truth, but at least it was the truth.

"I want to meet him," Grace said immediately. My face must've gone funny, because she said, "Beck, I mean. He's practically your dad, isn't he?"

I rubbed my fingers over the steering wheel, eyes glancing from the road to my knuckles pressed into a white grip. Strange how some people took their skin for granted, never thought of what it would be like to lose it. *Sloughing my skin / escaping its grip / stripped of my wit / it hurts to be me.* I thought of the most fatherly memory I had of Beck. "We had this big grill at his house, and I remember, one night, he was tired of doing the cooking and he said, 'Sam, tonight you're feeding us.' He showed me how to push on the middle of the steaks to see how done they were, and how to sear them fast on each side to keep the juices in."

"And they were awesome, weren't they?"

"I burned the hell out of them," I said, matter-of-fact. "I'd compare them to charcoal, but charcoal is still sort of edible."

Grace started to laugh.

"Beck ate his," I said, smiling ruefully at the memory. "He said it was the best steak he'd ever had, because he hadn't had to make it."

That felt like a long time ago.

Grace was smiling at me, like old stories about me and my pack leader were the greatest thing in the world. Like it was inspirational. Like we had something, Beck and me, father and son.

In my head, the kid in the back of the Tahoe looked at me and said, "Help."

Grace asked, "How long has it been? I mean – not since the steaks. Since you were bitten."

"I was seven. Eleven years ago."

She asked, "Why were you in the woods? I mean, you're from Duluth, aren't you? Or at least that's what it said on your driver's licence."

"I wasn't attacked in the woods," I said. "It was all over the papers."

Grace's eyes held me; I looked away to the dim road in front of us.

"Two wolves attacked me while I was getting on to the school bus. One of them held me down, and the other one bit me." Ripped at me, really, as if its only goal had been to draw blood. But of course, that *had* been the goal, hadn't it? Looking back, it all seemed painfully clear. I'd never thought to look beyond my simple childhood memory of being attacked by wolves, and Beck stepping in as my saviour after my parents had tried to kill me. I had been so close to Beck, and Beck had been so above reproach, that I hadn't *wanted* to look any deeper. But now, retelling the story to Grace shoved the unavoidable truth right at me: my attack had been no accident. I'd been chosen, hunted down, and dragged into the street to be infected, just like those kids in the back of the Tahoe. Later Beck had arrived to pick up the pieces.

You're the best of them, Beck's voice said in my head. He had thought I'd outlive him and take over the pack. I should've been angry. Furious at having my life ripped away from me. But there was just white noise inside me, a dull hum of nothingness.

"In the city?" Grace asked.

"The suburbs. There weren't any woods around. Neighbours said they saw the wolves running through their back yards to escape afterwards."

Grace didn't say anything. The fact that I'd been deliberately hunted felt obvious to me, and I kept waiting for her to say it. I kind of wanted her to say it, to point out the unfairness. But she didn't. I just felt her frowning at me, thinking.

"Which wolves?" Grace asked finally.

"I don't remember. One of them might've been Paul, because one of them was black. That's all I know."

There was silence for several long moments, and then we were home. The driveway of the house still stood empty, and Grace blew out a long breath.

"Looks like we're on our own again," she said. "Stay here until I get the door unlocked, OK?"

Grace jumped out of the car, letting in a blast of cold air that bit my cheeks; I turned the heater up as high as it would go to prepare myself for the journey inside. Leaning on the vents, feeling the heat sting my skin, I squeezed my eyes shut, trying to will myself back into the distraction I had felt earlier. Back when I was holding Grace against me in the candy shop, feeling her warm body searing against mine, watching her smell the air, knowing she was smelling me – I shivered. I didn't know if I could stand another night with her, behaving myself.

"Sam!" called Grace from outside. I opened my eyes, focusing on her head poking out of the cracked front door. She was trying to keep the entryway as warm as possible for me. Clever.

Time to run. Shutting off the Bronco, I leaped out and bolted up the slick pavement, feet slipping a bit on the ice, my skin prickling and twisting.

Grace slammed the door shut behind me, locking the cold outside, and threw her arms around me, lending her heat to my body. Her voice was a breathless whisper near my ear. "Are you warm enough?"

My eyes, starting to adjust to the darkness in the hall, caught the glimmer of light in her eyes, the outline of her hair, the curve of her arms around me. A mirror on the wall offered a similarly dim portrait of the shape of her body against mine. I let her hold me for a long moment before I said, "I'm OK."

"Do you want anything to eat?" Her voice sounded loud in the empty house, echoing off the wood floor. The only other sound was the air through the heating vents, a steady, low breath. I was acutely aware that we were alone.

I swallowed. "I want to go to bed."

She sounded relieved. "I do, too."

I almost regretted that she agreed with me, because maybe if I'd stayed up, eaten a sandwich, watched TV, something, I could've distracted myself from how badly I wanted her.

But she hadn't disagreed. Kicking off her shoes behind the door, she padded down the hallway in front of me. We slipped into her dark bedroom, no light but the moon reflecting off the thin layer of snow outside the window. The door closed with a soft sigh and *snick* and she leaned on it, her hands still on the doorknob behind her. A long moment passed before she said anything. "Why are you so careful with me, Sam Roth?"

I tried to tell her the truth. "I – it's – I'm not an animal."

"I'm not afraid of you," she said.

She didn't look afraid of me. She looked beautiful, moonlit, tempting, smelling of peppermint and soap and skin. I'd spent eleven years watching the rest of the pack become animals, pushing down my instincts, controlling myself, fighting to stay human, fighting to do the right thing.

As if reading my thoughts, she said, "Can you tell me it's only the wolf in you that wants to kiss me?"

All of me wanted to kiss her hard enough to make me disappear. I braced my arms on either side of her head, the door giving out a creak as I leaned against it, and I pressed my mouth against hers. She kissed me back, lips hot, tongue flicking against my teeth, hands still behind her, body still pressed against the door. Everything in me buzzed, electric, wanting to close the few centimetres of space between us.

She kissed me harder, breath huffing into my mouth, and bit my lower lip. Oh, hell, that was amazing. I growled before I could stop myself, but before I could even think to feel embarrassed, Grace had pulled her hands out from behind her and looped them around my neck, pulling me to her.

"That was so sexy," she said, voice uneven. "I didn't think you could get any sexier."

I kissed her again before she could say anything else, backing into the room with her, a tangle of arms in the moonlight. Her fingers hooked into the back of my jeans, thumbs brushing my hip bones, pulling me even closer to her.

"Oh, God, Grace," I gasped. "You – you greatly overestimate my self-control."

"I'm not looking for self-control."

My hands were inside her shirt, palms pressed on her back, fingers spread on her sides; I didn't even remember how they got there. "I – I don't want to do anything you'll regret."

Grace's back curved against my fingers as if my touch brought her to life. "Then don't stop."

I'd imagined her saying this in so many different ways, but none of my fantasies had come close to the breathless reality.

Clumsily, we backed on to her bed, part of me thinking we should be quiet in case her parents came home. But she helped me tug my shirt over my head and ran a hand down my chest, and I groaned, forgetting everything but her fingers on my skin. My mind searched for lyrics, words to string together to describe the moment, but nothing came. I couldn't think of anything but her palm grazing my skin.

"You smell so good," Grace whispered. "Every time I touch you, it comes off you even stronger." Her nostrils flared, all wolf, smelling how much I wanted her. Knowing what I was, and wanting me, anyway.

She let me push her gently down on to the pillows and I braced my arms on either side of her, straddling her in my jeans.

"Are you sure?" I asked.

Her eyes were bright, excited. She nodded.

I slid down to kiss her belly; it felt so right, so natural, like I'd done it a thousand times before and would do it a thousand times again.

I saw the shiny, ugly scars the pack had left on her neck and collarbone, and I kissed them, too.

Grace pulled the blankets up over us and we kicked off our clothes beneath them. As we pressed our bodies against each other, I shrugged off my skin with a growl, giving in, neither wolf nor man, just Sam.

Forty-Five
Grace

-1°C

The phone was ringing. That was the first thing I thought. The second thing I thought was that Sam's bare arm was lying across my chest. The third thing was that my face was cold where it was sticking out from under the blankets. I blinked, trying to wake up, strangely disoriented in my own room. It took me a moment to realize that my alarm clock's normally glowing face was dark and that the only lights in the room were coming from the moon outside the window and the face of the ringing mobile phone.

I snaked a hand out into the air to retrieve it, careful not to disturb Sam's arm on me; the phone was silent by the time I got to it. God, it was freezing in here. The power must've gone down with the ice storm the forecasters had promised. I wondered how long it would be down and if I'd have to worry about Sam getting too cold. I carefully peeled back the covers and found him curled against me, head buried against my side, only the pale, naked curve of his shoulders visible in the dim light.

I kept waiting for this to feel wrong, his body pressed up against mine, but I just felt so alive that my heart hammered with the thrill of it. This, Sam and me, this was my real life. The life where I went to school and waited up for my parents and listened to Rachel vent about her siblings – that felt like a pale dream in comparison. Those were just things I had done while waiting for Sam. Outside, distant and mournful, wolves began to howl, and a few seconds later, the phone rang again, notes stepping down the scale, a strange, digital echo of the wolves.

I didn't realize my mistake until I held it to my ear.

"Sam." The voice at the other end was unfamiliar. Stupid me. I had taken Sam's phone from the nightstand, not mine. I debated for two seconds how to respond. I contemplated snapping the phone shut, but I couldn't do that.

"No," I replied. "Not Sam."

The voice was pleasant, but I heard an edge beneath his words. "I'm sorry. I must've dialled wrong."

"No," I said, before he could hang up. "This is Sam's phone."

There was a long, heavy pause, and then: "Oh." Another pause. "You're the girl, aren't you? The girl who was in my house?"

I tried to think of what I might gain by denying it and drew a blank. "Yes."

"Do you have a name?"

"Do you?"

He gave a short laugh that was completely without humour but not unpleasant. "I think I like you. I'm Beck."

"That makes sense." I turned my face away from Sam, who was still breathing heavily, my voice muffled by his arms over his head. "What did you do to piss him off?"

Again the short laugh. "He's still angry with me?"

I considered how to answer. "Not now. He's sleeping. Can I give him a message?" I stared at Beck's number on the phone, trying to remember it.

There was another long pause, so long that I thought Beck had hung up, and then he breathed out audibly. "One of his . . . friends has been hurt. Do you think you could wake him?"

One of the other wolves. It had to be. I ducked down into the covers. "Oh – of course. Of course I will."

I put the phone down and gently moved Sam's arm so that I could see his ear and the side of his face. "Sam, wake up. Phone. It's important."

He turned his head so that I could see that his yellow eye was already open. "Put it on speaker."

I did, resting it on my belly so that the camera's face lit a small blue circle on my vest top.

"What's going on?" Sam slid up on to one elbow, made a face when he felt the cold, and jerked the blankets up around us, making a tent around the phone.

"Someone attacked Paul. He's a mess, ripped to shreds."

Sam's mouth made a little *o*. I don't think he was thinking about what his face looked like – his eyes were far away, with his pack. Finally, he said, "Could you – have you – is he still bleeding? Was he human?"

"Human. I tried to ask him who did it – so I could kill them. I thought . . . Sam, I really thought I was going to be calling you to tell you he died. It was that bad. But I think it's closing up now. But the thing is, it was all these little bites, all over, on his neck and on his wrists and his belly, it was as if—"

"—as if someone knew how to kill him," Sam finished.

"It was a wolf who did it," Beck said. "We got that much out of him."

"One of your new ones?" Sam snarled, with surprising force.

"Sam."

"Could it have been?"

"Sam. No. They're inside."

Sam's body was still tense beside me, and I mulled over possible meanings for that phrase: *One of your new ones.* Was Jack not the only new one?

"Will you come?" Beck asked. "Can you? Is it too cold?"

"I don't know." I knew from the twist of Sam's

mouth that he was only answering the first question. Whatever it was that had distanced him from Beck, it was powerful.

Beck's voice changed, softer, younger, more vulnerable. "Please don't be angry with me still, Sam. I can't stand it."

Sam turned his face away from the phone.

"Sam," Beck said softly.

I felt Sam shudder next to me, and he closed his eyes.

"Are you still there?"

I looked at Sam, but he still didn't speak. I couldn't help it – I felt sorry for Beck. "I am," I said.

There was a long pause, completely devoid of static or crackling, and I thought Beck had hung up. But then he asked, in a careful way, "How much do you know about Sam, girl-without-a-name?"

"Everything."

Pause. Then: "I'd like to meet you."

Sam reached out and snapped the phone shut. The light of the display vanished, leaving us in the dark beneath the covers.

Forty-Six
Grace

7°C

My parents didn't even know. The morning after Sam and I – spent the night together, it seemed like the biggest thing on my mind was that my parents had no idea. I guessed that was normal. I guessed feeling a little guilty was normal. I guessed feeling giddy was normal. It was as if I had thought all along I was a complete picture, and Sam had revealed that I was a puzzle, and had taken me apart into pieces and put me back together again. I was acutely aware of each distinct emotion, all fitting together tightly.

Sam was quiet, too, letting me drive, holding my right hand in both of his while I drove with the other. I would've given a million dollars to know what he was thinking.

"What do you want to do this afternoon?" I asked, finally.

He looked out of the window, fingers rubbing the back of my hand. The world outside looked dry, papery. Waiting for snow. "Anything with you."

"Anything?"

He looked over at me and grinned. It was a funny, lopsided grin. I think maybe he was feeling as giddy as I was. "Yes, anything, as long as you're there."

"I want to meet Beck," I said.

There. It was out. It had been one of the puzzle pieces stuck in my head ever since I'd picked up the phone.

Sam didn't say anything. His eyes were on the school, probably figuring that if he waited just a few minutes, he could deposit me on the pavement and avoid discussion. But instead he sighed as if he was incredibly tired. "God, Grace. Why?"

"He's practically your father, Sam. I want to know everything about you. It can't be that hard to understand."

"You just want everything in its place." Sam's eyes followed the knots of students slowly making their way across the car park. I avoided finding a parking place. "You just want to perform magical matchmaking on me and him, so that you can feel like everything's in its place again."

"If you're trying to irritate me by saying that, you won't. I already know it's true."

Sam was silent while I circled the car park another time, and finally, he groaned. "Grace, I hate this. I hate confrontation."

"There won't be confrontation. He wants to see you."

"You don't know everything that's going on. There's *awful* stuff going on. There'll be confrontation, if I have any principles left. Hard to imagine after last night."

I found a parking place in a hurry, one on the furthest end of the car park so that I could face him without curious eyes watching us on the way to the pavement. "Are you feeling guilty?"

"No. Maybe. A little. I feel ... uneasy."

"We used protection," I said.

Sam didn't look at me. "Not that. I just – I just – I just hope it was the right time."

"It was the right time."

He looked away. "Only thing I wonder, is ... did you have s – make love – to me to get back at your parents?"

I just stared at him. Then I grabbed my backpack from the back seat. I was suddenly furious, ears and cheeks hot, and I didn't know why. I didn't recognize my voice when I answered. "That's a nice thing to say."

Sam didn't look back at me. It was like the side of the school was fascinating to him. So fascinating he couldn't look me in the eyes while he accused me of using him. A new wave of anger washed over me.

"Do you have such crap self-esteem that you think I wouldn't want you just for you?" I pushed open the door and slid out; Sam winced at the air that came in, though it couldn't have been cold enough to hurt him. "Way to ruin it. Just – way to ruin it."

I started to slam the door, but he reached far across the seat to keep the door from shutting all the way. "Wait. Grace, wait."

"*What?*"

"I don't want to let you go like this." His eyes were pleading with me, their absolute saddest. I looked at the goosebumps raising on his arms, and the slight tremble of his shoulders in the cold draught. And he had me. No matter how angry I was, we both knew what could happen while I was in school. I hated that. The fear. I hated it.

"I'm sorry I said it," Sam blurted out, rushing to get out words before I left. "You're right. I just couldn't believe something – someone – so good could happen to me. Don't leave mad, Grace. Please don't leave mad."

I closed my eyes. For a brief moment I wished with all my heart that he was just a normal boy, so that I could storm away with my pride and indignation. But he wasn't. He was as fragile as a butterfly in autumn, waiting to be destroyed by the first frost. So I swallowed my anger, a bitter mouthful, and opened the door a bit more. "I don't want you to ever think something like that again, Sam Roth."

He closed his eyes just a little bit when I said his name, lashes hiding his yellow irises for a second, and then he reached out and touched my cheek. "I'm sorry."

I caught his hand and tangled his fingers in mine, fixing my gaze on his face. "How do you think Beck would feel if you went away mad?"

Sam laughed, a humourless, self-deprecating laugh that reminded me of Beck's on the phone the night before, and dropped his eyes from mine. He knew I had his number. He pulled his fingers away. "We'll go. Fine, we'll go."

I was about to leave, but I stopped. "Why are you angry at Beck, Sam? Why are you so mad at him when I've never seen you angry at your real parents?"

Sam's face told me he hadn't asked himself this question before, and it took him a long time to answer. "Because Beck – Beck didn't have to do what he did. My parents did. They thought I was a monster. They were afraid. It wasn't calculated."

His face was full of pain and uncertainty. I stepped up into the car and kissed him gently. I didn't know what to say to him, so I just kissed him again, got my backpack, and went into the grey day.

When I looked back over my shoulder, he was still sitting there, gaze silent and lupine. The last thing I saw was his eyes half-closed against the breeze, black hair tousled, reminding me for some reason of the first night I'd ever seen him.

An unexpected breeze lifted my hair from my neck, frigid and penetrating.

Winter suddenly felt very close. I stopped on the

pavement, closing my eyes, fighting the incredible desire to go back to Sam. In the end, duty won out, and I headed into the school. But it felt like a mistake.

Forty-Seven

Sam

6°C

After Grace got out of the car, I felt sick. Sick from arguing with her, sick from doubt, sick from the cold that was just warm enough to keep me human. More than sick – restless, unsettled. Too many loose ends: Jack, Isabel, Olivia, Shelby, Beck.

I couldn't believe that Grace and I were going to see Beck. I turned up the heat in the Bronco and rested my head on the steering wheel for several long moments, until the ridged vinyl started to hurt my forehead. With the heat turned up all the way, it didn't take too long for the car to become stuffy and hot, but it felt good. It felt far away from changing. Like I was firmly in my own skin.

I thought at first that I might just sit like that all day, singing a song under my breath – *Close to the sun is closer to me / I feel my skin clinging so tightly* – and waiting for Grace, but it only took me a half-hour of sitting to decide that I needed to drive. More than that, I needed to atone for what I'd said to Grace. So I decided to go to Jack's house again. He still hadn't turned up, either dead or in the newspapers, and it was the only place I could think of starting the search again. Grace would be happy to see me trying to put everything into place for her.

I left the Bronco on an isolated logging road near the Culpepers' house and cut through the woods. The pines were colourless with the promise of snow, their tips waving slightly in a cold wind that I couldn't feel down below the branches. The hair on the back of my neck tingled uncomfortably; the stark pine woods reeked of wolf. It smelled like the kid had peed on every tree. Cocky bastard.

Movement to my right made me jump, tense, drop low to the ground. I held in a breath.

Just a deer. I caught a brief glimpse of wide eyes, long legs, white tail, before she was gone, surprisingly ungraceful in the underbrush. Her presence in the woods was comforting, though; her being here meant that Jack wasn't. I had nothing as a weapon except my hands. Fat lot of good they would do against an unstable new wolf with adrenaline on his side.

Near the house, I froze at the edge of the woods, listening to the voices carrying through the trees. A girl and a boy, voices raised and angry, standing somewhere near the back door. Creeping into the shadow of the mansion, I slid around a corner towards them, silent as a wolf. I didn't recognize the male voice, fierce and deep, but instinct told me that it was Jack. The other one was

Isabel. I thought about revealing myself but hesitated, waiting to hear what the argument was about.

Isabel's voice was high. "I don't understand what you're saying. What are you saying sorry for? For disappearing? For getting bitten in the first place? For—"

"For Chloe," the boy said.

There was a pause. "What do you mean, 'for Chloe'? What does the dog have to do with all this? Do you know where she is?"

"Isabel. Hell. Haven't you been listening? You're so stupid sometimes. I told you, I don't know what I'm doing after I've changed."

I covered my mouth to keep from laughing. Jack had eaten her dog.

"Are you saying that she's – you – God! You're such a jerk!"

"I couldn't help it. I told you what I was. You shouldn't have let her out."

"Do you have any idea how much that dog cost?"

"Boo hoo."

"So what am I supposed to tell the parental units? Mom, Dad, Jack's a werewolf, and guess what, you know how Chloe's been missing? He ate her."

"Don't tell them anything!" Jack said hurriedly. "Anyway, I think I've stopped it. I think I've found a cure."

I frowned.

"Cure." Isabel's voice was flat. "How do you 'fix' being a werewolf?"

"Don't you worry your blonde brain about it. I just – give me a few more days to make sure. When I'm sure, I'll tell them everything."

"Fine. Whatever. God – I can't believe you ate Chloe."

"Can you please shut up about that? You're starting to irritate me."

"Whatever. What about the other ones? Aren't there other ones? Can't you get them to help you?"

"Isabel, shut *up*. I told you, I think I've figured it out. I don't *need* any help."

"Don't you just think—"

A noise, sharp and out of place. A branch snapping? A slap?

Isabel's voice sounded different when she spoke again. Not as strong. "Just don't let them see you, OK? Mom's at therapy – because of *you* – and Dad's out of town. I'm going back to school. I can't believe you called me out here to tell me you ate my dog."

"I called you to tell you I fixed it. You seem so excited. Yeah. Not."

"It's great. Wonderful. Bye."

Barely a moment later, I heard Isabel's SUV tear down the driveway, and I hesitated again. I wasn't exactly eager to reveal myself to a new wolf with an anger management problem until I knew exactly what my surroundings were, but I needed to either get back to the car or into the warmth of the house. And the house was closer. I slowly crept around the back of the building, listening for Jack's position. Nothing. He must've gone inside.

I approached the door I had broken into earlier that week – the window had already been fixed – and tried the knob. Unlocked. How thoughtful.

Inside, I immediately heard Jack rummaging around, loud in the otherwise still house, and I slunk down the dim hallway to a long, high-ceilinged kitchen, all black-and-white tiles and black countertops as far as the eye could see. The light through the two windows on the right wall was white and pure, reflecting off white walls and sinking into the black skillets hanging from the ceiling. It was as if the entire room were in black and white.

I vastly preferred Grace's kitchen – warm, cluttered, smelling of cinnamon and garlic and bread – to this cavernous, sterile room.

Jack had his back to me as he crouched in front of the stainless steel fridge, digging through the drawers. I froze, but his hunt through the fridge had covered up the sound of my approach. There was no wind to carry my scent to him, so I stood for a long minute, assessing him and my options. He was tall, wide-shouldered, with curly black hair, like a Greek statue. Something about the way he carried himself suggested overconfidence, and for some reason, that irritated me. I swallowed a growl and slid just inside the door, silently lifting myself on to the counter opposite. Height would give me a slight advantage, if Jack got aggressive.

He stepped away from the fridge and dumped an armload of food on to the shiny-topped kitchen island. For several long minutes, I watched him construct a sandwich. He carefully layered the meats and the cheeses, slathered the bread with Miracle Whip, and then he looked up.

"Jesus," he said.

"Hi," I replied.

"What do you want?" He didn't look afraid; I wasn't big enough to frighten by looks alone.

I didn't know how to answer him. Hearing his conversation with Isabel had changed what I wanted to know. "So what is it you think will cure you?"

Now he looked afraid. Just for a second, and then it was gone, lost in the self-assured set of his chin. "What are you talking about?"

"You think you've found a cure. Why would you think that?"

"OK, dude. Who are you?"

I really didn't like him. I didn't know why; I just felt it in my gut and I really didn't like him. If I hadn't thought he was a danger to Grace and Olivia and Isabel, I would've said the hell with him and left him there. Still, my dislike made it easier to confront him. It made it easier to play the role of the guy who had all the answers. "Someone like you. Someone who got bitten." He looked about to protest, and I held up my hand to stop him. "If you're thinking you're going to say something like 'You've got the wrong guy', don't bother. I've seen you as a wolf. So just tell me why you think you've found a way to stop it."

"Why should I trust you?"

"Because, unlike your father, I don't stuff animals and put them in my hall. And because I don't really want you showing up at the school and on people's doorsteps and exposing the pack. We're just trying to survive with the crappy lot we've been given. We don't need some smarmy rich punk like you revealing us to the rest of the world, so they can come after us with pitchforks."

Jack growled. It was a little too close to animal for my taste, and my thought was confirmed when I saw him shiver slightly. He was still so unstable – he could change at any time. "I don't have to worry about it any more. I'm getting a cure, so you can get the hell away from here and leave me alone." He backed away from the island, towards the counter behind him.

I jumped down from my counter. "Jack, there is no cure."

"You're wrong," he snapped. "There's another wolf that was cured."

He was edging towards the knife block. I should've run for the door, but his words froze me. "What?"

"Yeah, it took me all this time, but I figured it out. There's a girl who was bitten and got cured, at school. Grace. I know she knows the cure. And she's about to tell me in a hurry."

My world reeled. "Stay away from her."

Jack grinned at me, or maybe it was a grimace. His hand was on the counter, feeling backwards towards the knives, and his nostrils flared, taking in the faint odour of wolf that the cold had brought to my skin. He said, "Why? Don't you want to know, too? Or has she already cured you?"

"There *is no cure*. She doesn't know anything." I hated how much my voice revealed; my feelings for Grace felt dangerously transparent.

"You don't know that, man," Jack said. He reached for a knife, but his hand was shaking too much to grasp the handle on the first try. "Now get out of here."

But I didn't move. I couldn't think of anything worse than him confronting Grace about a cure. Him trembling, unstable, violent; and her, unable to give him the answers he was looking for.

Jack managed to grab a handle and pulled out a wicked-looking knife, the edge serrated and reflecting the black and white of the kitchen in a dozen different directions. He was shaking so badly that he could barely hold the blade towards me. "I asked you to get out."

My instincts urged me to leap on him like I would on one of the wolves, growl over his neck and make him submit. To make him promise to stay away from her. But that wasn't how it worked when you were a human, not when your adversary was so much stronger. I approached him, eyes on his eyes instead of on the knife, and tried a different tactic. "Jack. Please. She doesn't have the answer, but I can make this easier for you."

"Get away from me." Jack took a step towards me, then back, before stumbling to one knee. The knife fell on to the tiles; I winced before it landed, but its landing was surprisingly muffled. Jack made almost no sound at all when he followed the knife to the floor. His fingers were claws, curling and uncurling on the black-and-white squares. He was saying something, but it was unintelligible. Lyrics formed in my head. They were supposed to be for him, but they were really about me. *World of words lost on the living / I take my place with the walking dead / Robbed of my voice I'm always giving / thousands of words to this nameless dread.*

I crouched next to him, pushing the knife away from his body so that he wouldn't hurt himself on it. There was no point asking him anything now. I sighed and listened to him groan, wail, scream. We were equals now, me and Jack. For all his privilege and nice hair and confident shoulders, he was no better than me.

Jack whimpered.

"You should be happy," I told the panting wolf. "You didn't throw up this time."

Jack regarded me for a long moment with unblinking hazel eyes before leaping up and bolting for the door.

I wanted to just leave, but I didn't have any choice. Any possibility of leaving him behind had disappeared as soon as he'd said Grace's name.

I jumped after him. We scrambled through the house, his nails slipping on the hardwood floor and my shoes squeaking behind him. I pelted into the hall of grinning animals close behind him; the stench of their dead skins filled my nostrils. Jack had two advantages: he knew the house and he was a wolf. I was betting on him using the well-known surroundings to hide instead of relying on his unfamiliar animal strength.

I bet wrong.

Forty-Eight
Grace

9°C

Sam had never been late before. He had always been waiting in the Bronco by the time I got out of class, so I'd never had to wonder where he might be or what to do while I waited.

But today I waited.

Today I waited until the students loaded on to the buses. I waited until the lingering students headed out to their cars and disappeared in ones and twos. I waited until the teachers emerged from the school and climbed into their cars. I thought about taking my homework out. I thought about the sun creeping down towards the tree line and I wondered how cold it was in the shade.

"Your ride late, Grace?" Mr Rink asked kindly, on his way out. He had changed shirts since class and smelled vaguely like cologne.

I must've looked lost, sitting on the brick edge of the little mulched area in front of the school, hugging my backpack in my lap. "A little."

"Do you need me to call someone?"

Out of the corner of my eye, I saw the Bronco pull

into the lot, and I allowed myself a long breath. I smiled at Mr Rink. "Nope. They just showed up."

"Good thing, too," he said. "It's supposed to get really cold later. Snow!"

"Yippee," I said sourly, and he laughed and waved as he walked out to his car. I yanked my backpack on to my shoulder and hurried out to the Bronco. Pulling open the passenger-side door, I jumped in.

It was only a second after I'd shut the door that I realized that the smell was all wrong. I lifted my eyes to the driver and crossed my arms over my chest, trembling.

"Where's Sam?"

"You mean the guy who's supposed to be sitting here," Jack said.

Even though I'd seen his eyes peering out of a wolf's body, even though I'd heard Isabel say she'd seen him, even though we'd known he was alive for weeks, I wasn't prepared for seeing Jack in the flesh. His curly black hair, longer than when I'd last seen him in the halls, his darting hazel eyes, his hands clinging to the steering wheel. Real. Alive. My heart kicked in my chest.

Jack's eyes were on the road as he tore out of the car park. I imagined he thought I wouldn't try to get away if the Bronco was moving, but he didn't have to worry. I was fixed in place by the unknown: where was Sam?

"Yes, I mean the guy who's supposed to be sitting there." My voice came out as a snarl. "Where is he?"

Jack glanced over at me; he was nervy, shaking. What was the word Sam had used to describe new wolves? Unstable? "I'm not trying to be the bad guy here, Grace. But I need answers, and soon, or I'm going to get bad really fast."

"You're driving like an idiot. If you don't want to get pulled over by the cops, you'd better slow down. Where are we going?"

"I don't know. You tell me. I want to know how to stop this and I want to know *now* because it's getting worse."

I didn't know whether he meant it was getting worse as the weather got colder, or worse right this second. "I'm not telling you anything until you take me to wherever Sam is." Jack didn't answer. I said, "I'm not playing around. Where is he?"

Jack jerked his head towards me. "I don't think you get it. I'm the one driving and I'm the one who knows where he is and I'm the one who can *rip your head off* if I change, so it seems to me you're the one who ought to start pissing herself and telling me what I want to know."

His hands were clamped on the steering wheel, bracing arms that were shuddering. God, he was going to change soon. I had to think of something to get him off the road.

"What do you want to know?"

"How to stop it. I know you know the cure. I know you were bitten."

"Jack, I don't know how to stop it. I can't cure you."

"Yeah, I thought you'd say that. That's why I bit your stupid friend. Because if you won't fight to cure me, I know you'll do it for her. I just had to make sure she was really going to change."

The staggering sense of it stole my breath; I could barely get my voice out. "You bit Olivia?"

"Are you an idiot? I just said that. So now you'd better start talking because I'm going to *ahh*." Jack's neck jerked, wrenching awkwardly. My wolf senses screamed *danger fear terror anger* at me, emotions rolling off him in waves.

I reached out and spun the heating dial up. I didn't know how much of a difference it would make, but it couldn't hurt.

"It's the cold. The cold changes you to a wolf and the heat stops it." I was talking quickly, trying to keep him from getting a word in, trying to keep him from getting any angrier. "It's worse when you first get bitten. You change back and forth all the time, but it gets more stable. You get to be human for longer – you'll get the whole summer—" Jack's arms spasmed again, and the car fishtailed in the gravel of the shoulder before tracking back on to the road. "You can't be driving right now!

Please. I'm not going to run away or whatever – I want to help you, really I do. But you've got to take me to Sam."

"Shut up." Jack's voice was part growl. "That bitch said she wanted to help me, too. I'm done with that. She told me you were bitten and that you didn't change. I followed you. It was cold. You didn't change. So what is it? Olivia said she didn't know."

My skin was burning from the blasting heater and the force of his emotion. Every time he said *Olivia* it was like a punch in the gut. "She *doesn't* know. I was bitten, she was right. But I never changed, not even once. I don't have a cure. I just didn't change. I don't know why, nobody knows why. Please—"

"*Stop lying to me.*" It was hard to understand him now. "I want the truth *now* or you're going to get hurt."

I closed my eyes. I felt like I had lost my balance and the whole world was spinning away from me. There had to be something I could say to him that would make this better. I opened my eyes. "Fine. OK. There's a cure. But there's not enough of it for everyone, so nobody wanted to tell you about it." I winced as he smacked the steering wheel with dark-nailed fingers. My mind's eye whirled away from the alien reality to an image of the nurse sliding the syringe with the rabies shot into Sam's skin. "It's a vaccination, sort of, it goes right in your veins. But it hurts. A lot. Are you sure you want it?"

"*This hurts,*" snarled Jack.

"Fine. If I take you to where it is, will you tell me where Sam is?"

"Whatever! Tell me where to go. So help me God, if you're lying, I'll kill you."

I gave him directions to Beck's and prayed he'd make it that far. I retrieved my phone from my backpack.

The Bronco swerved as Jack's attention focused on me. "What are you doing?"

"I'm calling Beck. He's the guy with the cure. I have to tell him not to give the last of it away before we get there. Is that all right?"

"You seriously had better not be lying to me..."

"Look. This is the number I'm dialling. Not the police." Beck's number came back to me; I was better at numbers than words. It began to ring. *Pick up. Pick up. Let this be the right decision.*

"Hello?"

I recognized the voice. "Hi. Beck, this is Grace."

"Grace? Sorry, your voice sounds familiar, but I—"

I talked over the top of him. "Do you still have some of the stuff? The cure? Please tell me you didn't use the last of it."

Beck was silent.

I pretended like he'd answered. "Thank goodness. Look. Jack Culpeper has me in the car. He has Sam somewhere and he won't tell me where he is unless he gets some of the cure. We're, like, ten minutes away."

Beck said, very softly, "Damn."

For some reason, that made my chest shake; it took me a moment to realize it was a swallowed sob. "Yes. So will you be there?"

"Yes. Of course. Grace – you still there? Can he hear me?"

"No."

"Be confident, OK? Try not to be afraid. Don't look him in the eyes, but be assertive. We'll be waiting at the house. Get him inside. I can't come out or I'll change and then we're all screwed."

"What's he saying?" Jack demanded.

"He's telling me what door you should come in when you get there. To get you in the fastest, so you won't change. He can't use the cure on you if you're a wolf."

"Good girl," Beck said.

For some reason, Beck's unexpected kindness was hard to bear – it made tears prick my eyes where Jack's threats hadn't.

"We'll be there soon." I snapped the phone shut and looked at Jack. Not right at his eyes, but at the side of his head. "Pull straight into the driveway and they'll have the front door unlocked."

"How do I know I can trust you?"

I shrugged. "It's like you said. You know where Sam is. Nothing's going to happen to you, because we have to know where he is."

Forty-Nine
Sam

4°C

Cold clung to my skin. Earthy darkness pressed against my eyes, so heavy that I blinked to clear it from my irises. When I did, I saw a dull white rectangle in front of me – the crack of a door. Without any other shapes to gauge by, I couldn't tell if it was desperately close or horribly far away. Smells crowded around me, dusty, organic, chemical. My breathing was loud in my ears, so wherever I was had to be small. A tool shed? A crawl space?

Crap. It was *cold*. Not cold enough for me to change, not yet. But it would be soon. I was lying down – why was I lying down? I staggered to my feet and bit my lip, hard, to keep from gasping aloud. There was something wrong with my ankle. I tried it again, carefully, a fragile fawn on new legs, and it gave underneath me. I crashed sideways, arms wheeling, feeling for some kind of support. My palms raked across a legion of spiked instruments of torture hung on the walls. I had no idea what they were – cold, metallic, dirty.

For a moment I stayed on all fours, listening to my

breathing, feeling blood well on my palms, and thinking about giving up. I was so tired of fighting. It felt like I'd been fighting for weeks.

Finally, I pulled myself back up and limped to the door, arms stretched out in front of me to protect my unarmoured body from more surprises. Icy air seeped in through the crack in the door. Trickled into my body like water. I reached for a handle, but there was nothing but ragged wood. A splinter stuck into my fingers and I swore, very quietly. Then I leaned my shoulder into the door and pushed, thinking, *Please open please if there's any justice in this world*.

Nothing.

Fifty
Grace

4°C

I picked up my backpack. "This is it."

It seemed stupid, somehow, for Beck's house to look exactly the same as when Sam had brought me here to walk me to the golden wood, because the circumstances were so wildly different, but it did. The only difference was Beck's hulking SUV in the driveway.

Jack was already pulling to the side of the road. He took the keys out of the ignition and looked at me, eyes wary. "Get out after I do." I did as he said, waiting for him to come around and pull the door open. I slid out of the seat and he grabbed my arm tightly. His shoulders were thrust too far together and his mouth hung slightly open – I don't think he even noticed. I guess I should've worried about him attacking me, but all I could think was, *He's going to change and we won't know where Sam is until too late.*

I prayed Sam was somewhere warm, somewhere out of winter's reach.

"Hurry up," I said, tugging my arm against Jack's

grip, almost jogging towards the front door. "We don't have any time."

Jack tried the front door; it was unlocked, as promised, and he shoved me in first before slamming the door behind us. My nose caught a brief hint of rosemary in the air – someone had been cooking, and for some reason, I remembered Sam's anecdote about cooking the steaks for Beck – and then I heard a shout and a snarl from behind me.

Both sounds came from Jack. This wasn't the silent struggle of Sam trying to stay human that I'd seen before. This was violent, angry, loud. Jack's lips tore into a snarl and then his face ripped into a muzzle, his skin changing colour in an instant. He reached for me as if to hit me, but his hands buckled into paws, nails hard and dark. His skin bulged and shimmered for a moment before each radical change, like a placenta covering a terrifying, feral infant.

I stared at the shirt that hung around the wolf's midsection. I couldn't look away. It was the only detail that could convince my mind that this animal really had just been Jack.

This Jack was as angry as he had been in the car, but now his anger had no direction, no human control. His lips pulled back from his teeth and formed a snarl, but no sound appeared.

"Stand back!"

A man tore into the hall, surprisingly agile given his

height, and ran directly at Jack. Jack, off guard, crouched down defensively, and the man landed on the wolf with all his weight.

"Get down!" snarled the man, and I flinched before I realized that he was talking to the wolf. "Stay down. This is *my* house. You are *nothing* here." He had a hand around Jack's muzzle and was shouting right into his face. Jack whistled through his clenched jaw, and Beck forced his head to the ground. Beck's eyes flitted up at me, and though he was holding a huge wolf to the ground with one hand, his voice was perfectly level. "Grace? Can you help?"

I'd been standing perfectly still, watching. "Yes."

"Grab the edge of the rug he's sitting on. We're going to drag him to the bathroom. It's—"

"I know where it is."

"Good. Let's go. I'll try to help, but I have to keep my weight on him."

Together, we pulled Jack down the hall and to the bathroom where I'd forced Sam into the bathtub. Beck, half on the rug and half off, got behind Jack and shoved him into the room, and I kicked the rest of the rug in after him. Beck leaped back and slammed the door, locking it. The doorknob had been reversed so that the lock was on the outside, making me wonder how often this sort of thing had happened before.

Beck heaved a deep breath, which seemed like an

understatement, and looked at me. "Are you all right? Did he bite you?"

I shook my head, miserable. "That doesn't matter, anyway. How are we going to find Sam now?"

Beck jerked his head for me to follow him into the rosemary-scented kitchen. I did, looking up warily when I saw another person sitting on the counter. I wouldn't have been able to describe him as anything other than *dark* if anyone had asked me later. He was just dark and still and silent, and smelled of wolf. He had new-looking scars on his hands; it had to be Paul. He didn't say anything, and Beck didn't say anything to him as Beck leaned against the counter and picked up a mobile phone.

He punched in a number and put it on speakerphone. He looked at me. "How angry is he with me? Did he get rid of his mobile phone?"

"I don't think so. I didn't know the number."

Beck stared at the phone and we listened to it ring, small and distant. *Please pick up.* My heart was skipping uncontrollably. I leaned on the kitchen island and looked at Beck, at the square set of his shoulders, the square set of his jaw, the square line of eyebrows. Everything about him looked safe, honest, secure. I wanted to trust him. I wanted to believe that nothing bad could happen because Beck wasn't panicking.

There was a crackle at the other end of the line.

"Sam?" Beck leaned close into the phone.

The voice was badly broken up. "Gr – t? . . . you?"

"It's Beck. Where are you?"

"—ack. Grace. . . Jack to – co." The only thing I could understand was his distress. I wanted to be there, wherever he was.

"Grace is here," Beck said. "It's under control. Where are you? Are you safe?"

"*Cold.*"

The one word came through, terribly clear. I pushed off from the island. Standing still didn't seem to be an option.

Beck's voice was still even. "You aren't coming through very well. Try again. Tell me where you are. Clearly as you can."

"Tell Grace . . . call I – bel . . . in . . . shed some . . . re. I heard . . . ago."

I came back to the counter, leaned over the island. "You want me to call Isabel. You're in a shed on their property? She's there?"

"—es." Sam's voice was emphatic. "Grace?"

"What?"

"—ove you."

"Don't say that," I said. "We're getting you out."

"Hur—"

He hung up.

Beck's eyes flicked to me, and in them, I could see all the concern that his voice didn't reveal. "Who's Isabel?"

364

"Jack's sister." It seemed to take too long to pull off my backpack and get my mobile phone out of one of the pockets. "Sam must be trapped somewhere on their property. In a shed, or something. If I get Isabel on the phone, maybe she can find him. If not, I'm going now."

Paul looked at the window, at the dying sun, and I knew he was thinking that I didn't have enough time to get to the Culpepers' before the temperature dropped. No point thinking about that. I found Isabel's number from when she'd called me before and hit SEND.

It rang twice. "Yeah."

"Isabel, it's Grace."

"I'm not an idiot. I saw your number."

I wanted to reach through the phone and strangle her. "Isabel, Jack's locked up Sam somewhere near your house." I cut off the beginning of her question. "I don't know why. But Sam's going to change if it gets much colder, and wherever he is, he's trapped. Please tell me you're at your house."

"Yeah. I just got here. I'm in the house. I didn't hear any commotion or anything."

"Do you have a shed or something?"

Isabel made an irritated noise. "We have six outbuildings."

"He has to be in one of them. He called from inside a shed. If the sun gets down behind the trees, it's going to get cold in, like, two seconds."

"I get it!" snapped Isabel. There were rustling sounds.

"I'm getting my coat on. I'm going outside. Can you hear me? Now I'm outside. I'm freezing my ass off for you. I'm walking across the yard. I'm walking across the part of the grass my dog used to pee on before my damned brother *ate her*."

Paul smiled faintly.

"Can you hurry it up?" I demanded.

"I'm jogging to the first shed. I'm calling his name. Sam! Sam! Are you in there? I don't hear anything. If he's turned into a wolf in one of these sheds and I let him out and he rips my face off, I'm having my family sue you."

I heard a dim, faint crack. "Hell. This door is stuck." Another crack. "Sam? Wolf-boy? You in here? Nothing in the lawnmower shed. Where is Jack, anyway, if he did this?"

"Here. He's fine for now. Do you hear anything?"

"I doubt he's really fine. He's seriously screwed up, Grace. In the head, I mean. And no, I'd tell you if I heard something. I'm going to the next one."

Paul rested the back of his hand on the glass of the window over the sink and winced. He was right. It was getting too cold.

"Call Sam back," I begged Beck. "Tell him to shout so she can hear him."

Beck picked up his phone, punched a button, and held it to his ear.

Isabel sounded a little out of breath. "I'm at the

next one. Sam! You in there? Dude?" There was a nearly inaudible squeak as the door opened. A pause. "Unless he's turned into a bicycle, he's not in here, either."

"How many more of them are there?" I wanted to be there at the Culpepers' instead of Isabel. I'd be faster than she was. I'd be screaming my lungs out to find him.

"I told you. Four more. Only two more close. The others are way out in the field behind the house. They're barns."

"He has to be in one of the close ones. He said it was a shed." I looked at Beck, who had his phone up to his ear still. He looked back at me, shook his head. No answer. *Sam, why aren't you picking up?*

"I'm at the garden shed. Sam! Sam, it's Isabel, if you're a wolf in there, don't rip my face off." I could hear her breathing into the phone. "The door's stuck like the other one. I'm kicking it with my expensive shoe and it's pissing me off."

Beck slammed his phone down on the counter and turned away from Paul and me. He linked his arms behind his head. The motion was so *Sam* that it pierced me.

"I've got it open. It stinks. There's crap everywhere. There's nothing – oh." She broke off, and her breathing came through the phone, heavier than before.

"What? *What?*"

"Wait a sec – shut up – I'm taking my coat off. He's

here, OK? Sam. Sam, look at me. Sam, I said, look at me, you bastard, you're not turning into a wolf right now. Don't you dare do this to her."

I sank slowly down beside the counter, cupping the phone against my head. Paul's face didn't change; he just watched me, still, quiet, dark, wolf.

I heard a smacking sound and a softly breathed swear word, then wind roaring across the speaker. "I'm getting him inside. Thank God my parents aren't home tonight. I'll call you in a few minutes. I need both my hands now."

The phone went silent in my hands. I looked up at Paul, who was still watching me, wondering what I should say to him, but I felt like he already knew.

Fifty-One
Grace

3°C

Sleet danced off my windshield as I turned down the Culpepers' driveway, and the pines seemed to swallow the headlights. The hulking house was nearly invisible in the darkness except for a handful of lights shining in the windows of the ground floor. I pointed the Bronco towards them like I was steering a ship towards lights on shore, and pulled up next to Isabel's white SUV. No other cars.

I grabbed Sam's extra coat and leaped out. Isabel greeted me at the back door, leading me through a smoky-smelling mud-room full of boots and dog leashes and antlers. The smoky smell only increased as we left the mud-room and made our way through a beautiful, stark kitchen. An uneaten sandwich sat, abandoned, on the counter.

Isabel said, "He's in the living room next to the fire. He just stopped throwing up before you got here. He puked all over the carpet. But that's OK because I *like* having my parents pissed off at me. No point interrupting a constant pattern."

"Thank you," I said, more intensely grateful than the phrase conveyed. I followed the smell of smoke to the living room. Luckily for Isabel and her non-existent fire-building skills, the ceiling was very high, and most of the smoke had drifted upwards. Sam was a curved bundle next to the hearth, a fleece blanket wrapped around his shoulders. An untouched mug of something sat beside him, still steaming.

I rushed over, flinching at the heat of the fire, and stopped short when I smelled him: sharp, earthy, wild. A painfully familiar smell that I loved so well – but didn't want to smell right now. The face he turned to me was human, though, and I crouched beside him and kissed him. He took me carefully, as if either I or he might break, and closed his arms around me, laying his head on my shoulder. I felt him shiver intermittently, despite the small, smoky fire that was nonetheless hot enough to burn my shoulder nearest to it.

I wanted him to say something. This deadly quiet scared me. I pulled away from him and ran my hands through his hair for a long minute before I said what needed to be said. "You aren't OK, are you?"

"It's like a roller coaster," Sam said softly. "I climb and climb and climb towards winter, and as long as I don't get to the very top, I can still slide back."

I looked away, into the fire, watching the very centre of it, the very hottest part, until the colours and light lost meaning, burning my vision to white dancing lights. "And now you're at the very top."

"I think I might be. I hope not. But God – I feel like hell." He took my hand with frigid fingers.

I couldn't stand the silence. "Beck wanted to come. He couldn't leave the house."

Sam swallowed, loud enough for me to hear it. I wondered if he was feeling sick again. "I won't see him again. This is his last year. I thought I was right to be angry at him, but it just seems stupid now. I just can't – I just can't wrap my head around it."

I didn't know if he meant wrapping his head around whatever had made him angry with Beck, or the roller coaster he was riding. I just kept staring at that fire. So hot. A tiny little summer, self-contained and furious. If only I could get that inside Sam and keep him warm for ever. I was aware that Isabel was standing in the doorway of the room, but she seemed far away.

"I keep thinking about why I didn't change," I said slowly. "If I was born immune, or something. But I wasn't, you know? Because I got that flu. And because I still am not really – normal. I can smell better and hear better." I paused, trying to collect my thoughts. "And I think it was my dad. I think it was when he left me in the car. I got so hot, the doctors said I should've died, remember? But I didn't. I lived. And I didn't turn into a wolf."

Sam looked at me, his eyes sad. "You're probably right."

"But see, it could be a cure, couldn't it? Get you really hot?"

Sam shook his head. He was very pale. "I don't think so, angel. How hot was that bathwater you had me in? And – Ulrik – he tried going to Texas that year – it's one hundred and three and one hundred and four degrees out there. He's still a wolf. If that's what cured you, it's because you were little and because you had a crazy-high fever that burned you from the inside out."

"You could induce a fever," I said suddenly. But as soon as I said it, I shook my head. "But I don't think there's a medication to *raise* your temperature."

"It is possible," Isabel said from the door. I looked to her. She was leaning against the door frame, arms crossed over her chest, the sleeves of her sweater filthy from whatever she'd had to do to get Sam out of the shed. "My mom works in a low-income clinic two days a week, and I heard her talking about a guy who had a fever of one hundred and seven. He had meningitis."

"What happened to him?" I asked. Sam dropped my hand, turned his face away.

"He died." Isabel shrugged. "But maybe a werewolf wouldn't. Maybe that's why you didn't die as a kid, because you were bitten right before your idiot dad left you in the car to cook."

Beside me, Sam scrambled to his feet and started coughing.

"Not on the frigging rug!" Isabel said.

I jumped up as Sam braced his hands on his knees and retched without throwing anything up. He turned around to me, shaky, and something that I saw in his eyes made my stomach drop out from under me.

The room stank of wolf. For a dizzying moment, it was me and Sam, my face buried in his ruff, one thousand miles from here.

Sam squeezed his eyes shut for a second, and when he opened them, he said, "Sorry. Grace – I know this is an awful thing to ask. But could we go to Beck's? I have to see him again, if this is—" He stopped.

But I knew what he'd been about to say. The end.

Fifty-Two
Grace

Driving on cloudy nights had always unsettled me. It was as if the low cloud cover not only hid the moonlight but also robbed the headlights of any power, siphoning away their light the second it hit the air. Now, with Sam, I felt like I was driving down a black tunnel that kept getting ever narrower. The sleet tapped the windshield; both my hands gripped the wheel as the car tyres bucked on the slick road.

The heat was on absolute high, and I wanted to believe that Sam looked a little better. Isabel had poured his coffee into a travel mug, and I'd forced him to drink it as we drove, despite his nausea. It seemed to be helping, more than the external heat sources had, anyway. I took this as a possible reinforcement of our new theory of internal heat.

"I'm thinking more about your theory," Sam said, as if reading my mind. "It makes a lot of sense. But you'd have to get your hands on something to induce the fever – maybe meningitis, like Isabel said – and I'm thinking that's going to be unpleasant."

"Aside from the fever itself, you mean?"

"Yeah. Aside from that. Like dangerously unpleasant. Especially considering you can't exactly do animal testing first to find out if it's going to work." Sam glanced at me quickly to see if I had got the joke.

"Hardly funny."

"Better than nothing."

"Granted."

Sam reached over and touched my cheek. "But I'd be willing to try it. For you. To stay with you."

He said it so simply, so unaffectedly, that it took me a moment to get the statement's full impact. I wanted to say something, but I felt like I had no breath at all.

"I don't want to do this any more, Grace. It's not good enough any more to watch you from the woods, not now that I've been with you – the real thing. I can't just watch any more. I'd rather risk whatever could happen—"

"Death—"

"Yeah, *death* – than watch all this slip away. I can't do that, Grace. I want to try. Only – I think I'd have to be human for it to have a chance. It doesn't seem like you could kill the wolf while you *were* the wolf."

I was trembling. Not because it was cold, but because it sounded possible. Horrible, deadly, awful – possible. And I wanted it. I wanted to never have to give up this feeling of his fingers on my cheek or the sad sound of his voice. I should've told him, *No, it's not worth it*, but that would've been a lie of such epic proportions that I couldn't do it.

"Grace," Sam said, abruptly. "If you want me."

"What?" I said, and then realized what he had said. It seemed impossible that he had to ask. I couldn't be that hard to read. Then I realized – stupid, slow me – that he wanted to hear it. He told me all the time how he felt, and I was just . . . stoic. I don't think I'd ever told him. "Of course I do. Sam, I love you, you know I do. I've loved you for years. You *know* that."

Sam curled his arms around himself. "I do. But I wanted to hear you say it." He reached towards my hand before realizing I couldn't take it off the wheel; instead he made a knot of my hair around his fingers and rested his fingertips against my neck. I imagined I could feel his pulse and my pulse syncing up through that tiny bit of contact. *This could be mine for ever.*

He slouched back in his seat, looking tired, and leaned his face on his shoulder to look at me while he played with my hair. He started to hum a song, and then, after a few bars, he sang it. Quietly, sort of half-sung, half-spoken, incredibly gentle. I didn't catch all the words, but it was about his summer girl. Me. Maybe his forever girl. His yellow eyes were half-lidded as he sang, and in that golden moment, hanging taut in the middle of an ice-covered landscape like a single bubble of summer nectar, I could see how my life could be stretched out in front of me.

The Bronco lurched violently, and a heartbeat later, I saw the deer roll up over the hood. A crack raced across the windshield, exploding a second later into a thousand spiderwebbed fractures. I hit the brake, but nothing happened. Not even a whisper of a response.

Turn, Sam said, or maybe I imagined him saying it, but when I turned the wheel, the Bronco kept going straight, sliding, sliding, sliding. I remembered, in the back of my head, my dad saying, *Steer into the skid*, and I did, but it was too late.

There was a sound like a bone breaking, and there was a dead deer on the car and *in* the car and glass was everywhere and God, a tree shoved through my hood, and there was blood on my knuckles from the glass, and I was shaking and Sam was looking at me with this look on his face like *oh, no*, and then I realized that the car wasn't running and there was frigid air trickling in the jagged hole in the windshield.

I wasted a moment staring at him. Then I tried the engine, which wouldn't even respond when I turned the key. I said: "We call 911. They'll come get us."

Sam's mouth made a sad little line, and he nodded, as if that really would work. I punched in the number and reported the accident, talking fast, trying to guess where we might be, and then I took off my coat, careful not to drag the sleeves over my bloody knuckles, and I threw it on top of Sam. He sat quietly, unmoving, as I grabbed a blanket from the back seat and threw it on top of him, too, and then I slid across the seat and leaned against him, hoping to lend my body heat to him.

"Call Beck, please," Sam said, and I did. I put it on speakerphone and set it on the dash.

"Grace?" Beck's voice.

"Beck," Sam said. "It's me."

There was a pause, and then, "Sam. I—"

"There's no time," Sam said. "We've hit a deer. We're wrecked."

"God. Where are you? Is the car running?"

"Too far. We called 911. The engine's dead." Sam gave Beck a moment to realize what that meant. "Beck, I'm sorry I didn't come by. There are things I need to say—"

"No, listen to me first, Sam. Those kids. I need you to know I recruited them. They knew. They knew all along. I didn't do it against their will. Not like you. I'm so sorry, Sam. I've never stopped being sorry."

The words were meaningless to me, but obviously not to Sam. His eyes were too bright, and he blinked. "I don't regret it. I love you, Beck."

"I love you, too, Sam. You're the best of us, and nothing can change that."

Sam shuddered, the first sign I'd seen of the cold acting on him. "I have to go," he said. "There's no more time."

"Goodbye, Sam."

"Bye, Beck."

Sam nodded to me and I hit the END button.

For a second he was still, blinking. Then he shook off all the blankets and coats so that his arms were free and he wrapped them around me as tightly as he could. I felt him shuddering, shuddering against me as he buried his face in my hair.

I said, uselessly, "Sam, don't go."

Sam cupped my face in his hands and looked me in the eyes. His eyes were yellow, sad, wolf, mine. "These stay the same. Remember that when you look at me. Remember it's me. Please."

Please don't go.

Sam let go of me and spread out his arms, gripping the dash with one hand and the back of his seat with the other. He bowed his head and I watched his shoulders ripple and shake, watched the silent agony of the change until that one soft, awful cry, just when he lost himself.

Fifty-Three
Sam

1°C

crashing into the trembling void
stretching my hand to you
losing myself to frigid regret
is this fragile love
a way
to say
goodbye

Fifty-Four
Grace

0°C

When the paramedics arrived, I was curled on the passenger seat in a pile of coats, my hands pressed against my face.

"Miss, are you all right?"

I didn't answer, just put my hands on my lap and looked at my fingers, covered with bloody tears.

"Miss, are you alone?"

I nodded.

Fifty-Five
Sam

I watched her, like I'd always watched her.

Thoughts were slippery and transient, faint scents on a frigid wind, too far away to catch.

She sat just outside the wood near the swing, curled small, until the cold shook her, and still she didn't move. For a long time, I didn't know what she was doing.

I watched her. Part of me wanted to go to her, though instinct sang against it. The desire sparked a thought which sparked a memory of golden woods, days floating around me and falling around me, days lying still and crumpled on the ground.

But I realized then what she was doing, folded there, trembling with the vicious cold. She was waiting, waiting for the cold to shake her into another form. Maybe that unfamiliar scent I caught from her was hope.

She waited to change, and I waited to change, and we both wanted what we couldn't have.

Finally, night crept across the yard, lengthening the shadows, pulling them out of the woods until they covered the whole world.

I watched her.

The door opened. I shrank further into the dark. A man came out, pulled the girl from the ground. The light from the house glistened off the frozen tracks on her face.

I watched her. Thoughts, distant, fled with her absence. After she disappeared into the house, there was only this: longing.

Fifty-Six
Grace

1°C

Their howls were the hardest thing to bear.

As terrible as the days were, the nights were worse; days were just listless preparations to somehow make it through another night populated by their voices. I lay in bed and hugged his pillow until there was no more of his scent caught in it. I slept in his chair in Dad's study until it had my shape instead of his. I walked barefoot through the house in a private grief I couldn't share with anyone.

The only person I could share with, Olivia, couldn't be reached by phone, and my car — the car I couldn't even bear to think of — was useless and broken.

And so it was just me in the house and the hours stretched out before me and the unchanging, leafless trees of Boundary Wood outside my window.

The night I heard him howl was the worst. The others began first, like they had for the last three nights. I sank down into the leather chair in Dad's study, buried my face in the last Sam-scented T-shirt of his that I had, and pretended that it was just a recording of wolves, not real wolves. Not real people. And then, for the first time since the crash, I heard his howl join in with them.

It tore my heart out, because I heard his voice. The wolves sang slowly behind him, bittersweet harmony, but all I heard was Sam. His howl trembled, rose, fell in anguish.

I listened for a long time. I prayed for them to stop, to leave me alone, but at the same time I was desperately afraid that they would. Long after the other voices had dropped away, Sam kept howling, very soft and slow.

When he finally fell silent, the night felt dead.

Sitting still was intolerable. I stood up, paced, clenched and unclenched my hands into fists. Finally I took the guitar that Sam had played and I screamed and smashed it into pieces on Dad's desk.

When Dad came down from his room, he found me sitting in the middle of a sea of splintered wood and snapped strings, like a boat carrying music had crashed on a rocky shore.

Fifty-Seven
Grace

1°C

The first time I picked up my phone after the crash, it was snowing. Light, delicate flakes drifted by the black square of my window, like flower petals. I wouldn't have picked it up, but it was the one person I had been trying to contact since the crash. "Olivia?"

"G-gr-r-ace?" Olivia, barely recognizable. She was sobbing.

"Olivia, shh – what's wrong?" That was a stupid question. I *knew* what was wrong with her.

"Re-remember I told you I knew about the wolves?" She was taking big gasps of air between the words. "I didn't tell you about the hospital. Jack—"

"Bit you," I said.

"Yes," Olivia sobbed out the word. "I didn't think anything would happen, because days went by and I felt the same!"

My limbs fell slack. "You changed?"

"I – I can't – I—"

I closed my eyes, imagining the scene. God. "Where are you now?"

"At the b-bus stop." She paused, sniffing. "It's c-cold."

"Oh, Olivia. Olivia, come over here. Stay with me. We'll figure this out. I'd come, but I don't have a car yet."

Olivia began to sob again.

I stood up and shut my bedroom door. Not that Mom would hear me; she was upstairs, anyway. "Olivia, it's OK. I'm not going to freak out. I saw Sam change and I didn't freak out. I know what it's like. Calm down, OK? I can't come and get you. I don't have a car. You're going to have to drive over here."

I calmed her down for another few minutes and told her I'd have the front door unlocked when she got there. For the first time since the crash, I felt closer to me again.

When she arrived, looking red-eyed and dishevelled, I pushed her towards the bathroom for a shower and got her a change of clothes. I sat on the closed toilet lid while she stood in the hot water.

"I'll tell you my story if you tell me yours," I told her. "I want to know when Jack bit you."

"I told you how I met him, taking pictures of the wolves, and how I fed him. It was so stupid that I didn't tell you — I was just so guilty about fighting with you that I didn't tell you right away, and then I started cutting classes to help him out, and then I felt like I couldn't tell you without...I don't know what I thought. I'm sorry."

"It's water under the bridge now," I said. "What was he like? Did he force you to help him?"

"No," Olivia said. "He was pretty nice, actually, when things went his way. He got pretty angry when he changed, but it looked painful. And he kept asking about the wolves, wanting to see photos, and we talked, and after he found out that you'd been bitten—"

"Found out?" I echoed.

"OK, I told him! I didn't know it was going to make him crazy! He went on and on about a cure after that, and he tried to get me to tell him how to fix him. And then he, um, he. . ." She wiped her eyes. "Bit me."

"Wait. He bit you when he was human?"

"Yeah."

I shuddered. "God. How awful. Sick bastard. So you've been dealing with this all the time, by yourself?"

"Who would I tell?" Olivia said. "I thought Sam was one, because of his eyes – because I thought I recognized them from my wolf photos – but he told me he was wearing contacts when I met him. So I knew I either had it wrong or he just wasn't going to help me, anyway."

"You should've told me. I already told you about the werewolves, anyway."

"I know. I was just – guilty. I was just –" she shut off the water – "stupid. I don't know. What can I do, anyway? How was Sam human so much? I saw him. He waited in the Bronco for you all the time, and he never changed."

I handed her a towel over the top of the curtain. "Come into my room. I'll tell you."

Olivia stayed with me overnight, shaking and kicking so much that she eventually made a nest of blankets and my sleeping bag next to the bed so that we could both sleep. After a late breakfast, we went to get Olivia some toothpaste and other toiletries – Mom had ridden to work with Dad so that I could use her car. On the way back from the store, my mobile phone rang. Olivia picked up the phone without answering the call and read the number off to me.

Beck. Did I really want to do this? I sighed and held out my hand for the phone. "Hello?"

"Grace."

"Yes."

"I'm sorry to call you," Beck said. His voice sounded flat. "I know the last couple days must've been hard for you."

Was I supposed to say something? I hoped not, because I couldn't think of anything. My brain felt cloudy.

"Grace?"

"I'm here."

"I'm calling about Jack. He's doing better now, he's

more stable, and it won't be too long before he changes for the winter. But he's still got a couple of weeks of swapping back and forth, I think."

My brain wasn't too cloudy to realize how much Beck was trusting me at this point. I felt vaguely honoured. "So he's not still locked in the bathroom?"

Beck laughed, not a funny laugh, but nice to hear, anyway. "No, he's graduated from the bathroom to the basement. But I'm afraid, um, I'm going to change soon – I almost did this morning. And that would leave Jack in a very bad place for the next few weeks. I hate to ask you this, because it puts you in danger of getting bitten – but maybe you could keep an eye on him until he changes?"

I paused. "Beck, I've been bitten already."

"God!"

"No, no," I added hurriedly. "Not recently. Many years ago."

Beck's voice was strange. "You're the girl that Sam saved, aren't you?"

"Yeah."

"And you never changed."

"No."

"How long have you known Sam?"

"We only met in person this year. But I've watched him ever since he saved me." I pulled into the driveway but didn't turn the engine off. Olivia leaned over, cranked up the heat, and lay back in her seat with closed eyes. "I'd like to come over before you change. To just talk, if that's OK."

"That would be more than OK. But it'll have to be soon, I'm afraid. I'm just getting to the point where I can't turn back now."

Crap. My phone was beeping another call through. "This afternoon?" I asked. When he agreed, I said, "I have to go – I'm sorry – someone is calling me."

We said goodbye and I clicked over to the other call.

"Holy crap, Grace, how many times were you going to let it ring? Eighteen? Twenty? One hundred?" It was Isabel; I hadn't heard from her since the day after the crash, when I'd filled her in on where Jack was.

I replied, "For all you know, I was in class, and I was being murdered for my phone ringing during it."

"You weren't in class. Anyway. I need your help. My mom saw another case of meningitis – the worst sort of meningitis – at the clinic where she works. While I was there, I drew the guy's blood. Three vials."

I blinked several times before I figured out what she was saying. "You what?! Why?"

"Grace, I thought you were at the top of the class. Clearly the sliding scale has done wonders for you. Try to focus. While Mom was on the phone, I pretended to be a nurse and I drew his blood. His nasty, infected blood."

"You know how to draw blood?"

"Yes, I know how to draw blood! Doesn't everyone? Are you not getting what I'm saying? Three vials. One for Jack. One for Sam. One for Olivia. I need you to help me get Jack over to the clinic. The blood's in the fridge there. I'm afraid to take it out in case the bacteria die or whatever it is that bacteria do. Anyway, I don't know where this guy's house is, where Jack is."

"You want to inject them. To give them meningitis."

"No, I want to give them malaria. Yes, stupid. I want to give them meningitis. The main symptom is – ta*da* – a fever. And if we're being honest, I don't give a crap if you do it to Sam and Olivia. It probably won't work on Sam, anyway, because he's a wolf already. But I figured I had to get enough blood for all of them if I wanted to get you to help me."

"Isabel, I would've helped you, anyway." I sighed. "I'm going to give you an address. Meet me there in an hour."

Fifty-Eight
Grace

5°C

Being in Beck's basement made me both the happiest and the saddest I'd felt since Sam had changed into a wolf, because seeing Beck there, in his own world, was like seeing Sam again. It started when we left Olivia puking in the bathroom and met Beck at the top of the basement stairs – it was too cold for him to meet us at the front door – and I realized that Sam had inherited so many of his mannerisms and movements from Beck. Even the simplest gestures: reaching over to brush up a light switch, inclining his head for us to follow him, awkwardly ducking to avoid a low beam at the bottom of the stairs. So much like Sam that it hurt.

Then we reached the bottom of the stairs and I caught my breath. The large, main room of the basement was filled with books. Not just a few. It was a *library*. The walls were lined with recessed shelves that climbed to the top of the low ceiling, and they were stuffed full. Even without getting close to the shelves, I could see that they were categorized: tall, fat atlases and encyclopaedias on one shelf; short, colourful paperbacks with rumpled edges on several others; big photo books with block letters on their spines; hardcover novels with glistening dust jackets. I stepped slowly into the middle of the room and stood on the dusky orange carpet, turning slowly to see them all.

And the smell – the smell of Sam was everywhere in this room, like he was here with me, holding my hand, looking at all these books with me, waiting for me to say "I love it".

I was about to break the silence by saying something like "I can see where Sam got his reading habit" when Beck said, almost apologetically, "When you spend a lot of time inside, you do a lot of reading."

I remembered, then, abruptly, what Sam had told me about Beck: this was his last year as a human. He would never read these books again. My words were stolen from me, and then I just looked at Beck and managed, stupidly, "I love books."

He smiled, like he knew. Then he looked at Isabel, who was craning her neck as if Jack must be stuffed on one of the shelves. "Jack's probably in the other room, playing video games," Beck said.

Isabel followed Beck's gaze to the doorway. "Will he tear out my throat if I go in there?"

Beck shrugged. "No more than usual, I'd think. That's the warmest room in the house, and I think he feels more comfortable in there. Though he still changes every so often. Just pay attention."

It was interesting how he talked about Jack — more animal than human. As if he were advising Isabel on how to approach the gorillas at the zoo. After Isabel had vanished into the other room, Beck gestured towards one of the two squashy red chairs in the room. "Have a seat."

I was glad to settle down into one of the chairs. It smelled of Beck and a few other wolves, but mostly of Sam. It was so easy to imagine him down here, curled in this spot, reading and developing an obnoxiously large vocabulary. I rested my head against the side of the chair to pretend I was curled in Sam's arms and turned to look at Beck, who sat down in the chair opposite. Not properly, but crashed back into it with his legs kicked out. He looked tired. "I'm sort of surprised Sam kept you a secret all this time."

"Are you?"

He shrugged. "I guess I shouldn't be. I didn't tell him about my wife."

"He knew. He told me about her."

Beck laughed, short and fond. "I shouldn't be surprised about that, either. Keeping a secret from Sam was impossible. Not to be clichéd, but he could read people like a book."

We were both referring to him in the past tense, like he was dead. "Do you think I'll ever see him again?"

His face was faraway, unreadable. "I think this year was his last. I really do. I know it's mine. I don't know why he got so few years. That's just not normal. I mean, it varies, but I was bitten a little over twenty years ago."

"*Twenty?*"

Beck nodded. "In Canada. I was twenty-eight, a rising star at my firm, and I was hiking on vacation."

"What about the rest of them? Where are they from?"

"From all over. When I heard that there were wolves in Minnesota, I thought there was a good chance they could be like me. So I went looking, found out I was right, and Paul took me under his wing. Paul's—"

"The black wolf."

He nodded. "Do you want coffee? I could murder for coffee, if you don't mind the expression."

I was intensely grateful. "That would be wonderful. If you point me in the direction of the pot, I'll make it." He pointed it out, hidden in a cranny between the shelves, next to a tiny refrigerator. "And you can keep talking."

He sounded humoured. "What about?"

"The pack. What it's like, being a wolf. Sam. Why you changed Sam." I paused, coffee filter in hand. "Yes. That one. I want to know that one in particular."

Beck crumpled his face in his hand. "God, the worst one. I changed Sam because I was a selfish bastard without a soul."

I measured coffee grounds. I heard the regret in his

voice, but I wasn't letting him off the hook. "That's not a reason."

Deep sigh. "I know. Jen — my wife — had just died. She was a terminally ill cancer patient when we met, so I knew it was going to happen, but I was young and stupid and thought maybe a miracle would happen and we'd live happily ever after. Anyway. No miracle. I was depressed. I thought about killing myself, but the funny thing about having wolf in you is that suicide doesn't seem like a very good idea. Did you ever notice that animals don't kill themselves on purpose?"

I hadn't. I made a note of it.

"Anyway, I was in Duluth in the summer, and I saw Sam with his parents. God, this sounds awful, doesn't it? But it wasn't like that. Jen and I talked all the time about having kids, even though we both knew it would never happen. Hell, she was only supposed to live for another eight months. How could she have had a baby? Anyway, I saw Sam. There he was, with his yellow eyes, just like a real wolf, and I was totally obsessed with the idea. And — you don't have to tell me, Grace, I *know* this was wrong — but I saw him with his silly, vapid parents, them just as clueless as a pair of pigeons, and I thought, I could be better for him. I could teach him more."

I didn't say anything, and Beck leaned his forehead into his hand again. His voice was centuries old. I didn't say anything, but he groaned. "God, I know, Grace. I know. But you know the stupid thing? I actually *like* who I am. I mean, not at first. It was a curse. But it came to be like someone who loves summer and winter. Does that make sense? I knew that eventually I'd lose myself, but I came to terms with that a long time ago. I thought Sam would get over it, too."

I found the mugs in a little cubby hole above the coffe maker and pulled two of them out. "But he didn't. Milk?"

"A little. Not too much." He sighed. "It's hell for him. I made a personal hell for him. He *needs* that sort of self-awareness to feel alive, and when he loses that and becomes a wolf . . . it's hell. He is absolutely the best person I've ever met in the world, and I absolutely ruined him. I have regretted it every day for years."

He might've deserved it, but I couldn't let him get any lower. I brought him a mug and sat back down. "He loves you, Beck. He may hate being a wolf, but he loves you. And I have to tell you, it's killing me to sit here with you, because everything about you reminds me of him. If you admire him, it's because you made him who he is."

Beck looked strangely vulnerable then, his hands wrapped around the coffee mug, looking at me through the steam above it. He was silent for a long moment, and then he said, "The regret will be one of the things I'll be glad to lose."

I frowned at him. Sipped the coffee. "Will you forget everything?"

"You don't forget anything. You just see it differently. Through a wolf's brain. Some things become completely unimportant when you're a wolf. Other things are emotions wolves just don't feel. We lose those. But the most important things – we can hold on to those. Most of us."

Like love. I thought of Sam watching me, before we had met as humans, and me watching back. Falling in love, as impossible as it should've been. My gut squeezed, horribly, and for a moment, I couldn't speak.

"You were bitten," Beck said. I'd heard this before, this question without a question mark.

I nodded. "A little more than six years ago."

"But you never changed."

I related the story of getting locked in the car, and then explained the theory of a possible cure Isabel and I had developed. Beck sat quietly for a long moment, rubbing a small circle in the side of his mug with one of his fingers, staring blankly at the books on the wall.

Finally, he nodded. "It might work. I can see how it might work. But I think you'd have to be human when you got infected for it to work."

"That's what Sam said. He said he thought if you were killing the wolf, you shouldn't be a wolf when you were infected."

Beck's eyes were still unfocused as he thought. "God, but it's risky. You couldn't treat the meningitis until after you were sure the fever had killed the wolf. Bacterial meningitis has an incredible fatality rate, even if you catch it early and treat it from the beginning."

"Sam told me he'd risk dying for the cure. Do you think he meant it?"

"Absolutely," Beck said, without hesitation. "But he's a wolf. And likely to stay that way for the rest of his life."

I dropped my eyes to my half-empty mug, noticing the way the liquid changed colour just at the very edges of the rim. "I was thinking we could bring him to the clinic, just to see if he'd change in the heat of the building."

There was a pause, but I didn't look up to see what expression Beck wore during it. He said gently, "Grace."

I swallowed, still looking at the coffee. "I know."

"I've watched wolves for twenty-odd years. It's predictable. We get to the end . . . and it's the end."

I felt like a stubborn child. "But he changed this year when he shouldn't have, right? When he was shot, he made himself human."

Beck took a long drink of coffee. I heard his fingers tapping the side of the mug. "And to save you. He made himself human to save you. I don't know how he did it. Or why. But he did. I always thought it must have had something to do with adrenaline, tricking the body into thinking it was warm. I know he's tried to do it other times, too, but he never managed it."

I closed my eyes and let myself imagine Sam carrying me. I could almost see it, smell it, feel it.

"Hell." Beck didn't say anything else for a long time. Then, again: "Hell. It's what he would want. He'd want to try." He drained his coffee. "I'll help you. What were you thinking? Drugging him for the trip?"

I had been thinking about it, in fact, ever since Isabel had called. "I think we'll have to, right? He won't stand it otherwise."

"Benadryl," Beck said, matter-of-fact. "I've got some upstairs. It'll make him groggy and put him enough out of it that he won't go crazy in the car."

"The only thing I couldn't work out was how to get him here. I haven't seen him since the accident." I was cautious with my words. I couldn't let myself get hopeful. I just couldn't.

Beck's voice was certain. "I can do it. I'll get him. I'll make him come. We'll put the Benadryl in some hamburger or something." He stood up and took my coffee mug from me. "I like you, Grace. I wish Sam could've had—"

He stopped, put his hand on my shoulder. His voice was so kind I thought I would cry. "It might work, Grace. It might work."

I could see that he didn't believe it, but I saw, too, that he wanted to. For right now, that was enough.

Fifty-Nine
Grace

A thin layer of snow dusted the ground as Beck walked into the back yard, his shoulders dark and square underneath his sweater. Inside, Isabel and Olivia stood with me by the glass door, ready to help, but I felt like I was alone, watching Beck slowly walk out into his last day as a human. One of his hands held a gob of red, raw meat laced with Benadryl, and the other shook uncontrollably.

A dozen metres from the house, Beck halted, dropped the meat to the ground, and then walked several paces towards the woods. For a moment he stood there, his head cocked in a way that I recognized. Listening.

"What is he *doing*?" Isabel demanded, but I didn't answer.

Beck cupped his hands around his mouth, and even inside, I could hear him clearly.

"Sam!" He shouted it again, "*Sam!* I know you're out there! Sam! Sam! Remember who you are? *Sam!*"

Shaking, Beck kept shouting Sam's name to the

empty, frigid woods, until he stumbled and caught himself just before falling.

I pressed my fingers to my lips as tears ran down my cheeks.

Beck shouted Sam's name one more time, and then his shoulders hunched up, buckling and twisting, his scrambling hands and feet scarring the layer of snow around him. His clothing hung on him, vast and tangled, and then he backed out of it, shaking his head.

The grey wolf stood in the middle of the yard, looking towards the glass doors, his eyes watching us watching him. He stepped away from the clothing he would never wear again, and then he froze, turning his head towards the woods.

From between the stark black pines, another wolf emerged, head low and cautious, snow dusted over his ruff. His eyes found me, behind the glass.

Sam.

Sixty
Grace

The evening was steel grey, the sky an endless expanse of frozen clouds waiting for snow and for night. Outside the SUV, the tyres crunched along salted roads, and sleet tapped on the windshield. Inside, behind the wheel, Isabel kept complaining about the "wet mutt smell", but to me it was pine and earth, rain and musk. And behind it, the sharp, contagious edge of anxiety. In the passenger seat, Jack kept whining softly, halfway between animal and human. Olivia sat beside me in the back seat, her fingers knotted so tightly in mine that it hurt.

Sam was behind us. When we had lifted him into the SUV, his body was heavy with drug-induced sleep. Now, his breaths were deep and uneven, and I strained to listen to them over the sound of slush spraying from the tyres, to maintain some kind of connection with him when I couldn't touch him. With him drugged, I could've sat with him and run my fingers through his fur, but it would've been torment for him.

He was an animal now. Back in his world, far away from me.

Isabel pulled up in front of the little clinic. At this hour, the car park was dark and unlit; the clinic itself was a little grey square. It didn't look like a place to work miracles. It looked like a place you came when you were sick and had no money. I pushed the thought out of my head.

"I stole the keys from Mom," Isabel said. To her credit, she didn't sound nervous. "Come on. Jack, can you try the hell not to savage someone before we get inside?"

Jack muttered something unrepeatable. I looked in the back; Sam was on his feet, swaying. "Isabel, hurry up. The Benadryl's wearing off."

Isabel wrenched up the parking brake. "If we get arrested, I'm telling them you all abducted me."

"Come on!" I snapped. I opened my door; Olivia and Jack both winced at the cold. "Hurry up – you two need to run."

"I'll come back to help you with him," Isabel told me, and leaped out of the SUV. I turned back around to Sam, who rolled his eyes up towards me. He seemed disoriented, groggy.

I was momentarily frozen by his gaze, remembering Sam lying in bed, nose to nose with me, eyes looking into mine.

He made a soft noise of anxiety.

"I'm sorry," I told him.

Isabel returned, and I came around back to help her. She pulled off her belt and expertly twisted it around Sam's muzzle. I winced, but I couldn't tell her not to. She hadn't been bitten and there was no guarantee of how Sam would react to this process.

Between the two of us, we lifted him and crab-walked to the clinic. Isabel kicked open the door, which was already slightly ajar. "The exam rooms are that way. Lock him in one of those and we'll do Olivia and Jack first. Maybe he'll turn back again, if he's in the heat long enough."

Isabel's lie was extraordinarily kind; we both knew he wasn't changing without some kind of miracle. The best I could hope for was that Sam had been wrong – that this cure wouldn't kill him when he was a wolf. I followed Isabel to a little supply room, cluttered and stinking with a sort of medicinal, rubber scent. Olivia and Jack were already waiting there, heads ducked together as if they were talking, which surprised me. Jack lifted his head when we came in.

"I can't stand this waiting," he said. "Can we just get this the hell over with?"

I looked at a bin of alcohol wipes. "Do I need to prep his arm?"

Isabel gave me a look. "We're intentionally infecting him with meningitis. It seems pointless to be worried about infection at the injection site."

I swabbed his arm, anyway, while Isabel retrieved a blood-filled syringe from the fridge.

"Oh, God," Olivia whispered, her eyes frozen on the syringe.

We didn't have time to comfort her. I took Jack's cold hand and turned it so that it was palm up, like I remembered seeing the nurse do before our rabies shots.

Isabel looked at Jack. "You're sure you want this."

He lifted his teeth in a snarl. He stank of fear. "Just do it."

Isabel hesitated; it took me a moment to realize why. "Let me do it," I told her. "He can't hurt me."

Isabel handed me the syringe and ducked aside. I took her place. "Look the other way," I ordered Jack. He turned his head away. I stuck the needle in, then smacked his face with my free hand as he jerked back around towards me. "Control yourself!" I snapped. "You're not an animal."

He whispered, "Sorry."

I depressed the syringe fully, trying not to think too hard about the bloody contents of it, and pulled out the needle. There was a dot of red at the injection site; I didn't know if it was Jack's blood or infected blood from the syringe. Isabel was just staring at it, so I turned around, grabbed a Band-Aid, and stuck it over the site. Olivia let out a low moan.

"Thank you," Jack said. He hugged his arms around himself. Isabel looked sick.

"Just give me the other one," I said to Isabel. Isabel handed it to me and we turned to Olivia, who was so pale that I could see the vein running over her temple; nerves shook her hands. Isabel took over my duty of swabbing the arm. It was like an unspoken rule that we both had to feel useful to make the hateful task possible.

"I changed my mind!" Olivia cried. "I don't want to do it! I'll take my chances!"

I took her hand. "Olivia. Olive. Calm down."

"I can't." Olivia's eyes were on the dark red of the syringe. "I can't say that I'd rather die than be this way."

I didn't know what to say. I didn't want to convince her to do something that could kill her, but I didn't want her to not do it, out of fear. "But your whole life – Olivia."

Olivia shook her head. "No. No, it's not worth it. Let Jack try it. I'll take my chances. If it works on him, then I'll try it. But I . . . can't."

"You do know it's nearly November, right?" Isabel demanded. "It's freezing cold! You're going to change soon for the winter, and we won't get another chance until spring."

"Just let her wait," Jack snapped. "There's no harm. Better her parents think she's missing for a few months than find out she's a werewolf."

"Please." Olivia's eyes were full of tears.

I shrugged helplessly and put down the syringe. I didn't know any more than she did. And in my heart, I knew that, in her position, I'd make the same choice – better to live with her beloved wolves than die of meningitis.

"Fine," Isabel said. "Jack, take Olivia out to the car. Wait there and keep an eye out. OK, Grace. Let's go see what Sam's done to the exam room while we were gone."

Jack and Olivia headed down the hallway, pressed against each other for warmth, trying not to shift, and Isabel and I turned to go to the wolf who already had.

Standing just outside the exam room where Sam was, Isabel put her hand on my arm, stopping me before I turned the door handle. "Are you sure you want to do this?" she asked. "It could kill him. Probably will kill him."

Instead of answering, I pushed open the door.

In the ugly fluorescent lighting of the room, Sam looked ordinary, doglike, small, crouched beside the exam table. I knelt in front of him, wishing that we'd thought of this possible cure before it was probably too late for him. "Sam." *I don't want to stand before you like a thing, shrewd, secretive. . .* I had known that the heat wouldn't change him back to human. It was nothing but selfishness that had made me bring him to the clinic.

Selfishness, and a fallible cure that couldn't possibly work for him in this form. "Sam, do you still want to do this?"

I touched his ruff, imagining it as his dark hair. I swallowed unhappily.

Sam whistled through his nose. I had no idea how much he understood of what I said; only that, in his semi-drugged state, he didn't flinch under my touch.

I tried again. "It could kill you. Do you still want to try?"

Behind me, Isabel coughed meaningfully.

Sam whined at the noise, eyes jerking to Isabel and the door. I stroked his head and looked into his eyes. God, they were the same. It killed me to look at them now.

This has to work.

A tear slid down my face. I didn't bother to swipe it away as I looked up at Isabel. I wanted this like I'd never wanted anything. "We have to do it."

Isabel didn't move. "Grace, I don't think he stands a chance unless he's human. I just don't think it will work."

I ran a finger over the short, smooth hair on the side of his face. If he hadn't been sedated, he wouldn't have tolerated it, but the Benadryl had dulled his instincts. He closed his eyes. It was unwolflike enough to give me hope.

"Grace. Are we doing this or not? Seriously."

"Wait," I said. "I'm trying something."

I settled on the floor and whispered to Sam, "I want you to listen to me, if you can." I leaned the side of my face against his ruff and remembered the golden wood he had shown me so long ago. I remembered the way the yellow leaves, the colour of Sam's eyes, fluttered and twisted, crashing butterflies, on their way to the ground. The slender white trunks of the birches, creamy and smooth as human skin. I remembered Sam standing in the middle of the wood, his arms stretched out, a dark, solid form in the dream of the trees. His coming to me, me punching his chest, the soft kiss. I remembered every kiss we'd ever had, and I remembered every time I'd curled in his human arms. I remembered the soft warmth of his breath on the back of my neck while we slept.

I remembered Sam.

I remembered him forcing himself out of wolf form for me. To save me.

Sam jerked away from me. His head was lowered, tail between his legs, and he was shaking.

"What's happening?" Isabel's hand was on the doorknob.

Sam backed away further, crashing into the cabinet behind him, curling into a ball, uncurling. He was peeling free. He was shaking out of his fur. He was wolf and he was Sam, and then he

was

just

Sam.

"Hurry," Sam whispered. He was jerking, hard, against the cabinet. His fingers were claws on the tiles. "Hurry. Do it now."

Isabel was frozen by the door.

"Isabel! Come *on*!"

She snapped out of her spell and came over to us. She crouched beside Sam, next to the bare expanse of his back. He was biting his lip so hard that it was bleeding. I knelt, took his hand.

His voice was strained. "Grace – *hurry*. I'm almost gone."

Isabel didn't ask any more questions. She just grabbed his arm, turned it, and jabbed the needle in. She depressed the syringe halfway, but it jerked out of his arm as he seized violently. Sam backed away from me, tugging his hand from mine, and threw up.

"Sam—"

But he was gone. In half the time it had taken him to become human, he was a wolf. Shaking, staggering, nails scratching on the tiles, falling to the floor.

"I'm sorry, Grace," Isabel said. That was all she said. She laid the syringe on the counter. "Crap. I hear Jack. I'll be right back."

The door opened and closed. I knelt next to Sam's body and buried my face in his fur. His breaths were ragged and exhausted. And all I could think was — *I killed him. This is going to kill him.*

Sixty-One
Grace

Jack was the one who opened the exam-room door. "Grace, come on. We have to go – Olivia's not doing so good."

I stood, embarrassed to be found with tear-stained cheeks. I turned to tip the used syringe into the hazardous waste container by the counter. "I need help carrying him."

He scowled at me. "That's why Isabel sent me in here."

I looked down, and my heart stopped. Empty floor. I spun, ducking my head to look under the table. "Sam?"

Jack had left the door open. The room was empty.

"Help me find him!" I shouted at Jack, pushing past him into the hallway. There was no sign of Sam. As I pelted down the hall, I could see the door wide-open at the end of it, black night staring in. It was the first place a wolf would've run to, once his drugs wore off. Escape. The night. The cold.

I spun in the car park, looking for any sign of Sam

in the slender finger of Boundary Wood that stretched behind the clinic. But it was darker than dark. No lights. No sound. No Sam.

"*Sam!*"

I knew he wouldn't come, even if he heard me. Sam was strong, but instincts were stronger.

It was intolerable to imagine him out there somewhere, half a vial of infected blood mixing slowly with his.

"*Sam!*" My voice was a wail, a howl, a cry in the night. He was gone.

Headlights blinded me: Isabel's SUV, tearing up beside me and shuddering to a stop. Isabel leaned over from the driver's side and shoved open the passenger-side door, her face a ghost in the lights of the dashboard.

"Get in, Grace. Hurry the hell up! Olivia is changing and we've been here way too long already."

I couldn't leave him.

"*Grace!*"

Jack climbed into the back seat, shuddering; his eyes pleaded with me. They were the same eyes I'd seen at the very beginning, back when he'd first been turned. Back before I'd known anything at all.

I got in and slammed the door shut, looking out of the window just in time to see a white wolf standing by the edge of the car park. Shelby. Alive, just like Sam had thought. I stared in the rearview mirror at her; the wolf stood in the car park and gazed after us. I thought I saw triumph in her eyes as she turned and disappeared into the darkness.

"Which wolf is that?" Isabel demanded.

But I couldn't answer. All I could think was *Sam, Sam, Sam.*

Sixty-Two
Grace

4°C

"I don't think Jack's doing well," Olivia said. She sat in the passenger seat of my new car, a little Mazda that smelled like carpet cleaner and loneliness. Even though she wore two of my sweaters and a stocking cap, she was still shaking, her hands wrapped around her stomach. "If he was doing well, Isabel would've called us."

"Maybe," I said. "Isabel isn't the calling sort." But I couldn't help but think she was right. This was day three, and the last we'd heard from Isabel was eight hours ago.

Day one: Jack had a splitting headache and a stiff neck.

Day two: headache worse. Running a temperature.

Day three: Isabel's voicemail.

I pulled the Mazda into Beck's driveway and parked behind Isabel's giant SUV. "Ready?"

Olivia didn't look like she was, but she got out of the car and bolted for the front door. I followed her in and shut the door behind us. "Isabel?"

"In here."

We followed her voice into one of the downstairs bedrooms. It was a cheery little yellow bedroom that seemed at odds with the decomposing odour of *sick* that filled the space.

Isabel sat cross-legged on a chair at the foot of the bed. Deep circles, like purple thumbprints, were pressed beneath her eyes.

I handed her the coffee we'd brought. "Why didn't you call us?"

Isabel looked at me. "His fingers are dying."

I'd been avoiding looking at him, but I did, finally, where he lay on the bed, curled like a half-done butterfly. The ends of his fingertips were a disconcerting shade of blue. His face was shiny with sweat, his eyes closed. My throat felt too full.

"I looked it up online," Isabel told me. She held up her phone, as if that explained everything. "His headache is because the lining of his brain is inflamed. The fingers and toes are blue because his brain isn't telling his body to send blood there any more. I took his temperature. It was one hundred and five."

Olivia said, "I have to throw up."

She left me in the room with Isabel and Jack.

I didn't know what to say. If Sam had been here, he would've known the right thing to say. "I'm sorry."

Isabel shrugged, eyes dull. "It worked the way it was supposed to. The first day, he almost changed into a wolf when the temperature dropped overnight. That was the last time, even when the power went down last night. I thought it was working. He hasn't changed since his fever got going." She made a little gesture towards the bed. "Did you make an excuse for me at school?"

"Yes."

"Fantastic."

I gestured for her to follow me. She stood up from her chair as if it was difficult for her and trailed me into the hall.

I pulled the bedroom door almost shut so that Jack, if he was listening, wouldn't overhear. In a low voice, I said, "We have to take him to the hospital, Isabel."

Isabel laughed – a weird, ugly sound. "And tell them what? He's supposed to be dead. You think I haven't been thinking about this? Even if we give a fake name, his face has been all over the news for two months."

"Then we just take our chances, right? We'll come up with some story. I mean, we have to at least try, right?"

She looked up at me with her red-rimmed eyes for a long moment. When she finally spoke, her voice was hollow. "Do you think I want him to die? Don't you think I want to save him? It's too late, Grace! It's hard for people to survive this kind of meningitis even if they've had treatment from the very beginning. Right now, for him, after three days? I don't even have painkillers to give him, much less anything that might do something for this. I thought the wolf part might save him, like it saved you. But he doesn't have a chance. Not a chance."

I took the coffee cup out of her hands. "We can't just watch him die. We'll take him to a hospital that won't know him right away. We'll drive to Duluth if we have to. They won't recognize him there, at least not right away, and by then, we'll have thought of something to tell them. Go clean up your face and get whatever of his stuff you want to bring. Come on, Isabel. *Move.*"

Isabel still didn't answer, but she headed for the stairs. After she'd gone, I went into the downstairs bathroom and opened up the cupboard, thinking there might be something useful in there. A houseful of people tended to accumulate a lot of meds. There was some acetaminophen and some prescription pain pills from three years previously. I took all of it and went back to Jack's room.

Kneeling by his head, I said, "Jack, are you awake?" I smelled puke on his breath and wondered at the hell he and Isabel had been living in for the past three days; it twisted my stomach. I tried to convince myself that he somehow deserved this for making me lose Sam, but I couldn't.

It took a very long time for him to answer. "No."

"Can I do anything for you? To make you any more comfortable?"

His voice was very small. "My head's killing me."

"I have some pain pills. Do you think you can keep them down?"

He made a vaguely affirmative noise, so I took the glass of water from beside the bed and helped him swallow a couple of capsules. He mumbled something that might've been "thank you". I waited fifteen minutes, until the meds started to kick in, and watched his body relax a little.

Somewhere, Sam had this. I imagined him lying somewhere, brain exploding with pain, fever ravaging, dying. It seemed like, if something happened to Sam, I ought to know it, in some way: feel a tiny prick of anguish the moment he died. On the bed, Jack made a small noise, an unintentional sound of pain, a little whimper in his fitful sleep. All I could think of was injecting Sam with the same blood. In my head, I kept seeing Isabel pushing it into his veins, a deadly cocktail.

"I'll be right back," I told Jack, even though I thought he was sleeping. I went out into the kitchen and found Olivia leaning on the island, folding up a piece of paper.

"How is he doing?" she asked.

I shook my head. "We have to take him to the hospital. Can you come?"

Olivia looked at me in a way that I couldn't interpret. "I think I'm ready." She pushed the piece of folded paper towards me. "I need you to find a way to give that to my parents."

I started to open it and she shook her head. I raised an eyebrow. "What is this?"

"It's the note telling them I'm running away and not to try to find me. They'll still try, of course, but at least they won't think I was kidnapped or something."

"You're going to change." It wasn't a question.

She nodded and made another weird little face. "It's getting really hard not to. And — maybe it's just because it's so unpleasant, trying not to change — but I *want* to. I'm actually looking forward to it. I know that sounds backwards."

It didn't sound backwards to me. I would've given anything to be in her place, to be with my wolves and with Sam. But I didn't want to tell her that, so I just asked the obvious question. "Are you going to change here?"

Olivia gestured for me to follow her into the kitchen and together we stood by the windows to the back yard. "I want you to see something. Look. You have to wait a second. But look."

We stood at the window, looking out at the dead winter world, into the tangled underbrush of the woods. For a long moment I saw nothing but a small, colourless bird that fluttered from naked branch to naked branch. Then another slight movement caught my eye, lower to the ground, and I saw a big, dark wolf in the woods. His light, nearly colourless eyes were on the house.

"I don't know how they know," Olivia said, "but I

feel like they're waiting for me." I suddenly realized that the expression on her face was excitement. It made me feel oddly alone.

"You want to go now, don't you?"

Olivia nodded. "I can't stand waiting any more. I can't wait to let go."

I sighed and looked at her eyes, very green and bright. I had to memorize them now so that I could recognize them later. I thought I ought to say something to her, but I couldn't think of what. "I'll give your letter to your parents. Be careful. I'll miss you, Olive."

I slid open the glass door; cold air blasted us.

She actually laughed as the wind ripped a shiver from her. She was a strange, light creature that I didn't recognize. "See you in the spring, Grace."

And she ran out into the yard, stripping sweaters as she did, and before she got to the tree line, she was a light, light wolf, joyful and leaping. There was none of the pain of Jack's or Sam's change – it was as if she had been meant for it. Something in my stomach twisted at the sight of her. Sadness, or envy, or happiness.

It was just the three of us then, the three of us who didn't change.

I started the car's engine to warm it, but in the end it didn't matter. Fifteen minutes later, Jack died. Now it was just the two of us.

Sixty-Three
Grace

-5°C

I saw Olivia after that, after I'd left her note on her parents' car. She moved lightly in the twilight woods, her green eyes making her instantly identifiable. She was never alone; other wolves guided her, taught her, guarded her from the primitive dangers of the desolate winter wood.

I wanted to ask her if she'd seen him.

I think she wanted to tell me "no".

Isabel called me a few days before Christmas break and my planned trip with Rachel. I didn't know why she called me instead of just coming over to my new car; I could see her right across the school car park, sitting in her SUV by herself.

"How are you doing?" she asked.

"I'm OK," I replied.

"Liar." Isabel didn't look at me. "You know he's dead."

It was easier to admit on the phone, rather than face-to-face. "I know."

Across the frosty grey car park, Isabel snapped her phone shut. I heard her put her SUV in gear and then she drove it to where I stood by my car. There was a *click* as she unlocked the passenger-side door and a *whirr* as the window rolled down. "Get in. Let's go somewhere."

We went downtown and bought coffee, and then, because there was a parking place in front, we went to the bookstore. Isabel looked at the storefront for a long time before getting out of the car. We stood on the icy pavement and stared at the display window. It was all Christmas stuff. Reindeer and gingerbread and *It's a Wonderful Life*.

"Jack loved Christmas," Isabel said. "I think it's a stupid holiday. I'm not celebrating it any more." She gestured to the store. "Do you want to go in? I haven't been in here in weeks."

"I haven't been here since—" I stopped. I didn't want to say it. I wanted to go in, but I didn't want to have to say it.

Isabel opened the door for me. "I know."

The bookstore was a different world in this grey, dead winter. The shelves, blue and slate, had taken on a different hue. The light was pure, pure white. Classical music played overhead, but the hum of the heater was the real soundtrack. I looked at the kid behind the counter – dark-haired, lanky, bent over a book – and for a moment, a lump rose in my throat, too thick to swallow.

Isabel wrenched my arm, hard enough to hurt. "Let's

find books on getting fat."

We went to the cookbook section and sat on the floor. The carpet was cold. Isabel made a huge mess, pulling out a stack next to her and putting them back in the wrong order, and I lost myself in the neat letters of the titles on the spines, absently pulling the books out so that they were flush with one another.

"I want to learn how to get fat," Isabel said. She handed me a book on pastries. "How does that look?"

I paged through it. "All the measurements are in metric. And no cups. You'd have to get a digital scale."

"Forget that." Isabel put it back in the wrong place. "Try this one."

This one was all on cakes. Beautiful chocolate layers bursting with raspberries, yellow sponges smothered with fluffy buttercream, cloying cheesecakes drizzled with strawberry nectar.

"You can't take a piece of cake with you to school." I handed her a book on cookies and bars. "Try that."

"This is perfect," Isabel accused, and set the book aside in a different pile. "Don't you know how to shop? Being efficient isn't a good thing. It doesn't take enough time. I'm going to have to teach you the art of browsing. You're clearly deficient."

Isabel taught me browsing in the cookbook section until I was restless, and then I left her behind and wandered through the store. I didn't want to, but I climbed the burgundy-carpeted stairs to the loft.

The snow-clouded day outside made the loft seem darker and even smaller than it had before, but the love seat was still there, and the little waist-high bookshelves Sam had searched through. I could still see the shape of his body curled in front of them, looking for the perfect book.

I shouldn't have, but I sat on the couch and lay back on it. I closed my eyes and pretended as hard as I could that Sam was lying behind me, that I was secure in his arms, and that any moment I would feel his breath move my hair and tickle my ear.

I could almost smell him here, if I tried hard enough. There weren't many places that still held his scent, but I could almost detect it – or maybe I just wanted to so badly that I was imagining it.

I remembered him urging me to smell everything in the sweet shop. To give in to who I really was. I picked out the scents in the bookstore now: the nutty aroma of the leather, the almost perfumey carpet cleaner, the sweet black ink and the petrol-smelling colour inks, the shampoo of the boy at the counter, Isabel's fragrance, the scent of the memory of me and Sam kissing on this sofa.

I didn't want Isabel to find me with my tears any more than she wanted me to find her with hers. We shared a lot of things now, but crying was one thing we never talked about. I wiped my face dry with my sleeve and sat up.

I walked to the shelf where Sam had got his book, scanned the titles until I recognized it, then pulled the volume out. *Poems* by Rainer Maria Rilke. I lifted it to my nose to see if it was the same copy. *Sam.*

I bought it. Isabel bought the cookbook on cookies, and we went to Rachel's place and baked six dozen thumbprint cookies while carefully not talking about Sam or Olivia. Afterwards, Isabel drove me home and I shut myself in the study with Rilke, and I read and I wanted.

> *And leaving you (there aren't words to untangle it)*
> *Your life, fearful and immense and blossoming,*
> *so that, sometimes frustrated, and sometimes*
> *understanding,*
> *Your life is sometimes a stone in you, and then,*
> *a star.*

I was beginning to understand poetry.

Sixty-Four
Grace

-9°C

It wasn't Christmas without my wolf. It was the one time of year I'd always had him, a silent presence lingering at the edge of the woods. So many times, I'd stood by the kitchen window, my hands smelling of ginger and nutmeg and pine and one hundred other Christmas smells, and felt his gaze on me. I'd look up to see Sam standing at the edge of the woods, golden eyes steady and unblinking.

Not this year.

I stood at the kitchen window, my hands smelling of nothing. No point baking Christmas cookies or trimming a tree this year; in twenty-four hours, I'd be gone for two weeks with Rachel. On a white Florida beach, far away from Mercy Falls. Far away from Boundary Wood, and most of all, far away from the empty back yard.

I slowly rinsed out my travel cup, and for the thousandth time this winter, lifted up my gaze to look to the woods.

There was nothing but trees in shades of grey, their

snow-laden branches etched against a heavy winter sky. The only colour was the brilliant flash of a male cardinal, flapping to the bird feeder. He pecked at the empty wooden base before wheeling away, a red spot against a white sky.

I didn't want to go out into the back yard with its unmarked snow, devoid of pawprints, but I didn't want to leave the feeder empty while I was gone, either. Retrieving the bag of birdseed from under the kitchen sink, I pulled on my coat, my hat, my gloves. I went to the back door and slid it open.

The scent of the winter woods hit me hard, reminding me fiercely of every Christmas that had ever mattered.

Even though I knew I was alone, I still shivered.

Sixty-Five

Sam

-9°C

I watched her.

I was a ghost in the woods, silent, still, cold. I was winter embodied, the frigid wind given physical form. I stood near the edge of the woods, where the trees began to thin, and scented the air: mostly dead smells to find this time of the season. The bite of conifer, the musk of wolf, the sweetness of her, nothing else to smell.

She stood in the doorway for the space of several breaths. Her face was turned towards the trees, but I was invisible, intangible, nothing but eyes in the woods. The intermittent breeze carried her scent to me again and again, singing in another language of memories from another form.

Finally, finally, she stepped on to the deck and pressed the first footprint into the snow of the yard.

And I was right here, almost right within reach, but still one thousand miles away.

Sixty-Six
Grace

-9°C

Every step I took towards the feeder took me closer to the woods. I smelled the crisp leaves of the undergrowth, shallow creeks moving sluggishly beneath a crust of ice, summer lying dormant in unnumbered skeleton trees. Something about the trees reminded me of the wolves howling at night, and that reminded me of the golden wood of my dreams, hidden now under a blanket of snow. I missed the woods so much.

I missed him.

I turned my back to the trees and set the bag of birdseed on the ground beside me. All I had to do was fill the feeder and go back inside and pack my bags to fly away with Rachel, where I could try to forget every secret that hid inside these winter woods.

Sixty-Seven

Sam

-9°C

I watched her.

She hadn't noticed me yet. She was knock, knock, knocking ice off the bird feeder. Slowly and automatically following the steps to clean it and open it and fill it and close it and just look at it as if it was the most important thing in the world.

I watched her. Waited for her to turn and glimpse my dark form in the woods. She pulled her hat down over her ears, blew out a puff of breath to watch it swirl a cloud in the air. She clapped the snow from her gloves and turned to go.

I couldn't hide any more. I blew out a long breath as well. It was a faint noise, but her head turned immediately towards it. Her eyes found the mist of my breath, and then me as I stepped through it, slow, cautious, unsure of how she would react.

She froze. Perfectly still, like a deer. I kept approaching, making hesitant, careful prints in the snow, until I was out of the woods and I was standing right in front of her.

She was as silent as I was, and perfectly still. Her lower lip shook. When she blinked, three shining tears left crystal tracks on her cheeks.

She could've looked at the tiny miracles in front of her: my feet, my hands, my fingers, the shape of my shoulders beneath my jacket, my human body, but she only stared at my eyes.

The wind whipped again, through the trees, but it had no force, no power over me. The cold bit at my fingers, but they stayed fingers.

"Grace," I said, very softly. "Say something."

"Sam," she said, and I crushed her to me.

Acknowledgements

These acknowledgements will suck. I'm just warning you. Once a project gets as big as *Shiver* (both in length of manuscript and length of writing), the list of people to thank becomes a cast of thousands. I know y'all don't want to read about a cast of thousands, so I'll keep this brief. If your name is supposed to be on here and isn't, I'm sorry – I either forgot it in a senior moment or can't remember how to spell it.

First of all, I'd like to thank the person who safeguarded my sanity and changed my life in about two weeks flat, my agent, Laura Rennert, whose talents are legion.

Next, the truly amazing Scholastic team, with special mentions to editors Abby Ranger and David Levithan, who worked exhaustively to make *Shiver* the best it could be and tolerated my various neuroses, and also to Rachel Horowitz and Janelle DeLuise, who perform magic.

I also need to thank the friends who got me through this: Tessa Gratton and Brenna Yovanoff, the Merry

Sisters of Fate, who are the best crit partners in the world (and no, you can't have them) – the universe doesn't contain enough chocolate to express my gratitude. Also Naish, a tireless friend and supporter, and Marian, who has opened her home to me countless times. Everyone should have friends like these.

An appreciative nod to early readers Cyn and Todd, for their insight and suggestions, and also to Andrew "Yoda" Karre, for showing me how to write what I wanted to write. Andrew, I wish you many Luke Skywalkers in your career.

And finally, I have to thank my family, without whom I would be a drooling, incoherent person unable to do anything but watch *Top Chef* reruns. Especially my father, who while he worked, fielded endless phone calls to the ER in order to discuss ailments that made you run a fever, and my sister Kate – Kate, I rely on your advice more than you know.

And last of all, Ed. You're my best friend and the reason why the love stories in my novels ring true at all.

Look out for the
heart-stopping sequel to
Shiver...

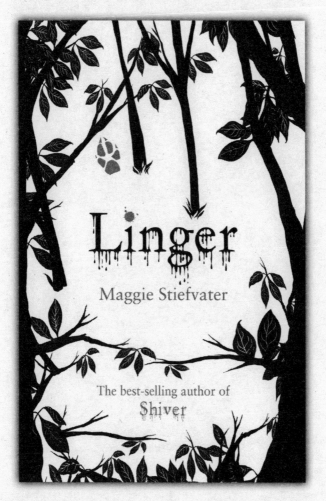

The final book in the trilogy

Forever

COMING SUMMER 2011

www.maggiestiefvater.com